Your Christmas begins at the Gingerbread Cafe

A Gingerbread Cafe Christmas

REBECCA RAISIN

CARINA™

This edition is published by arrangement with Harlequin Books S.A. CARINA is a trademark of Harlequin Enterprises Limited, used under licence.

Published in Great Britain 2015
by CARINA, an imprint of Harlequin (UK) Limited,
Eton House, 18-24 Paradise Road,
Richmond, Surrey, TW9 1SR

A GINGERBREAD CAFÉ CHRISTMAS © 2015 Harlequin S.A.

Christmas at the Gingerbread Café © 2013 Rebecca Raisin
Chocolate Dreams at the Gingerbread Café © 2014 Rebecca Raisin
Christmas Wedding at the Gingerbread Café © 2014 Rebecca Raisin

ISBN 978-0-263-91803-8

98-1015

Harlequin's policy is to use papers that are natural, renewable and recyclable products and made from wood grown in sustainable forests. The logging and manufacturing processes conform to the legal environmental regulations of the country of origin.

Printed and bound by
CPI Group (UK) Ltd, Croydon, CR0 4YY

Rebecca Raisin is a true bibliophile. This love of books morphed into the desire to write them. She's been widely published in various short-story anthologies and in fiction magazines and is now focusing on writing romance. The only downfall about writing about gorgeous men who have brains as well as brawn is falling in love with them—just as well they're fictional. Rebecca aims to write characters you can see yourself being friends with. People with big hearts who care about relationships and, most importantly, believe in true, once-in-a-lifetime love.

Follow her on Twitter @jaxandwillsmum or visit her website to keep up to date with every 'once in a lifetime' romance, www.rebeccaraisin.com.

Christmas
at the
Gingerbread Cafe

Thank you seems too simple a sentiment for the amount of support and encouragement that I've received from my writer friends. They are an inspiration to me and my first port of call to celebrate or commiserate and I feel blessed to have them in my life. I read their work and am in awe of their talent.

Thank you, Lisa Swallow, for everything. None of this would have happened without you. There's nothing better than knowing you're an e-mail away to laugh, shout, or discuss hot guys with—purely for research! You're the best. And your success spurs me on.

Julie Davies, I feel like I've known you forever. But maybe that's the sign of an extraordinary writer. Feeling as though you're connected because their words have touched you.

Thank you to the Carina UK team. Victoria, you've been amazing and I felt immediately like we were on the same wavelength. I look forward to working with you on the next book!

EWG-The Word Cult: Laura, Jake, Lisa, Alyssa and Deb, I love you guys.

To Clare and Liz from Dymocks Ellenbrook. You are the sweetest girls, ever.

Ashley, thanks for coming home and not mentioning it when the house looks like it's been burgled, and you have to make dinner because writing has taken precedence.

And Mum, you're the best proof-reader I know, and very cheap (free). You drop everything and set to work. I love you. Rachel, all I have to do is ask, until our pesky twin ESP kicks in, and you're there, thank you.

My extended family: Aunty Norma, Uncle Alex & Toni, Aunty Jen, Uncle Ronald, Jason & Liesel, Emma, Marg & Kim, Lisa Raisin, Tracy, Cathy, Sam, Tone, Joss, Jules, Jo bear, and Roz (I'm claiming you)—thanks for all your Facebook messages, and 'likes' and 'shares' and your constant support. Pretty lucky to have my own cheer squad.

Lastly, William and Jaxson—You're the reason I'm following my dreams. You guys have taught me so much about life and love and what truly counts. I love you, my precious (zombie) boys.

CHAPTER ONE

Amazing Grace blares out from the speakers above me, and I cry; not delicate, pretty tears, but great big heaves that will puff up my eyes, like a blowfish. That song touches me, always has, always will. With one hand jammed well and truly up the turkey's behind I sing those mellifluous words as if I'm preaching to a choir. Careful, so my tears don't swamp the damn bird, I grab another handful of aromatic stuffing. My secret recipe: a mix of pork sausage, pecans, cranberries and crumbled corn bread. Punchy flavors that will seep into the flesh and make your heart sing. The song reaches its crescendo, and my tears turn into a fully-fledged blubber-fest. The doorbell jangles and I realize I can't wipe my face with my messy hands. Frantic, I try and compose myself as best I can.

"Jesus Mother o' Mary, ain't no customers comin' in here with this kinda carry-on! It's been two years since that damn fool left you. When you gonna move on, my sweet cherry blossom?"

CeeCee. My only employee at the Gingerbread Café, a big, round, southern black woman, who tells it like it is. Older than me by a couple of decades, more like a second mother than anything. Bless her heart.

"Oh, yeah?" I retort. "How are you expecting me to move on? I still love the man."

"He ain't no man. A man wouldn't never cheat on his wife. He's a boy, playing at being a man."

"You're right there." Still, it's been two lonely years, and I ache for him. There's no accounting for what the heart feels. I'm heading towards the pointy end of my twenties. By now, I should be raising babies like all the other girls in town, not baking gingerbread families in lieu of the real thing.

I'm distracted from my heartbreak by CeeCee cackling like a witch. She puts her hands on her hips, which are hidden by the dense parka she wears, and doubles over. While she's hooting and hollering, I stare, unsure of what's so damn amusing. "Are you finished?" I ask, arching my eyebrows.

This starts her off again, and she's leg slapping, cawing, the whole shebang.

"It's just…" She looks at me, and wipes her weeping eyes. "You look a sight. Your hand shoved so far up the rear of that turkey, like you looking for the meaning of life, your boohooing, this sad old music. Golly."

"This is your music, CeeCee. Your gospel CD."

She colors. "I knew that. It's truly beautiful, beautiful, it is."

"Thought you might say that." I grin back. CeeCee's church is the most important thing in her life, aside from her family, and me.

"Where we up to?" she asks, taking off her parka, which is dusted white from snow. Carefully, she shakes the flakes into the sink before hanging her jacket on the coat rack by the fire.

"I'm stuffing these birds, and hoping to God someone's going to buy them. Where's the rush? Two and a bit weeks before Christmas we're usually run off our feet."

CeeCee wraps an apron around her plump frame. "It'll happen, Lil. Maybe everyone's just starting a little later this year, is all." She shrugs, and goes to the sink to wash her hands.

"I don't remember it ever being this quiet. No catering booked at all over the holidays, aside from the few Christmas parties we've already done. Don't you think that's strange?"

"So, we push the café more, maybe write up the chalkboard with the fact you're selling turkeys already stuffed." This provokes another gale of laughter.

"This is going to be you in a minute—" I indicate to the bird "—so I don't see what's so darn amusing."

"Give me that bowl, then."

We put the stuffing mix between us and hum along to Christmas music while we work. We decorated the café almost a month ago now. Winter has set in. The grey skies are a backdrop for our flashing Christmas lights which adorn the windows. Outside, snow drifts down coating the window panes and it's so cozy I want to snuggle by the fire and watch the world go by. Glimmering red and green baubles hang from the ceiling, and spin like disco balls each time a customer blows in. A real tree holds up the corner; the smell from the needles, earth and pine, seeps out beneath the shiny decorations.

In pride of place, sitting squarely in the bay window, is our gingerbread house. It's four feet high, with red and white candy-cane pillars holding up the thatched roof. There's a wide chimney, decorated with green and red jelly beans, ready for Santa to climb down. And the white chocolate front door has a wreath made from spun sugar. In the garden, marshmallow snowmen gaze cheerfully out from under their hats. If you look inside the star-shaped window, you can see a gingerbread family sitting beside a Christmas tree. The local children come in droves to ogle it, and CeeCee is always quick to invite them in for a cup of cocoa, out of the cold.

I opened up the Gingerbread Café a few years back, but the town of Ashford is only a blip on the map of Connecticut, so I run a catering business to make ends meet. We cater for any party, large or small, and open the café during the week to sell freshly made cakes, pies, and whatever CeeCee's got a hankering for. But we specialize in anything ginger. Gingerbread men, cookies, beverages, you name it, we've made it. You can't get any more comforting than a concoction of golden syrup, butter, and ginger baking in the oven in the shape of little bobble-headed people. The smell alone will transport you back to childhood.

CeeCee's the best pie maker I've ever known. They sell out as quickly as we can make them. But pies alone won't keep me afloat.

"So, you hear anything about that fine-looking thing, from over the road?" CeeCee asks.

"What fine thing?"

She rolls her eyes dramatically. "Damon, his name is. The one opening up the new shop, remember? You know who I mean. We went over there to peek just the other day."

"I haven't heard boo about him. And who cares, anyhow?"

"You sure as hell wouldn't be bent over dead poultry, leaking from those big blue eyes of yours, if he was snuggled in your bed at night."

I gasp and pretend to be outraged. "CeeCee! Maybe you could keep him warm—you ever think of that?"

"Oh, my. If I was your age, I'd be over there lickety-split. But I ain't and he might be just the distraction you need."

"Pfft. The only distraction I need is for that cash register to start opening and closing on account of it filling with cold hard cash."

"You could fix up those blond curls of yours, maybe paint your nails. You ain't got time to dilly-dally. Once the girls in town catch on, he's gonna be snapped right up," says CeeCee, clicking her fingers.

"They can have him. I still love Joel."

CeeCee shakes her head and mumbles to herself. "That's about the dumbest thing I ever heard. You know he's moved on."

I certainly do. There's no one in this small town of ours that doesn't know. He sure as hell made a mockery of me. Childhood sweethearts, until twenty-three months, four days and, oh, five hours ago. He's made a mistake, and he'll come back, I just know it. Money's what caused it, or lack thereof. He's gone, hightailed it out of town with some redheaded bimbo originally from Kentucky. She's got more money than Donald Trump, and that's why if you ask me. We lost our house after his car yard went belly up, and I nearly lost my business.

"Lookie here," CeeCee says. "I think we're about to get our first customer."

The doorbell jangles, and in comes Walt, who sells furniture across the way.

"Morning, ladies." He takes off his almost-threadbare earmuff hat. I've never seen Walt without the damn thing, but he won't hear a word about it. It's his lucky hat, he says. Folks round here have all sorts of quirks like that.

"Hey, Walt," I say. "Sure is snowing out there."

"That it is. Mulled-wine weather if you ask me."

CeeCee washes her hands, and dries them on her apron. "We don't have none of that, but I can fix you a steaming mug of gingerbread coffee, Walt. Surely will warm those hands o' yours. How'd you like that?"

"Sounds mighty nice," he says, edging closer to the fire. The logs crackle and spit, casting an orange glow over Walt's ruddy face.

CHAPTER TWO

CeeCee mixes molasses, ginger, and cinnamon and a dash of baking soda. She sets it aside while she pours freshly brewed coffee into a mug. "You want cream and sugar, Walt?"

"Why not?" Walt says amiably.

CeeCee adds the molasses mix to the coffee, and dollops fresh cream on top, sprinkling a dash of ground cloves to add a bit of spice. "Mmm hmm, that's about the best-looking coffee I ever seen. I'm going to have to make me one now."

"So, I guess I'm stuffing these birds by myself?" I say, smiling.

"You got that right." She winks at me, and walks to the counter handing Walt the mug. He nods his thanks and drinks deeply, smacking his lips together after each gulp.

"What can I get for you?" CeeCee asks.

"Janey sent me in for a ham, and a turkey, not too big but not too little, neither." He rubs his belly for emphasis.

"Sure thing," CeeCee says. "How's about one with Lil's special stuffing? Janey won't need to do a thing, 'cept put it in the oven, and baste it a few times."

"Yeah? Then maybe we'll have a peaceful Christmas morning."

"Doubt that," CeeCee says. "If she can't get all het up at her husband Christmas Day, it just ain't Christmas."

"You think?" Walt tilts his head, and smiles. "So, you girls still busy, what with the new guy, an' all?"

I look sharply at Walt. "What do you mean?"

"I heard he's selling turkeys and hams, just like you."

"Say what!" CeeCee says, barely audible with her head pushed deep into the chest fridge. All I see is her denim-clad rump poking out.

"What, you don't know?" Walt says and averts his eyes suddenly sheepish.

"But I thought he was a small goods shop?" My heart hammers—the last thing I need is more competition.

"Yeah, he is—what did you think small goods was?"

I sigh inwardly. "Well, small goods, with an emphasis on the small—"

CeeCee butts in. "Maybe a few cheeses, some o' that fancy coffee. What, he gonna start making gingerbread houses too now, and pumpkin pies, and whatnot?" She places her hands on her hips, and is getting up a full head of steam. "That just ain't how we do business round here."

Walt scratches the back of his neck. "I thought you knew. He's been advertising in the paper…"

I castigate myself for not being more observant, but I don't want to make Walt feel any more uncomfortable than he already is.

"That's OK, Walt. I might have a little chat with him, later on. CeeCee made a nice batch of apple pies yesterday. I'm going to give you one for Janey. You tell her we appreciate her custom, OK?"

CeeCee adds a pie to the box with Walt's ham and turkey. "Nice big chunks of apple, too. You make sure you heat it up first, OK?"

He takes his wallet out and hands CeeCee some cash. "Thank you, girls. She surely will appreciate that."

"You have a good Christmas, if we don't see you before," I say, nodding to him.

"Same goes for you. And thanks, I hope you sort it all out."

"Don't you even think of it," CeeCee says.

We wait for Walt to leave, and I expel a pent-up breath. "Well, no wonder!" I pace the floor and silently curse my own stupidity.

CeeCee wrings her hands on a tea towel. "Lookie here, maybe he just don't know. You should go on over there and tell him."

"How can he not know? It's a small town—any idiot can work it out. You think he's going to start catering too?"

I walk to the window and stare out. There he is, waving like a fool. At me. I glare at him and stomp back to the bench. "He's trying to make nice. Well, that won't wash. I'm going over there to tell him what I think of him!"

CeeCee sighs. "Wait, don't go over there and have a hissy fit. That ain't gonna help matters."

"He's got no business stealing our customers. And I'm going to tell him that."

I bundle my apron, fling it on a table, and march out of the shop. The cold air stings my skin, and I rue the fact I didn't put my jacket on. Damon sees me coming, and smiles; his big brown puppy-dog eyes look kindly at me, but that doesn't stop me for a minute. He's a shark. A charlatan. And I'm going to tell him so.

He walks out to the stoop of his shop. "Hey," he says, sweet as pie. "I was going to come over and introduce myself this afternoon."

"Who do you think you are?" I stuff my hands into the pockets of my jeans, and resist the urge to stamp my foot.

"Sorry?" His forehead creases, adding to his rugged good looks. He sure can play the innocent, all right.

"You think you can just move into town and steal my customers? Don't think I don't know what you're doing!" The street comes alive as shoppers stop to watch. This'll be spread round town before I'm even done talking.

He looks truly bamboozled, but I know it's an act. I've seen plenty of men like him. He's dressed like some kind of cowboy, tight denim jeans that hug in all the right places, a red checker shirt, unbuttoned one too many buttons, exposing his chest. This infuriates me. Good looks like that, he's going to be popular and I'm going to suffer for it. I can see the ladies of this town, frocking up, smearing all kinds of gloop on their faces, while they parade around his shop, pretending to be interested in whatever it is he's selling.

"I'm really not following, ah, Miss…" He rubs a hand through his sandy blond hair, which is too darn long for a man.

"Name's Lily, and you don't fool me, mister. Not for a minute."

"What are you talking about now? What have I done?" He grins; he actually *grins*.

"You've been selling turkeys. And Christmas hams! God only knows what else. You're using your looks to get the ladies in this town to spend their hard-earned money in your shop, and putting me out of business in the meantime."

"My looks?"

It's all I can do not to huff. "So, you've got nothing to say for yourself?"

He kicks the slushy ice on the pavement, as if he's trying to formulate some kind of lie.

"I'm sorry if I caused you this…upset. But I own a shop, and I sell all kinds of things for Christmas. I never thought it would affect you. Surely, there's enough room for both of us?"

"No, there darn well isn't! And I'm going to make sure you're not open long enough to find out, anyway." I spin on my heel and head back to the shop.

He calls out behind me, "I'm starting up cooking classes, Miss Lily. You want to book in to one?"

That stops me in my tracks. Shivering from the elements, I turn back, hovering in the middle of the road. "You what?"

He smirks at me, and for a moment I see my future—an empty shop. There's no way the ladies of this town will be able to resist him.

"I said, I'm starting cooking classes. You want to come to one?"

"Are you *trying* to bankrupt me?"

He rubs his chin, and widens those big brown eyes of his. "No. I'm just trying to earn a living."

My eyes are blazing, but I try to smile and act more confident than I feel. "You go on and do that, then. We'll see who is still in business by the new year."

Cars honk at me blocking their way. With their headlights trained on me I suddenly feel under the spotlight. I race back inside the shop, my hands shaking as if I've got the DTs.

"You gonna catch your death going outside like that!" CeeCee says. "Go warm up by the fire. Look at you, so white I'm gonna call you Casper."

I'm so worked up, I haven't realized I'm covered in snowflakes. My teeth chatter, as if they're holding a one-way conversation. I rush towards the grate, my hands outstretched to the flames.

"So? What'd he say?" CeeCee frowns, and massages her temples.

I rub my hands together, and turn my back to the fire. "You're not going to believe it. He's going to start cooking classes!"

CeeCee's face relaxes and she laughs. "That boy *know* he good-lookin'."

"Do you think it'll affect us?"

"Not likely, but who knows? I think we need to have some kinda sale up in here."

We look towards the window and gaze across. His shop is filled with customers. "Would you look at that?" I point to a small itty-bitty woman. "Rosaleen's over there, and in her church clothes." I knew this would get to CeeCee.

"I don't believe it. Church clothes on a Wednesday."

Before I know it, CeeCee is out front. "Hey, Rosaleen, shouldn't you be supporting members of your congregation?" she hollers over.

Rosaleen looks at us, her face pinched. "He is a part of our congregation. I already asked him."

CeeCee shakes her head and tuts, before walking back inside. "Dressed up like that, trying to impress him, at her age, no less." She harrumphs. "Right, sugar plum. What we gonna discount? Most o' those folk so tight they squeak. If we offer cut-price goods, they'll be back over here with their tail between their legs."

"Good idea. I'll get the blackboard, and we can write it up and face it directly towards his shop."

We giggle like schoolgirls, and I smile. We'll win, I know it. We have to. There aren't enough customers in this town for both of us.

CHAPTER THREE

The next morning, I get to the shop earlier than usual. I'm planning on baking some gingersnap-pear cheesecakes, after a friend of CeeCee's dropped in a pile of fresh pears. The scent of the ripe fruit hits me as soon as I open the back door, aromatic and sweeter than any perfume.

Thinking I may as well open the shop since I'm here anyway, I catch sight of Damon. His door is open and there's a flood of customers on his stoop. I peer over, and, lo and behold, he's got a chalkboard facing my way.

It reads: *Why did the turkey cross the road? Because the other side is better!*

Of all the dirty tricks. I edge away from the window, and try to calm myself. We sold nearly half our turkeys yesterday, but at half price, so there'll be almost no profit, but at least I won't be stuck with them. I thought surely that'd be the end of it, and he'd learn his lesson. I guess not.

I set to work peeling pears and try to think up a new strategy. It's finicky work, but cooking always calms me. That's probably why I run a business that makes next to no money.

An hour later, the fruit's peeled and sliced. I finely grate fresh ginger and mix it through the sliced pears, setting it aside so the flavors combine. I smirk when I realize I have the perfect payback for Mr Smarty Pants across the way.

"Where you at?" CeeCee waddles in from out back.

"Where am I? Cee, it isn't exactly big in here, you know."

"Now don't you be backchatting me. You won't believe what I just heard." She plonks her bag on a table, and unwinds her scarf, getting tangled on account of the fact she's wearing her mittens. She's out of breath and in a tizzy.

"What?"

"He's starting those cooking classes, and tonight he's making gingersnap-pear cheesecake!"

I gasp.

"That ain't all. They get to take whatever they bake *home* with them."

"How did he know we're baking that today?"

"He must have seen Billy come in with all those pears, or else someone told him."

"Who did we tell we planned on gingersnap-pear cheesecake?"

"We only told Reverend Joe, and Billy's mamma."

Yesterday we had a multitude of customers that came in to shoot the breeze. Anyone could have heard. We're going to have to watch everything we say in future.

CeeCee narrows her eyes. "I bet it was Billy's mamma. And she'll probably start taking their pears over to him."

"Is there any point even making it now?" Eyeing the amount of fruit I've spent so much time preparing, I sigh. "Be a shame to waste it."

CeeCee surveys the work I've done. "I have a hankering for it after all that talk yesterday. We make it, and then if they don't sell we halve the price by lunchtime. Maybe no one's booked in to his classes—you ever think of that?"

"Yeah, you're right. It's not like most of them don't know how to make cheesecake, anyway. Did you see his sign?"

CeeCee shuffles over to the window, muttering and cursing, though she doesn't hold with cursing, usually. "I don't believe it. He's trying to start a war with us! What we gonna do?"

I turn on the CD player and the gospel choir begin with *Silent Night*. The lights in the window flash green, red, and a luminescent white. The angel atop the tree seems to smile benevolently down on me. Steeling myself, I say, "We're going to appeal to their Christmas spirit."

CeeCee looks at me as if I've lost my marbles. "Here you go." I reach under the counter and produce a Santa hat and a bell I found in our box of old decorations.

"And what you expect me to do with this?" She widens her eyes, and jingles the bell.

"You, Mrs Claus, are going to drum up business by walking the length of the street, handing out candy canes, and some kind of coupon. *Buy one, get one free.* Or *Buy one, pay it forward*, and they can donate a free item to the church. What do you think?"

A grin replaces her consternation. "I didn't think you had it in you. How's about I walk on his side of the street?"

I know we should be feeling worried on account of giving so much away, but we're like schoolkids, and I'm having more fun than I care to admit. "Sounds like you know what you're doing, Mrs Claus."

CeeCee laughs, her big-bellied southern haw, and goes to our Santa display. "I'm just gonna borrow the fat man's jacket here for a minute—lucky we the same size." She wraps the dusty red jacket around herself and giggles, and tries to fit the hat over her thick black curls. "You gonna owe me a hair set, sugar plum. This hat sure gonna flatten my wave."

"Sure, I'll organize Missy to fix your hair up pretty for Christmas." I laugh.

"I look a sight!" she says, grinning at her reflection in the window. "Right, go print me some coupons, and I'll set to work."

Leaving Mrs Claus out front, I rush back to my shoebox-size office and hastily type some coupons. Everyone in town loves a bargain, and if they are seen doing something for the church, even better.

Let's see *him* try and outmaneuver me on *this*. I have the added bonus of being a local born and bred, and our town is more reserved with new folk.

With a sly grin on my face, I jog back out to the front, yelling, "That fool won't know what hit him," only to run straight into the damn fool.

"Who are you talking about?" Damon asks, rubbing his chin where my head has just connected.

"Ouch! Who creeps up like that? If you want me to feel the earth move, that isn't the way to go about it," I say, sure I'm going to be sporting a big lump on my head any minute now.

"Which *fool* are you talking about?"

I make a show of wincing, while I try and think of an answer. CeeCee's no help, standing there as a half-dressed Santa, her lips quivering as she tries to hold in laughter. I know she's going to lose it, and then the whole sorry story will come tumbling out of her mouth.

"Excuse me, mister, who said you could come in here and spy on us?"

His forehead creases, and that same sexy smile creeps back on his face. "Who said I was spying?"

"That smile might work on other girls, but it sure doesn't work on me. *I said* you're spying. Now get on out of here. Shoo." I wave my hand towards the door.

"Shoo? Not until you tell me who the fool is."

"You're as dumb as a bucket of rocks if you think I'm telling you anything."

"I see." He scratches his chin, which has a red mark from our collision. "I think you're cooking up another plan to steal my customers."

"Of all the…I think you're forgetting who was here first. You're stealing *my* customers—let's be clear on that." I try hard not to poke my tongue out at him. He brings out the worst in me, this newcomer. He's wearing those same tight jeans, and under his open jacket he's wearing another of those checker shirts, but has yet another button undone. I can see right down to his belly button and I happen to notice he's got quite the six-pack going on. The girls round here are going to swoon over him.

He edges backwards, his brown eyes sparkling with mirth. "Well, my family has lived here since before there was electricity, don't you know? And wouldn't the town folk love to know you're not giving me the same warm welcome that they are?"

CeeCee bustles over. "Oh, yeah? And who's your family, then? Ain't no one mentioned your people to me."

"My people, as you say, are the Guthries, born and bred right here in Ashford for as long as anyone can remember."

CeeCee and I inhale sharply. The Guthries are the oldest and richest family in our town. So rich, they don't live here any more. They follow the sun and never struggle through a winter unless they're skiing. They owned a fleet of cargo ships, and train lines, and had their fingers in all sorts of pies when it came to transport. A few years back they sold their businesses, raking in a fortune. They still own by and large a heap of properties around town, and are well-respected, church-going folk. Not that we ever see them in Ashford, any more.

It's all I can do not to cry. There's no way I can beat him if he's backed by that kind of money.

"Why you even bothering to work, then?" CeeCee asks. "We know most o' the Guthries don't do much 'cept sit on their porches and get fat off good 'ol American food, since they got no need for employment. They've got people to do their bidding."

"They're my family, but I make my own way." He crosses his arms and puffs out his chest like a prize cock. His jaw juts out, making me think there's more to the story than he's letting on.

"You the rotten apple?" CeeCee asks, tilting her head. I hope to God he is, then my shop might just have a chance.

"I don't like handouts, that's all."

CeeCee makes a show of clearing her throat. "Good to hear. Now we got cakes to make, but I guess you know all about that."

He ducks his head. "Well, all right. I was just coming to invite you over to my cooking class tonight. Free of charge."

My fighting spirit returns, and I paste on a smile. "Thanks all the same, but we've got *so* many orders to assemble. Yesterday was one of our busiest days ever, you see."

"I see. Not much money in half-price poultry, is there?"

"Well, you know how it is," I say. "We're full of Christmas cheer this time of year." CeeCee rings the bell maniacally. I nod to her, grinning. "And we like to look after folk around here."

"I'll say." He uncrosses his arms and leans over to me and whispers, "Bet my cheesecake is better than yours."

I reel, as if poked. "We'll see about that."

He walks away, cool as a cucumber, and tips a finger to his head as though he's wearing a hat. We watch him cross the street; he jogs, and jumps when he reaches the pavement. I can honestly say I've never seen a man's butt look so good in jeans before. They're so tight, every muscle is evident as his body pushes against the faded denim. It's like watching magic happen. I take a deep appreciative breath in.

"He sure ain't ugly, is he?" CeeCee says wistfully.

"No, ma'am."

He turns abruptly and catches us staring, jaws agape. I promptly close my mouth and busy myself at the counter.

"Well, I'll be," CeeCee says, shaking herself back to the present. "How did we not know he's a Guthrie?"

"I don't know. What do you think? That they'll bail him out as long as it takes to close us down?"

CeeCee drags her gaze from the window. "Sugar plum, I don't rightly know. He doesn't seem like that, though. He seems sweet as cherry pie."

"Here we go. You're getting all misty-eyed."

CeeCee glances at me, and I can tell she's debating whether to say what's on her mind.

"Just say it, Cee. What are you cooking in that mind of yours?"

"Hmm. I just got a feeling."

I groan. CeeCee thinks she's got second sight, sometimes. Second sight, only when it comes to me and whichever man she's trying to set me up with.

She shakes her head, and says, "I know, I know, but this time it's different. There's somethin' special about him. I saw the way he looked at you. Like electricity or somethin'. I could see sparks flying between you. It was like lightning. Like—"

"Like a thunderstorm," I interrupt. "Like a great big brooding cloud of despair. That's what you saw."

"Mark my words. He's different. He gonna pull you outta this funk."

Ignoring CeeCee, I walk to the bench. The pears have infused with the ginger. I toy with the ingredients for the cheesecake, fidgety all of a sudden.

"You think so too?" she asks hopefully.

"I think you're crazy, Cee. And Joel, what about Joel?" I'm hoping if I say it like a prayer, he'll come back. Joel would see straight through Damon's ploys. Yeah, so Damon may be flirting with me, but that's so I loosen up and let him ruin my business. Joel would know what to do about this situation. My heart lurches at the thought of spending Christmas Day alone. No Joel to open presents with. No Joel full stop. In fact, no family here at all this year.

My folks discovered cruising when they retired and are sailing around New Zealand, of all places. Damned if I know where they heard about it. My siblings got out of our small town as quick as they could after school was done. My brother lives in New York City, and leads some glamorous life, full of socialites, and parties. He's so far gone in that world, he doesn't make time for family any more. My parents pretend that they're happy for him, but it breaks my heart their own son doesn't visit. And my sister, Betty, has gone on to Michigan with her husband and had about a hundred babies.

"You thinking of Joel, again?" CeeCee demands. "Girl, when you gonna stop mooning over him? He just don't deserve that kinda attention. He up and divorced you, Lil..." Her voice softens. "I think it's time you realized that's about as finished as a marriage gets."

I didn't even see it coming. Thought it was a phase— maybe some married men get itchy feet. As devastating as it was, I'd give him another chance, once he knew the grass wasn't greener elsewhere. But instead, he served me divorce papers. Something I never wanted to see. My heart broke into about a million pieces that day.

I think back to our marriage, and the promises we made. When he stared into my eyes, and recited wedding vows, I believed him. When I said, 'Till death do us part' I truly meant it. How can one person have that kind of hold of your heart, and not feel the same any more? Marriage should be for ever—at least, that's what I was raised to believe. When you stumble, you work through it, together. But Joel, he's not on the same page as me, not yet.

CeeCee breaks my train of thought. "You OK, Lil? You look like you seen a ghost."

Pensive, I try and shake the memories away. "You're right, Cee. No time for mooning over what I can't change." I force a bright look on my face, and remember the challenge at hand. "So, you still going to be Mrs Claus, or what?"

CeeCee picks up a basket and stuffs it full of candy canes. "Surely am. Gimme those coupons, and let me go drum up some sales."

CHAPTER FOUR

That afternoon we're rushed off our feet. The folk in town are vying to pay it forward to the church so the reverend will look kindly upon them. They've got good hearts, and I hope, what with all the discounts, I'm still making some money. Everyone who comes in appreciates the gospel Christmas music. CeeCee hams it up in her soprano voice, and pitches and warbles to the customers, who join merrily in.

We sell our last Lane cake; the white iced fruit cakes are a Christmas tradition in Alabama, where CeeCee is from. She's got most of the town folk hooked on her southern food. Most of our gingersnap-pear cheesecakes are snapped up too. Dusting my hands on my apron as the final customer carries his box of goods out, I raise my eyebrows at CeeCee. She's gulping down iced-tea as if she's been stuck in the desert.

"I sure didn't expect such a flurry all at once."

She puts her empty glass down, and says, "I don't think I ever been that parched. Glory be, that was busier than I ever seen it before."

Glancing over the street, I see Damon. He's on his haunches scrawling something on his chalkboard. Guilt gnaws at me, as I see his shop is empty, and has been each time I had a minute to look his way. He's spent the morning sitting on a stool by the window reading the paper, or talking on his cell.

"What's he doin'?" CeeCee wonders.

"Probably advertising his cooking classes. They just aren't going to work. Folk 'round here can cook, anyway."

CeeCee grunts. "Yeah, but that's what folks said about you opening a shop to sell home-made food. They all said who was gonna buy from you when they been taught how to bake since they was knee-high to a grasshopper? But they did, they surely did. Maybe he ain't cooking home-made food. Maybe he's fixing to teach them something fancy. You see all those grown-up kids coming back from whatever big city they livin' in. They don't want their mamma's traditional meals—they want all that fancy stuff, like sushi or some such."

"But he's making *our* cheesecake. While it's mighty tasty, it isn't exactly fancy."

"Probably just to get them in. Show them he's one of us. Then he'll start on with all that seaweed, and raw fish." She screws up her face. "It's just disgusting."

Damon stands up, and dusts his hands on the seat of his jeans. He looks over his shoulder at us, and waves. He has big hands. Big, but graceful, as I imagine a piano player would have.

I'm lost for a moment thinking of whether his hands would be soft or rough and calloused from cooking, when CeeCee yelps. "Free! He's doing it free!"

I look at the blackboard.

"FREE cooking class. Baked food, made with LOVE. Take home what you make."

Damon does a mock salute and strolls back inside his shop.

"Pray tell, what's all that made with love about?" CeeCee asks, her forehead furrowing.

"You still think he's special now?"

"He's just playing a game with you." She takes off her Santa jacket and hat, both damp from the weather. Her hair lies flat on the top of her head; she runs a hand through it, musing. "Come by the fire." CeeCee says as I throw another log on, and watch it slowly take. We sit on the small sofa that faces the street.

CeeCee continues, "You like a daughter to me, you know that. So I'm going to speak to you like your mamma would. Look at that man." She points to Damon standing at the window, hands crossed over his chest, facing towards us.

"What?"

"I can tell a person's heart by their smile. And his smile goes all the way up to his eyes. Joel's smile stopped right under his nose. You see what I'm saying?"

"You're saying Joel looked down his nose at people?"

"Damn straight, I am."

I laugh at CeeCee's sincerity. She's trying to hypnotize me into agreeing with her. I shake my head. "Well, if he's giving out free classes, I might just stay open all night, and sell whatever I have left. I'll start a batch of butterscotch pies, and hope no one knows it's me who baked them."

CeeCee taps her nose with her finger, implying a secret. "They'll know it was you. But you go right on ahead. I'm just gonna sit here awhile and warm my old bones up."

"You do that. I might as well tell everyone our new closing time."

CeeCee's cackle follows me out of the door as I go to write on the chalkboard.

The wind has picked up. I shrug into my jacket, and fumble for the chalk in my pocket.

"You can't let up, can you?" I spin to look up at Damon, a mite scary, leaning over me while I'm squatting at the board.

"Not all of us have family money to fall back on, you know."

"That right?"

"Sure is."

"You don't hardly know a thing about me."

"I can say the same for you." I stand and gaze into his eyes. I try to look fierce, but it reminds me of staring competitions we had back in high school. We stared at each other until someone blinked, and they lost the game. I purse my lips, trying to keep my laughter in check but it barrels out of me, in a very unladylike way.

His eyes crinkle. "This funny to you?"

"A little. It's just, it reminded me…"

Damon's phone rings, a loud, startling tone. He checks the screen, and rushes off, head hunched as he answers it.

"Well, I'll be. Can't miss a phone call. Typical city slicker," I grumble.

By the time I finish the sign, complete with whorls of tinsel colored in chalk, CeeCee has cleaned the kitchen from the day's labors and has started making pastry. "So much for warming those old bones. You don't trust me to make the pies, I see."

"Sugar plum, you got enough going on, lest someone say, your pies ain't made with *love*."

I sidle up and hug her. I'd be lost without CeeCee in my life. "You're tired. We can leave the pies until tomorrow."

"It's OK, sugar. I'd rather be here with you than at home on my lonesome."

"You're too good to me." With CeeCee being so sweet, and me being reminded of all the things we've both lost, I well up again. I turn away from her and try and dry my eyes with the back of my hand but she knows me better than that.

"Don't you go getting all sentimental on me." I lose it completely when I see tears pool in her eyes. Again, I curse myself for being such a dramatic crier. I'm so sensitive sometimes it kills me.

CeeCee and her husband, Curtis, moved from Alabama to Ashford when their kids were just babies. Curtis worked on the railroads for most of his life, and that's how they wound up here. He spent his time to-ing and fro-ing on the train lines, with Ashford as their base. Train lines that the Guthries used to own. They swapped one small town for another. And then their kids, all grown up, moved out of town, like so many, gone to find better jobs in big cities. CeeCee lost Curtis to cancer, one winter, not three years back. When I think of her all alone in that old house of hers, I crumble.

"I know what you're thinking, but I'm fine, truly I am. I've got my church, and my friends. The kids are coming up for Christmas Day, and I'll see my grandbabies. That's all I want. I'm happy on my own. What about you? You wanna come over and spend the day with us? You know you part of the family."

I wipe my eyes, and take a deep breath. "Aw, no. I don't want to intrude, and I know what you're going to say, so don't bother. You cuddle those grandbabies of yours. I'm going to sloth on the couch all day, and watch a bunch of soppy Christmas movies. I won't even get out of my PJs. It'll be nice not to have to get up and rush in here."

CeeCee clucks her tongue. "What about dinner? You can at least come over and let me feed you."

"We'll see." As much as I love CeeCee, I don't want her thinking she has to entertain me. She'll have her own kids there, and her grandbabies who she loves more than anything. A day by myself doesn't sound so awful. I plan on crying along to cheesy flicks on TV and eating ice cream straight from the tub.

"Would you look at that?" CeeCee says, pointing to across the road.

Damon's back on the stool by the shop window looking dejected. He's bent over, cradling his head in his hands.

"That poor man," CeeCee says. "Breaks your heart just looking at him."

I bite my lip, and ponder. Is he just playing a game here, or what?

CeeCee's rolling out big balls of pastry without even looking; it's second nature to her. "Go on over there, Lil. Looks like he could use a friend."

"What? Are you falling for this? He's angling for sympathy, that's all."

"And why not, pray tell? He's like a movie star, those fine chiseled cheekbones and that curly hair—don't you just want to run your hands through it?"

Like an expert chef, CeeCee's flinging the pastry all over the place, while her eyes don't move from Damon.

"No, I don't want to run my hands through his hair. I'm sure it's all tangled. That only happens in books, Cee. Sounds like you've been reading one too many bodice rippers, if you ask me." I was all talk. He truly did look sad, sitting there as if he had the weight of the world on his shoulders.

"Get on over there, and make that boy smile. Go on, get."

I'm one of those people who always feel guilty. If someone bangs into me, I apologize. If someone drives up the footpath and runs over my shoe, I say sorry I was in the way. And here I am, feeling guilty robbing this man of his customers, yet it's going to cost me too, this whole competition. I sigh; I'm not made for war.

"Fine. I'll go. And what should I say, do you think?"

A huge smile lights up CeeCee's face, and I wonder if those two are in cahoots together. It sure wouldn't surprise me. She pretends to be really interested in her pastry all of a sudden. "Take him a pecan pie. I'm going make another batch tomorrow, anyways."

It's all well and good joking about it, but what am I going to say to the man? I begin to wonder if it was the phone call that's made him so morose.

While I'm wrapping the pie, CeeCee mutters to herself. I know she's fixing to tell me something, so I take my time, and wait for her to mull it over.

"You know, this might sound crazy, but why don't you two join forces?"

"Are you on about the matchmaking thing again?"

"No, no." She shakes her head. "I mean, why not join forces with the Christmas rush? Instead of competing against each other—work together. You never know what might happen. You've been trying to find someone to help you cater for as long as I can remember. And lookie here, that fine thing might just be the man for the job."

"And how's that going to work? Have you been drinking the sherry when you're baking those cakes?"

"Just a nip to fortify me," she says, and laughs. "But I don't see why you can't work together. You know, you could run some cooking classes for him—there's not much you don't know about baking. He can supply you with those ingredients you ship in for your catering customers. He sells a whole lot of things you don't, and vice versa. You can work together. You could expand catering to bigger customers in towns further out, if you had another pair of hands—hands like his." She looks meaningfully at me.

"And when did this come to you? Don't tell me you just thought about it." My palms are sweaty, and I realize CeeCee might be right about venturing further out. If Damon can actually cook it might just be a possibility. On my own, I have no hope of catering for larger customers.

And there aren't too many folk interested in working for me, who can cook, and work under pressure, or who want to lose their weekends to do it, either. I've been hoping for some extra help, so I can take on more clients, but catering's hard work. So far, all of the avenues I've tried to find staff have turned into a dead end.

CeeCee's idea spins through my mind. If we worked together, I could surely double the catering side of things, and we'd use products we both sold. It could really work. I stop short; what am I thinking?

"You can thank me later," CeeCee says. "Now get on over there and see what's bothering him."

I fossick through my handbag for my lip gloss, and slick it on.

"Well, I'll be, make-up too?" CeeCee raises her eyebrows.

"A girl's got pride, Cee. There's no reason for me to go over there looking downright disheveled. It has nothing to do with him."

"'Course it don't." She hums the wedding march as I grab the pie and walk out of the door.

"Oh, please." I roll my eyes heavenward.

"Cherry blossom?"

"Yeah?" I hold the door open.

"You forgetting your jacket again? Someone sure is distracted these days."

I scoff, and walk back inside to the coat rack.

CHAPTER FIVE

Once I'm out and walking across the road it dawns on me: I'm nervous. I never meant to hurt him by having these sales; I only wanted to stay afloat. Always me and the guilt. It's a gift of mine to blame myself. Balancing the pie, I take small steps; the road is icy, and slippery.

"Well, hello," I say as Damon walks to the front to meet me. He looks up, his eyes vacant. And for a second I'm truly worried. Has someone died? He looks hollowed out, his shoulders are slumped, and his usual grin is replaced with a tight line.

"What you got there?" he asks, his voice barely audible.

"Some of CeeCee's famous pecan pie. Free, and made with love, no less."

That provokes a slight lift at the corners of his mouth.

"And what's with the change of heart?" he says, taking the proffered pie. "This got horse laxatives in it or something?"

Laughter bubbles out of me. "I wish I'd thought of that. Nope. This is a peace offering. The proverbial olive branch."

I edge closer to the step, about to walk up when I slip on a pile of sleet, and scramble like some kind of roller-skater before I land smack bang into Damon's arms. He holds me tight, his face trained down towards me. His aftershave wafts over, something tangy and spicy. I try to hold myself back from outright sniffing him. So, I've got a thing with aftershave.

"You always throw yourself at men like that?" he asks, grinning.

"You wish," I say, realizing I should probably try to extricate myself from his embrace. It's just that he's so warm. "I think you really need to salt and shovel your steps. Not hard to tell you're new around here."

"What, and miss all the fun?"

Untangling myself from Damon, I try to stand without slipping. I notice he still holds the pecan pie, which somehow didn't get squashed in the fracas.

Pulling my jacket together, I say, "So, what do you say—friends?"

"Why are you doing this?" he asks, his voice husky.

"I'm no good at fighting. I can't be angry for longer than ten minutes, and this has lasted two days. I'm exhausted. And seeing you over here all glum, well, it's just not me, causing this kind of reaction in a man."

He leans back against the window and looks up at the sky. He's silent for too long; an awkward pause hangs between us, making me fidget.

"OK, well, I'm going to get back—"

"Wait," he says, touching me lightly on the hand. "Don't go. You want to come inside for coffee?" There is something different about him, a sadness in his eyes. It dawns on me it might not be the business causing it.

"Sure. Love to."

We amble inside and my breath catches. "Wow, you sure do know how to decorate." We'd peeked in when he was setting up, but now the shop is decked out with half whiskey barrels filled with straw, a bed for jars of preserves. Old wagon wheels are varnished and hitched to the walls, with a variety of goods hanging from the spokes on thin golden hooks. On the decked floor, little round up lights shine, making the place sparkle. It's like something from a Western movie, a bygone era, and it has a real homely feel. The delicious smell of rich coffee beans lingers in the air. In the corner is a huge fireplace with mahogany Chesterfield lounges to each side. The only Christmas decorations are a string of lights along the counter, and a small plastic tree on a coffee table.

"This is really something," I say.

"Thanks, Lil. Can't take much credit for it, though. It's an exact replica of the shop I had back in New Orleans. Someone else designed it."

"So you have two shops?"

He moves behind the fancy coffee maker, which is the size of a small car. He presses some buttons and pulls a lever; it coughs and splutters like someone drowning. "Cappuccino OK?"

"Sure," I say and sit on a bar stool in front of him.

After much gurgling from the machine, Damon walks through a shroud of steam and hands me a cup jiggling on a saucer.

"I hope you like it strong."

"Just like my men," I say and feel myself color. It just slipped out as if I were joking with CeeCee.

He pretends to flex his muscles, and my blush deepens. "So, do you still have the shop in New Orleans?" I repeat in order to get back to a safer topic.

His eyes cloud. "Nope. That's all finished. I'm here for good, now."

A heavy silence fills the room. I can hear my heartbeat thump.

He looks forlorn staring into his cup. "Do you want to join forces?" I ask, before I can change my mind and think about anything remotely sensible, like, *I hardly know the man.*

He looks lazily over his cup to me. "What do you mean?"

Darn it. Too late to recant. "How many people are booked in for the class tonight?"

He takes a sip of his coffee. "Three. The three Mary-Jos."

The three Mary-Jos are infamous for being flirts. They're teenagers. They all grew up together, some kind of cousins, twice removed or some such. Their moms all staked their claim to the name Mary-Jo and wouldn't budge. And now our small town has three blond-haired, blue-eyed mischief-makers, who share the same name. It can get confusing.

"You're not going to make any money with the Mary-Jos. Can you cook?" I ask.

"Yeah, the Mary-Jos are my best customers, 'cept they've never actually bought a thing. What do you mean can I cook? Sure I can."

His phone blares out from the pocket of his jeans. He sure does receive a lot of calls.

He looks at the screen and frowns. "I gotta take this." He struts away, and answers the phone, speaking what sounds all lovey dovey to me. As if he's trying to soothe someone. He's obviously got a girl back in New Orleans. Maybe they're trying to mend the bridges, or something. Not that it matters; I still love my Joel. I'm only here on business, I tell myself, and drink the steaming coffee, which tastes bitter now.

I'm about to leave when Damon strolls back in, rubbing his face. He seems jittery, nervous. I don't think it's my place to ask, but I am from a small town, which means it's kind of in my blood to question.

"You OK?"

He looks startled, as if he forgot I'm here. "Oh, right. Lil, where were we?"

"You sure you're OK?"

"Nothing time can't fix," he says, mysteriously.

His demeanor worries me, but I figure I'll talk shop and eventually he'll tell me what's really going on. Call it female intuition, but there's something happening in Damon's life that takes the sparkle from his eyes after each of those phone calls. "OK, then." I sit back and explain CeeCee's idea.

The moon is winking behind clouds by the time I cross the street back to CeeCee. I know she'll be baking up a storm; anything to keep herself from marching over to Damon's to see what's taking so long.

Opening the front door, I'm assailed with the scent of butterscotch from CeeCee's pies. It's rich and comforting, so buttery, and wholesome, I almost want to take one back to Damon.

CeeCee jumps out from behind the fridge, scaring me half to death. "So, what'd he say?"

"He said yes. I hope I made the right decision." Fumbling with my apron strings, I decide I'm going to spruce up the shop. I clean when I'm nervous.

"Why you all twitchy like that?"

"You should see the inside of his shop. It's got polished oak floors, a big old wooden bar, and these tiny little lights that shine right on down to all the bottles perched there. And some imbedded in the floor too. It's just so warm, what with all that dark wood. He's got all sorts of things you just can't get around here. Makes me think this place—" I glance around at the bare white walls, and the long silver benches we use to roll out dough "—is a little stark. You know, once we put the Christmas decorations away…"

CeeCee plants her hands on my shoulders. "So we flick some paint over the walls, and buy some lamps, but what'd he say about the business side of things?"

"Oh, right. Yeah, we discussed it, and we're going to give it a three-month trial. We'll expand the catering, and he'll get someone to run his shop, like you do here, and see if we can venture out further afield. It was the darnedest thing, though…"

"Sit down," CeeCee says. "You're all fluttery like some kind of butterfly."

We move to the lounges, and I take a few deep breaths. I think I've overdone it with those fancy coffees of his.

"What's making you nervous?" CeeCee asks.

"Well, we were discussing all the ins and outs, and what we'd expect from each other, you know, trying to lay some ground rules out before we agree to start, and he kept taking phone calls. Every two, three minutes. In the end, he didn't say anything, just rushed off with the phone, and then came back with this defeated look on his face."

"You ask him who it was?"

"I asked him if he was OK. He kept changing the subject."

CeeCee mutters to herself, and starts wringing her hands. "I don't believe it! Oh, Lord." She looks up at the ceiling. "Why you do this to me?"

"What are you talking about, Cee?"

"I seen the signs." She points to the spot between her eyes. "I seen you two…together."

I slap my leg and laugh. "Oh, Cee. Is that why you dreamt up this business venture? So I could get a boyfriend?"

"Why o' course!"

"I should know better than to trust you when it comes to me and single men. I'm nervous, because what if he does have a girlfriend, some kind of long-distance relationship or something? He can't be running off every two minutes to speak on the phone. And what about if he up and walks out, once I get a bunch of customers?"

"He ain't like that," CeeCee says knowingly. "He a Guthrie, after all. They good people. You just say it delicately, maybe phone calls are better left for after work, like that." She lets out a squeal. "I knew it. I knew this was gonna be your year."

I laugh along with her, but I'm plagued by doubt. Who would call someone so many times? What's his secret?

CHAPTER SIX

"I've tallied up the takings. We gone and had our best day yet." CeeCee hands me the banking.

"Why, thank you." We didn't discount anything, and I sure haven't seen a pile of cash this big in a long time. Things are definitely looking up for us.

"Head on over to Damon. Here's his money for those gift baskets we made with all his goodies."

It's been nearly two weeks since we began working with Damon. He used our pork shoulder cuts in a cooking class, and we sold out of them the very next day. We've swapped and shared products for Christmas party orders, and gift baskets. It was CeeCee's idea to make Christmas hampers with all beautiful jars of produce Damon stocked, and a selection of our baked goods. We fancied them up with ribbons, and wrapped the baskets in Christmas colors. They're selling like hot cakes. And tomorrow, Damon and I cater our very first soirée together. I have something to ask him before I begin preparations for the party. "You going to be OK if I go over there?" I ask CeeCee.

"I'll jingle that big bell if I get run off my feet," CeeCee says, looking down her glasses at me. "You go. I'm going to start on some more Lane cakes for folk to have Christmas Day. Take your time." She wanders off singing under her breath.

The Christmas spirit is alive and well in our small town. It's impossible not to smile when young kids come in, their eyes lit up like fairy lights when they see the gingerbread house, and we give them a marshmallow snowman and a handful of candy canes.

Grabbing my scarf and jacket from the coat rack, I wrap myself up, and wave to CeeCee. "Shout if you need me."

"Get," she says, shooing me away like a fly.

I smirk, closing the door softly behind me. The street is busy with families doing last-minute shopping, mothers wearing frantic looks, searching for gifts before the shops shut for good.

I step into Damon's shop. Customers are milling, picking up things and fussing over the sheer variety he stocks.

"Why, hello, pretty lady," he says. My heart flutters. It truly does. He's so darn attractive and it's beginning to prove difficult not to flirt right back.

"Ho, ho, ho. I bring you a gift." I hand over the banking bag.

"Thank you." His smile does go all the way up to his eyes, I notice, just as CeeCee said. He puts the bag under the bench, and pulls out a box. "I also have a gift for you."

I color. "Oh, what? But mine isn't really a gift—it's your money from the baskets." He hands me a beautifully wrapped box, complete with a big gold bow.

"Go on, open it."

I rip off the expensive-looking paper then stop. Gosh, darn it, I should have tried to do it delicately, as a lady would. Save the paper, at least. I lift the lid of the box, and when I see it laughter tumbles out of me.

"You shouldn't have."

"Oh, I think I should have."

"What's it do?"

"It's a shrilling turkey. See?" He takes the plastic yellow turkey from my hands and presses a button. It starts hawing like a turkey on helium.

I pretend to wipe a tear from my eye. "That's about the nicest thing anyone ever gave me. How did you know?"

"When I saw it, I thought of you."

"A plastic, limp, bright yellow turkey reminds me of you, too."

Customers look at us like we're crazy, so I turn the shrilling turkey off and sit down.

"Coffee?"

"Sure."

He's hidden by the steam for a moment, while the noisy machine does its thing.

"Ma'am." He places the cup down and ambles around the bench to sit beside me.

"I was…"

"I was…" we say in unison.

"You go…"

"You go…" We laugh; suddenly it's really hot in here.

I motion for him to speak.

He looks at his coffee, and then up at me. "I was just wondering if you wanted to go to the Christmas carols with me? I hear it's quite the show."

"Sure, I'd love to." I say, quickly, before my voice gets shaky like my hands are. A grin splits his face. "What were you going to ask?"

I wave my hand. "Aw, I was just going to ask if you'd heard about the Christmas carols. It's quite the show."

We smile awkwardly at each other, then take comfort in staring into our coffees.

I make a mental note to pull out my red dress, and dust off my boots. Jeans and sweaters are OK for work, but not so much for Christmas Eve. And not for a date with Damon. *Not that it's a date.*

I rush back into the shop, feeling guilty about how long I've left CeeCee on her own. She's in a state, fanning her hands at her face, and looking all faint. "You OK?"

She sobs as if she's gone and lost her best friend. "Cee, what is it?"

Lifting her head, she walks to me, throws her arms around my shoulders, like a bear. "I'm just as happy as a hog in slop! I heard you gone said yes to a date with Damon!"

The joys of living in a small town. "Seriously, how did that get to you so quick?"

"Emma Mae was over there, and heard you twos giggling like children. She said you were snuggled up, all cozy-like." Her eyes twinkle with unshed tears.

"Emma Mae's a busybody. It's not a date. We're just going to the carols together. As friends. No one even mentioned the D word. Plus that phone of his started bleating out all over the place again. Makes me wonder what he's hiding. Kind of puts a pall over things."

Knitting her brow, she glances over at the shop, as if she can discern from here what Damon's secret is. "Surely someone knows something about why he suddenly back."

I follow her gaze. Damon's gesticulating wildly to the local sheriff, probably about the boys attempting to shoplift earlier that day. Poor kids, trying to get their mamma a present on account of their daddy walking out not so long ago. At least Damon had a heart once he heard their story. He gave them a box of small goods to take home to their mamma, as long as they promised never to steal again.

"I think," CeeCee says, dragging her eyes back to mine, "he's probably just tying up loose ends back in New Orleans. You said he had a shop there, right?"

"CeeCee, it doesn't matter, anyway. I'm just happy to go to the carols with someone other than myself. Plus, it'll set tongues wagging, so that's a bonus too."

She nods. "Sure as shooting will. Now you all ready for that fancy shindig tomorrow?"

"I think so. I'm going to stay back tonight and do as much prep as I can, then Damon and I'll head on over about lunchtime to set up. You sure you'll be OK by yourself? It's been busy these last few days."

"I'm sure. If I get stuck Walt said Janey's just a phone call away. Folk 'round here won't mind waiting if there's a queue. I'll ply them with candy-cane coffee, or some such. You don't worry 'bout a thing, 'cept Damon."

"'Cept Damon?" I copy, arching my eyebrows.

CeeCee fusses with her hair, and tries to look innocent. "You know what I mean."

CHAPTER SEVEN

"So far so good," Damon says, setting down a tray of empty Chinese soup spoons that moments before had been filled with tuna and mango ceviche.

"Wow, that was quick. Are we making enough?" We're halfway through, and so far it doesn't look as though people are slowing down with the food.

Damon winks. "We'll have plenty, don't you worry. The noise level goes up every time I go out there, and I hazard a guess that the alcohol consumption is rising right along with that noise. People are starting to dance. I think I saw the mayor doing Gangnam Style…"

"Oh, golly! I can't wait to see pictures of that."

Damon's right. If anything we've over-catered. I want to make sure we're known for quality food, and plenty of it.

"What's next?" Damon says, standing so close I feel his breath on my neck. Goose bumps break out on my skin, and I blush at the thought of him noticing them.

I clap my hands together. "OK, we need to slice the turkey and cranberry tart, and assemble the choux pastries—"

"With rare beef and horseradish?" Damon interrupts.

"Yes, good memory. Be careful with the choux…"

"I know, I'll treat it like I would a lady, gentle and lovingly."

I scoff and roll my eyes at Damon. "Can you get any cheesier?"

He grins back at me and I notice when he's really smiling he has these teeny tiny little dimples, which are inordinately adorable on a fully grown man.

Damon takes the tart from the oven, and begins slicing it. The scent of roasted turkey makes my mouth water. Before I know it, Damon's beside me again. "Here, try it." He slides a small corner of the tart into my mouth. It takes me by surprise and, in a rush to close my mouth lest I stand gawping, I feel my lips brush his fingertips. He leaves them there for what feels like for ever.

"Good?" he asks.

I nod. Unable to speak and not only because I'm chewing.

His expression changes, to something more serious. "You have to try new things once in a while, don't you think?"

I mumble agreement, and look down to the smoked-salmon blinis I'm making. Damon knows I always try my food before I send it out, so I know he isn't talking about the canapés. He goes back to the tart, and I let out a breath I've been holding.

The evening progresses so fast, I'm almost sad to think we're just about done.

Damon has a tea towel slung over his shoulder and is busy stacking the multitude of dishes into the industrial-sized dishwasher.

"Glad to see you know how to work one of those," I say. "You'll make someone a mighty fine husband one day."

He takes the tea towel from his shoulder and hangs it on the oven rail. "Oh, yeah? A man who cooks and cleans— you think there's a market out there for that?"

"Depends—what else can you do that might satisfy a lady?" The words tumble from my mouth before I'm able to stop them. I spin on my heel and head to the bathroom before he can respond. As I reach the door, laughter spills from me. *I can't believe I just said that.*

CHAPTER EIGHT

Christmas Eve and the excitement is palpable. The magic of Christmas never fails to amaze me. I bawled like a baby not two hours ago, when we delivered our gingerbread house to the children's hospital in Springfield. Damon came up with the idea when we were musing what to do with it. Those courageous kids' eyes went so wide when they saw four of us carry it in. We set it up nice and pretty in the games room. CeeCee made the kids gift bags full of treats, and they were so excited, it made my heart skip a beat. Just thinking of them being away from home at Christmas, and being so brave, made me appreciate everything I had in my life. I gave them all great big hugs before we left, and promised them we'd return for new year with some party supplies.

It's arctic out. I shrug down into my jacket as CeeCee and I close the shop, and breathe a sigh of relief. That's work over for us for a few days. No more baking and no more late nights.

"So," CeeCee says. "I'll see you tonight at the carols. I'm gonna make us a little feast, so you two lovebirds don't worry about a thing. Just concentrate on getting yourself prettied up." She casts a cursory glance from my head to my toes. "You not gonna wear jeans, sugar plum."

"Firstly, we're not lovebirds. Secondly, I'm planning on wearing a dress, but not if you're going to make it into something it isn't." I arch my brow, and try to stare CeeCee down, but I know from experience I won't win this battle.

"Most the girls in town would give their eye teeth to have your figure, and you hide it behind those old jeans, and scruffy sweaters. You got it, flaunt it, I say."

"Oh, please, CeeCee…"

"There's not a man gonna be able to resist you, especially the fine thing across the way, mmm hmm."

"You sound like you want to eat him."

She guffaws, her beautiful face crinkling up like paper. "You got that right—like gooey caramel, that boy."

Laughter barrels out of us, and I know we don't sound very gentle.

"You go on now, and get yourself ready. I'll see you at the town hall."

I lean down to kiss CeeCee's soft cheek; she smells like cinnamon and honey. "Thanks, Cee. I'll meet you there later, then."

Damon's shop is dark. He must have locked up while we were hooting and hollering.

Walking home from town, I notice it's gone quiet, sleepy. People have left for home to get ready for tonight; the schoolkids on holidays are probably toasting marshmallows by the fire. It's a nice feeling, the town relaxing in on itself. There's something incredibly sweet about small towns at this time of year. People look out for one another, and any tensions fall by the wayside. It's a nice place, old Ashford, and I can't imagine living anywhere else.

Jogging the few blocks to my house, I feel light as a feather. My weary legs don't ache any more. Funny how knowing I have a few days off energizes me.

Inside, my red dress lies sprawled over my lounge like a crimson wave, and my boots sit patiently on the floor. I know I'll be toasty warm inside the town hall; it'll just be a matter of not turning into an icicle walking there. We used to suffer in an amphitheater, year after year, each hoping the carols would end so we could go home and warm up. Until last year it was decided the carols, and all the Christmas festivities, would be held in the town hall from now on. It's a wonder no one thought of it sooner.

I head straight to the tub for a good soak. Who knows, I might even consider putting some gloop on my face. Just a small amount, mind.

Once the bath is run, I undress and survey my body in the mirror. I'm not thin; I have proper country-girl curves, but they seem to suit me, I think. I rub the soft swell of my belly, thinking about Joel, and our plans to start trying for babies just before he walked out. I wonder if that's what frightened him off, all that responsibility. He was never one to be tied down, always scheming to make millions. Grand plans to get rich quick. I listened to him intently, and I supported him, because he loved me.

I've never been attracted to the bright lights of a big city. All I crave is a happy, simple life. I have my job, and good friends, and family. Babies would be nice somewhere down the track. There's nothing I don't have right here in Ashford. Well, except love. And babies.

I scold myself for all this soppy thinking, and plunge myself into the bath. Tonight the town will come together and we'll sing and be content with what we have, and it'll be enough.

My red dress fits snugly, and my boots clack as I walk around fussing with the rest of the outfit. I'm not sure about the gloop. Scarlet lipstick smears my lips, and it just feels wrong, as if I've gone and dunked my mouth in lard. Mascara coats my lashes and it's all I can do to see past them; I get the heebie-jeebies when I glance upward and it looks as if I've got spiders' legs poking out of my eyes. And do women do this every day?

A knock at the door startles me. Damon. Groaning, I peep at myself once more. I'm worried I look like a clown with so much stuff on my face. And I've spritzed on too much perfume, I'm sure of it.

I fan myself with my hands to dispel the scent as I walk to the door.

"Well, look at you." His gooey caramel-colored eyes hone in on my face.

"Too much?" I ask. He ignores me and his gaze travels down my body, making me squirm.

"You look beautiful. Truly beautiful."

"Thank you."

I shift my feet and try not to stare at the floor. It's not a date; it's simply an escort to a public event. *It's not a date.* Damon's grinning like a fool, and he's dressed up for the occasion too. He's still wearing super-snug jeans, which I don't rightly oppose, but he's swapped those awful checker shirts for a tight sweater that stretches over his stomach. I can see the outline of his muscles. He's holding a thick black jacket over his shoulder. And a grey woolen scarf is wound expertly around his neck. He smells divine, like something sweet and sugary. Something edible. I retreat to grab my coat. An uncomfortable heat spreads through my body and if I didn't know better I'd say it was desire.

"Ready?" he asks.

"Sure am." I'm debating whether to hold his hand when his phone rings. I force a smile on my face as he motions to the cell and walks back down the driveway. Who in the hell keeps calling him? I'm feeling about as smart as tree bark even entertaining the thought of going out with Damon. It's as if I have a gift of picking men who want to break my heart.

Hold his hand? *Goddamn it, girl.* While I wait for him to finish, I head back to the bathroom and roughly wipe off the lipstick. Who was I trying to be anyhow? It's just not my thing. My eyes prick with tears, and I wonder what's got into me.

"Lil. Lil?"

"I'm coming," I say with one last look at the girl in the mirror.

Damon frowns when he sees me. "What happened?"

"Nothing. Let's go—we don't want to be late."

He goes to speak then changes his mind.

We walk to the town center, and Damon chatters away about inconsequential things. I nod, and say, "Mmm," but my heart isn't in it any more. I'm annoyed at myself for being upset. *Joel, remember, you love Joel.* But I begin to wonder if that's true. Maybe I just like the idea of being married because it means someone loves me above all else.

"Have I done something to upset you?"

An awkward silence hangs between us, while I walk a pace ahead. "Why do you say that?"

"You seem distant, and before you were positively glowing."

"I'm fine. Just tired. I might call it a night. I'll introduce you round, then head on home."

He catches up and puts his hands in his pockets. "Aw, what? What's upset you, Lil?"

I pull my coat tight and cross my arms. "Nothing, it's been a long day, that's all." There's an edge to my voice and I can't seem to disguise it. I hope I don't start crying on account of this fool.

He slaps his head. "Was it the phone call?" Stopping in front of me, he holds my face and forces me to look into his eyes. Lowering his voice to a husky whisper, he says, "Was it?"

"The call? Don't you mean *calls*? You sure are popular on that damn cell. Don't you know that's a lot of radiation going in your ear, right into that brain of yours?"

"Is that what's bothering you, all the calls?" He looks truly concerned, but that doesn't wash with me. Joel's phone was ringing off the hook near on a month before he walked out. I know what this is.

"It's nothing to do with me. Your phone is your business."

"Lil, I'm not going to lie. I like you. I like you a lot. But there's things you don't know about me. And I was gonna tell you…"

"What? That you've got a girl back in New Orleans that you're stringing along?"

He has the audacity to laugh. I glare up at him.

"No! There is no girl…well, there is a girl…"

Storming forward, I push past Damon, and head towards the town square.

"Wait! Would you wait?" he says, pulling me back by my elbow. "Let me explain."

Feeling utterly stupid, I brush tears away with my sleeve. "You don't owe me any explanation."

He groans, looks up at the sky. "You're making this hard."

I open my mouth to respond and he leans forward and cups my face with those big hands of his. "God, you're beautiful."

Before I know it, he's planted his lips on mine and I'm truly lost. Warmth spreads through me, while our lips collide. My body betrays me; my legs feel like jelly. My heart hammers against my chest as I pull him closer. I melt into him, and move my hands to his face, until my brain clicks back into gear.

There is a girl.

I step back, and glower at Damon. "What do you think you're doing? You got a girl back home and you're—"

"I sure do." He's grinning at me like a damn fool again. What is he playing at? He's got this love-struck, goofy look on his face.

"Are you drunk?"

He touches a finger to his lips, as if he's reliving the memory of our kiss before smiling at me again. "Come on, let's walk, and I'll tell you all about the girl back in New Orleans."

I snatch my hand away when he tries to clasp it. "Shoot."

"Her name's Charlotte, and she's as pretty as a picture." He darts me a look that says wait. "She's got these blond, itty-bitty curls, kind of like yours…"

"Get to the point, Damon. You aren't exactly winning me over here."

"She's turning seven next month. Charlotte, or Charlie as I call her, is my daughter."

A million thoughts flash through my mind, and I try to pluck one as they rush past. "Is that who keeps phoning you?"

"Yeah. I gave her a cell phone, and told her to call whenever she's missing me."

"She must be missing you a lot."

He clasps my hand and I let him this time, as I brush a stray curl from my face. "And what about her mamma?"

"We were married, happily for a while. The plan was always to come back here, once we had Charlotte. This is where my family are from, and I like small towns. I want Charlie to grow up safe, to be able to run around till dusk without worrying something bad is going to happen. But Dianne won't have it. She landed a corporate job, personal assistant to some bigwig, and everything we planned went out the window. Work took over her life—at least I thought it was work. Turns out Dianne was doing more than just typing for her boss."

His expression darkens for a second, as if he's revealed too much, my heart breaks for him: it really does. I know what he's been through, and it hurts. It sounds just like me and Joel, except he's got a baby girl to think about. "It must be hard not seeing Charlotte every day."

"Harder than I could ever imagine. And you know, I could've forgiven Dianne—well, I would have tried to, for Charlie's sake. But she's changed. I don't recognize her at all any more, and I know I can't live that kind of lie."

"What will you do? About Charlie?"

"She'll be here the day after Christmas for a week, and I guess that'll be it from now on. Holidays and weekends, and whenever I can convince Dianne to let her visit. Once Charlie's older she can decide for herself where she wants to live."

"I don't understand why you didn't stay in New Orleans, so you could be closer to her."

He looks curiously at me. I get the strangest sensation, as if he's come back here for me. But we didn't even know each other. My heart starts to pound. I've been listening to CeeCee's babble about second sight for too long.

"I belong here, in Ashford. And this is where I'm staying. Do you mind if I kiss you again?" Without waiting for a reply he bends and kisses me, so softly I swoon. I run my fingers through his too-long hair, and smile inwardly when they don't get tangled. Maybe those bodice-ripper books are right, after all.

We break apart. "You are sweeter than sugar," Damon says, his voice soft.

He gently kisses the tip of my nose and pulls me to him. I embrace his warmth, and love the feeling of his strong arms around me. I can worry about all kinds of things tomorrow, but for tonight I'm going to pretend he's mine, and there are no other complications, and I'm going to enjoy it.

We cross the icy road and see practically the whole town gawping at us. They're all circled around a bonfire that's a few feet in front of the town hall. A cheer goes up, and I flush red right to the very roots of my hair. How did we not notice them? I must've been spellbound by the damn man.

CeeCee is milling at the front of the crowd, near the bonfire, as we amble on over. Tears spill down her face, and I gather her in my arms. "I knew it. I knew that boy were special."

"It was one kiss, Cee," I whisper to her.

"I bought mistletoe, so don't you worry," she says, brandishing the leaf in front of me. We both sputter through our hands. She truly thinks of everything. We huddle around the fire, trying to keep warm while delicate flakes of snow drift down upon us. Children run and play as if it's the middle of summer, not feeling the cold the way we adults do.

I see kids I recognize from the café, scrambling over the big old fiberglass sleigh that Walt sets up. We're down to one reindeer now, poor old Rudolph, whose nose gets kissed by just about every family in town for luck. The children's laughter and squeals punctuate the air, and I smile for them, remembering my own excitement at this time of year when I was their age.

We move inside and make our way to Janey, who's handing out cups of eggnog. I wave at familiar faces; most wink back as if we're in a conspiracy. Damon clasps my hand as we mill about waiting for the show to start. At this moment I'm as happy as I can ever remember. CeeCee hands us both a candle as the choir assembles.

The music for *Amazing Grace* begins, and this time I smile. I know there'll be no crying tonight.

CHAPTER NINE

Muted light peeks through the blinds the next morning, and I lazily arch my back. I feel drowsy as a cat, on account of getting no sleep. Damon's beside me, curled around the flannelette sheets. I ease out of bed and head for the bathroom to brush my teeth and wash. The girl in the mirror looks flushed, radiant.

While I'm scrubbing the vestiges of the gloop from my face, I hear Damon wake. He pads around the room looking for his clothes. I stifle a giggle as I remember that they're somewhere near the front door. So, things kind of moved quickly after the carols last night. My ears burn, and I know the town folk are talking about us already.

I'll say he simply came back here for a glass of wine, and that was it. Being Christmas morning, there's more chance he can sneak out without anyone knowing he stayed over. Dizziness grips me when I think of Damon naked. That man's a fine specimen of the human form, and I just couldn't say no. Anyone would have done the same.

"Lil?"

I wander back into the bedroom. There he is, all propped up on the bed, shirtless, and pantless by the look of the bulge under the sheet.

"Good morning," I say, walking back into the room with only a towel on.

"I got you another present." He winks and pats the bed.

"Oh, yeah? Didn't you give me that a number of times last night?"

"That was only practice. And today is actually Christmas Day, so I'm going to need to start all over again."

I drop the towel and walk to the bed. He whistles appreciatively as I join him under the sheet.

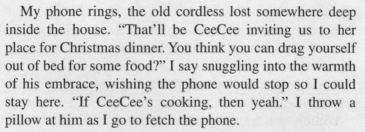

My phone rings, the old cordless lost somewhere deep inside the house. "That'll be CeeCee inviting us to her place for Christmas dinner. You think you can drag yourself out of bed for some food?" I say snuggling into the warmth of his embrace, wishing the phone would stop so I could stay here. "If CeeCee's cooking, then yeah." I throw a pillow at him as I go to fetch the phone.

As I scramble past the lounge I pick up an old throw rug and wrap it around myself. The phone continues to ring, and I find it on the kitchen bench.

"We're coming, Cee. Give me—"

"It's not Cee."

I nearly faint when I hear him speak. After all this time, my heart lifts, and I will it not to.

"What is it you want, Joel?" Can't imagine he's ringing to wish me a Merry Christmas. We haven't spoken since he left, and that wasn't because I didn't try. But a girl's got pride, and when he ignored my calls, my pleading texts, I stopped. Waiting for a reply, for any word, was devastating when I was met with silence.

"How are you, Lil?" He sounds off, as if he's forcing himself to sound chipper.

"I'm great, Joel. What can I do for you?" I'm aware of Damon not ten feet away, naked and waiting.

It seems wrong to leave him there, *and* wrong to have him there.

"I miss you."

I shake my head. Of all the times for him to call; if he'd called yesterday, things would have been markedly different.

"Oh, yeah? And what does your redhead have to say about that?"

"That's all over. Has been for a while now. I've spent this Christmas break mulling it over, and I know I made a mistake. A huge mistake."

A movement behind startles me. Damon's searching the floor for his clothes. He pulls his jeans on, and raises his eyebrows at me.

"Now's not a good time, Joel. I'm going to have to talk to you later."

Damon motions to the door. He looks bewildered, and I realize he must know who Joel is. I hold my hand up, so he knows to wait.

"Can I call you back? In the morning?" Joel says, his voice beseeching.

"I don't know about that. You take care now." I hang up the phone, and place it back on the counter.

"I'm gonna go," Damon says, a hurt look plastered on his face.

"Wait, why? I thought we were going to CeeCee's."

He stares at me for a length of time, waiting for me to speak. I haven't told him about Joel, but figure in this small town of ours he probably already knows.

"Was that your husband?" he asks, his voice breaking.

"Ex-husband."

"Sounds like you got some unfinished business there, Lil."

My eyes averted, I spin the phone, and desperately try to think.

"Please, Damon. Let's go to Cee's and enjoy the night."

He searches under the lounge for his sweater. He finds his boots and stuffs them on.

I shiver, cold despite the rug wrapped around me. He walks over, and holds me tight. We stay squeezed together for an age. Lightly, he kisses the top of my head, cups my face and stares into my eyes. "Lil, I'm going to give you some space to decide what you want. I know all about Joel. Rosaleen told me." He has the grace to blush. "So no pressure, OK? You need to do what's right for you. I'll always be here for you, no matter what."

His heartfelt plea breaks me. Tears spill as I watch him walk away. He's right, and that's what hurts most of all.

The phone rings again, and I let it go to the message bank. I don't want to talk to Joel again until I've decided how I feel. I head to the shower. I'll go to CeeCee's. Being in the bosom of her happy family will be just the distraction I need. Being alone is too much right now, especially with the scent of Damon still on my skin.

CHAPTER TEN

"Merry Christmas, sugar plum." CeeCee embraces me, and I will myself not to cry. Way to ruin Christmas, I think glumly to myself. I force a smile on my face as we break apart.

"And where is that fine-looking man?" She looks over my shoulder into the inky night.

"He's not here."

She searches my face. "And why not, pray tell?" She ushers me inside. The sound of children's laughter rolls down the hallway, and I can hear a TV blaring in the distance.

"He's got other things to do. Where is everyone? I want to say hello."

"Oh, no, you don't. Not before you tell me what's going on." CeeCee pushes me into her formal sitting room, a chintzy affair with floral lounges, and floral curtains, her fine china on display.

"It's nothing, Cee. I've got gifts for the—"

"Stop right there. Now, how long have I known you? And you think you can waltz in here with that pasty smile of yours, and those puffy red crying eyes, and I won't know somethin's wrong?"

Damn my crying eyes. I need to learn to sob silently, to un-puff.

"You gonna tell me or am I gonna have to march over to Damon's and find out myself?"

And she would. "It's not Damon. It's Joel."

"What you mean 'Joel'?"

"Joel rang, while Damon was there. He says he made a mistake, he's not with the redhead any more…"

"And what? He wants to come back to you?"

"I guess." I pluck at a tassel on the cushion. It's hard not to compare the two men, and the only thing that keeps me from running back to Damon is the fact that Joel and I have so much history. I hardly know Damon.

CeeCee's trying really hard not to let loose what's going on in her head but I can gather she's none too happy, by the grunting and sighing she's doing.

"Sugar plum, there ain't nothing I can say that's gonna change your mind. You have to decide, but I just want you to know, if you lie down with dogs, you gonna get fleas!"

I cackle along with CeeCee, and the mood lightens. "You certainly have a way with words."

"So, how you feel?"

"I don't know. Last night with Damon was magical. But Joel and I were together since we were kids, you know?"

"I know. And you the forgiving type. Sometimes when a man does wrong, you have to make him accountable, Lil. That man don't see what we see. He looks around this town, disdain on his face, like he better than most folk. I just wonder if he's really ready to move back here. You and I both know this place hasn't changed none in two years, and surely won't any time soon."

She's right. Pining for Joel these last two years, I realize I've been pining for what we lost, by him breaking my trust. And the fact that Joel always wanted a bigger, better life than what we had.

"You know, it's funny, Joel sounds exactly like Damon's ex-wife. They think small towns are full of hicks that don't know any better."

"I know all about her. Rosaleen told me everything at church today."

"She must have sore jaws what with all her yapping."

"She used to it, what with all the practice. And what about Damon? He has a baby girl?"

I remember Damon's Christmas gift then. I'd forgotten in the drama of the afternoon. A gingerbread-house kit. Complete with all the trimmings, ready for father and daughter to assemble when they get some time together. "Yes, he's got a little girl named Charlie. She's all set to visit after Christmas. And that's who's calling him every five minutes. Poor baby, she's missing him like crazy."

CeeCee nods, "I can imagine him as a daddy. I bet he's great with kids."

"But that's just it, Cee. What if his ex-wife decides she's made a mistake, just like Joel's done? And she wants to come back after a while? They've got a little girl—they'd have to try for her sake. And then what? I'm left all alone. I just don't know if I can go through that kind of heartbreak again."

"Really, sugar? You'd stop yourself from falling truly in love in case of a 'what if'? That ain't no way to live your life. Who knows what the future holds? But don't put your life on hold on account of one fool who weren't good enough for you."

Listening to CeeCee, so fervent and so right, I know. Everyone else has moved on, and it's time I did too.

"How do you think the little girl will feel about her daddy having a girlfriend?"

"A girlfriend who owns a shop that specializes in gingerbread men? Pretty darn good! If she don't love you from the get-go, we'll sure as shooting find a way to her heart."

"Doesn't that sound a little Hansel and Gretel to you?"

CeeCee slaps her leg, and laughs. When she's composed she says in a more serious tone, "Sounds as though you know what's in your heart, Lil. I'm a let you stew on it a bit more." She pulls me up from the lounge. "Come help me in the kitchen. I promised your mamma I was going to look after you. We need to get some meat on those bones of yours."

"I got plenty of meat on these bones, Cee."

"You could use a little more."

We enter the small kitchen. The table is laid with a red tablecloth, and small green candles sit in the center. Gold Christmas crackers are neatly lined up next to the cutlery. The delicious smell of turkey wafts out from the oven. I think of calling Damon. I can see him sitting here, carving up the meat, and joking with CeeCee. But I don't, just in case he says no.

"You want me to baste it?" I ask.

"Sure thing, honey. And I'm gonna start the gravy. I'll call the kids in to come say hello."

I yawn as I park the car in my driveway. It's nearly two a.m., and fatigue hits me like a brick. CeeCee and I got to talking and time raced away, as it does. One by one, the kids disappeared and the house grew quiet, until it was just the two of us sitting at the table, drinking gingerbread coffees.

The truck door creaks with protest as I push it open and hop down from the seat. I jump, startled, as I see a figure on the porch.

"Sorry, I scared you."

"No, it's OK."

"I couldn't stay away," he says.

"Oh, yeah?"

Heat floods my body as I run to him. I lift my face to his and kiss him full on the mouth. My heartbeat quickens as he moves his hands around my hips and pulls me closer. Cupping my face, he stops to gaze at me. "Yeah. If he wants you, he's going to have to fight me for you."

We laugh. "I've seen those muscles of yours. I think we'd better appoint the winner now, and save all the bloodshed."

He nuzzles into my neck, and I break out in goose bumps. We stand under the light of the moon, and look at each other, grinning like fools. "I missed you like crazy," he says, and bends to kiss me.

Joel and the memory of the years we spent together drift into the night, forgotten. From now on in, I only want the real thing. I'm not settling for second best any more.

Before I forget, I go to the truck, and retrieve Damon's present. He unwraps it delicately and I frown at the memory of myself wrenching the paper off the gift box when he gave me the turkey.

When he sees what it is, he stares at me, with that same all-knowing look, as if we've done this before. "She's going to love that."

"I hope so," I say. "After all, she's the most important person in your life, and I just want you to know I respect that. To me, your child, no matter what the circumstance, should be number one."

Damon embraces me, and whispers, "How'd I get to be so lucky?"

I lead him inside, past the Christmas tree with its flashing lights, so bright and colorful as if it's shrieking congratulations to us. I hold that thought in my heart, and vow never to forget this moment.

I pull Damon to the bedroom; all I want to do is fall asleep in the comfort of his arms. I can't wait to tell CeeCee. By now, she's probably planning the wedding; what with her second sight and all, she'll already know the date, the location, and what kind of dress I'll be wearing.

Chocolate Dreams at the Gingerbread Cafe

To Alyssa Davies,
it wouldn't have happened without your
spider-girl powers, so thank you.

CHAPTER ONE

"Good morning, pretty ladies. I come bearing gifts on this picture-perfect spring day," Damon says mock-formally, and bows. He steps through the doorway of the Gingerbread Café, brandishing an almighty postal tube like a sword. My heartbeat quickens at the sight of him. His wavy hair is lit by the sunshine behind casting a golden glow over him, like a spotlight.

My only employee, CeeCee, fluffs her curls, before giving him a great big launch hug that nearly knocks him off his feet and makes him groan with delight. She's a big bundle of southern exuberance, and is more like a friend and mother-figure to me.

"And pray tell, what is it?" she asks, pointing to the plain white packaging.

"Well, it's not a shrilling turkey, let's just say that." He winks.

I smile and glance over at the cash register where the God-awful bright yellow shrilling turkey he gave me at Christmas sits, like a mascot.

Damon walks to me and lands a soft kiss on my cheek. Woozy, that's how I feel when he's near me. I go jelly-legged and google-eyed, not my best look. It's so easy to get lost staring at his face, his lips. I fight the urge to launch myself at him too. Who knew love could feel like this? A dreamy, intoxicating, passion-fest.

retrieve another package. It's an odd shape and is wrapped haphazardly in newspaper.

As usual I forget to be delicate but figure it's only newspaper as I tear it to shreds to see what's underneath.

"How do you do it?" I pretend to be dazed with wonder. "I'm going to have the best collection of...*ugly* going round!" I smile as I press a small button to switch it on. An evil-eyed bunny rabbit starts hopping maniacally across the silver bench, singing out of tune about hot cross buns. Laughter barrels out of us as we watch the demented toy.

"I think this may trump the shrilling turkey!" CeeCee hoots.

"You, my friend, just started another war." I sidle up to Damon, and hug him loosely around his hips. "You know that, right?" My lips twitch with the urge to kiss him.

He drapes his arm over me and lands a kiss on the top of my head. "A war on...*unique* seasonal collectibles? That so? Well, before I leave you to attend to the customers who, by the looks, are waiting patiently on my stoop, there's one thing you should know—seems there's a teeny tiny fault with the hopping bunnies. The salesperson was basically giving them away. I mean, I just had to buy it at that bargain-basement price..."

I give him a playful shove. "Get on with it, what's the fault?"

"It seems Peter Rabbit here doesn't have an off switch. He can keep that joyful noise up *all* day long."

"Joyful noise? That what you call it?" CeeCee says. "Sounds more like this bunny got his foot caught in a rabbit trap to me."

"You can thank me later," he says, edging towards the door while I pretend to lob the rabbit at him.

We watch him stride across the street; as usual our eyes are glued to his butt, which looks all sorts of perfect under a pair of tight denim jeans. His shirt lifts in the breeze and I see the tanned, smooth skin of his lower back. The memory of running my hand along his naked body makes me shiver. I shake the thought away, not wanting to look like some kind of love-struck idiot, my mouth hanging open, ogling him from the window. I pull myself together and gaze over at CeeCee, who's uncharacteristically lost for words, staring at him too.

"Hmm, that fine-looking thing sure do know how to please a woman," CeeCee says, as if she's in a daze and we giggle. Every time she brings Damon into a conversation she calls him 'that fine-looking thing' which always reduces us to laughter.

"Yes, ma'am, he sure does," I say sarcastically, holding my hands over my ears. "But I've got a bad feeling this bunny rabbit is about to have a tragic accident."

She smirks. "It's funny, I thought the very same thing." CeeCee picks it up and studies the underside. "There must be an off switch. Surely he was only playin'."

The cordless phone trills, making us jump. "I'll take it in the office so I can hear. It's probably *that fine-looking thing* calling to gloat," I say, jogging to the back of the café to the small office.

Still smiling, I answer, "The Gingerbread Café, Lil speaking." And wait for Damon's velvety voice to talk back.

"Lily-Ella, it's me." It's a velvety voice all right, but it's not Damon's. The way Joel rolls the Ls of my full name takes me back to my old life. Closing my eyes, I picture him, his thick black hair pushed back from his face while he rakes his fingers through it, a subconscious mannerism. I stiffen; it's been months since we talked. And two years since we divorced. I make my voice businesslike. "How are you, Joel?"

"I've been better." He lets out a short hollow laugh.

"So you got the boxes I sent?" The detritus of Joel's life with me had been stashed around my house, things I stopped seeing because they'd been there for an age, but Damon noticed as soon as he moved in a few weeks back. A baseball glove in the hall closet, old clothes in the spare room, used car parts in the shed. Goes to show just how quick Joel upped and left. Damon didn't say a word about it but I could see a shadow of doubt cross his face as he kept stumbling across Joel's things so I decided it was high time I de-cluttered my old life.

"Yeah, I got them. None of it means anything 'cept the photos. Spent a whole night staring at them."

"Don't talk like that. They're just pictures. Nothing more."

I'd sent Joel half of our wedding pictures with the boxes, because it meant something back then, and there's no point pretending it didn't happen. When I divvied them up, I spent some time looking through them too, but all I felt was a sort of sadness that those two bright-eyed lovers staring back at me weren't so suited after all.

He sighs. "Look, Lil, I know I made all kinds of mistakes, but I'm a changed man. Totally different from the one who left…"

"Stop, Joel. That sounds like a line."

CeeCee calls out, "Well, is it Damon? Tell him I think I've figured out a way to stop it. Can't barely hear it from the depths of the chest freezer…" Her cackle follows me into the office.

"Well, it's coming from my heart, Lil," Joel says, in a slightly offended tone.

"*You* did this, Joel. You made your choice, and it wasn't me."

Two years I pined for him after he walked out. Just after he managed to lose our house, and his car yard in one of his get-rich-quick schemes. He took a gamble with our finances and lost without breathing a word of it to me until it was too late. I struggled to keep the Gingerbread Café going, and held on through some truly bad times. But he didn't care; our home was taken by the bank, and we were forced to rent a tiny cottage. He walked away without a backward glance, right into the arms of another woman. To think I waited for him *for two years* ready to forgive. I was a damn fool, and I'm sure as hell not going to make that mistake again.

"Look, baby, I know you're with some other guy—"

"That's none of your business!"

"So our history doesn't count for anything? You can't honestly say it wasn't one helluva marriage before things went…pear-shaped."

The saccharine timbre of his voice reminds me that he can't be trusted. He's a salesman through and through. CeeCee says he could sell fire to Satan if you gave him half a chance. "Pear-shaped? Is that what you call it?" It's impossible to keep the sarcasm from my voice. "And you're right, it was one helluva marriage, emphasis on the *hell*. I have to go."

"Lil, can we meet? There's something I really need to discuss with you."

Exasperated, I exhale down the line. "I think we've discussed everything."

"I'm out at Old Lou's…"

I groan inwardly. Old Lou owns a big property on the outskirts of Ashford. It looks more like a junk yard than a place where someone lives. I lower my voice, "How long have you been here?"

"A couple of days. I was planning to go check out that new shop in town; you know the one, sells small goods…"

Damon's shop. There's an abrasiveness to Joel's voice; he obviously knows all the details of my new relationship.

I pinch the bridge of my nose as my head begins to ache. I wonder what he's scheming in that great big melon head of his. One thing I know for sure is that it's never black and white when it comes to Joel.

Maybe I can nip this in the bud before it blooms into trouble. "Stay away from that shop. I'll give you ten minutes tonight, and that's it, Joel. And you're right, I am with someone else, so if it's about reconciliation forget it." I end the call so he can't respond.

Worry gnaws at me. What's he up to?

"Sugar plum?" CeeCee yells. "Are we doing these eggs or not?"

"Coming!" I put the phone back in the cradle on the desk and pray he doesn't call again.

Heading back to CeeCee, I see she's laid the bench with everything we need to make Paschal eggs. Real eggs that we're going to drain and dye in a rainbow of colors so the children of Ashford can paint them at the chocolate festival.

"What'd he say?" She smirks up at me. "Did you tell him the bunny is suffering a severe case of frostbite?"

I grin in spite of myself when I hear the muffled drone of the bunny from the square chest freezer, winding down as if its battery is almost flat. "It wasn't Damon. It was someone…about a catering job. Just a quote." The lie catches in the back of my throat. I look away so she doesn't notice my hesitation.

"Another one? You two are surely making it big in the catering world."

Damon and I joined forces at Christmas time to cater parties outside Ashford. I was catering alone before but was missing out on the bigger jobs because I couldn't do it by myself. With Damon's help, we've managed to spread our wings further afield, and have secured lots of corporate events in the bigger towns that border Ashford, Connecticut. Our town, while pleasant to live in, doesn't have much of a call for canapés, or any of the fancy dishes we make to order. Luckily we don't have anything booked until after the festival, otherwise I don't know how we'd manage.

"So," I say, hoping to distract CeeCee from asking for more details about the phone call. "Who's doing what here?" I gaze down at the huge bowl of eggs and wonder how long it's going to take us to drain them all.

"I'm not one to beg off, Lil, but I picture how those eggs came to be and I can't imagine myself puckerin' up to blow the contents out. You get my drift?"

"Cee! Now I'm picturing the chicken laying the egg. That's just plain gross!" I look at her, bemused, and slightly queasy at the thought.

"Mind, I washed 'em good. You'll be OK." Her lips wobble and a second later she doubles over; her big-bellied southern haw rings out, making it damn near impossible not to join in.

For the first time ever the Gingerbread Café is flourishing. We've had extra money to invest in more supplies and let our creativity loose. Our window display is a show-stopper, crafted to look like a magical forest. We have trees made with fluffy green cotton candy and dark chocolate trunks. We've set up a bed of burnished hay made from toffee-like spun sugar where our chocolate bunnies nest. And tiny yellow chicks, made from fondant icing, are 'hatching' out of white chocolate eggs. The intricate display has drawn in kids and adults alike, the heady smell of molten chocolate has worked wonders on passers-by, who can't help but wander in and see what we're up to.

Semi-composed from the thought of tasting raw egg yolk, I glance back at Cee, who's moved away and is slapping her hand on the bench every time laughter gets the better of her. "Is this going to continue?" I say, arching my eyebrows. "Every time I put my lips on an egg?" I'm supposed to poke a hole in each end of the egg and blow down so the liquid spills out. Now she's got me picturing the origins of the egg, and it's kind of disgusting. CeeCee certainly has a way of lightening my mood, and I chortle along with her.

I scrutinize the egg up close and she shrieks; her brown skin is almost purple from laughter; she's gasping for breath and gripping her belly. "OK...OK, I'm nearly done." She glances back at the eggs, and manages to hold in her merriment as tears stream from her eyes. "Glory be, I'm too old for this."

"Oh, yeah? If you don't stop I'm going to make you suck eggs."

"*Suck eggs*! You meant to be blowing!" This starts us off again. "It's a wonder we get any work done with this kinda carry on!" CeeCee manages, before her guffaw carries to the street where a few people walking past stop to gawp at us, with quizzical expressions.

We manage to control ourselves enough to set to work. CeeCee fills up a saucepan with warm water and adds a dash of vinegar and a hefty squirt of red food coloring, ready to dye the eggshells.

I pierce the first egg and glance over at Cee. She sputters into her hand and walks away, her shoulders shaking. "I can't watch. I just can't!"

By the time she wanders back I've done five eggs. "Only ninety-five to go." I wipe my forehead in exaggeration.

CeeCee takes the empty shells, and gently drops them in the pot of scarlet water. She stirs softly so they dye evenly before taking them out to dry in an empty egg carton.

We work quietly, and my mind drifts back to Joel. He hasn't been back to Ashford since we split; it seems odd he'd come back now. I wonder if he's going to try to make trouble for me, but most of all I worry about what Damon will make of it. Joel can be pigheaded—if he sets his mind to something he usually figures a way to get it. I can't help feeling anxious he's back and clearly with some kind of agenda.

I curse under my breath as I break an egg. My jittery hands are no match for the delicate shell, and I end up holding a yolky mess.

"Don't think that's how you're goin' to get out of doing them, Lil," CeeCee jokes.

"Got to admit it's much faster," I reply as I use paper towels to wipe away the goo. A breeze wafts in, making the pages of our magazines flutter on the tables. The glorious floral-scented spring air pulls people from their homes like magic after winter finally packed up and left for another year. It won't be long before we're inundated with customers who want to idle away the morning soaking up the soft sun from the comfort of an outside table. Earlier this morning CeeCee made a batch of buttermilk pies, which bake nice and slow in the oven. The occasional burst of vanilla essence floats outside, tempting people to stop in and ask how long they'll be.

"Cherry blossom…" CeeCee's voice is soft with concentration "…can you pass me the blue dye?"

"Sure, give me a sec." I stand over the bin and shake the rest of the gooey egg off my hands. "Blue, and what comes next?"

"That little bottle of sunshine right there." She points to the yellow dye, her face lit up.

I break another egg and this time my curse rings out.

"Glory be, sugar plum, you sure do got butterfingers today. You want me to have a go?"

"No. It's OK, I'll go slower." Damn Joel. I'm worried. I don't want him to cast a pall of ugliness over my new life. And what else can he be here for, except to make trouble?

"Mmm hmm," she says distractedly as she spoons an egg out of the pot and rests it next to the others in the carton. She stares straight at me and says, "What's botherin' you? You suddenly got the clumsies. It ain't like you to make mistakes no matter how finicky the job is."

Moving to the sink to wash my hands, I laugh her off. "It's nothing, Cee."

CeeCee doesn't pry into it again and I'm grateful my back is turned so she doesn't try to stare me down. I confess all when she does that and she knows it. We don't usually keep secrets from each other. But for now, it's better if she doesn't know Joel's back. She'd probably drive out to Old Lou's and holler at him something fierce. There's no love lost between those two. CeeCee is protective of me, like a mother hen, and for that reason, I won't tell her about Joel just yet.

CHAPTER TWO

I head outside to update the chalk board and to clear the tables of empty coffee cups.

Bending down, I write about the buttermilk pies, and the chocolate-dipped strawberries, we made earlier. I turn as someone lightly taps me on the shoulder. I hear a little giggle as I feel a tap on the other shoulder. I spin the other way and look into the deep azure eyes of Charlie. She giggles again, a high chipmunk-like sound.

"Tricked you."

I take her into my arms. Her gorgeous blonde curls tickle my nose as I bury my face in her hair. "Charlie bear, you're here!"

"Yep, for a whole week! Daddy said we're going to paint eggs and do lots of fun stuff…"

"We sure are." I glance across the way at Damon, who stands to watch she's crossed the street safely. I wave at him and point to the café as I take Charlie's hand and lead her inside. Damon's daughter, Charlotte, or Charlie as we call her, first came to Ashford just after Christmas. I kept my distance so she could enjoy her time with her daddy but it didn't take long for her to toddle over the road and ask for a gingerbread man. Soon enough she was helping cut out the figures and stayed most days to bake alongside us, before leaving to go back to her mom, and return to school in New Orleans.

It was decided Charlie would spend the Easter break with us because her mom was taking a trip to Vegas, and it's not the kind of place suitable for a seven-year-old.

"You know what else we're going to do?" I ask as I set her up on a stool by the bench.

"What?"

"We're going to have a chocolate festival! The whole town is getting involved, even your daddy, so we might need someone to be our taste tester…"

She squeals and claps her hands. "I can!"

I look solemnly at her. "OK, you're our quality control. And do you know what else? If you're really lucky, you might meet the Easter bunny!"

She slaps her hands on her cheeks and says, "The real Easter bunny?"

"Of course!"

CeeCee and I cackled like witches when we found an adult bunny-rabbit dress-up online, and even more so when they only had one in stock in pink *and*…in Damon's size. It was our finest moment, presenting him the suit complete with ginormous rosy rabbit head with flippy-floppy ears. So we might have sung a nursery rhyme or two to convince him it was for the children…when in actual fact it was for our amusement.

"I can't wait!"

"And then on Sunday we have the town egg hunt. It's going to be great fun. You'll have a basket to hold all the lovely eggs the Easter bunny hid."

"We might need a map." Her little mouth puckers.

I grin and bend down to hug her small frame. "A map might be a good idea. Now let me fix you a snack. CeeCee'll be back soon, and she was going to ask you to help her bake some hot-cross-bun cake pops, but it's a very tricky job. I wasn't sure if you were up to the task…"

"I am! I am! I love cake pops. CeeCee said I'm the best helper she's ever had."

"She's right." I pour Charlie a glass of milk. "Now, how about you go look in that fridge over there, and see what you want to eat?" Her eyes light up as she sees the variety of chocolate lining the shelves.

"They're all so pretty. Can I have the gingerbread-man one?" She points to an egg wrapped in the special foil. I kiss the top of her head before taking it out for her. "Good choice," I say.

Cee returns not long after and yelps when she sees Charlie helping me ice a chocolate crepe cake.

"Oh, my sweet little angel! Come here and give me a great big hug!" Charlie slips off the stool and races into her arms. CeeCee adores the little girl and seems to have adopted her as another grandbaby.

Once we're all settled down, CeeCee tells Charlie what they need to make hot-cross-bun cake pops.

"They gonna be a little taste explosion," CeeCee tells her. "You pop the square of fruity cake in your mouth, and *bam*, it's a mini hot-cross bun on a stick! With a nice coating of chocolate, mind."

"Just like a hot-cross bun?"

"The very same with the white cross and everythin'."

Charlie looks serious as she helps CeeCee pull out the ingredients they'll need.

The Gingerbread Café resembles a chocolate shop by the time CeeCee and I finish the day's work. Square ganache-filled truffles shine from their perch in the glass display fridge. We've made a range of flavors, from simple dark chocolate to the more time-consuming white chocolate with Earl-Grey-tea-infused ganache. For those, we candied the delicate tea leaves and used tweezers to prop them on top of the small squares of perfection. There are caramel pecan truffles with honeyed pecans on top, because we figured some people would appreciate some more extravagant flavors.

We drag ourselves away from the fridge and tidy up as the soft sunlight begins to fade. The street empties as town folk make their way home at the end of the day. Charlie wandered off home with one of the older kids who live next door to us to watch movies but more likely take a nap after a busy day baking.

"I'm going to go ahead and bring the tables inside," I say to CeeCee. Outside the air has cooled, and I hug my cardigan tight. Flowers bloom from our pots, bright red roses so vivid I can't help but stare at them, enjoying the way they sway slightly in the breeze, almost as if they're waving. I fold a small wooden table, and go to lift it when Damon appears.

"Let me take care of that," he says, lifting it as if it weighs nothing.

He hoists it over his shoulder and navigates the doorway, careful not to knock it into the newly painted walls. In his wake, his aftershave and the mix of scents that perpetually envelop him drifts to where I stand. The usual Damon smell of coffee beans, and something spicy with a hint of cinnamon; he's downright edible, and it makes my pulse quicken.

When he returns for another table, he glances at me and stops. "What is it?" Concern etches his face. "You look so pale, Lil." He rubs his strong hands up and down my arms.

"Just enjoying the view," I say, giving him the once-over, but my voice sounds strange, even to me.

He pulls me to him, and holds me tight. Resting my face against his chest, I hear the steady thrum of his heart.

It's comforting and in some cheesy way I imagine it beats just for me. I know I need to confide in him about Joel. Damon's not one to tell me what to do, but I owe it to him to explain so he knows it's about closure once and for all and nothing more.

He clasps my face, rains kisses on my forehead, the tip of my nose, and then ever so softly on my lips. I close my eyes, and kiss him back, harder with more urgency. We pull apart and I gaze up at him; his eyes are lit with a question. He tilts his head, like a sign to start talking.

"It's Joel," I say. "He's back and he wants to see me. Says he's got something to discuss." Damon's hands fall to the crook of my back, and I shuffle closer to him. Arching slightly to see each other, we rest thigh to thigh, hip to hip, connected.

I continue: "I don't want you to think it's anything more than it is. I feel absolutely nothing for him except pity, if you can even call it that."

He searches my face before replying. "What do you think he feels for you, though, Lil?"

"Whatever it is it'll only be a passing thing. He's at a stopgap right now, and that's got something to do with it. But I won't go if it makes you second-guess us." I gesture to the small space between our hearts.

Damon lets out a gruff sigh. "Nothing'll make me second-guess us, Lil. If you feel you need to do this, you go on and do it. I trust you, Lil, I *know* you. And that's all that matters to me. Plus we don't call you feisty Lil for nothing. I know you can look after yourself."

I slap him playfully across the arm. "Who calls me feisty Lil?"

He shrugs. "You know…everyone."

I grin up at him. "They do not!"

"OK, they don't." His face softens with laughter.

"Well, I'm glad you trust me, and I just know it'll be easier to see him face to face and sort this out once and for all."

"If he hurts you in any way, you know I'll kill him, right?" Damon says, his voice light, but I can still make out the serious undertone.

"You'll have to get in line behind Cee. Who I haven't told, by the way," I add quickly.

He runs a hand through my hair, tucking it behind my ear. He's so gentle in everything he does; I get to wondering how I'm so lucky. "You think that's wise?" he asks. "I happen to know from experience it doesn't take long for news to spread around town."

I blush, thinking back to Christmas Eve when Damon and I first kissed. No way we could keep it to ourselves when we embraced passionately in front of the town hall where almost all of the residents of Ashford stood, waiting for the carols to begin. I blame Damon for that public display of affection. He's got a way of making me forget where I am and what the hell I'm doing.

"Lil?"

I blink away the memory of kissing him in the snow. "I'll tell her tomorrow, when he's gone. CeeCee's liable to hunt out Curtis's old shotgun if she knows he's here."

"How's her aim?" he jokes, embracing me once more.

Back inside, I banish the thought of the impending visit with Joel as CeeCee and I do the usual clean-up. She stacks the magazines and resets the tables, and I give the kitchen a mop.

"Sugar?"

"Mmm?"

"I had an idea 'bout the chocolate festival. We sure gonna be busy serving folks, and all we've got organized for the l'il ones is painting those eggs. Why don't we do some more activities for them so their parents can enjoy the day while we occupy the kids in here? You know, maybe some face painting or some such…"

"Great idea, Cee! We can do all sorts of things. I was going to make gingerbread Easter bunnies—they can decorate them with tubes of icing. And what about egg-and-spoon races? And egg rolling? This'll be so much fun for Charlie!" I put the mop back in the bucket and swish it around.

"Right," CeeCee says, blustering over with a bout of enthusiasm. "We better make a list. We've only got a few days to prepare."

"I'll ask the Mary-Jos to bring their face-painting kits. They're like children themselves—I know they'll have a great time." Nothing has changed with the three Mary-Jos; cousins who look the same, talk the same, and hang around Damon's shop, fluttering their eyelashes at him in the cutest case of puppy love going around. They're sweet teenagers, just bored in Ashford.

They delighted in making posters for the chocolate festival, I think mainly so they could drive to the bigger towns and gawk at the teenage boys as they handed them out.

"Surely they'll jump at the chance to do something other than look pretty," CeeCee mutters. "Let's start on those gingerbread bunnies."

Glancing at the clock, I see it's almost six. I don't want to get out to Old Lou's too late and have Damon's mind racing at where I am. My stomach flips having to lie again to CeeCee. "Let's leave it for today. I'll come in early tomorrow and make a start. How does that sound?"

She yawns and pads over the wet floor, careful not to slip. "You right, I got all excited on account of those kids comin' here. Let's start tomorrow, and you see 'bout asking the Mary-Jos if they can drag themselves away from Damon's stoop to help out on Saturday."

I nod and fumble with my apron strings.

"We done?" She surveys the café; everything except the mop bucket is as it should be.

"Looks like it. Head on home, and I'll see you tomorrow. Don't forget your scarf." This time of the evening there's a chill in the air.

"Shoot, then I got to cross over your nice clean floor again. No matter, I'll get it tomorrow. You go see that fine-looking thing now, you hear? Don't fuss around here no more."

"Yes, ma'am." I hug her tight and promise myself I'll tell her all about Joel tomorrow.

CHAPTER THREE

The wind wails softly as I step outside to empty the bucket and wash the mop. I go to put the cleaning equipment back in the small storage shed when I'm blinded by the headlights of a wide old car pulling in the car park. The engine rumbles like some kind of beast.

I shield my eyes from the glare of the lights before the car crawls into a space, and the bright headlights shine on the fence instead. I don't recognize the car, but can guess by the classic model it's something belonging to Old Lou. Cars like this are spread all over his property dying a slow rusty death from being pummeled by the elements.

The car shudders to a halt, and out steps Joel.

My stride falters when I see his familiar lopsided smile. He's dressed in low-slung denim jeans, and a tight black sweater. His dark hair is swept back, as always, making his olive skin and deep brown eyes the first thing a girl might notice. But all I see is the same expression on his face when he was close to making a sale at the car yard, and I steel myself.

"Thought you might've got cold feet." He saunters over to me, and pecks me on the cheek. Up close, I see dark circles under his eyes, and take a step back at the stale smell of cheap wine that cloaks him. "Figured I'd drop by and see you instead, and your…empire." He waves a hand towards the café.

"Let me lock this up." I point to the storage shed. "Go on inside." I'm surprised to feel absolutely nothing from seeing him again. I thought maybe there'd be some kind of wistful flutter of the memory of our love but instead, there's just numbness. I guess the spell he had over me is long gone.

He moves to hug me but I sidestep him. "Joel, I warned you about that. I'm with someone else now."

Putting a hand to his chest, he feigns surprise. "It was just a hello hug between old friends."

"Go on in," I say more forcefully.

"OK, don't run away now." He winks, and runs a hand through his hair.

I ignore him, and turn back to the shed as I hear his heavy footfalls on the back steps.

Taking a deep breath, I remind myself to give him ten minutes, and then send him on his way. Damon will be waiting for me. Longing races up my spine when I think of going home and showing him just how much he means to me.

When I walk back into the café Joel's standing by the cash register shaking the shrilling turkey. "What are you doing?" I ask, snatching it away from him.

"Whoa, you sure are defensive these days, Lil. I was wondering what the hell it does, that's all."

There's no way I want him anywhere near Damon's gift; silly as it sounds, it's special to me, that goddamn turkey, and the memory it holds.

I stuff the turkey back on his spot, and cross my arms over my chest. "So, what is it you had to discuss with me?"

He rubs his hands together and surveys the kitchen. "Coffee first? Or maybe, a glass of something stronger?"

"Everything's switched off. And we don't keep alcohol here."

He clucks his tongue, and slowly wanders around the café, picking up things as if he's in a store. "I like what you've done with the place. It looks...cozy. No more stark white walls, and only a stick or two of furniture."

I itch to say it'd taken a good two years and a lot of hard work to be able to afford luxuries such as paint and the odd assortment of shabby-chic secondhand furniture we'd acquired slowly. But I bite my tongue. He's stalling for time, and I don't want to drag this visit out any longer than I have to.

"Joel, I really have to go. So can we get down to it?"

When he turns to me, I hold my breath; something in his eyes scares me. "You know I left here with only the clothes on my back. I didn't ask for anything from you."

I return his glare. He can't be serious. "That's because there was nothing *to* take from me, Joel. Remember?"

"Is it serious between you and Damon?"

I rack my mind wondering who would have told him about Damon. Joel isn't exactly popular in Ashford, and Old Lou never ventures into town. Even Rosaleen, the town know-it-all, wouldn't stoop so low as to tell Joel anything.

"It sure is." I pick up my handbag, and fling the strap over my shoulder. "If that's all you came to discuss then your question is answered. I hope you have a nice life."

He laughs, a low, mean sound. "I do have a question for you, Lil. How much does the café make these days? I've seen flyers all over the place advertising your so-called chocolate festival. Word is you've got yourself a nice little earner..."

The malice in his voice leaves me cold. "That's none of your concern now, Joel."

"No?" He steps behind the register and presses the button to spring it open. When I see his face drop, I hide my smile. The takings are safely tucked away in the freezer in an empty box of frozen peas. CeeCee and I figure no one would look there, not that there's much crime around Ashford anyway.

"What, Joel, do you need a loan or something?" I try to keep the disdain from my voice. "You think you can walk in here and act like some kind of evil cameo from a Batman movie and I'm just going to stand here and take it? You really need a trench coat or some gloopy black eyeliner to be believable."

He slams the cash register shut. "I'll cut to the chase, then, silly Lily." His voice is hard, and his eyes no longer hold the close-the-deal look; they're icy with anger. "When I left you for the glamorous Rita, I'll admit it was for her sizeable assets." He holds his hands out in front of his chest.

I scoff. "Oh, please. As if I care."

"It wasn't just the double-D cups that had me hooked. It was also her healthy bank balance. Anyhow, that's all finished. And it pains me more than you know to say she didn't set me up like she promised. So what do I do? You gotta spend money to make money, right? Speculate to accumulate?"

I purse my lips; he's a walking cliché. What did I ever see in him? "What is it you want, Joel?"

"Well, I got to thinking where can I get some money fast to start another car yard… Any idea?"

I cross my arms over my chest. "No idea."

"And then I thought…actually, yes! The quaint little Gingerbread Café, a veritable money spinner of late. I got to remembering how this café came about. Do you remember, Lil?"

My throat tightens, and I blink back tears. There's no way I'm giving him the pleasure of seeing me cry. "What are you saying, Joel?" It's all I can do not to hiss the words.

"I set you up, Lil. I paid for all of this…stuff." He turns, his arms outstretched. "As I recall I *loaned* you twenty grand to get this place started. That oven is mine, that fridge; hmm, I think I paid for that dishwasher too."

"You lost everything we had, Joel. *Everything.* I managed to hang onto the café by sheer hard work. I don't owe you a cent." I hear the tremor in my voice and hate myself for it. It's true Joel gave me the money to set up the kitchen in the café, but I didn't consider it a loan, since I supported him financially most of my adult life before moving on to start the Gingerbread Café.

He sneers, and I resist the urge to slap the look from his face. "It was just bad timing, Lil. The whole global financial crisis thing. We both lost things we loved. But the money I loaned you wasn't mine—it was…family money, you could say."

"You've got to be kidding me, Joel. This is low even for you." I shake my head, wondering how a man I once loved could be as cold and as calculating as this. *Family money.* I want to rage at him. Before he died, Harry, Joel's father, was a loan shark, who cost a lot of people their homes with his exorbitant rates. I should have known better that any money from him would come with strings attached.

"But I need to make a fresh start. And far as I see, this is the only way I can do it. You've got a Guthrie now…very clever, Lil. You won't want for anything again, will you?" I scowl at him for all I'm worth.

Damon's family is from old money. The Guthries made their fortune from transport: they owned a fleet of cargo ships and train lines back in their heyday, but have since sold their empire, and now live off the profits. Some place more hoity-toity than Ashford, but they're good people, and are well respected in this town on the rare occasions they visit. Damon works off his own bat, doesn't take handouts from them. He's got his pride, unlike Joel here.

"I would never borrow a dime off Damon or his family! Now, get out! You'll get nothing from me." Fury makes my hands shake and my voice rise an octave.

"Maybe it's time to sell this place, then?" He walks to the back door then stops and turns, pulling an envelope from his back pocket. "Here, some light reading for you. I've already been to a lawyer, and, as you'll see, you owe me. Twenty large, Lil. Plus interest. It's been three years you've sat on my money." He throws the envelope on the bench and slams the door behind him.

I listen to the low rumble of the car as it leaves the car park before I let the tears flow. Sitting at a table, I cradle my head in my hands and blubber until I can't see straight. I've never been a pretty crier, and this time isn't any different. Loud choking sobs make me hiccough, and sputter, but I let it all out. Even just the *threat* of having to sell the Gingerbread Café is enough to make me dizzy with worry. He couldn't have picked a worse time to drop this on me; there's still so much to organize for the festival, and now this will hang over me like a black cloud.

Regret sits heavy in my heart about keeping Joel's visit from CeeCee. She'll be fit to kill when she knows I met him without telling her. And Damon? What will he think about the mess I'm in? I sit there for an age, thinking of all the things I should have said.

The moon shines bright in the dark night. I walk to the window and stare up at it. I think of telling CeeCee and know her retort would be, *"There's not a snowball's chance in hell you losing the Gingerbread Café, not on account of that damn fool, anyways."*

CHAPTER FOUR

My old truck whines as I pull into the driveway; another thing I was all set on replacing this year, but I guess that may not happen now. I jump down from the cab, and head up the porch. Light from inside peeks out through the thick lace curtains. I take a deep breath and brace myself to tell Damon.

Inside, I throw my bag and keys on the buffet, and head towards the kitchen.

Damon's there, his back towards me, a tea towel slung over his shoulder as he stirs something that smells tangy, in a pot.

"Hey," I say, edging towards him.

He turns to me as he pulls the tea towel from his shoulder and tosses it on the bench. His smile disappears when he glances at my face, which is probably puffy and ruddy, and all sorts of ugly.

"Hey, you." He takes me in his arms, and I want to kick myself when the tears start again. This time they fall silently without the great big chest heaves. He doesn't ask anything, just holds me tight. I close my eyes, and thank God I have a man who loves me right.

I tilt my head and show him my face. "Lil." He wipes my tears away, and leans down to kiss me softly on the lips.

He exhales slowly and squeezes me tight once more, before stepping back, and pouring a glass of red wine. "You need to unwind. Take this—" he hands me the glass "—and go soak in the tub. It's all ready for you. How about I finish up in here, and come talk to you while you relax?"

I take a sip of wine, and feel myself go heavy with relief. "Sounds great." I kiss his cheek. "Where's Charlie bear?"

"She's asleep. She spent the rest of the afternoon up in the treehouse with the kids next door." His face softens, and I know he's thinking of the lifestyle here for his little girl. He wants her to be able to roam free and explore safely, the way kids in small towns can. A place where they make their own fun, like we did at their age, before computers and technology took over.

"She must be exhausted. Did she have some dinner?"

"Home-made fish fingers." He grins as he sees my eyes light up. "And I made some for us too."

"You're never too old for fish fingers. What's in the pot?" I motion to the burgundy syrup he's stirring.

"Plum sauce—thought I'd try the recipe out before the festival. It's to go with the deep-fried Camembert dish."

"My mouth's watering. I hope you're making some Camembert to go with my fish fingers…"

"Surely am. Taste this first." He holds the spoon to my lips; the sauce is sweet, and tart at the same time.

"It's good," I say.

He drops the spoon in the pot, and kisses the taste from my mouth.

His voice is husky. "You better get in the bath before you drive me to distraction."

Heat flushes my face as I shuffle to the bathroom, listening to the sound of Charlie's soft snores as I walk past her bedroom.

Moments later, he's there, perched on the white-tiled ledge of the bath watching me submerge myself under the soft water. I push my wet hair back, take a deep breath and tell him all about Joel, and what he wants.

He leans his head against the wall, and stares up at the ceiling. I can tell he's angry at Joel by the way he clenches his jaw. Feeling mighty silly to be in such a predicament, I push the bubbles around the bath so I don't have to see his expression.

"Do you think you'll have to pay him?"

"I don't see why I'd have to. The only worry I have is that it was from his father's bank account. At the time he gave me a bunch of reasons for that…we were married, we shared everything. I lost *more* than twenty thousand when he made all those bad business deals. As far as I'm concerned that money is mine, always was. I supported him financially for most of our marriage, because I was so naïve, and then he lost it all. Except the café, and that's only because of how hard I fought to keep it."

I take a huge gulp of wine, which spills from the side of my mouth. Goddamn it, just once I'd like to feel like one of those sophisticated women, who wear gloop and drink wine in the bath looking as glamorous as a movie star—but, no, I manage to muck it up.

"If it comes to it I don't have enough to pay him even if I wanted to." I shudder, even thinking about the remote possibility of having to sell the Gingerbread Café.

"I can give you the money."

"No, no way."

Damon frowns. But I don't want anyone to bail me out. That's what got me into the mess in the first place. Easier if I pretend it's no big deal in front of Damon and CeeCee until I plan exactly how to extricate myself from Joel's clutches.

He sighs softly. "You can call it a loan if that makes you feel better."

"Thanks, but I need to sort this out myself. Once and for all."

"I forgot—feisty Lil." He leans forward to kiss me. I grab the scruff of his shirt and pull him in the water fully clothed. He yelps, and then gives in, lying atop me, just at the right angle for serious smooching.

"Feisty, did you say?" I challenge him.

"Feisty and beautiful," he murmurs. I kiss the words from his lips, and pull at the buttons of his drenched jeans.

Tidying the last of the dinner dishes away, I hear the patter of little feet behind me. Charlie's blond hair's a tangled mess from sleep and she clutches an old teddy, so worn out it's mostly gray in color.

"Hey, kiddo, you OK?" I ask gently.

She lifts a hand to shield her eyes from the light.

"I woke up and forgot where I was." Her bottom lip trembles slightly—I think of how hard it must be for her, this new life, without her parents together under the same roof.

Careful not to overstep my mark, I motion to the family room. "Why don't you go on in to your daddy, and I'll make you a nice cup of hot cocoa?"

She looks over her shoulder, then shakes her head. "Can you read me a story?"

I wipe my hands on the tea towel, and nod. "I sure can. Let's tell your daddy I'm going to tuck you in."

"OK."

We hold hands, and my heart swells. She truly is the most beautiful little girl—I wonder how Damon can stand to be parted from her when she leaves.

"Charlie." He sits up as we enter the dimly lit room. The TV flashes in the darkness. "Did you have a bad dream?"

"No." She falls into his arms. He lifts a hand and pushes the soft curls from her face. "It's the room. I woke up, and got a little bit confused..."

He closes his eyes and kisses the crown of her head. "How about I get you a night light tomorrow? That might help."

She nods her head. Their sleepy embrace is about the sweetest thing I've ever seen.

"Lil's gonna read me a book."

I make a mental note to buy some pretty things for Charlie's room so it feels as if she belongs here, and not so much as if she's a guest in our lives.

"That sounds mighty nice," Damon says. "Sleep tight, I'll kiss you goodnight when I come past." He tilts his head almost imperceptibly and gives me a look as if to check I'm happy to be the one to put her back to bed. I smile, and nod.

Back in the small room, I switch on the bedside lamp and tuck her in snug.

"Lil?"

I select a book from the small pile stacked on the shelf. "Mmm?"

"If I say I love you, that doesn't mean I don't love my mommy, right? I mean...she won't be hurt, will she?"

I perch on the edge of the bed and weigh up how to answer. "You know...no one can replace the love you have for your mom or dad. By saying you care for other people as well as them just means you've got a big heart—" I tap her chest "—with enough love in there for everyone. I think your mom would be happy to know that you feel safe and loved here. That's all that would matter to her."

"So she won't mind?"

I flash her a smile. "Seems to me she'd be pretty proud of you. And you can tell her how much you miss her while you're here, because I'm sure she's missing you."

Charlie nods sagely. "I do miss her, but I miss you and Daddy when I'm gone too."

"We do too, but that only makes it so much more fun when you come back."

"I love CeeCee too. My mommy says she sounds like a funny lady."

We giggle. "See? Sounds like your mom is happy that you're having fun while you're here."

"OK." Charlie puts her teddy bear under her arm. "Will you do special voices when you get to the part about the wolf?" She points to the book.

I relax against the bedhead. "I sure can."

CHAPTER FIVE

Birds chirp from the tree outside my window, making me
bolt out of bed. *Shoot!* Sunlight streams in; I've overslept.
Damon's side of the bed is empty, and I take a second to
wonder why. It's not like him to leave without waking me;
most mornings we sit together over a cup of coffee that's
so strong it makes my eyes *boing* open. For a moment I
wonder if he's rethinking our relationship because of Joel's
sudden presence, then dismiss the ridiculous thought.

I curse as I pull clothes from the cupboard. My mind
races with all the things we need to do for the chocolate
festival, and the activities for the kids on Saturday.
I also want to buy a few things for Charlie's room, cute
little girly things: pink sheets, a lamp, maybe some Barbie
dolls.

I throw on a loose tee shirt, and pull up some jeans.
CeeCee will be wondering where I am; I promised to get
in early to make the gingerbread rabbits. In the bathroom
I assess my reflection in the mirror: a mite pale, but a
lot better than I looked last night. The thought of Joel's
letter sitting in my bag galvanizes me. I have to make an
appointment with Mr Jefferson, a semi-retired lawyer, and
the only one in Ashford to boot, for some legal advice.

A quick splash of cold water on my face is all I have
time for. Make-up isn't my thing anyway. Ripping

open the letter from Joel, I read a whole bunch of legal gobbledegook. My shoulders slump. I'm not sure if it's because this lawyer's on Joel's side, but it sounds as though I will have to pay. He must have planned it so he'd always have a way to get the money back.

CeeCee's hollering away at someone as I walk through the back door of the Gingerbread Café. She's slamming her hands on the bench and looks all ruffled.

I rush over. "Cee, are you OK? What is it?"

She puts a hand on her heart. "There you is. Glory be, I been so worried! I had to go on over to Damon and make sure you were OK. Rosaleen told me Joel was here last night!"

I look sharply at Rosaleen, who averts her eyes on account of getting caught gossiping. "You don't miss a trick, do you?" I say to her, fighting the edge in my voice. I have no idea how she manages to discover every tidbit in this town, but she does, and then she spreads the gossip like a game of Chinese whispers.

"I better go." She picks up a bag of cookies. "I hope everything works out and that…well, you know…" Her voice trails off as she nods to CeeCee and scurries away quick as a mouse. We watch her scrawny frame retreat before turning to each other.

"I nearly done had a heart attack when I heard that snake was here when you all alone! What'd he want? I couldn't get a word outta Damon, his mouth shut so tight I worry it'd been superglued!" She's so riled up she speaks in exclamation marks.

I take the envelope from my bag. "Let's sit on the sofa." I trudge to it, knowing CeeCee's going to be worried.

"He called yesterday, said he wanted to meet. Cut a long story short, he wants the money back I used to set up the café."

"He what? That man as crooked as a dog's hind leg! But he owes you a whole lot more than that! He lost your house and everythin'." Sweat breaks out above her lip; she picks up a magazine and uses it like a fan.

"I know." I pat her knee. "Don't worry, please, Cee. I'm going to see about an appointment with Mr Jefferson, and figure out what to do." I try my hardest to sound bright, as if I'm not concerned, and hope it fools her.

"I got a bad feeling about this, Lil. He ain't gonna let up so easy, lawyer or no."

"It's fine, Cee. We'll keep going like we always do. I'll work out something. You want a gingerbread coffee?"

Her eyes are glassy and I realize she's about to cry. "Cee, it's OK. Really, don't cry."

"It just ain't right. You worked your butt off to make this place into a business."

"We've *both* worked our butts off. Don't you worry. I'm not going to give in without a fight." I kiss her soft, plump cheek. "Put your feet up for a bit. I'll bring you a coffee and a piece of pie."

"OK, just for a minute, then." She keeps up a one-way conversation, muttering to herself, and shaking her fists.

Once the shock wears off, CeeCee's back to her bustling, busy self. I try and put Joel out of my mind as we get to work. It's hard, though, when I picture his sneering face, and think of how cunning he is.

We line the wicker baskets by the front door with greaseproof paper, and fill them with freshly baked hot-cross buns. Within minutes we have customers three deep as the smell travels out to the street.

"I knew that was a good idea!" CeeCee says, pointing to the baskets. "It's like bees to a honeypot." And I have to agree. The café is more appealing with all the touches we've added recently. Damon built a bookshelf on the wall closest to the fireplace. We filled it with cookbooks, and paperbacks, and hunted out gingerbread coloring-in books for kids.

CeeCee found the wicker baskets at a church fête, and we used all our knowledge of DIY to mount them on the wall. We must have looked a sight that day, two women with nails hanging out of our mouths, drills in hand, as we tried to attach them to the wall. So they hang a little crookedly, but with the amount of nails we used they certainly won't fall down. Over the Christmas break we painted the walls a dark chocolate color and hung gingerbread-man bunting and fairy lights along the edge of the cornice. It's chintzy and sweet, and I'm proud of what we've accomplished.

The customers trickle away once the hot-cross buns are sold so we stop to catch our breath and plan the rest of the day. I make a quick call to Mr Jefferson, who tells me to fax over the letter from Joel's lawyer and that he'll call me as soon as he's done some investigating into it.

Joining CeeCee on the old sofa by the bookshelves, I take a minute to watch the world go by outside the Gingerbread Café. I could easily grab a book off the shelf and while the day away reading, and gawping out of the window after each chapter.

"I faxed the documents to Mr Jefferson," I say idly, noticing Damon's shop is filled with customers. He sells a range of small goods, and does cooking classes once a week, which all manner of local women get themselves glammed up for. Seems once Damon moved to town girls from eighteen to eighty suddenly forgot how to cook.

I watch him wander around the shop, speaking to customers, and get the same tingly feeling I always do when I lay eyes on him. Even when he wears those ridiculous checker shirts he loves so much. They are growing on me, I guess, especially when he leaves one too many buttons open, exposing his chest. I blink the sleepy desire away, and try and look at though I'm not lost in some kind of fantasy world.

CeeCee sighs loudly. "I feel better knowing that he's gonna help. He'll see you right. Guess there's no chance Joel will just up and disappear, is there?"

"You never can tell," I say, wishing it were true.

CeeCee uncrosses her arms. "If I sit here any longer I'll fall asleep. Let's bake something new."

I stretch, yawning. "Like what?"

"Let's make some dark chocolate crème brulées. Then that's one less thing to do for the festival."

"That's if we don't eat them all," I say, following her back to the kitchen. I can almost taste the rich creamy dessert with its caramelized sugar topping, just by picturing it.

With the crème brulées made, and only two or three missing, as temptation got the better of us, we spend the rest of the morning serving customers and planning our range. Trying to organize what can be made ahead, and what needs to be done as late as possible.

CeeCee's busy concocting a huge slab of macadamia and white chocolate fudge—I can't even look at it after the amount we've eaten today.

A lanky man strolls through the doors, looking almost as if he's lost something. He takes in the walls, the ceiling, as if he's a repairman.

"Can I help you?" I ask. He's not from around here—that much I know.

He strides to the counter. "Name's Dennis. I heard this place was for sale. Joel told me to come and meet with you—he was a bit sketchy on the details…"

Anger clouds my mind, and I can't help but glare at the damn fool in front of me, whether he's innocent or not. What in the hell kind of game is Joel playing sending someone out like some kind of tire-kicker to look over the place?

"This place most certainly is not for sale!" I yell, indignant.

His eyes widen. "But Joel said…"

CeeCee storms over. "You go back and tell that nasty piece of work this kinda carry-on ain't gonna wash with us! Go on, get." She shoos him away. He takes one look at her and spins on his heel.

She turns to me. "This ain't gonna stop, Lil, till he gets his way."

"I'll call Mr Jefferson back. But I'm not going to let him bully me into paying, Cee. I'm just not."

We're distracted as Charlie runs through the door out of breath. "Daddy said you were making Easter eggs today!" I glance at CeeCee, who in a tacit wave of her hand knows instinctively not to discuss what just happened in front of Charlie. We lock eyes for a moment longer; I can tell CeeCee's still reeling from Joel's latest attempt to intimidate me. I mouth the words, "It's fine."

CeeCee purses her lips, and pulls the little girl into her arms. "Wanna help us make some eggs?"

Her cornflower-blue eyes widen in excitement. "Yes please! Daddy bought me an apron and everything." She opens up her pink backpack and pulls out a brown apron.

"Would you look at that?" Cee says. "It's got gingerbread men all over it. Your daddy sure knows how to buy gifts all right." We giggle, thinking of the shrilling turkey and the manic bunny. CeeCee helps Charlie fix the strings of the apron, and sets her up on a stool.

"So, Lil's gonna temper the chocolate," CeeCee says, "which is a fancy way of saying she's going to melt it. Now give me a minute here to read this recipe." She plonks her glasses on the bridge of her nose, while she reads. "Oh, this is gonna be fun! Says here, we can pipe in white chocolate first to make little patterns in the molds, like dots or squiggles, then, once that sets, we coat with the dark chocolate. They gonna look pretty as a picture."

I heft up a big bag of dark chocolate buttons, and cut it open. The rich scent of cacao hits me, and it takes all my might not to grab a handful and start eating, no matter that my overfull belly screams in protest.

"Lil needs to set up a saucepan with an inch or two of water and wait for it to simmer. Then she gonna fill a big metal bowl with the dark chocolate buttons atop, so it acts like a bain-marie."

Charlie crinkles her nose. "What's that?"

"Kinda like a bath with a bowl on top." Charlie looks a mite confused at Cee's description, but shrugs her shoulders and watches our every move. Following CeeCee's instructions, we wait for the water to heat.

"Ready?" I say to them as I add the chocolate buttons to the bowl.

Charlie ogles it as if it's something magical. "I've never seen so much chocolate," she whispers, awestruck.

CeeCee cackles. "That bag almost as big as you!"

I stir the molten chocolate, making sure to hold the bowl so it doesn't drop into the water underneath.

"That smells like heaven itself," CeeCee says. "I'm gonna melt a tiny bit of white chocolate so we can pipe it into the molds. You can decorate the eggs however you want, Charlie."

She drags her gaze from the gooey pot of chocolate and claps her hands. "Really? I'm going to do love hearts!"

"Sounds perfect." I smile.

We work quickly. I check the temperature—it's almost at the right heat. CeeCee's done in no time and sets up the piping bags and molds on the bench. She wipes the oval-shaped molds out with a paper towel, which will help make the chocolate eggs glossy when they're set.

With oven mitts on, I take the bowl of lusciously liquefied chocolate off the saucepan and put it between us on the bench. CeeCee's used piping bags to swirl thin strands of white chocolate in the molds, which have set. Charlie tries her best to make hearts but they look more like scribbles. She sticks her tongue between her lips as she concentrates.

"You're doing a great job, sugar."

She beams. "Now what?"

CeeCee says, "OK, we give it a minute to set, then we lightly brush in the dark chocolate, a real thin layer, and when that's dry we fill the molds up with chocolate and tap so there ain't no air bubbles."

Charlie takes a brush and watches us before attempting her own eggs.

"Real thin, mind." CeeCee stands behind her and holds the mold so she can brush the first layer over the hearts. "Now you ready for the fun part?"

Charlie puts the brush to her mouth and paints her lips with it. "I can't help it!" she says when she notices us staring at her mouth, which is coated brown as if she's wearing lipstick. CeeCee hoots. "You keep that brush just for your eggs now."

We spoon in the chocolate to completely fill the molds and then tap the sides.

"Sounds like a horse gallopin' to the finish line!"

I laugh with CeeCee as I survey the bench; we've spilt chocolate all over it and it dries quickly in all sorts of obscure dribbles.

"Here comes the messy part." I rip off a layer of baking paper, and spread it on the clean end of the bench. We laugh as we upend the molds and watch the excess chocolate fall out like lava, leaving only the thin shell. Charlie immediately dips her finger into turned-out chocolate.

"They look perfect already," CeeCee says, admiring the even, half shells before she puts them in the fridge to set.

We get through three more batches of chocolate eggs, some tiny ovals, some huge as gridiron balls, before we decide to take a break, and sample some of our creations. Charlie hugs us before tottering back to Damon's shop. Not before taking a handful of treats as she leaves.

"I'll make us a couple o' gingerbread milkshakes to go with our chocolate—what do you say?"

I groan in mock protest. "I can see this little fad adding a few inches to my hips."

CeeCee harrumphs as she mixes up our drinks. "You too skinny anyways."

"Pfft. You would say that even if I was as big as a barn."

CeeCee dips the milkshake glasses into honey, then coats the rim with gingerbread crumbs before filling them up. She mooches over and hands me a glass, and we flop to the sofa. I take a big gulp, and close my eyes at the sheer deliciousness of it. The ice cream makes the drink thick, it's spicy from the ginger, and sweet from the gooey treacle mixed through.

CeeCee smacks her lips together and says, "Glory be, that about as good as a cuddle from yo' mamma."

CHAPTER SIX

"That's the prettiest thing I ever seen." CeeCee tilts her head, and stands back to get a better look at the window display. We've added the newly decorated eggs, including one of Charlie's, which looks as if she's scrawled white hieroglyphics on the dark chocolate shell. We added a chocolate honeycomb wall and little bees made from licorice adorn it.

The display looks like a fancy barnyard, with the spun sugar glinting under the small down lights, and all the cute little animals we made out of chocolate or fondant peering up at us. Easter eggs of every shape and color look downright mouth-watering littered throughout the magical setting.

"Let's go check it from the street." CeeCee grabs my arm, and pulls me into the bright day.

"Would you look at that?" I say. "Walt's shop is closed again—that's the third time in a week or so. Why do you suppose that is?"

CeeCee crosses her arms and follows my gaze. "I don't rightly know."

"You think sales are slow?"

She turns back to our Easter display, and says, "Could be."

Walt's shop is dark. His display window is filled with colorful one-off pieces of furniture he lovingly hand-crafts.

He uses wood recycled from old boats, their assorted paints faded and chipped, and mismatched to produce the most beautiful eclectic pieces you've ever seen. He says his furniture tells a story. The wood he uses has sailed around the world and seen more life than most of us ever will. My heart aches thinking Walt and Janey might be suffering financially.

"Maybe we should make him a box of goodies tomorrow, Cee. There's nothing one of your famous pies can't fix."

She nods. "That surely will help."

I know firsthand how hard it is to stay afloat in such a small town. We've seen plenty of businesses come and go but Walt and Janey's furniture shop is one of the oldest. They've been here forever. Walt is the event organizer for Ashford. He arranges the Christmas carols every year, and all the festivals and gatherings we have throughout the seasons. It strikes me how odd it is he hasn't been more involved in the chocolate festival. And CeeCee's uncharacteristically quiet about it all; she's Janey's best friend, and surely knows what's going on. Though, it could be a pride thing—I'm sure if it's a financial problem they don't want everyone knowing.

"Once I get this Joel mess sorted out, why don't we look at buying a few more of his tables for out front here?" I motion to the pavement, where we have a motley mix of wooden tables, and mix-matched chairs.

"You a good girl, Lil. I think that'd be nice."

We stare at Walt's store for a while longer. I realize I haven't seen Janey in town over the last week or so. Usually Janey comes in to shoot the breeze and sit with CeeCee while they talk about their church and their grandbabies.

"Did you play bridge with Janey this week?" I ask CeeCee.

"Nope. I got word from Rosaleen it were off because we had odd numbers. Happens all the time. We'll see if Walt turns up tomorrow." CeeCee bustles back inside before I can respond.

Later that day, we decide to shut the café a tad earlier than usual. All these early starts and late evenings have taken a toll. The street has gone sleepy with so few people about. Everyone is conserving their energy for the weekend festivities; well, I hope so, at any rate.

"Sugar plum, you try and put the thought of Mr Jefferson's verdict out of your pretty little head. Go on and enjoy the night with that fine-looking thing, and worry about it in the a.m."

I couldn't seem to get hold of Mr Jefferson on the phone all day. The niggly feeling he's going to have bad news for me hasn't been far from my mind. "I'll be fine, Cee. Bet you he's found a way to fix it, and will call with the good news tomorrow. Why don't you take a few bunnies home? Not sure we taste-tested them enough."

She haws, loud and high, and pats her handbag. "Already done. I never tried the white chocolate rabbits—can't go selling the merchandise if I haven't tasted it for myself."

I pat my bag. "I've got a helping of caramel-filled eggs. You never can tell when you'll get a sugar craving."

"It's a wonder we ain't bigger!" She guffaws, and pats her rounded belly. "Wait a minute! You the only skinny one—that just ain't fair!"

I scoff. CeeCee's got a real thing about calling me skinny, when in actual fact I've got proper country-girl curves, which are only getting bigger with all the chocolate I've been eating.

I shut off the lights and we head out of the front door into the balmy air. Damon's shop is still open, and I wave to him as CeeCee and I stroll up the street. "You gonna walk?" I ask. CeeCee usually hitches a ride with Sarah when she closes her book store. "Yeah, sugar, after all that chocolate today, I think I might need to make it a regular thing. Plus we're early. You go on ahead. I'll see you tomorrow." She pecks me on the cheek.

"I'll pop in and tell Sarah you're walking home." CeeCee lives a bit further out on the other side of town from me, a good twenty-minute walk.

"You tell her I need another selection of those bodice rippers you keep teasing me over," CeeCee says.

Laughing, I nod and walk into the tiny bookshop.

As usual Sarah is propped up behind the cash register, her head in a book, jeans-clad legs crossed and perched on a stool. "Hey, Lil." She dog-ears the page of her book, and closes it.

I smile in greeting as she stretches and shakes away the dozy look on her face. "Cee's going to walk today on account of how much chocolate we've consumed."

Her tinkling laughter rings out. She's tiny, and looks like a doll with her smooth black bobbed hair, and perfectly cut bangs that hang just above her eyebrows.

"You know, the smell of melted chocolate travels all the way over here. I planned on coming over but I got to reading…"

I run a hand over the cover of the old hardback book. "That good?"

"A classic…"

Plunging my hand into the depths of my handbag, I scrabble around for the box of caramel eggs and offer them to Sarah. "Here's something to keep your energy up."

She laughs, and takes the eggs, unwrapping one and popping it into her mouth. "Gosh…wow."

"Keep going, plenty more where they came from." I walk around the small shop looking for cookbooks. The small space has an otherworldly feel about it. It's dusty and dingy with books piled on top of each other or double stacked on shelves. Old books mixed with new, a veritable treasure trove of wonder. Sarah knows instinctively where everything is, but it's fun to mosey your way around and find something hidden, a gem for yourself.

"So you all organized for the festival?" Sarah asks.

All the coordinating was done weeks ago. All that's left to do is the fun part. "I think so. We've made most of the eggs, and the truffles, now we're making the medley of cakes, and fudges, and slices…"

"Stop! You're making me salivate… How can you stand to cook like that without gorging on it all day?"

"We do gorge! Trust me, we do. It kind of goes on all day till I can't fit another thing in. Maybe I should have opened a salad shop…" I pinch my love handles.

Sarah scoffs. "Lucky for us, you didn't. Can't see us getting a town full of shoppers for a potato salad festival, can you?"

I grin and say, "Well, what about a Caesar salad festival?"

She clicks her fingers. "A coleslaw festival!"

I giggle at the thought.

Her expression turns mock serious. "Are you telling me there's not going to be a three-bean salad festival?"

I drop my bottom lip and shake my head sadly. "Not for a few weeks anyway."

"Ha ha, I'll hold you to that!" She leans under the counter and pulls some thin white books from a box. "I got these in especially for CeeCee. She sure can get through them at a rate of knots."

I smile, thinking of CeeCee reading so many romance books a week, then talking about the characters as though they're real. She's got me hooked on them, after talking up so many buff men, and glamorous women. Though there's not much chance I'll ever be like the heroines, with their perfectly made up faces, and their sky-high confidence.

I poke around the box of books and find an old French dessert cookbook. As I flick through the pages my belly rumbles loud enough for Sarah to hear. "You can't be hungry and run a café. That just doesn't make sense." She laughs.

"I think it's living on a diet of sugar that's doing it."

"Take that book, Lil. I got it in for you."

"Thank you. I can see us trying some of these recipes out tomorrow. Soon enough we're going to need another pair of hands. We sure are getting busier these days."

"You've worked hard for it. And I don't know if it's just the advertising we've done for the festival, but Ashford sure seems busier these last few weeks."

The talk of customers reminds me of Walt, and I suddenly feel guilty talking about business improving when his shop sits closed next door.

"You know why Walt and Janey aren't open?"

"No." She frowns. "It's not like them, though, is it?"

I shake my head. "CeeCee says she doesn't know either, but I kind of felt like she did. Maybe I'm reading too much into it. I'm beginning to sound like Rosaleen!"

Sarah puts a palm to her face. "Speaking of which, I heard about Joel."

"Rosaleen, already?"

Sarah smiles ruefully. "You got it. What are you going to do?"

"I've faxed Mr Jefferson the letter from Joel's lawyer, so I'm hoping he has some magical potion that'll make it all disappear."

"I'm sure he will. And shout out if you need anything."

I gather up CeeCee's books, and go to pay but Sarah waves me off. "I'll swap books for chocolate," she says, grinning.

"Deal! Mosey on over when you need a fix."

We hug, before I head outside into the fading sunlight. I take in the surroundings, the little town I love so much, with its old federation-style buildings, and the neat shops, and clean sidewalks. Aesthetically nothing much has changed here over time, other than a few cosmetic make-overs; a building gets a flick of paint, or some bright flowers sing out from new terracotta pots, but all in all Ashford stays the same.

CHAPTER SEVEN

I'm languishing in the tub when Damon gets home. It seems to be my go-to place in times of stress. There's something about feeling weightless and submerging yourself that makes all your worries ebb away momentarily. He wanders in, his lazy, sexy smile not failing to make my pulse race.

"You some kind of mermaid or what?" he says, trailing a hand in the water.

"I think so." I grip the edge of the bath and pull myself over the edge to kiss him hello.

"Charlie's out with the kids next door again. She loves it here." He sits on the tiled ledge.

"Did she talk to you about how she feels guilty loving people as well as her mom?"

He smiles. "She did, and she told me what you said, which was pretty sweet. I think she feels better now. I rang Dianne, and told her to speak to Charlie, to put her mind at ease. It's one thing I'm grateful for, that there's no animosity between me and Dianne any more. She's happy with her new life, and I am more than happy with mine. Makes it easier to put Charlie's needs first."

I arch my eyebrow. "So you're happy, you say?" My heart races when I watch his expression as his gaze travels up the length of my naked body.

"Hmm, I'd say right now I'm…distracted. What's say we go take a lie-down before dinner?" Before I can answer he's holding my hands and pulling me out of the bath.

I smirk as I say, "Oh, I'm not tired."

His voice is gruff with desire. "That right? Well, you won't be sleeping." He carries me to the bedroom, as if we're some kind of honeymooning couple.

Still smiling from Damon's so-called lie-down, I change into old sweats. They're too large, and are stained from cooking, or more likely from eating, but as comforting as a safety blanket.

In the kitchen, Damon's at the table, his hands clasped together, looking out of the window as though he's mesmerized by the sinking sun. Two glasses of white wine sit waiting, condensation running off the cool glasses.

"Hey, pretty lady," he says lazily. "Don't you just look adorable dressed like that?"

"Yeah, it's the latest look. You know the whole sloth vibe…"

"I don't know about that…you make sweats look good."

I sigh inwardly. His flirty, sexy voice makes me want to ravish him again, but I know Charlie will be home soon. I can't remember ever feeling this intoxicated by love before. It's so powerful, like a drug, it makes it difficult to focus on anything other than him.

We sit quietly, listening to the sounds of the children's shrieks as they play chase outside. It's one of those very rare times when you suddenly realize nothing else could make this moment any more perfect. I'm flushed with love; it feels extraordinary, as if we're the only ones in the world who've loved like this.

"So." He turns to me, and by the look in his eyes I know what the topic is going to be. "Did you hear anything back from Jefferson?"

I shake my head. "No, not yet. I have this horrible feeling I'm going to have to pay Joel back. But, you know, I have some money saved, and hopefully the revenue from the festival will be enough to keep him at bay until I can work something out."

He folds his arms and goes to speak then stops. Guess he's weighing up what he ought to say and what he really wants to say. Truly, I am angry at Joel, and will be more so if I have to pay. But I don't want Damon to think he has to save me. I don't want to be that girl that needs to be rescued.

"Lil, I know you're proud, and you don't want to take the money from me. But can't you see…? To me, it's not about the money. It's about you."

"I know. I do. But I can't have people fighting my battles. I should have known better when it comes to him and his family, so I'll take it on the chin, and work my way out of it. I've done it before, I can do it again."

He frowns as he sips his wine. "But what if you don't make enough at the festival? Will you accept the shortfall from me?"

I try to look composed, confident. "No, there'll be enough. I'm sure of it." There's no chance I'll make enough to cover the twenty thousand, and the exorbitant amount of interest he wants to slug me, but if Mr Jefferson says I have to pay, I'll get a loan or something before I even think of borrowing off Damon or selling the café. People might call me a fool not accepting his help, but there comes a time when you have to be in control of your own life. And nearing the big three oh, I can't expect to be bailed out.

"I won't keep hounding you, Lil, but what if he doesn't leave? What if you have to sell the café, all on account of something as stupid as that idiot?"

"It won't come to that. I promise," I say hopefully. "And if all else fails, I'll open up a chocolate shop." My joke falls flat as I see his frown deepen.

"Really?"

"Easter eggs all year round, I say. No, not really—the café is my life. I'd be lost without it."

"I wish you'd reconsider taking the money. I'd happily pay it to get him out of town and away from you." His voice has a slightly harder tone and I realize maybe Damon does feel slightly threatened by the scurrilous Joel.

"He'll go. I'll work out a way, and I'll fight to keep the Gingerbread Café. Either way I'm going to add chocolate to our repertoire. There's something hypnotic about tempering chocolate and molding it into something completely different. I think of all the flavors and textures I can add…"

"Sounds like your mind is made up. We could incorporate it into the catering too. Chocolate martinis with a side of truffles. Say, we could even do chocolate buffets, set it out all pretty on a table and let people help themselves."

"See? Now we're thinking ahead. It's much better than mooning about things I can't change."

He nuzzles into my neck; his warm breath on my skin gives me goose bumps. "Well, OK. I'm still learning that you can be stubborn as a mule."

I let out a donkey-like haw, and we laugh together as the sun sinks completely, the orange hue replaced by soft sepia light. Shadows stretch on the floor beside us, and I get lost in the blackness of them, wondering how Joel managed to creep into my perfect moment, and break the spell.

CHAPTER EIGHT

The next morning at the Gingerbread Café, CeeCee is swamped with customers. I look on in awe as I jog past the window, and see a long queue inside. I'm late again on account of picking up some more supplies for the festival.

I rush in and don my apron.

"Sugar plum, glory be, it's been hectic!" CeeCee has a sheen of sweat on her brow, and is smiling as if she's won lotto. I grin back at her. From the looks of it everyone is here for chocolate and a rush of pleasure surges through me.

I serve customers, who are mostly local, and chat while I get their orders together.

CeeCee's guffaws ring out when she tells the story about me blowing out the Paschal eggs. Seems she just has to tell everyone, including people who don't ask.

"You shoulda seen her face, oh, it were priceless..."

I shake my head, and laugh at her hooting and hollering. CeeCee is always excitable when we're busy. Everyone laughs along with her. "You should've been a stand-up comedian, Cee."

With each order we slip in a free gingerbread rabbit, sweet-smelling biscuits that look cute with their white icing whiskers, and ruby-red bow ties.

Once the last customer strolls out with a backwards wave, we plonk down on the sofa for a break.

"I'm beat!" CeeCee hoists her legs up and closes her eyes.

"I've never seen it so busy. Seems like the whole town wandered in this morning."

"There's only a handful of chocolate eggs left. We're going to have to make more tonight."

"More? Gosh, we're going to need a holiday after this festival." I sigh, thinking of a summer holiday somewhere seaside with Damon. Cheesy love songs spring to mind. I envisage him chasing me along a white sandy beach. I grin when I realize I'm fantasizing about my life as if it's one of CeeCee's novels. They sure do give a girl inspiration.

"What you grinnin' at?"

"Nothing. Just thinking of a holiday one of these days." There's no way I'm telling her I'm picturing a beach run while a song plays in my mind. She'll think I'm cuckoo.

"So you heard from that snake?" she asks, narrowing her eyes at me.

And there it is again: Joel, the total mood killer. "Not a peep. I can't believe I wasted so much time with a man like him." It's so hard to see what I found attractive in him, now that I have Damon to compare him to. "I must have been a dumb fool not to see him for what he really is."

She glances at me, her face softening. "You ain't dumb *or* a fool, Lil. The heart sees what it needs to see. You ever think that maybe it happened the way it did was so when that fine-looking thing came into your life you could recognize real love? Plus, you still so young, not even thirty, you got the rest of your life to spend with a real man. One who adores you just the way you are. Gloop-less, baggy clothed, and ponytailed."

I laugh. "Amen to that." I just can't be that girl that gets excited about hair and make-up. And form-fitting clothes are just not me. Jeans and tees are about as fancy as I get most days. Cee's always at me: "Let down those gorgeous blond curl o' yours, show off that figure." It feels wrong, though, as if I'm pretending to be someone I'm not. Plus I can't see straight when I've got that amount of gloop on my face. Feels like glue drying and I can't stand it.

"So what you think Joel gonna do?"

I try to keep the worry from my voice. "Don't rightly know. I just want him gone. Out of my life for good."

"Me too, sugar plum, me too."

People wave as they stroll past, some with an eyebrow raised seeing CeeCee and me lazing on the sofa as if we're on holiday.

"Did you hear from Janey, yet?" I ask idly.

CeeCee jumps up. "No, not yet."

I watch her retreating back, and wonder what the heck she's not telling me. Seems like we're both guilty of keeping secrets.

The phone rings, startling me awake. From my bed the alarm clock reads 5.49. Time to get up anyway. I shake the grogginess away, and answer. "Hello?"

"You got the money, yet?"

I flop back in the bed and close my eyes. Thankfully Damon's side of the bed is empty so he doesn't have to hear this. I reach out and feel the groove in the mattress where he sleeps; it's cold to touch. It makes me anxious we're not spending our mornings together all of a sudden.

"Well?" Joel says again, interrupting my train of thought.

I exhale all the hurt and the worry in one long gust of breath. "I can give you three thousand, Joel. But that's all I have. And it's more than you deserve." I don't mention the festival proceeds just in case he agrees on my paltry savings.

Paltry to him, certainly not to me. But there's no way I'll be handing over any cash until I hear back from Mr Jefferson.

"You're just going to have to sell, then, Lil. I'm not playing a game here. I'm serious. I'll give you one more day to organize something or I'll file with a lawyer," he threatens.

"One day? This isn't a movie, Joel."

"Don't be smart, Lil. In the meantime, I'd hate to see a fuse blow at your precious café. Imagine that—all your fridges off for the night...all those cakes for the festival, ruined. You've got *one* day." He slams down the phone.

I let out a barrel of expletives and only wish Joel were still on the phone to hear them.

CeeCee's at the café when I arrive, slamming her palms into pastry dough as if it's a punching bag.

"Why are you here so early?" I ask.

"Thought I'd make a start on these pies."

"Sure, but you didn't need to come in early. Let me help."

I take a ball of dough.

"Damon left early this morning too. Hope it's not my morning breath that's scaring him away."

"Hmm, don't think it's that," CeeCee says.

"Do you think it's weird, Cee? That he's been leaving in the morning without me? We usually have coffee and mosey on down together. Now he's up and gone before I'm even awake."

CeeCee looks at me sternly. "What you gettin' at?"

I shrug. "I just hope Joel hasn't made him rethink things, that's all." I'm not used to the range of emotions that swim inside me, when it comes to Damon. I almost want to cling to him, because he's so much more than I've ever had.

She tuts and tosses down the dough. "So Damon's left early a couple days this week? Days Charlie's been here? Kids that age are up before sparrows, that's what it is. I seen the way you two carry on—all that huggin' and kissin' you do when you think no one's watchin'…"

A blush rises up my cheeks. "Whoops."

"Yeah, whoops, all right." She sighs, big and dramatic. "Young love, it's a beautiful thing."

"Young? Why, thanks, Cee. Has Mr Jefferson called back yet?" I pummel the pastry.

"Nope," she says. "And I checked that fangled machine for messages, nothin'."

"Joel called this morning, said I have one day to sort something out. He's really hamming up that whole bad-guy act." I don't mention his threat about the fuses—CeeCee would be at Old Lou's before I could say boo.

"One day? What you s'posed to do in one day?"

I shrug. "Exactly."

CeeCee grunts, and shakes her head. "Put it out of your mind, sugar. Oh, before I forget, another delivery of chocolate buttons arrived. We can get started on the rest of the Easter eggs. I thought we could fill up the smaller ones with some zany flavors for kids, like sherbet, that kinda thing. What you think?"

"Sherbet? Sounds amazing!"

"Folks certainly won't find that anywhere else. I wanted to leave early today on account of running some errands."

"Errands? You want me to do them?" I usually help CeeCee with her shopping because she doesn't own a car.

"No, no," she says quickly. "Just some things I need to sort out. It won't take long."

"OK. Take your time, Cee. I thought I'd organize those make-at-home choc-chip cookies in a jar, for the festival."

CeeCee wraps the balls of dough in cling film, and sets them in the fridge to rest. "You want me to pick up some pretty ribbons to tie around them while I'm out?"

"Sure."

After the lunch rush, I walk out to the office to return Mr Jefferson's call. He phoned earlier when we were knee-deep in customers, and I could tell by the tone of his voice the news wasn't good.

"Mr Jefferson, it's Lil."

He sighs, a long drawn-out sound. "Lil, I got some bad news. He's wrapped you up tight with this. By the looks you're going to have to pay him. From what I can see, the loan has gone through his dad's business, so technically you owe the twenty thousand, plus interest."

"Even though his dad's passed on?"

"Yes, ma'am. Seems Joel is the beneficiary of his dad's estate, and is chasing everyone who still owes them. Not that there's many with anything tangible left. They got some nerve, that family, sending people broke with the amount of interest they charged. No one could afford that kind of money. They preyed on desperate people."

I rest my head against the cool of the wall. "That they did. What should I do? See about getting a loan…"

Mr Jefferson clears his throat. "We can see about getting a payment plan of some type. There's a host of things we can legally do. You can fight it, it's just the cost of that if you lose…"

"No, I don't have the energy to fight him. Let's see about some kind of payment terms, then. You think you can hold him off for a little while?"

"I do, Lil. Let me contact him, and see about negotiating."

CHAPTER NINE

We've made over a hundred small eggs, filled with various flavored luscious ganaches to replenish our stock for the last time before the festival. We dust the tops of each egg with colored sugar crystals to differentiate the flavors.

Our jam jars are filled with all the dry ingredients to make chocolate-chip cookies. We've tied star-shaped cookie cutters to the jars with gingerbread ribbon. A cute little gift idea we couldn't resist trying.

"I'm going to add a few of these to the window display," CeeCee says.

I nod distractedly as I tidy the bench.

A moment later CeeCee rushes back in, her eyes wide, hand on her chest.

"What, Cee? You OK?"

She is breathless, and points to Damon's shop. "He's there, out front with Damon!"

"Who?" As soon as the word leaves my mouth I realize. I rush to the window to gaze out. Joel. He's pointing a crooked finger into Damon's face.

"Oh, my gosh, I better go over…"

But CeeCee tugs my arm. "No. Leave it. That's what he wants. He trying to scare you. Damon's not a coward. He can stand up for himself."

My heartbeat speeds up. "Yeah, but he shouldn't have to, Cee. This has nothing to do with him."

"Leave them be."

My hearts leaps as I see Joel poke and prod his finger into Damon's checker shirt. Damon stands there looking a lot more dignified than Joel, who's yabbering and yelling like a fool. Damon shakes his head at whatever venom Joel's spewing out.

"Cee, what if they fight?"

"If he don't leave soon, it's gonna be *me* who marches over there." Cee looks determined.

Joel's voice carries over on the wind. He's so angry he's spitting.

"Cee," I say urgently, "this is escalating. I have to go…" I trail off when Joel pushes Damon hard in the chest, making him stumble backwards.

Damon regains his balance and steps forward, grabbing Joel by the collar of his shirt. A crowd has gathered to watch, including the local shopkeepers, who yell at Joel to leave. Joel's face is red with anger as he snarls at the crowd, and angrily flips Damon's hands off his shirt. He lunges forward at Damon, pushing him hard in the chest. Damon lifts a fist, ready to strike Joel just as Charlie wanders out to the stoop, her face pinched with fear. He shakes his head, as his anger is replaced with concern at seeing his little girl so scared.

"Charlie…" I gulp.

"Is that all you got?" Joel barks at him.

"That's it!" Cee beats me to the punch; before I've even turned to look at her she's powering across the street yelling all manner of things.

"I don't hold with cuss words, Joel, but you making me rethink that! You get your grubby paws offa Damon this minute…"

Joel's eyes are wide with surprise at CeeCee's volley of abuse. I walk to the front and call for Charlie; she takes one look at her daddy, and races across the road. I pick her up, and murmur soothingly to her. She turns back to watch out of the window, her little heart beating quickly through the fabric of her dress.

"It's OK, Cee," Damon says, holding a hand up. "Joel's just leaving, right?"

"Oh, no, he ain't!" CeeCee steps between the two men. "Not till I've said what needs to be said. And don't think I won't smack you upside the head if you don't listen!"

Joel scowls at her. "Oh, yeah? I'd like to see that."

"Glory be, you nasty. You could start an argument in an empty house." She turns to Damon. "You go on in now."

Damon shakes his head.

"Go and see Charlie bear, make sure she's OK."

He's glued to the spot, not wanting to leave CeeCee by herself. I wave him in, wanting him as far away from Joel as possible. Seeing him literally fight my battles is not something I want on my conscience, no matter how much Joel deserves it. Plus I don't want Charlie to witness anything so frightening.

"You forget I've known this boy since he was knee high to a grasshopper, so get." From the window I can see give Damon give her an imploring look. She waggles a hand at him to leave.

He takes his time ambling across the street, looking back over his shoulder to make sure CeeCee is safe.

"Hey," he says, walking into the café. He takes Charlie from me, and kisses her nose. "You OK?" he asks her.

She looks up at him, her blue eyes wide. "I'm good. Was that man going to hit you?"

"No, honey, no."

"I'm so sorry," I say. We clasp hands and watch CeeCee unleash a tirade at Joel. He takes a step back from her but listens to whatever it is she's saying.

"She's certainly got his measure," Damon says.

"It's not right. I should be the one out there, not either of you."

"That's what he wants, Lil. So he's not having it. Better he knows you have a whole town behind you, ready to back you up. Quicker he learns that, the better."

CeeCee lowers her voice, but her arms flail as she gesticulates wildly.

"Think he'll be scared off now?"

"We can only hope," Damon says.

CeeCee marches back into the café puffing and panting as if she's been to aerobics.

"I'm glad I told that snake exactly what I think o' him." She takes a few deep breaths and stands at the window like a sentry. "It's been a long time coming."

Damon scoops up Charlie from the stool, where I set her up with a piece of carrot cake. "I better get back, ladies. You keep an eye out. If he comes back make sure you holler over."

I hug them and watch Damon carry his daughter across the road.

Turning back to Cee, I ask, "What'd you say to him?"

"Plenty! Never mind, cherry blossom. I'm parched like some kinda camel."

Guilt surges through me as I hug her. It seems everyone is fighting my battles. It's time I got rid of Joel for good. I decide I'll call the bank, see if I can get a credit card or some kind of loan. While I'm there I'll withdraw my savings and see if that amount tides him over for now. There's no point drawing it out; I just want him out of all of our lives.

Rushing to the kitchen, I mix up a big glass of iced tea and take it back to CeeCee. "At least sit down, Cee." She's staring out of the window. I can't read her expression.

"Cee?"

"Yeah?"

"Why don't you sit down for a bit?"

"I need to go run those errands." She takes a big gulp of iced tea. "You want anything done while I'm out?"

"You sure you're OK to be going barreling around town after that?"

She laughs, her big-bellied haw. "Never been better. Righting a wrong sure is good for the soul."

"Well, OK. If you're sure, Cee. Maybe take a few hours, see about visiting Janey?"

"I won't be long." She straightens her dress, and pats down her hair before heading out.

Uneasy. That's how I feel when I hang up the call with the local bank manager. Worry sits in my belly as heavy as a brick. He can fix me up with a credit card, but only for a few thousand. And it'll take a fortnight before I can draw on it. This is like a bad dream that never goes away.

CHAPTER TEN

The morning of the chocolate festival rolls around. I'm jittery with nerves. I hope everything goes as planned, and that there are no spectacular cooking mishaps. It's one thing to muck up a recipe in the café but quite another to do it in front of almost the whole town. Most of our chocolate recipes are prepared; it'll just be a matter of keeping up and replenishing, with only a few things made fresh, like chocolate soufflés, which we'll bake in batches, and I pray they rise into a gooey, chocolaty cloud.

I get to work early, and find an army of volunteers sitting on the chairs out front sipping mugs of something spicy. "Morning, everyone," I say, leaning close to peer into their drinks.

Sarah from the bookshop speaks up. "It's a hot cup of gingerbread cocoa. You missed the little gingerbread men Cee perched on top. We ate them up first!"

I laugh as CeeCee wanders out with a tray of more drinks, and offers me one.

"Thanks, Cee." I feel almost sad crunching into the cute little button-nose gingerbread man who floats amongst the whipped cream.

"You got the tables, Lil?" CeeCee asks.

"In the truck. I'll bring it around and we can set them up when you're ready." I borrowed trestle tables from the town hall. We're going to line them up under umbrellas, and each station will serve a selection of chocolate-themed deliciousness. The road will be closed for the entirety, so we can spread tables down the length of the street.

Damon walks out from his small goods shop with Charlie in tow. She skips over to CeeCee and hugs her tight. "My little angel, you go on inside. There's a special milkshake on the bench for you." Charlie squeals and runs inside to investigate.

I clap my hands. "Before we start, CeeCee and I wanted to thank you all for helping out today, and, remember, you can eat as much as you want! So feel free to take a break from your table and sample everything that's on offer. We'll be running things inside, and making sure you're stocked up out here in the event everything sells."

Our volunteers let out a whoop, and gather together to help set up. I force myself to look cheerful, but I have a horrible feeling Joel might turn up and ruin things. He said I had one more day, so I expected another pre-dawn phone call from him threatening me. But so far, nothing. A tiny ray of hope runs through me—maybe Mr Jefferson's involvement scared him off. Maybe he is gone for good. Or is that just wishful thinking?

The Gingerbread Café explodes with noise as we cram in as many kids as we can to help paint the Paschal eggs. Laughter rings out as they crack almost as many as they manage to paint. CeeCee and I grin at each other. "At least they're empty of goo this time," she says, yelling above the din.

The streets are crowded with people milling about, sampling all the chocolate desserts on offer. We cover a few of the tables with newspaper and wave to a bunch of kids, who eagerly run up and take a seat. I direct them all to the cotton wool, and paper plates, the pink cardboard and colored pipe cleaners.

"Right, kiddiewinks." I hold up a finished bunny-rabbit mask. "So you glue each piece in order as they are on the table, then, once you're done, I'll tie a length of elastic through these tiny holes here—" I indicate "—and then you can hang them on the pegs Cee's left on the string line out back, to dry…" Before I'm finished talking, hands spring from every direction, eager to get their crafts started.

The Mary-Jos arrive in a hail of glitter. They're dressed in frou-frou pink gowns, and wear plastic tiaras. One of them, hard to tell which under all that make-up, swishes a wand around, and says, "You, you, you, follow me for face painting!"

The children push their chairs back, and chase after her.

It's midday when I'm zigzagging through the throng of the festival, and notice Walt's shop is closed. I stand still as people sidestep me, and watch the shop for movement. Maybe he's taking a break and has closed the doors for some peace and quiet. I think back to the morning, searching my memory to whether I saw Walt's shop open at all. I don't think I did. And why hasn't Janey stopped by the café? CeeCee's been her best friend since they were girls, there's just no way even a squabble would keep Janey away, and if they did bicker the furniture shop would still be open.

I march back into the café and search for CeeCee.

She's leaning against the door jamb, watching Charlie paint a nest made out of shredded brown paper.

"Where are they?" I ask more abruptly than I mean to.

She pretends not to hear me, but I see her face fall slightly.

"Have you ever seen a girl concentrate so hard?" she murmurs.

"Cee."

She shakes her head, and I see her eyes glisten with tears.

"We just gonna head out back for a minute, Charlie bear, OK?"

I follow CeeCee outside to the car park.

She leans her bulk against a rusty old car, and takes a deep breath. I wait patiently, my mind spinning possible scenarios.

"I was goin' to tell you after the egg hunt tomorrow. I wanted you to have a good weekend and be able to focus on the business and what with that conman Joel and everythin'…"

"Tell me what?"

When she looks at me, it's almost as if she's another person, there's such a sadness in her eyes, and without her usual smile it doesn't look like Cee.

"Janey's been diagnosed with cancer. From what they know, it seems one o' those aggressive types…" She breaks off as her words become a jumble when the tears finally spill.

I wrap my arms around her, knowing there's nothing I can say that will ease her heartbreak in the slightest, and because I'm so shocked. I think of Janey, with her ever-present smile, silver hair always tied up in an orderly bun. She keeps the town social life ticking over as she buzzes around organizing events, and fundraisers. She's so vital and vibrant it's hard to picture her as anything less. Surely it can't be?

"Will she be OK? I mean, modern medicine is so good these days, right?"

I lean on the car next to CeeCee.

"They gonna try, sugar plum, and I been praying for her."

"Where is she, Cee? Up in Springfield?"

CeeCee nods as she wipes her tears.

"Why don't you go to her? Surely she needs you more than anything right now."

She takes a long shuddery breath in. "I was going to wait and see what Walt had to say. He's coming back some time this weekend to drop off the keys for the store. I told him we'd find a way to keep it open, like maybe do a roster system with the other shopkeepers on the street. That way they still got some money comin' in."

Once people find out about Janey, there'll be all sorts of help lined up, from bulk trays of casseroles, to people tending their garden, and anything else they can think of that might ease their burden. Ashford will band together in a show of support for Janey and Walt.

"I'm sure there'll be no shortage of helpers. We better make up a basket of chocolate for them too." It's the only thing I know to do in a crisis. Ply people with food and hope it brings a small level of comfort somehow.

My heart breaks for them, and for CeeCee, who was trying so hard to keep it from me when she must have been slowly dying inside.

"We can sort out his shop, Cee. You should go to her."

CHAPTER ELEVEN

By early afternoon the kids finally lose their zeal. We've sold out of almost everything as the festival went on merrily outside, while the children played inside. My head throbs with the sudden silence but I brace myself for them to get their second wind as the Easter bunny is moments away from arriving to spread some cheer and hand out eggs we'd secreted out. I stop for a moment, and look over at Walt and Janey's shop, and can't help but miss them. I know CeeCee will put on an act, pretending to be all bubbly and happy for everyone's sake, but really her heart's broken into about a million pieces.

CeeCee wanders over to me and whispers, "He's here." She nods to the back door.

I find Charlie in the crowd and get set to watch her reaction.

CeeCee claps her hands to get their attention. "We just wanna say thank you for coming to play here at the Gingerbread Café today. We surely have enjoyed it. If you wouldn't mind doing me one last favor…"

The kids sit cross-legged on the floor, staring up at her.

"Can anyone tell me who that is at the back door?"

Their heads swivel to door as the Easter bunny walks in holding a basket filled with eggs. They immediately jump up and race towards him screaming, "The Easter bunny!"

Damon in his pink fluffy bunny suit is well disguised, but I can almost feel him laughing under the bobbly head as they launch themselves at his knees. Charlie is at the back of the crowd, her face lit with wonder.

Parents shade their faces as they peer through the glass. They've been relegated outside and seem happy to watch from the street.

Damon tries to hand out eggs but can't pick them up with his huge paws. He muffles, "A little help here?"

We giggle and edge the kids back so we can get through and help him.

"Have you been a good girl?" he asks me.

"Isn't it Santa who asks that?"

"You're on the naughty list. I'll deal with you later," he says, stepping forward and shaking hands with the kids as they stand stunned. I try and wipe the goofy, lovey-dovey look off my face, but find it impossible. CeeCee's right: I had to kiss a toad before my knight in a bright pink bunny suit found my heart. I watch Charlie pick the foil off her egg slowly and delicately before popping it into her mouth, beaming.

"It just ain't the same without Janey and Walt here," CeeCee says sadly. We're up before the sun, hiding the eggs for the Easter egg hunt in shrubs along the streets of Ashford. Sarah and Damon are helping; they're further ahead, chatting as they walk on opposite sides of the street.

"I know," I say softly. "Feels hollow without them."

CeeCee goes to speak but chokes up. She takes a minute then says, "You know, Lil, the only thing that matters in life is having good friends and family around you. When you get to the twilight of your life, like me, you realize that. Money, fancy clothes, none of that matters. When you're sitting alone in the dark of night, the things that make your heart happy are simple. Charlie's smile when she bit into that cake pop. You and me laughing ourselves silly every day. My grandbabies, my kids, who all done me proud. And Janey. Our friendship's spanned decades. There ain't a thing we don't know 'bout each other, and that counts for more than anythin'. I know she gonna pull through, I know it. But if she don't, it means that God got other plans for her, and, as sad as that be, I trust Him. And I'll be ever grateful for havin' a friend like Janey. Life doesn't always have a happy ending, and that makes it even more important to love and cherish what you got. So you just remember that, Lil, OK?" She wipes tears from her eyes, and nods at me before turning away and walking up the quiet street. Times like this I know she wants to be alone. Her words replay in my mind. I can't help but wonder what else she means.

My heart's heavy as I walk the other way, placing eggs into the underbrush of plants that line the street. Things don't often change in Ashford, but it suddenly seems as though they will. The people I look up to and respect are all advancing in years, and I just can't picture my life without them. I try and shake the blues away. Everything is always sadder before the sun comes up. Picturing Janey and Walt about to face their biggest struggle puts the Joel fiasco into perspective. As CeeCee says, it's only money. Once I pay him, I'll never have to see him again, and that's worth more than anything. My friends need me now, and I need to be strong for them, not lost inside my mind with Joel, and his toxic threats.

Since Walt isn't here, Damon takes over as the egg-hunt organizer. He lines the kids up along a makeshift start line, painted hurriedly at daybreak, when we realized we'd forgotten.

"OK, does everyone have a basket?" he hollers above the excited chatter.

Their "yes sirs" ring out high into the fresh morning air.

"Great! Now we have a few little ones here today. It'd be nice if the bigger kids buddy up and make sure they find just as many eggs as you."

The line wobbles as the tweens move places to stand next to the younger kids to shadow them.

"On your marks, get set, GO!"

We watch them race every which way, their yelps punctuating the morning.

CeeCee and I head on into the café, and get to making gingerbread coffee for the parents, who stumble in groggy from such an early start.

The kids have all moseyed on home as I close up shop for the day. CeeCee tallied up the takings, including the festival, and it looks as though we've made more than we anticipated. All our hard work was worth it in the end.

I'm just about to lock the front door when Damon pushes against it. Charlie stands behind him, gripping the edge of his shirt.

"Hi," I say, confused. We'd planned to close up and meet at home so Charlie could have a nap after running around town most of the day. I'd planned on guzzling a big glass of wine.

"I forgot to give you something," he says, stepping into the café. He hands me a small silver-wrapped egg.

"Hey!" I say. "We didn't have silver eggs. Where did you get this one?"

"We made it. Go on, see if you like it."

I take my time unwrapping the egg, which is not like me at all but I figure if Charlie, a seven-year-old, can be delicate, I can certainly try.

Once the foil is off I see a smattering of letters embossed into the chocolate. "What does it say?" I peer closer.

They stand silently.

And then I see it. I feel my cheeks color, and I do the silly jump-clap dance again.

The teeny, tiny words spell: *Will you marry me?*

"Yes!" I scream and collapse into Damon's arms. Charlie looks up, her smile dazzling as I pull her into the hug.

Damon's face shines as he says, "Open the egg."

I go to smash the egg in my palm as I normally do, when he grabs my hand to stop me. "Maybe just bite the top off first."

Why can't I be ladylike, just once? I take a small bite and the shell crumbles. Amidst the chocolate rubble lies an antique-looking diamond ring. It's so feminine, and delicate I immediately love it. He reaches for the ring, and slides it on my finger. I hold my breath, hoping it's not too small; he inches it over my knuckle—a perfect fit. In fact, it looks as if it's always been there. I can't help grinning at my finger, which I'm sure looks downright silly.

"I knew the very moment I met you, I was going to marry you," Damon says softly.

I bite my lip as I think of all the things that spun through my mind when I first clapped eyes on Damon, and, if I'm honest, I thought he was as delectable as one of CeeCee's pies, but wouldn't have thought of telling a soul. "Is this why you've been leaving the house before daybreak?"

"Surely was. I had to enlist CeeCee's help to make the egg, and then there was the matter of getting her approval on the right ring…"

Charlie toddles off to help herself to a snack. With one last look at the ring, I put my hands in Damon's back jean pockets and pull him close. "I thought it was my bed hair that had you running scared in the mornings."

"There's not one thing I don't love about you, Lil. Not even the way you choke over the coffee I make you in the mornings…"

"Oh, you noticed that?"

He throws his head back and laughs. "It's like you're forcing yourself to down a cup of poison."

I feel myself color and I laugh. "OK, so I can go back to instant coffee now." Damon's coffee machine is like his other child; I didn't have the heart to tell him how bad it tastes to me.

He nods. "I can't wait to tell the world you said yes."

"I can't wait either."

He leans down and kisses me, and I feel as though my life has just begun. I was only practising before. This is the real deal. We stand back gawping at each other, mirroring the same goofy look.

CeeCee pokes her head through the door. "Is there a Mrs Guthrie here?" she asks, pretending to be someone else. And that's when I lose it. I'm a laughing, sobbing, shrieking mess of happiness.

CHAPTER TWELVE

I flick the bedside light off, and tiptoe from Charlie's room. Back in our room, Damon's propped up in bed reading a book.

"Hey," he says, smiling. He closes the book and pats the bed. "You sure you're OK reading to Charlie every night?"

I creep under the covers next to him, and slide up against his warm body. "I'm sure. How can I refuse those big blue eyes of hers?"

He laughs. "I know that feeling. But maybe we'll take it in turns. Don't want your wolf voice to burn out."

"Oh, you heard? She said I had to sound gruffer, and more snarly when the wolf speaks."

"Wait until you read the dinosaur one. She'll make you act out their roars."

We lay back on the pillows, facing each other. "I think I better get Sarah to order me some princess books, pronto."

"Mmm." Damon traces my lips with a finger. "Lil, do you believe in soulmates?"

I think back to when I met Damon at Christmas time. I had the strangest sensation, as if we already knew each other, and that he'd come back to Ashford just for me. "Do you?" I ask, not willing to be the first to say it.

"I didn't before I met you. I know this is going to sound corny, but I get this whole body-melt sensation when I'm near you. It's not just how pretty you are, or your gorgeous curves, or your goofiness, it's something more than all of that combined. Like there's an energy around you that pulls me in your orbit. It's the strongest feeling, like my soul recognizes yours. Gosh, that sounds stupid."

"No, it doesn't." Before a blubber-fest happens I cup his face, close my eyes, and kiss him as if we're the last people on earth.

After the excitement of the weekend, there's not much that can steal the smile from my lips. I tell Cee I have to run errands, so I can nip off to the bank, and withdraw the money for Joel. With my savings and the weekend takings I have almost six thousand. I'll apply for the credit card, and do whatever I can to pay him and get his noxious presence out of my life.

Picking up my handbag, I see my engagement ring sparkling under the light. Excitement sweeps me over every time I think of marrying Damon. We stayed up late discussing what kind of wedding we'd like and both agree on something simple. I may even wear gloop, just that once.

I say goodbye to CeeCee and walk outside. It's just after nine, and people mill lazily about on the streets. Everyone is probably pooped after yesterday's celebrations. Funny how my weariness has been replaced with wonderment.

The bank is quiet as I walk to a teller.

"Hey," Alyssa greets me. "We were just talking about you."

"Oh, yeah? Good or bad?" I joke as I reach for my bank card.

"I was raving to Marlene here about the pie CeeCee brought in. She said it was a secret recipe…"

"A secret recipe? You must have had the orange-kissed strawberry and rhubarb pie, then. Tastes as good as summer holiday."

"It surely does. Didn't last too long, I can tell you."

"They never do when it's one of CeeCee's."

Alyssa smiles. "What's going on with Cee? Is she moving or something?"

"No, why do you ask?" I frown remembering her spiel about friendships, and the importance of them, the morning of the egg hunt. A lump forms in my throat, I hope CeeCee isn't planning on moving. Her kids live out of town— maybe she wants to be closer to them. Maybe finding out about Janey has made her rethink her priorities. I couldn't imagine my life without CeeCee.

Alyssa continues, "She took out a bundle of cash. We can't think of where she'd spend so much money in Ashford. But she wouldn't tell. She closed her account and everything."

Grabbing my bank card, I race for the exit.

Alyssa yells out behind me, "You OK, Lil? What'd I say?"

I lift an arm to wave and head out to the street back to the Gingerbread Café.

Out of breath, I spill inside the café. CeeCee is alone, mixing something over the stove. She turns when she hears my clumsy footsteps.

"Lil, you beetroot red. What…you taking up running now? You already too skinny!"

"CeeCee, you can't do it. That money is for your retirement." I know Curtis, Cee's husband, left her a modest amount of money when he passed. Money he'd saved for exactly that reason, so she would have a nest egg and wouldn't need to work if she chose not to.

Her face tenses. "Do what?"

I tilt my head. "I've just been to the bank, Cee."

She clucks her tongue. "Mother o' Mary, no one can have any secrets in this town. They had no right telling you that!" Her face darkens. "It's my money, and it ain't up to you how I spend it."

"But, Cee…"

She holds a hand up. "No, Lil. I don't need that money. And that snake was never goin' to leave you alone. He's gone now. The loan's paid off and all done right. Mr Jefferson made it so. Joel won't bother you again, and of that I can be certain."

"Is that what you talked about the day he turned up over the road?"

She waves a hand. "Can't remember."

I gulp back tears. "So you paid him already?"

"I surely did. Couldn't get there quick enough."

"I'll go to the bank. I can pay some of it back right now, Cee. Then I'll…"

She shakes her head. "I don't need it, Lil. It wasn't a loan. *It was a gift*. Because that's what friends do. When Curtis died I figured my whole life was finished. I couldn't jump over that grief, Lil. But then you came along. Dragged me outta that house, and into the café. Made up some pretense about needin' help, when you surely didn't. Even made me take a wage when you were so broke you couldn't pay attention! Well, things like that I ain't never gonna forget. So now we even."

She shuffles to a table and sits heavily, motioning for me to join her.

"But, Cee…"

"Hush. It ain't important. You ever wonder why people trying to help you, Lil?"

I go to respond but she holds a hand up.

"Because you always helpin' people first. You got a good heart, Lil, and it's even better cause you don't know it. You just think that's how things should be. So take it when it comes back to you."

I'm lost for words, wondering how she could be so generous. I'm going to have to plot some clever way for her to take the money back as soon as I get it.

"I'm going to go visit Janey today. You be all right here without me?" Her mask of composure cracks for a moment, as I see such pain in her eyes.

I quickly reassure her. "I'll be fine. I think it'll be quiet after such a big weekend."

"OK, maybe I'll call Walt, and see what he needs."

I nod, knowing Walt will be happy to have CeeCee's effervescent presence around at such a sad time. And as they say, laughter is the best medicine. "Why don't you stay a while with Janey? I can get someone to help me here. Don't think there's anything more important than that right now."

"You sure, Lil?"

"More than sure."

"There's a change on the wind, ain't there?"

I know exactly what she means: things seem so different from how they were just a few days back. "Seems like it, Cee. I feel blazing happiness one minute, then so sad the next."

"Sugar plum, I know, but you gotta enjoy every moment with that fine-looking thing… Time goes so fast, Lil. So fast…" She breaks off, her eyes glazing over, as she stares across the road. Damon's sitting on the bench out front of his shop reading a newspaper. CeeCee looks sharply back to me, then over at Damon again. She jumps up suddenly and claps a hand over her heart. "I seen it! I seen it!" she says, her hands shaking.

I glance quickly at Damon, but can't see anything unusual. "What, Cee?"

"A baby! You gonna have a baby!" She scrunches her eyes closed.

I roll my eyes dramatically. "Oh, Cee! We're not even at that stage yet!"

Her eyes snap open. "It's the second sight! Was I wrong about you and Damon?" she screeches.

"No, ma'am." I grin back. Butterflies swarm in my belly at the thought of having children, but I don't say anything. I just smile, and shrug. "We'll see."

"It's gonna be a little boy, oh, he as cute as a button," she says. "We better hurry up and get you married. I had this idea for your wedding cake…"

I watch CeeCee scramble from the table, her eyes bright with excitement. I rub my belly once, just in case she's right.

Christmas Wedding at the Gingerbread Cafe

For Sophie Hedley because I love you.

CHAPTER ONE

Ten days

The fluffy white meringue hypnotizes me as it swirls around the mixer into soft valleys and peaks. A chocolate cake cools on the stainless-steel bench ready for me to layer with meringue, which will look like fresh snow for the cheery-faced fondant reindeers to graze in. High-pitched voices interrupt my reverie, and I turn to see the small children of Ashford making their way along the icy street, caroling.

It's almost nightfall; through the tinseled window and flashing fairy lights I watch them sing, their faces lit up with the excitement of Christmas. I switch off the mixer, and dust my hands on my apron. Edging closer to the door, I listen to them pitch and warble. I sing along, enraptured by the catchy festive songs.

A couple of young stragglers pull away from the crowd of carolers, and race to the window of the Gingerbread Café. They push their tiny red noses against the glass; their breath fogs up the view. I duck my head around the door. "See those marshmallow snowmen? CeeCee made them especially, so when you're finished caroling you can take as many as you want. Tell your friends too." Their eyes go wide, as they squeal and dash back to the group, gesticulating wildly back to the sweet treats on display.

Smiling at their exuberance, I glance back to the window, and see why they're so animated. At their age and height it must look like a monolithic ode to gingerbread. CeeCee insisted we make our own Christmas tree this year…out of gingerbread. It took us the better part of three weeks to work out how exactly to bake the pieces so they'd fit together to form branches. There were plenty of mistakes made, which were hastily eaten up by our regular customers.

We felt like the most accomplished engineers when it was finally erected and we'd decorated it with golden candy floss 'tinsel', and 'baubles' made from scarlet toffee. The 'ground' is made from marshmallow, and the Christmas presents made from chocolate dusted with edible glitter sit afoot the tree. All the late nights baking seem like nothing when a crowd of children stop and ogle it as if it's something magical. I can't wait for Damon's daughter, Charlie, to see it. For a moment I picture her, with her beautiful blond curls, following the kids along the street, singing. I miss her when she's gone, almost as if she's my own child.

The doorbell jingles, catching me mid-chorus. I turn, half expecting the tiny revelers to rush in. "Oh, golly, that's the voice I love," Damon teases. His hands snake behind my jacket and he rubs the warmth of my back. "Operatic, and dramatic."

"Very funny." I grin. "I would have tried a bit harder if I knew I had an audience." So, my singing leaves a lot to be desired. I blame my mamma—she's sings as if she's being strangled and unfortunately I inherited that gene.

"And I get to wake up to the sound of that voice every day until…for ever."

Gazing up at him, my mouth hanging open like a love-struck fool, I say, "*Ten days* until I'm Mrs. Guthrie.

Ten days until I swan down that aisle. I'm tingly with excitement even if I do have to wear gloop on my face, and be tortured with hair devices to make my curly hair... curly."

He laughs so hard little dimples appear on his cheeks. "I'm tingly too, in more ways than one." He half groans as he leans down and kisses me full on the mouth. I close my eyes as my whole-body throb reaches swoon level. This *fine-thing* sure knows how to kiss a girl, all right.

Slightly breathless, we pull apart, silent for a moment until the blood rushes back to wherever the hell it's supposed to be. We stare hard at each other, but I don't dare kiss him again. We're likely to close up shop and jump into bed for the evening. As tempting as that is, I have cakes to bake.

But...no.

I have cakes to bake.

Damon runs his hands through his hair. "Let's just close..."

Jelly-legged from his presence, I fight to stay strong. "Nope."

He hooks his fingers through the belt loops of my jeans and pulls me against him. I step back, but he pulls me close again in an effort to convince me. "Lil..."

"Nope."

His lips part slowly, and my restraint almost crumbles. *Cakes, think of the cakes.*

He moans low. "You're a temptress..."

I laugh. "It's a hard life."

"Very hard," he agrees, winking. He makes a show of exhaling, and shakes away the desire that is plain on his face. Composed, he says, "Let's stop *canoodling* in the doorway before we end up in some compromising photos on CeeCee's Spacebook."

I imagine a picture of us wrapped together squid-like, flushed, for the world to see on Facebook. I giggle and drag Damon close to the fireplace when my friend Missy ducks her head in and says, "Hello, lovebirds! You're looking mighty sweet all tangled like that."

"Come out of the cold, Missy." I wave her over to the fire. She struts in. Despite being heavily pregnant, she still manages to saunter rather than waddle.

Missy, who owns The Sassy Salon, has all these grand plans for my wedding hair and make-up, and, while it's not usually my thing, it's hard not to get caught up in her excitement. She is an expert, after all.

I rub her belly before giving her a hug. As always she smells sweet with perfume and hair products, her heavily made-up face perfection as she fluffs her big auburn curls. "I don't intend to interrupt you two from whatever it is you were doing…" she arches an eyebrow, and grins "… but I wanted to give you these, Lil." She hands me a brown paper bag. "Some make-up samples, *colorstay*, so no matter how much toying you do to your pretty little face, it should stay put."

I go to protest, but she shakes a finger. "Before you start shaking your head, hear me out. You need to decide what colors you like…so just try it, OK? I know make-up is not your thing, but you'll get used to it if you try it out a few times before the wedding."

Damon lets out a huge belly laugh. I pivot, hands on hips, and give him a fake pout, he stops immediately and claps a hand over his mouth. "You think this is funny?" I tease; ruing the fact that at almost thirty years of age I still don't understand the basics of applying make-up. I've tried, but it feels so unnatural, as if I've cemented my face, that I can't help but mess with it, as a child would.

"No, no!" Damon holds his palms up, stifling a laugh. "Definitely not funny." I give him a shove with my hip and turn back to Missy.

"I just hope I'm not going to look like a Dolly Parton impersonator."

Missy rolls her eyes heavenward. "There's nothing wrong with Dolly Parton, Lil. That woman knows what real beauty is."

I guffaw.

"She's my people and I won't hear a bad word about her!" Missy laughs. I grin back. Missy dresses similar to Dolly Parton, all tight miniskirts, bold prints, the odd sequin or two. She's vibrant and sassy and has a heart of pure gold.

"OK, no more Dolly jokes. So are there instructions with this stuff?" Doubt creeps in as I survey the bag full of colorful vials and tubes used for God knows what. Missy knows I'm erring on the side of natural rather than full-on war paint, but so far all I see are pinks and reds so bright they make my eyes hurt.

Missy scoffs. "No, there aren't instructions! At least try the lipsticks and see which shade you prefer. We can sort the rest at the make-up trial, OK?"

"OK."

"I better go and close up shop or else Tommy'll think I've run off with another man."

Laughter barrels out of us at the thought of a heavily pregnant woman running anywhere, least of all off with another man. "See you tomorrow, and thanks." I hold up the bag. Missy air kisses us both and struts away. From behind you can't even tell she's pregnant—all the gingerbread men and slices of pie she's consumed have obviously gone straight to the baby.

"Only ten more days…" Damon's voice brings me back to the present as he kisses the top of my head.

Ten more days marks our one-year anniversary, *and* our wedding day.

I wasn't searching for love a year ago, far from it, when it fell in my lap—or rather my café—in the form of this tight-jean-wearing, curly-haired, six-packed, glorious man. Some days it *still* doesn't feel real, that this kind of passionate, all-consuming love could just happen, in the blink of an eye, but thank my lucky stars, it did.

Nipping my fingers into Damon's back pockets, I pull his hips close. "Look at them…"

Ashford's mini carolers huddle together as they wait to cross the road. They're bundled up in woolen scarves and beanies, their mittened hands holding candles. They chorus *Amazing Grace*, and I stiffen in Damon's arms. *Oh, no.* I bite the inside of my cheek. I wiggle my toes. Isn't that what people do to stem their tears? It's too late. My eyes well up; it's no use. That song kills me. It's the very heart of Christmas and it speaks to me like nothing else.

"Lil?" Damon says. "You OK?"

I half laugh, half hiccough. "It's that darn song. It's even more of a tear-jerker when six-year-olds are singing it." My voice comes out a little strangled as I try to laugh it off.

"How could I forget?" he says wistfully. "The *Amazing Grace* blubber-fest exactly one year ago today."

I cock my head. "Wait…what? You saw that?" This time last year I had my hand wedged well and truly up a turkey's behind, stuffing the damn poultry to sell in the café as I sang my little heart out to *Amazing Grace*, laughing-shrieking-sobbing with the sadness of one whose life wasn't going as planned. And that very same day, I met Damon.

Damon smacks his forehead. "Whoops. So I may have been spying on you long before you marched across the road to shout at me for stealing your customers."

The memory makes me smile. I'd been all riled up when this handsome newcomer strode into town selling the same things as my beloved Gingerbread Café. It hadn't helped matters he was gorgeous and instantly had a shop full of ladies, single or not, flicking their shiny hair, and strutting about, trying to make his acquaintance.

"You were *spying* on me?" I ask, mock seriously.

He puts a hand to his chest and does his best to keep his face straight, but his lip wobbles as he gulps back laughter. "I fell in love with you that very second. I thought, if a girl can stuff a turkey, simultaneously cry, and laugh, and sing like it's the only thing that'll save her, then she's the one for me." He presses a fist to his mouth, no doubt reliving the scene in all its sob-fest glory.

I laugh and blush to the roots of my hair. I really did make a spectacle of myself that long-ago wintry morning in the café. I had no idea anyone could see me in such a vulnerable state. "I'm surprised—" I hit him playfully on the arm "—that you've never mentioned this before."

He raises his eyebrows. The deep brown of his eyes is so easy to get lost in, I forget for a moment what we're even discussing. "You were upset, and I didn't want you to know I'd seen. I only wanted to make you smile. Little did I know that you'd take offence to my mere presence in town, and that it would become a bit harder than I'd first thought."

Thinking back to that day, I'm caught up in a rush of mixed feelings. Back then, I was pining for my ex-husband Joel, too naïve to know he was no good, not realizing it was just the *idea* of love I missed—and not actually him. And that very day, I'd vowed to run Damon out of town because I'd seen him as a threat to my business, and without the café I would have been lost *and* broke. That version of me, sad and lonely, seems like a lifetime ago.

Shaking my head, I marvel—what a difference a year makes. It hadn't taken long for me to fall in love with Damon; he truly was a Christmas miracle. And now, we're about to get married! I resist the urge to pinch myself.

When a man turns every notion you had of love upside down, and shows you what a genuine heart he has, it's almost impossible not to well up, and again it makes me wonder why I let my ex-husband treat me callously for so long. Silently, I thank the universe he's out of my life for good, and instead focus on the wonderful man in front of me.

And next year, I vow, I'll only listen to *Amazing Grace* when I'm alone, and can bawl for the full five minutes and afterwards will feel strangely refreshed, and altogether festive.

"Where's CeeCee?" Damon asks, glancing around the café.

Frowning, I push a tendril of hair back. "She dashed out to get some Christmas presents for her grandbabies." I glance at my watch and shrug. "But that was a while ago. She's probably bumped into someone."

You can never really *dash* anywhere in Ashford. Everyone knows everyone—you can't get down the main street without stopping to chat to people. Even the inclement weather doesn't deter the locals from stopping to shoot the breeze.

Outside snow drifts down like white confetti, pitching in the wind, and settling on the square window panes. The sight makes me want to curl up and watch the world go by. With that in mind, I push Damon towards one of the old sofas in front of the fireplace, and sit with my legs over his lap. He's impossible to resist and the cakes can wait, for five minutes, at least. The fire is stoked up, and crackles and spits as if it's saying hello. Damon groans. "I'm beat.

You don't realize till you stop for a minute." He covers his mouth as he yawns, which immediately makes me yawn.

"How'd today go?" I ask. Damon owns a small goods shop across the road, and hosts cooking demonstrations as well as sorting out the finer details of our catering business. No matter what you do, money is tight for shopkeepers in Ashford purely because it's such a small town. Though the lead-up to Christmas is frantic for us all.

"Busy. I must have made a hundred cups of coffee…"

I smirk. Damon's fancy coffee tastes like tar to me, but women still flock there, and grimace their way through a cup. He's totally clueless they're ogling him as he dashes behind the counter, while they stare, mouths hanging open. I don't blame them. I'd spend my morning at his coffee bar and stare too if I could.

"Any catering enquiries for January?"

He shakes his head. We decided not to take any bookings for the catering over Christmas because of the wedding but we'd hoped to get some parties booked for the new year. Our catering business is what keeps us afloat in the times the streets are quiet, especially over winter. "They'll come, Lil. Don't worry; let's just focus on Christmas and the wedding and having our families all in one place."

I bite a nail, before catching myself, hearing Missy in my mind berating me. "I hope we haven't made a mistake turning clients away."

He shrugs. "It's our wedding, Lil. I'm sure everyone understands."

We've chosen a Christmas Eve wedding for sentimental reasons; it will be a year exactly that we've been a couple, and it seems fitting to make the commitment on that date. Plus, it's when Charlie visits, and my parents are finally back from an extended round-the-world-trip. And a winter wonderland wedding—well, you can't get more romantic than that.

But…it's also a busy time for the café until December twenty-fourth and then we're suddenly deader than a doornail, as people hibernate for the remaining winter. By turning catering clients away after a steady year of building the business into almost-flourishing, I do step back and wonder if we've made the right choice. I don't have anyone to fall back on financially if ends don't meet, and that's enough to keep me awake at night sometimes. Damon's family are wealthy, but he stubbornly refuses to take handouts from them, which is one of the reasons I love him. He makes his own way. But a small part of me sometimes thinks that's why he doesn't seem overly concerned when his business doesn't make enough to cover costs. He does have that back-up if he ever needs it, despite saying he'd never ask them for money.

Maybe it's just one of our differences: he's a little more relaxed about his future, whereas I tend to plan ahead. It's a good thing, in some respects—he brings me back to earth, the times I'm fiddling with the calculator, my paperwork piled in front. He'll massage my shoulders before gently taking away my pen, and telling me to leave it for a while. That my furious adding and subtracting won't change anything at ten minutes to midnight.

Secretly, I've been trying to save. I want to pay CeeCee back for the Joel fiasco, but she won't have any of it, so I've been squirrelling money into an account, which I'll put aside for her grandbabies. I also have another account, reserved especially for future wages for another staff member for the café. We'll need an extra pair of hands if, make that *when*, I fall pregnant. I want to be squared away financially when it does happen. I'll still work in the café, but I'd like to spend some time at home too. A baby needs routine, and I'm determined to find a way I can make it work. Just the thought of nursing a baby makes me warm inside. We've been trying since Easter, with no luck, but I know it'll happen. Just like Missy, it'll happen when I least expect it.

Outside the young carolers cross the icy street their voices carrying over on the wind, pure and sweet like tiny angels.

"And anyway," Damon says, his lazy smile in place, "unless we renew our vows every December, it's the only time we'll turn clients away."

I flash him a grin. He's right. I should be focusing on the wedding, not getting all angsty over the business side of things. He takes my hand and laces his fingers through mine.

It won't be long before friends and family arrive in Ashford for the week. There have been flurries of phone calls and emails about where they'll stay and what they'll do. I can't wait for them to sit at the kitchen bench nursing steaming cups of gingerbread coffee, while I bake for them.

I wonder what they'll make of my business. The café, with its dark-chocolate-colored walls and gingerbread-man bunting, looks enchanting at nightfall, when the fire throws shadows over the space, and the Christmas decorations shine under the fairy lights. It's cozy and warm, the kind of place you can loll about and forget your troubles. And celebrate love, and friendship and everything in between.

Excitement dazzles me for a moment, as I think about baking beautiful cakes for people I love. Baking has always been more like a meditation for me. Life makes sense when I'm clasping a wooden spoon, and have a bowl of batter cupped under an arm. And it's infinitely more magical when I make a sweet treat with a friend or family member in mind. When they exclaim about the presentation of a gateau, and, with fork poised mid bite, roll their eyes heavenward *oohing* over the flavors, it makes my heart sing. And that's why I run a café that struggles as much as it flourishes. I need to. It's what I'm meant to do. Seasons come and go, and so do customers. Summer is busy, and Christmas is hectic, but between that we falter, just like all the shops in Ashford.

I snuggle close to the man I'm going to marry. The soft orange glow from the fire lights up his face, and again I have one of those overwhelming feelings that life is Christmas-card perfect.

"Now it's so close, are you nervous about the wedding?" Damon asks.

"No way, Jose. Are you?" I arch an eyebrow.

"Nope. It can't come quick enough for me. *Lil and Damon Guthrie…*"

My heart flutters at the words. "Lived happily ever after."

He grins. "The end."

I run through our wedding checklist in my mind, but Damon's sentiment has turned my brain to mush, making it hard to remember. Damon's been involved in almost every step of the wedding planning. We've grown closer, if that's even possible, while we've had our heads bent over our wish list.

"I've still got to organize the bouquets, the centerpieces for the tables, confer with the photographer, the dress fitting, the make-up trial…" I trail off as I think of the orders I need to finish for the café too.

He rubs the sandy brown stubble on his chin as though he's contemplating. "Oh! I spoke to Guillaume again. He's happy with our ideas, said it won't be any trouble."

Guillaume owns *L'art de l'amour*, a French bistro just outside Ashford. When we were pondering a venue for the reception I knew instantly I wanted to have it there. It's an intimate space that's just the right size for our guests. It's not showy, or glitzy, just classically French, with a chef who's passionate about his food, no matter how temperamental he is.

Translated, the name of the restaurant means *The Art of Love*, which I think is a good omen, but I keep that pearl of wisdom to myself. Guillaume's a genius when it comes to the culinary arts, and we trust his judgment explicitly, though I did ask Damon to massage Guillaume's ego so we could make a few suggestions. He's typically French and believes in his methods and recipes, so for him to even discuss our menu, well, Damon must have charmed the socks off him.

The rumor mill has settled down now, but when Guillaume appeared in town a few years back there was plenty of speculation about why such a formidable chef would choose the outskirts of Ashford to ply his exotic wares. And we're yet to figure it out. There's a story behind the great man, but he's not talking. All *we* care about is him making the night spectacular with his inventive cooking.

"What did it take to convince him?" I ask.

Damon bites down on his bottom lip, a gesture that makes me want to ravish him right there. "I might have bent the truth a teeny tiny little bit…"

I give him a shove. "Out with it."

"I said the menu suggestions were CeeCee's idea. His face glowed red, and he instantly agreed."

I throw my head back and laugh. Guillaume has a soft spot for our CeeCee. She doesn't seem to notice when he visits the café and blushes like a schoolboy in her presence. When he's around CeeCee his jaw loses the tense set to it, which is replaced by a wide grin. He fidgets, reverts to speaking French, usually making CeeCee holler at him, "Come now, Guillaume, do I hafta get my French dictionary out again?"

"Wait till I tell her that," I say.

Damon tuts. "If you tell her she can't pretend she doesn't know he's sweet on her."

I gasp. "You think she knows?"

"I think she does."

"Does Guillaume know that CeeCee knows?"

Damon's eyes shine bright with laughter. "You sound like a teenager."

I frown.

"OK, yes, I think Guillaume knows *she* knows, but doesn't know what to do about it."

"Wow, that's a lot of knows, when no one knows."

"I know," he deadpans.

Well, I'll be darned. CeeCee and I don't keep secrets from each other. It's almost impossible to at any rate. We know each other so well that we'll read each other's expressions and with a few foot stomps, or heavy sighs, we'll inevitably let the story tumble out. But the minx has kept this from me fairly easily.

I wonder if CeeCee *has* contemplated dating again? Maybe that's why she hasn't mentioned that she knows Guillaume is sweet on her? Curtis, CeeCee's husband, passed away four years ago, and she misses him with all of her heart. They had that rare once-in-a-lifetime kind of love. But saying that, some companionship might be just the thing for her. There's no way I'm broaching that particular subject with her though—she's liable to beat me over the head with a bread stick if I even mentioned it.

"Your mamma stopped by the shop today." My parents have only been back in Ashford a few weeks after an extended world trip. It seemed once they started traveling they couldn't get enough of exploring the world outside of our small town. I missed them desperately while they were gone, but I understood they were hit with wanderlust, and I was happy for them after a lifetime of living in one place.

"Oh? What did she stop in for?"

"She wanted a hamper of goodies for Reverend Joe…"

"Hmm." Oh, Lord, what's cooking in that mind of hers? It's not unusual for Mamma to support the church with hampers of food, especially at Christmas, but it's odd she didn't ask me to make one for her. Scampering over to Damon and asking him to make one can only mean one thing. She didn't want me to know. "What for? Is she trying to rearrange the church or something?"

Our ceremony is to take place in the hundred-year-old chapel in Ashford, a beautifully restored building, with huge stained glass arched windows that funnel in the most glorious light. So many memorable events have been held there, from weddings, to baptisms and funerals of those we've loved, it just seems right, as if we'll be a part of the fabric of that sacred place once we're married. Reverend Joe is a fan of our gingerbread and caramelized pear Bundt cake so I baked him one when we met him to discuss our nuptials. He's a sweet man who doesn't seem to age, just looks the same year in year out, almost as if he's otherworldly.

"No idea why she wanted the hamper." Damon throws his palms up in an effort to bamboozle me, but I can tell when he's bending the truth. He gets this tiny little wrinkle on one side of his mouth, probably in his effort to hold back a smile.

"You've got your lying face on…"

"My what?" He narrows his eyes.

"Your lying face. I can read you like a book."

He scoffs. "Is that so?"

"Yep." He presses his cheek against mine; his breath tickles my skin.

"Well, it's…a surprise." He smiles, and continues holding me close.

"Give me a clue."

"Nope." He clucks his tongue. "You, pretty lady, are just going to have to wait and see."

"Fine." I cross my arms in mock annoyance, hoping he'll give in.

Instead he laughs, and says, "Fine."

"*Fine*. I think I might just pay a visit to the church…"

"It's closed." Damon grins and gathers me in his arms. He stares into my eyes long enough to make me giddy. "And anyway, you wouldn't guess the surprise even if you were staring straight at it."

"Really? I'm pretty clever when I want to be."

"That you are." He strokes my hair back and runs his fingers around my face.

"If you keep up with that, I'll fall asleep," I say as he continues.

"My parents phoned."

Damon's parents are due to fly in a few days before the wedding. Despite a few attempts for me to meet them earlier, it hasn't happened. Though Damon's often caught up with them in New Orleans when he's flown over for a weekend visit to see Charlie.

"What did they say?" I ask.

"They're excited to meet you. Mother wanted every minute detail about the wedding. I felt…I don't know, so excited to share it all with them, not just the wedding, but my life here, the shop, the town, *you*. I mean, of course they know about it all anyway, but it feels different now they're actually going to visit, you know?"

"They'll love it here and I can't wait to meet them." They're scheduled to arrive three days before the wedding, which is cutting it fine, so I've organized a morning tea so his mother can get to know us girls, and hopefully feel a little more included in the pre-wedding fun."

He nods, and pulls at his shirt—one of those God-awful checker types he insists on wearing as though he's some kind of cowboy. They do suit him, but it's a running joke between us, now, how much I hate his so-called cowboy style.

"I told Mother all about the chapel, and about Guillaume. She wanted to know what's left to do, and if we needed anything."

"Did she like the sound of it?"

He gives me a lazy smile. "She did. And she kept on about the menu—that's what reminded me to ring Guillaume and check our requests were OK."

I relax my shoulders. "Good. I'll sort out the flowers and the centerpieces, and those few other things and we are just about done!"

"I have a feeling there's not going to be a bridezilla for me," Damon says, half sadly.

I shove him playfully. "You sound disappointed."

He laughs. "Oh, you know, there's a lot to be said for those guys with eyes as big as headlights, sitting at Jerry's bar, nursing a beer, wondering when exactly the woman they met morphed into a screeching mass of nerves."

"Is this about *beer*?"

He drums his fists against his shirt. "Maybe I'd be better with whiskey, Lil," he says in a throaty voice as if he's a chain-smoking, whiskey-swilling tough guy. "Yep," he continues. "Thought I'd escape the crazy bride-to-be ramblings and head over there with Tommy. But there's no rambling. And no crazy bride. What the heck are we going to talk about?"

A giggle escapes me as I picture Damon trying to be one of those guys that hold up the bar at the run-down old pub the next town over. Sure, he'll be able to make conversation with anyone, but invariably he'll start talking about a three-day cassoulet he's set on making, or some new zany haute cuisine we're trying for our catering business, and the guys there will glance at each other over the top of his head and label him a sissy.

And Tommy as his so-called drinking buddy? Tommy is Missy's husband. While Missy is an exuberant, fast-talking sweetheart, Tommy is her polar opposite. He's quiet to the point of silent, but deep down he's just a really observant, intuitive guy who doesn't make small talk just for the sake of it.

"I wouldn't go to Jerry's if you paid me," Damon says.

"Well…I have some bad news for you." I wink at him. "A surprise, you could say." I grin wickedly.

He runs a hand through his sandy blond hair, and grimaces. "Please do not say the B word."

Bachelor party: it brings to mind all those connotations of men behaving badly, but around here the only mischief they get up to is the usual pranks you'd expect of teenagers.

"OK, I'll use the S word. The guys checked with me first—they really want to organize a stag party for you." Damon goes to speak but I halt him with a hand up. "It's just a small group. Something low-key."

Damon leans his head back on the sofa. "Low-key? Like a dinner party?"

I tap his leg. "No, siree. I'm afraid you're going to have to let them drag you out and shave off your eyebrows or whatever it is they do these days."

He groans. "Shooters of bourbon and tough-guy stories…"

"'Fraid so. Just don't let them tie you to a pole in the snow, or anything like that."

Damon's eyebrows shoot up. "What?"

CHAPTER TWO

Nine days

...?" CeeCee says, her voice soft with ... she wraps turkey, cranberry and ...parcels made with paper-thin filo pastry ...pecial.

...e the egg-wash?"

... bowl of beaten egg next to her and find ...aning over her shoulder as she wraps the ...ntemplate what they'll taste like once the ...my melted mess with th...

I hide my smile.

why smart folks don

Laughter rumble

chest. "Oh, you jes

"Enjoy!" I say c

"What about

something special

I gulp, sudden

say something ab

"A nightclub

strippers?"

This time I l

over his head o

are sealed. It's

While Fran

Christmas fro

collar of his s

"Cherry blossom

concentration as

Camembert into

for today's lunch s

"Mmm?"

"Can you pass n

I place the small

the pastry brush. Le

delicate pastry, I co

Camembert is a crea

and the crunch of the

"You breathin' d

jokes.

I giggle and tak

hungry."

"Well, why didn'

hungry my stomach

couple o' these in the

"You read my mi

baked around here;

the day where we br

While we wait

bench in preparat

café is quiet today, and the usual worry we're baking for ourselves sits heavy in my belly.

"What's those wrinkles popping up 'tween your eyes for?" CeeCee says.

I laugh. CeeCee's southern way of talking makes even the blackest moods fade. "Same old reason, Cee. Wondering where the heck everyone's got to, 'cause they sure aren't in town today."

She shrugs. "It's still early, Lil. They'll come. Especially when they see what I've got planned next." She waggles her eyebrows in an exaggerated fashion.

"Got something in your eye?"

She guffaws and slaps her leg. "No, I do not. I was trying to be mysterious!"

I laugh. "So what's going to draw the punters in today?"

"You're gonna put weight on just looking at the recipe, I swear it, but it's gonna be a showstopper." Fumbling in the pocket of her apron, she pulls out a square of paper and waves it at me.

I unfold it and read quickly. "A croquembouche?"

She snatches the piece of paper back, and pushes her glasses back on. "Not just any croquembouche, a *salted caramel* croquembouche with ricotta cream. Instead of making one big tower of profiteroles, I thought we could make say ten smaller towers. They sure are pretty, and if we flick toffee around them it'll look like tinsel 'round a Christmas tree."

Her enthusiasm is infectious, but I stand mute because it's a *French* recipe, from a *French* culinary magazine. CeeCee'll try baking anything once, but after Damon's chat about Guillaume my mind connects the dots, and the picture is a love heart.

"I think you're right, Cee." In the picture the little balls of choux pastry are stacked up into a cone shape, the salted caramel glaze dripped over them makes them shine, and some tendrils of spun toffee flicked over once they're assembled will draw in a crowd for sure. My mouth waters at the thought of biting into the luscious ricotta filling.

I sidle up to her and lean close. "So-o-o...where'd you get this recipe from?"

CeeCee makes a show of wiping her hands on her apron, and then bending over to take silver bowls from under the bench, though her brown cheeks blush so furiously they're almost purple.

"Cee?"

She stands, and pretends not to have heard me, but I can read her expressions as clearly as a road map. I snatch up the piece of paper. "You know..." I play with her "...I'm sure I remember Guillaume mentioning this recipe to me before..."

Her mouth opens and closes, and she drops the silver bowl, which clangs like a cymbal as it bounces on the floor.

"Did he now?" she eventually manages.

I'm just about to press her for information when the doorbell jingles.

"Well, lookie here," she booms. "If it ain't your daddy." Her voice is slightly manic with what? Relief?

My father strides in, flicking his braces over his big belly, which is a sure-fire sign he's hungry. "Hey, Dad." He hugs me tight.

"Hey, darlin'." I detect the faint whiff of cigar smoke on him, the same old dad, sneaking puffs out of Mamma's sight. If she knew he was still partial to the odd cigar, I'd hear her yelling all the way from home.

"Morning, CeeCee." He tips his head.

"Let me get you a candy-cane coffee." She bustles away, no doubt glad for the interruption.

"Hungry?" I say, remembering the parcels in the oven.

"Well…"

I edge him to a table. "Get comfy. You can try the turkey, cranberry and Camembert pastry that Cee's just made."

He laces his fingers together. "Don't tell your mamma." He winks.

"She's still making you diet?"

His face is glum as he counts on his fingers. "No sugar, no bread, no pasta, no rice. High protein, rabbit food only. And you know your mamma." He screws up his face. "Her idea of dinner is over-boiled carrots, and frozen peas, with a side of charred steak. At least my choppers stay sharp after all that grinding."

I laugh. He's always on about his teeth, as if the secret to longevity is how well his choppers are holding up. Mamma isn't the best cook in the world. In fact she's downright disastrous. Dad still marvels to this day how I managed to learn to cook since I share her genes, but my grandmother baked, and I spent a lot of my childhood in her kitchen.

"You're putting me in a predicament just being here," I joke. "What if she walks past and I've just gone and served you a plate of banned food?" I pop the pastries on two plates and take them to the table.

"She won't," he says. "I made sure of it." He lowers his voice as if he's plotting something more sinister.

CeeCee wanders over with mugs of candy-cane coffee and we sit at the table together. I slide a plate to each of them and take one of the steaming cups of sweet coffee.

"How'd you make sure of it?" I ask him.

"She said that Emma Mae invited her over for a game of Scrabble, and you know those two once they get to talking. I'll be lucky if she's home for dinner."

I swallow a sip of coffee and say, "What if she was lying? And she said that to test you, knowing full well you'd sneak into the café?"

His eyes go wide and he pushes the plate away as if it's on fire.

CeeCee pipes up, "I'm sure I seen her walk past not even a minute ago…" She cackles high and loud, and I smirk behind my hand.

He scoffs. "I *knew* you were joking—give me that plate back! And anyway, once a week, surely that's OK for a treat? I'm only human."

I cluck my tongue. "Dad, you come in every day."

"Small portions, Lil. That's the secret." Somehow he manages to keep a straight face. Dad visits at least once a day, fills up on whatever we're baking, and takes a few gingerbread men for the road. There's no sign of small portions anywhere near his dinner-sized plate.

A customer blows in just as I'm about to retort, a broody-looking stranger with dark eyes, and a fit physique. I go to stand and CeeCee says, "You catch up with your dad, Lil. I'll go."

I nod thanks, and sit.

"So," Dad says between forkfuls, "as the chief organizer of Damon's bachelor party, I thought I'd run a few things by you."

I grin. "How did you end up in charge of the bachelor do?"

He shrugs. "Damned if I know. Seems everyone's working and Tommy thinks I need to step away from daytime TV…"

Folding my arms and leaning my elbows on the table, I say, "Maybe that's a good idea." Dad retired just before he and Mamma went away; before that he worked with Tommy in the dairy. Almost forty years in the same place, and I think now he's home he misses the routine, and his friends there. Not so much the back-breaking labor, but the lack of physical work has definitely added to his waistline, hence Mamma's nagging. "But a few midday movie sessions aren't such a bad idea either."

He gives me a half-smile. "It was a novelty at first, but now…well, I'm under your mamma's feet all the time, and I'm kind of…bored. It was OK when we were traveling, but now, I need to find something to do." He flicks his braces. "So, first step; bachelor party, second step, something to fill my days…"

My dad's one of those people who like to keep busy. He retired on Mamma's say-so, but I don't think he was really ready for it. And I hate to think of him sitting at home trying to keep out of Mamma's way as she vacuums and dusts daily in her usual frenzy.

"You could do some volunteer work?"

He knots his bushy eyebrows. "That might be just the thing."

I rest my hand atop his. "Why don't you try the community center? I'm sure they'd love your help." We're both silent as we glance out of the snow-mottled window to Walt's empty furniture shop.

Walt and Janey usually run all the local events out of the community center, but we haven't seen them in an age. Janey was diagnosed with cancer back at Easter time. She and Walt moved to a small hotel in Springfield to be closer to the big hospital there while she receives treatment.

"I'll go in and see who's running things now, see if they need a hand." Dad clears his throat. "So, for the bachelor party, what'll it be? I was thinking I'd set up our front room like a casino. I'd be the croupier, of course. Do you think Damon would like that?"

"He'd love it." And he would. A night in, gambling pennies on cards, would suit him to a T. "What night are you thinking?"

"Maybe Monday night? Leaves a two days before the wedding in case someone dyes his hair red, or whatever it is they do these days."

"Blue's more his color."

Dad bellows so loud CeeCee glances over, and the newcomer does too. I mouth sorry, and exchange a smile with CeeCee.

"Possum," Dad says, reverting back to my childhood pet name. "Look at you."

I pat my hair down; my curls are probably a riot after dashing outside earlier.

Dad waves a hand at me. "No, Lil, I mean *look* at you." His face softens. "I don't think I've ever seen you so... radiant. Damon is a great guy. He's smitten with you. It's as obvious as the big nose on my face." He laughs. "What I'm trying to say is, your mamma and I are so proud of you, from the way you run the café, to the way you cherish your friends, and because you're marrying a man who is truly worthy of you. And I can't wait to walk you down that aisle, knowing that the man standing at the other end is a good one."

I rub the top of his hand. Dad doesn't often speak like this; usually he's more of a prankster, a joker. And I guess like most people he had his doubts about my ex-husband Joel. He never said anything directly, but he'd asked me the night before my first wedding if I was really sure I was making the right decision. And I *was sure*; it wasn't until much later that the marriage fell apart, and Joel changed into a different man from the one I married. But that part of my life taught me some valuable lessons about myself, and I wouldn't change it.

"That means a lot, Dad." I give his hand a squeeze.

"It's all true," he says. "Being away for so long, you know, we worried about you. When we heard that Joel had slunk back into town, we almost flew back. But CeeCee called and said she'd sorted it. It's a funny thing, parenthood—you'll always be my little girl no matter how old you are."

I stand and walk around to give him a hug. "I'm glad you didn't cancel your trip for that. I'm lucky to have a friend like CeeCee."

"That you are, darlin'. So…" he winks "…what's the chance of a slice of one of CeeCee's pies?"

"You're going to get me in trouble…" I amble over to CeeCee, who's packing a box of baked goods for the newcomer. I nod hello and he gives me a tentative smile. CeeCee pipes up, "This is Clay. He's gone and moved to the Maple Syrup Farm. Gonna do it up real nice, like it used to be."

"Nice to meet you, Clay. You'll be busy by the sounds of it." I picture the derelict farm. It needs a complete overhaul, that place.

Clay nods, and gives me a ghost of a smile.

"Dad wants a piece of pie, Cee. So just holler if you need a hand."

She shoos me away. "Your daddy dumber 'n a bucket of coal if he thinks your mamma won't find out. Ain't no way I'm serving him pie, neither!"

I massage her shoulders and laugh. "How will she find out?"

"She's a woman from a small town, cherry blossom. O' course she'll find out."

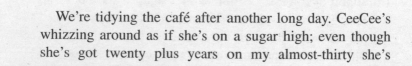

We're tidying the café after another long day. CeeCee's whizzing around as if she's on a sugar high; even though she's got twenty plus years on my almost-thirty she's as spritely as a teenager. I'm mopping the floors as she restacks the books on the shelves and tidies the tables near the fireplace. She's humming, and bopping along as she works.

We've been so busy in the lead-up to Christmas I'm as worn out as a rag doll but CeeCee's like a never-ending ball of energy. I clean slowly, and decide I'll reward myself with a nice long soak in the tub when I get home. And if Damon happens to wander in while I'm in there, all the better.

Blowing my hair from my face, I rest awhile using the mop as a prop to hold me. The street is almost deserted as shops close for the evening. It's almost seven, and snowing hard outside, when I see a couple of finely dressed people walk into Damon's small goods shop. There's something about them that catches my eye. They're not from around here by the looks of it: the woman is wearing a fancy fur coat, with a matching beret, and the gentleman is wearing a suit and scarf.

CeeCee goes out front to bring in our chalkboard. She races back inside, and dumps the A-frame against the wall. "It's cold enough out there to freeze the balls off a pool table!" She rubs her hands together to warm them. "Who's that over yonder?"

"I don't know." I dunk the mop, and swish it around the bucket when CeeCee says, "Well, we about to find out. Here they come now."

Damon holds onto the woman's elbow and escorts them over the icy street.

They stand just outside the café and shake the snow from their shoulders. Damon pushes against the door and motions for the couple to step in before him. Up close, I see the resemblance, and my chest tightens. Oh, golly, I wish I'd had some warning. They weren't supposed to arrive for another week! I run a hand through my hair, which is an unkempt mess, no doubt, after such a busy day. My apron is stained and I'm wearing the oldest pair of boots I own, which squeak as I walk. The woman is draped in pearls, and the silver bobbed hair under her beret is immaculate. The man is ruggedly good-looking, like an older Damon, with the same kind eyes.

"Lil, Cee," Damon says, shivering from the short walk across the road. "This is my mother, Olivia, and my father, George."

I'm too stunned to speak, ruing the fact their first impression of me is the way I look right now. I'm not a fancy dresser, nor do I care about hair and make-up, but these people are *Guthries* and no matter how much I pretend I don't care, I do. The Guthrie family has enough money to buy out a small country, and I just wish the first time I met them I were wearing something other than my bright scarlet Christmas sweater that reads: *Jingle all the way!* Not to mention my candy-cane earrings that flash intermittently. They must think Damon's gone mad to marry a girl who is so utterly disheveled.

CeeCee shoots me a look that says pull it together. With a surreptitious nod in return, I smile brightly and walk towards them to give them a welcome hug. Olivia immediately puts out a hand to shake. Fumbling, and unsure, I drop my outstretched arms, and hope my faux pas isn't noticeable.

Though CeeCee hasn't missed a trick and barrels past me, screeching, "That ain't how we say hello 'round here. Come on and give us a great big cuddle!" She launch hugs Olivia and nearly knocks her off her knee-high boots. I hide a smile, thanking the Lord again for CeeCee's ability to break the ice. God, I love this woman.

Olivia teeters for a moment and then says, "Thank you, CeeCee." She regains her composure, and stands tall.

"Well, it's certainly nice to meet you, Lil. We've heard so much about you."

"You too, Olivia." I find my voice. "This is a wonderful surprise!"

Damon rubs his mother's shoulders. "Come on, Mother, let's sit down. We've got a lot of catching up to do." He pushes his parents softly in the back and motions to the sofas before taking my hand and kissing me softly on the cheek. He whispers, "They were so excited they couldn't wait another day. They cut their holiday short."

They'd been holidaying somewhere sunny, so I'm chuffed they cut it short—their son's wedding should take precedence in my book, and they obviously agree.

George and Olivia hover near the fire and CeeCee says, "Go on and sit down, you makin' the place look crowded," and laughs her southern haw. "I'll fix us some drinks, while y'all get to talkin'."

Buoyed by CeeCee's confidence, and Olivia's radiant smile, I sink into the sofa. I pat the cushion, and Damon sits next to me, leaning close enough I can smell his aftershave, sweet and spicy, making me woozy with thoughts of him.

CeeCee bustles around the kitchen, humming *Jingle Bells*. Damon shoots me a smile. "I'll give CeeCee a hand with the drinks." He jumps up, leaving a Damon-sized dent in the sofa, which I quickly roll into. George and Olivia gaze around the café, taking in the bookshelves by the fire, and the display fridge filled with chocolate truffles neatly ordered in rows.

"Beautiful place you have here, Lil," George says, his voice so similar to Damon's. "Damon told us how hard you've worked to build the café up over the last few years."

"Thanks, George. Though it's not just me. I've got CeeCee here—she's the one with all the grand plans."

I tuck a tendril of hair back, hoping I don't look as bedraggled as I feel.

He smiles. "I'm sure you've had a hand in it too."

I return his smile, and say, "I'm so glad to meet you both."

"Us too," Olivia says, pulling down her beret and sweeping her hair back into place from CeeCee's rambunctious hug. "We managed to swap a few things around, and get a flight. We were worried about being delayed by the weather flying in, so figured it was best to get here early."

George rests his head on the back of the sofa, and folds his hands. "Though all that travel has surely caught up with me…" He closes his eyes.

Olivia lets out a small laugh. "Traveling through so many time zones, our body clocks don't know where we are." She pats George's hand, and he mumbles incoherently.

I laugh. "Will he sleep?" I click my fingers. "Just like that." George's chest rises and falls slower as slumber overcomes him. Sitting so close to the fire after a long day in transit has obviously zapped George.

Olivia sighs. "He can sleep anywhere, that man, on a plane, on a train, but not today it seems. He was too keyed up about finally seeing Damon."

"How long are you planning to stay in Ashford?" I ask as Olivia gazes at her slumbering husband, watching his lips flutter with each deep exhalation.

Finally she turns back to me. "Not long. We'll leave the day after the wedding."

I frown. "Oh, you're not staying for Christmas Day?" I'd thought it was a given that they'd stay. Charlie will be here, and we'd planned a week off in honor of spending the time as a family, instead of taking a honeymoon. CeeCee drops something in the kitchen; the clattering makes George's eyelids flutter momentarily. "Sorry!" Damon hollers out.

"No, Ashford's not my kind of town, Lil." She lets out a hollow laugh. "That's why we moved from here as quickly as possible. Neither of us can work out why Damon felt the urge to move back. He was only a toddler when we left, so it's not like he would have remembered the place."

I try not to blanch at her statement. "Ashford's changed a lot since then. You might like it a little more now."

"It hasn't changed a bit. The main street is still the same, and even the people are the same. Nothing changes here. We've come early to make sure Damon is…happy."

Golly. I double blink. "Happy?"

She tilts her head to the side, and slaps on a smile. "His sudden departure from New Orleans worried us, and the few times we've seen him since haven't allayed those concerns."

My mind whirls. Damon didn't leave New Orleans suddenly; he left after a long drawn-out divorce with his first wife, Dianne. In fact, he stayed in New Orleans a lot longer for his daughter's sake. Leaving her there and only being able to see her on school holidays and the odd weekend has been tough on him, there's no question, which is why he spent so long making the decision to move.

I clear my throat, suddenly not sure I'm on an even keel with Olivia any more. "You'll see, then, how happy Damon is here. He loves this place."

"Does he?" She lifts a brow. "Wonderful."

I glance over my shoulder wondering what's taking CeeCee and Damon so long. CeeCee is busy showing Damon our profiterole towers, and miming how we flicked the toffee on them.

Olivia shifts back on her chair. "Between us, Lil, he's always despised small towns. He's a vibrant, social person, so it makes us wonder if he's made the right choice. He's missing so much being away from his family."

I nod dumbly, the wind knocked right out of me. Damon told me he moved here specifically because it was a small town and that was what he wanted. His parents had lived here eons ago, and it felt like a special place to him. When his daughter visits she can roam the meadows, safe in a small-town environment.

Outside the night has turned an inky black. Christmas lights from the shops across the road reflect back on the windows of the café, reds and greens melting together, casting a festive glow over the room.

Olivia leans forward. "I know you'll keep this to yourself, but George and I worry a lot about Damon. Missing out on all those milestones with Charlie. There's the school plays, and her swim meets…you know, he can never get that time back."

I crane my neck to see if Damon's within earshot but he's still busy chatting away to CeeCee, throwing his hands in the air, and acting out some story, his face lit up with laughter.

"No…" I manage. "I suppose he can't. But Charlie does seem well adjusted to life here."

She shrugs. "Listen, it doesn't matter anyway. Damon was going to return, until…" She bites her lip and stares directly at me.

Whoa, whoa, whoa. "He was going to move back to New Orleans?" My voice comes out almost like a whine. "When was that the plan? We've been together since he stepped into Ashford and he was adamant he was staying for good." Olivia's put me on the back foot and it's been all of five minutes.

Olivia raises her eyebrows. "Really, what's the point of him being here? His business makes next to no money, his daughter is elsewhere, the town isn't exactly thriving…"

I resist the urge to cup my head in my hands. "*I'm* here, Olivia. And I love him with all my heart."

"But so does his seven-year-old daughter. Anyway, food for thought," she says as if she hasn't just dropped a bombshell on me. "Now, tell me about your dress…"

I stare ahead, mute with shock. Why would Damon go to all the effort of setting up a shop, having it professionally decorated, if he weren't planning on staying? It doesn't make sense. And surely he would have told me? I wonder if it's just wishful thinking on Olivia's part. Charlie and Damon miss each other, but is he pining for New Orleans and his old life?

"Lookie here." CeeCee finally walks back with a tray of eggnog and hands everyone a glass. She puts George's on the round side table next to him. "This is my special recipe. I surely hope you ain't driving afterwards." She cackles high and loud. Damon sits beside me again, and I gladly roll back into his warmth, my stomach recoiling slightly at the conversation Olivia and I just had.

"Thanks, Cee." I take a sip and even with the frothiness of the milk the amount of alcohol CeeCee's added gives my system a jolt. She winks at me, and I smile weakly. Maybe she figured a slight inebriation might help when meeting the future in-laws.

Olivia crosses her ankles as if she's a product from a deportment school. "Lil was just about to tell me all about her dress."

"Well, she can't now." Damon grins at me, and it takes all my might to return a half-hearted smile.

"I'm sure Lil can tell me later. I did want to say one thing, while we're all together: we have a big family, especially on the outskirts of Ashford, since we were all from here originally—"

CeeCee pipes up, "Since before there was electricity, don't ya know." She jerks a thumb towards Damon. "He told us that, already." She giggles. "Remember that, last year, Lil?" I nod, and smile at the memory of Damon strutting into the café when we'd gone to war with each other trying to steal each other's customers. I'd said he had no chance, folks round here were loyal, and he was just a newcomer, until he'd thrown into the conversation that he was a Guthrie.

In their heyday, the Guthries owned a bunch of transport, and shipping business in Ashford and its outskirts. They still own lots of property around here but with their businesses sold they had money to burn, and still do, by the looks. I was sure that his family would bail him out if we went head to head, business to business, but instead we fell in love, and worked together, propping each other's shops up.

CeeCee waddles over to the coat rack, and wraps her scarf, and takes her handbag down. "On that note, I'm gonna leave you kids to it. Nice meeting you, Olivia. Give George my respects. Be seeing y'all." It's late and CeeCee must be bushed. I know I am. I stand to hug her, and must hold on a little tight. "Whoa, cherry blossom, you gonna strangle me."

I let out a nervous laugh. "See you, Cee." She searches my face; she knows me so well, and intuits there's something off kilter.

"I'll be here bright and early, sugar plum." We exchange a knowing glance—she'll be here before the sun rises behind grey skies to find out what's stolen the smile from my face.

"Night, Cee."

"Lovely to meet you, CeeCee. I can't wait to find out more about the matron of honor." Olivia flashes her a wide smile. It's so charming I crumple a little inside; her tone's markedly different with Cee than it was with me.

"You too, Olivia. Tell that sleepy husband o' yours I said bye, now." Cee ambles outside, the door blowing closed behind her.

With an internal sigh, I sit back down. Beside me, Damon's grinning as if he's just won the lottery, oblivious to my mood. He's tapping his feet, and laughing, jittery with happiness like some kind of jumping bean. He stands again, moves to his father and shakes his shoulder. "Dad, you're here to get to know Lil!" George starts, and opens his eyes.

Damon chuckles. "Come on, old man, let me show you Lil's window display. It's a work of art." *Don't leave me,* I silently scream, but watch dumbstruck as they put their coats on and head back outside to admire it from the street.

They walk out to the dark night before Olivia continues: "As I was saying, I'm sure you didn't mean to, but somehow you've neglected to invite some of the Guthrie family… I know you probably don't know us well enough, but it's a little rude to leave them out."

With a deep breath I counter, "Oh? We wanted a small, simple wedding. We've only invited close friends and family. Damon hasn't seen the extended family in years, even decades, despite them living around here—we figured it wouldn't be a problem."

Olivia frowns and shakes her head. "Exactly—we haven't seen some of them for a long time, so now's the perfect opportunity to right that. No matter how *simple* you intend it to be."

The Guthrie family tree is rich in history as well as funds. There are branches of Guthries on the outskirts of town but we rarely see them. Occasionally they'll attend CeeCee's church and she'll bring news back of more Guthrie babies being baptized; other than that, they don't drop into town.

I scratch the back of my neck, feeling lost and alone all at once; without being able to pinpoint why, I think Olivia is baiting me. "We've only got so much room and I'd rather, *we'd* rather," I correct, "it be more intimate with just close family and friends."

Olivia does a little chortle again, as if I'm a child to be placated. "Damon won't tell you this, Lily, because he knows you want a small wedding, but he would prefer his family there. *All* of them. I do hope it won't be a problem... I can always help. It's late notice but I'm sure we can find a bigger venue, even a better chef, for that matter."

My breath catches. Would Damon seriously not have mentioned he wants the entire Guthrie clan at our wedding? And what's the talk about a better venue? Another chef? Glancing over to the window, I watch him talk with his dad. He's so animated, his face lit up with joy. They stand under the awning; Damon laughs, and his father pats him on the back. I can't hear what they're saying but happiness radiates from them both.

I mentally shake myself. I'm not going to sit here like a bamboozled fool. "Damon's been involved every step of the way with the wedding planning, and he's never once mentioned that he wanted to invite more people. And to be honest, Olivia, the venue is perfect and we're very lucky to have the chef we do. He doesn't usually cater weddings."

Olivia gathers her coat tighter. "Perhaps Damon doesn't know how to tell you. But I'm his mother and I know my son. Known him his whole life, in fact." Again she gives me that huge smile as if it'll take the sting out of her words.

An awkward silence hangs between us and I figure I'm going to have to try and compromise so we don't so much as get off on the wrong foot, as outright stagger. "Of course, Olivia, if it's important to you, and to Damon, we can try to accommodate more people."

Guillaume will throw a fit, but somehow we'll have to make it work. I'll get CeeCee to ask him. Damon must be catching his death outside, and for once I wish the display window wasn't such a talking point.

Perhaps Olivia just needs to be included more; then she'll see for herself how happy Damon is here and that our wedding, though simple, is going to be lovely. "Olivia, I'd love some help in choosing the centerpieces. I wanted poinsettias, maybe in rectangle planters, sort of Christmassy, and in keeping with the color theme. We've been so busy in the café the last few days the wedding preparations have kind of been pushed to the side."

"Your wedding has been pushed to the side? *Your wedding?*" she says, not managing to hide the incredulous edge to her voice.

"Not *my* wedding, *our* wedding. This is the busiest time of year for us—for all of us." I indicate to Damon outside too. "And there's no question work comes first, hence the need for a simple wedding."

The Christmas carols playing overhead finish, and we're suddenly sitting in silence.

Olivia says with a pained expression, "I don't mean to sound rude, but why on earth would you have a wedding at this time of year if you don't have time to plan it?"

Holding in an exasperated sigh, I say, "We decided to get married one year to the day we started out as a couple. And because it's when all of my family would be home, and when Charlie would be holidaying here." I'm sure she knows all of this. I've heard Damon on the phone to her a number of times, discussing the wedding, and the choices he's made.

"I do wonder if you've thought this through. While a snowy wedding is a lovely thought, you're taking people away from their warm homes at Christmas."

I'm on the back foot every single time Olivia opens her mouth. If it were anyone else I would have told them straight up that they were pushing my buttons. But out of respect, I bite back on any remarks that aren't friendly. I try once more to reassure her. "It's Christmas *Eve*, not Christmas Day, and we've only invited those we'd normally spend time with over Christmas anyway. They'd be happy if our wedding was in the middle of a field with a lame horse for a witness because they care about *us*. There's not much more to say about it. I'd love you to be involved in any planning that's left, but if not that's fine too."

The doorbell jingles as Damon and his dad walk inside. "Mighty fine window you've got there," George says.

"Thank you," is all I manage.

George rubs his gloved hands together and says, "If you ladies are finished discussing the upcoming nuptials, we might call it a night. It's been a long day of travel for us."

Damon stands and says, "Dad's right, you must be tired, Mother. How about I take you to our house and Lil can finish up here and meet us later?"

They're staying at our house? It'll be a squeeze when Charlie arrives. It's only a small cottage up the road from the Gingerbread Café.

"Damon," Olivia says, her voice saccharine, "we wouldn't like to impose. We'd planned on staying with Abe Guthrie—he's not too far from Ashford. We have *decades* of catching up to do." She glances squarely at me and I manage to ignore the jibe.

"Right, Mother." He grins. "How about I drive you there now, and we can meet for dinner tomorrow night?"

George pipes up, "We're busy tomorrow night. We went ahead and promised Abe that we'd spend the night with his family, but how about the following evening?"

Olivia nods. "I don't suppose there are any restaurants here yet?" She does a half-gasp, and laughs, as if she can't believe she said that out loud.

George and Damon join in the laughter. I don't see the funny side, but maybe that's because it sounded like an affront to Ashford. Damon's more relaxed and carefree than I've ever seen him, so I press on, hoping I've imagined this strange undercurrent from Olivia. "Why don't we have dinner here at the café? I'll knock something up." It's easier to cook at the café, and bigger than the kitchen at home.

"Perfect," Damon says. "I'll prepare the food, Lil. I'm doing a cooking demonstration so I'll make extra."

Olivia rubs Damon's back as moms do. "Lovely, darling. We've certainly missed your cooking. Haven't we, George?"

"That we have." George steps forward and shakes my hand. "We'd love to meet your parents, Lil. Maybe you could extend them an invitation too?"

"Of course," I say. "Looking forward to it." Mamma and Dad have been itching to meet Damon's parents. Mamma never stops with the queries about what Olivia's like, and if George really collects vintage cars. Things I have no clue about. Mamma visits Damon's shop regularly to sit at the coffee bar, and chat with him and her friends, so it feels almost as if she knows more about Olivia and George than I do. She's probably grilled poor Damon daily for information. Small-town folk, we're kind of nosey like that.

George says, "Maybe you should invite CeeCee too, Lil? From what we hear she's part of the family."

His sentiment stuns me for a moment. While Olivia is formal, George is relaxed and warm, so much like Damon.

"She is. She's like a mother and best friend all rolled into one. I'll ask her along."

Olivia fusses with her hair again. "It was lovely to meet you, Lil. We're blessed to have you in our family. You just let me know what else I can do to help." She beams at me before hugging me tight. In front of Damon she's all sweetness and light. Maybe I'm wrong, maybe she is just worried about Damon, and getting to know me will allay some of her concerns.

I pull at the bottom of my sweater. "It was great to meet you. At dinner perhaps we can go over some of the wedding preparations."

George yawns, and makes a show of stretching. His face is haggard from lack of sleep.

"I better get the old man home." Damon indicates to George. "You'll be OK?"

"I have the truck out back. I'll be fine." The thought of going home makes me smile in spite of it all. A steaming-hot bath always makes everything better.

Damon gives my jean-clad rear a cheeky tap before lacing his arm through Olivia's.

George says, "See you the day after tomorrow, Lil. Damon's given me a talking-to about falling asleep, my apologies." He nods goodbye.

Once the door blows shut, I blow out a breath.

Finding the cordless phone, I punch in CeeCee's number and fill her in to see what she makes of it. Once I get the whole sorry story out, I say, "So what do you think? Am I overreacting? She was sweet as cherry pie while dropping little bombs on me. Am I reading it wrong?"

"I sure as shootin' don't know, Lil. Maybe she's just thinking of her grandbaby, and it's only natural that she'd want her son closer to his daughter, but that ain't your fault, Lil. Damon's the one who made that choice when he moved here. And he ain't a fool—he planned a life here when he opened up that shop o' his."

I stand closer to the fire, which has burnt down; the glowing orange embers still warm the backs of my legs. "Yeah, I know. But she made it seem like he was running away from something, and that he'd move back to New Orleans once the dust had settled. I felt...like some kind of country hick rebound or something."

"That man loves you, Lil. Loves you something silly. I don't want to hear you talkin' that way, 'cause it ain't the truth." She clucks her tongue. "You gonna need to tell Damon what she said."

I grimace at the thought. "But, Cee, he was so happy to see them, so excited, like a kid or something. I don't want to ruin that high. Maybe I'll just wait and see what the next visit brings."

She sighs dramatically down the line. "I don't think keeping this to yourself is a good idea, Lil. But see what happens at dinner. Maybe she was out of sorts after a long-haul flight, who knows?"

"Yep, maybe that's it."

"You ain't a pushover, so stand your ground, an' be firm. Don't let her tell you how Damon feels. He ain't the type of man who bottles things up."

I pinch the bridge of my nose as a headache looms. "I guess."

"Don't worry that pretty head o' yours. I'll be here for you, Lil. Maybe she was expecting some kind of huge fancy everythin' wedding...She just needs to get to know you better."

Even though our wedding is deemed simple, it doesn't mean it's not going to be pretty. CeeCee and I have spent an age poring over websites for ideas. We've found bride and groom knife and fork sets that say: *Mr. and Mrs.* And the cutest recipe for gingerbread wedding favors decorated like a bride and groom. Small touches that have special meaning.

"Do you think Damon really does want to invite all those other family members?" He's often talked about cousins, and uncles who live not too far from Ashford, but he's never made any attempt to visit them, or even call them on the telephone as far as I know. I can't see him suddenly wanting them at the wedding. Or have I unintentionally pushed him into agreeing to keep the guest list small? As Olivia said, she's known Damon his whole life and I've only known him a year. Already tonight I've seen a different Damon, one who seems more energetic and animated, quick to laugh, and more...himself.

CeeCee says, "I don't rightly know, Lil. What I think is it's late, you've had a long day, and all this worry ain't gonna change a thing. Sleep on it, OK?"

The night has gone eerily quiet, with only the small crackle of the dying fire to keep me company. My earlier pre-wedding flush has faded away, replaced by a nervousness I can't quite shake. "You're right, CeeCee. A good night's sleep will help."

"Go home. Don't give it another thought."

"OK."

"Night, sugar plum."

"Night." I hang up, feeling slightly mollified. CeeCee's got a way of putting things in perspective, and I think maybe I've read it all wrong. I gather up the mop that leans against the table and swish it in the sudsy water, before finishing off the floors.

After I've packed the cleaning equipment away, I head on out back to my office. I open the drawer and pull out a jewelry box. Inside are wedding gifts I had made especially for our moms and my bridal party. Olivia's gift sits on top, a silver locket inscribed, *'Thank you for raising my Mr. Right.'* With a sigh, I wonder if it's something she'll like. Somehow after seeing the way she dresses, I can't imagine her wearing a silver locket, with a gushy sentimental inscription. Instead, I look for Charlie's gift, a necklace with a pearl pendant, and a card that reads: *Charlie, you may know the old saying a bride needs something old, something new, something borrowed, something blue, for good luck on her wedding day. But all I need is you. Will you be my flower girl?*

I smile, thinking of Charlie's radiant face, and how excited she'll be to find out she's part of the wedding. It was Damon's idea to surprise her. When she arrives, the day before the wedding, she'll walk into her bedroom to find a mink-colored gown hanging in her closet, with a faux-fur stole to match. Elegant little golden slippers sit at the foot of her bed, and a diamanté-encrusted clutch that glitters in the dim light. I want Charlie to feel special, and loved, not only included in our big day, but a huge part of it.

Am I the reason Damon lives so far away from his daughter? My heart hurts just thinking of it. I pack the box away. Would Damon keep his feelings secret? And if so, why?

After locking up the café, I jog to my beat-up truck out back. The icy wind takes my breath away, and I shiver, despite wearing a thick waterproof parka, and knitted scarf. The door of the truck creaks as I pull it open and jump up. Soon, I promise myself, I'll buy a new truck. It whines as I reverse, but I thank my lucky stars it even started. I only live up the street a way, but with all our late nights, and early mornings, there's no way I'm walking in a blizzard. Usually I have Damon for company on the sixty-second journey home, but he must have jogged home and picked up his car to ferry his parents around. As I wait for the truck to warm up, I idly wonder if he's back from dropping them off yet.

Finally the old truck sputters to life, so I loop to the main street. The town is deserted with only the Christmas lights to keep me company. Pushing my foot on the brake, I stare into Walt's furniture shop, which is directly across the road from the Gingerbread Café. It's the only window bare of flashing lights and shiny tinsel, when it's usually the opposite: the most decorated shop in town, with a life-size Santa inside, sitting on one of Walt's handmade chairs.

But now, it looks bereft, no decorations, and empty of Walt's one-of-a-kind furniture, and empty of the cheerful man and wife who'd usually be dashing around town at this time of year organizing the town's celebrations. CeeCee goes regularly to visit them in Springfield, and always comes back a smaller version of herself, as if her sadness is somehow shrinking her.

Tearful, I push the accelerator down, and head slowly home along the slick wet street.

As I pull into my driveway the porch light bathes the house in a cheery glow. Damon must be back. Fairy lights shine through the lace curtains, flashing green and red like little pulses.

I don't bother locking the truck, and head inside. Heat from the fire hits me as soon as I cross the threshold, and I race to stand in front of it, dropping my parka on a footstool, and unwinding my scarf as I go. In the corner of our small lounge sits a naked Christmas tree. The smell of the pine needles permeates the small room, and I gaze at it, picturing how it'll look dressed in decorations.

Being a festive-season fanatic, I'd normally have hung the ornaments a month ago in my excitement, but this year I want to wait for Charlie to do it. Her little cherub face will light up once she sees the gingerbread snowmen with bright silver button eyes and half-moon smiles that I baked and strung together to make a garland.

"Damon?"

"Glass of wine?" His voice carries out from the kitchen.

Carrying two glasses of red wine, he turns into the small room, and my breath hitches. I don't think I'll ever tire of gawking at him. Somehow the man is always tanned no matter what the season, blessed with the kind of olive skin I'd have to bake myself to achieve. But it's every little nuance of him, the way he walks, the sound of his voice, right down to the little muscle that runs up his forearm.

He smiles his big old warm smile that makes me melt like marshmallow in a fire.

"Red wine, OK?" I nod and take the proffered glass. I take a huge swig before catching myself. Delicacy isn't my thing.

He embraces me, and nuzzles into my neck. The heat from the fire and his breath on my skin is almost enough to make me swoon. "You taste like icing sugar," he says.

"I try my best."

"So," he says, "aren't they great?" Before I can respond he continues speaking in a rush. "Dad loved your window display, and Cee's eggnog. He's looking forward to meeting your parents, and having dinner. And Mother said she's all set to help out with the smaller details of the wedding, which will free you up for the café."

"I'm not so—"

"She sang your praises the whole drive out to Abe's place. And don't worry, I'll do dinner the day after tomorrow. I know you've got a few orders due. It'll be nice to cook for my parents. You forget how much they mean to you sometimes. Seeing them again has made me realize how important family is. And it'll be great for Charlie to spend some time with them too, when she gets here."

"Y-yes, it'll be great for Charlie…" I manage to stammer, my heart sinking while Damon looks as bright as I've ever seen him.

CHAPTER THREE

Eight days

When I wake this next morning, I'm alone. I touch Damon's half of the bed; the sheets are cold. Rolling out of bed, I find my robe and wrap it around me. The house is warm; he's stoked up the fire before he left.

Walking through the small hallway to the kitchen the air is rich with the scent of roasted coffee beans. I must have slept through his fancy coffee machine as it gargled its way into life this morning. It usually vibrates, and churns so forcefully, it's almost as if the ground is shifting.

There's a note by the kettle, where Damon knows I go each morning to make my much easier instant coffee.

Lil,

I left to have breakfast with my parents, I didn't want to wake you, you were completely zonked.

Damon. xxx

I laugh in spite of myself. Zonked is a nice way of saying my mouth was probably hanging open, my hair a tangled mess. But I wonder why he didn't wake me regardless. Maybe he wanted time alone with his parents? Half relieved, I dress quickly and head out front.

The truck takes for ever to start. I sit there with my breath fogging up the windscreen; eventually it sputters to life, and I reverse slowly on the icy driveway.

The main street is dark as I chug along, and head around the back of the café to park. A strip of light peeps out under the back door of the café. CeeCee. I hurry inside.

"There you are, sugar plum." She pours a cup of thick golden syrup into a bowl, and mixes it through the other ingredients.

"Gingerbread?" I ask.

"Gingerbread *cakes*," she replies. "With lemon sugar icing, and candied fruit."

"Let me help." I wash my hands and don my apron. CeeCee's laid the bench with the ingredients to make candied fruit, so I begin by chopping cherries in half and taking the pit out.

"I take it you didn't sleep on it like I told you?" She sizes me up over the rim of her glasses.

I continue with the cherries, trying to be delicate so I don't squash their flesh. "I slept fine."

She harrumphs. "Glory be, those bags under your eyes are so big I could carry my shopping home in 'em!"

I give her a rueful smile. "That so? I guess Olivia gave me a lot to think about, that's all."

She clucks her tongue. "Like what?"

"Like what if Damon's only staying here because of me?"

"Child! O' course he is! That man loves you! But he was set on staying here from the moment he opened that shop door. Don't you go obsessing over every little thing 'cause you getting the fever…" She purses her lips.

"What fever?"

"Mmm hmm, you getting the wedding fever. Don't think I don't know!" She waggles her finger at me.

Taking a pot from the hook above the stove, I mix sugar, honey and water and bring it to the boil. "What the heck is wedding fever supposed to mean?"

"You getting the jitters." She puts her big brown palm up. "Don't you start backchatting me neither. I know what you gonna say, so don't. You need to take some deep breaths and trust in the love you have for each other. Weddings…they send everyone a little cuckoo."

I laugh, picturing myself mopping my brow struck by some so-called wedding fever. "You're right, Cee. It's just…she made these off-the-cuff comments like Damon hates small towns, and stuff that's the complete opposite to what he said to me, you know, so one of us is wrong about Damon…"

"Who's been with Damon almost every day for the last year?"

"Me."

"Then you ain't the one who's wrong."

I shrug. "Maybe." I take an orange from the bowl, and peel it; the citrus scent is almost like a tincture.

"Hurry along with that fruit now. I'm going to bake these gingerbread cakes, and you still need to boil that batch in sugar syrup before we can dry it out in the oven."

I cut the orange peel into small slivers, and add it to the pot, along with some lemon rind, and some pineapple skin. Once the batch is boiled, absorbing the sweetness of the sugar syrup, we'll dry the slivers in the oven. Then we'll dust them with sugar crystals to sit atop the gingerbread cakes, a little shimmery goodness that'll make them sparkle under the fridge lights.

The gingerbread cakes cool on the bench; the scent of spicy ginger makes my mouth water. We've moved on to making cake pops. They've proved to be popular among the locals, adults and children alike. CeeCee's all set on decorating the chocolate pops with red sanding sugar and tiny snowflakes she's made from white chocolate. There's nothing sweeter than spending an age trying to get the cake pops to look uniform, and then customers pop the dainty mouthful in and, just like that, they're gone. The perfect bite-sized treat.

"So have you got your Christmas shopping sorted, Lil?"

I pour batter into the cake-pop molds, slowly so it doesn't spill over. "I have. I just need to find Charlie a few more things for her stocking, and that's about it."

"Ho, ho, ho," says a velvety voice behind me.

"I didn't hear you!" I say, turning, smack bang into Damon.

"I stopped the jingle from jangling, so I could surprise you." He kisses the tip of my nose, and then dips a finger into the batter. "Hazelnut?"

I nod. "And orange liquor. Strictly for the adults." Surveying him, I see he's all loose limbed again, unable to stand still. Maybe *he's* got the wedding fever.

"You're looking like the cat who got the cream," CeeCee says to Damon.

"Well, I surely did, didn't I?" He loops his arms around my waist, and smiles. "I'm sorry I didn't wake you this morning…figured it was too cold to be anywhere but in bed."

As I gaze into his bright eyes all the niggly worry I have evaporates. "You're as excitable as a puppy."

"That's because there's only eight more days until you become my wife! And…I wanted to know if I could sneak you out of the café early tonight?"

I raise an eyebrow. "Oh, yeah?"

"Yeah." He lowers his voice to a whisper. "Just you and me and a blazing fire."

Before I can say boo CeeCee says, "O' course you can! We got an early start this morning anyways…Lil can shoot through, and I'll close up."

"But, Cee…"

"No buts, you lovebirds need some time alone together."

I smile, grateful. In the last few weeks we haven't had time for much other than working. Often going home and falling into bed with a quick hug. "It's a date, Mr. Guthrie."

"That it is, Miss Lily."

"Go on and shoo, then," CeeCee says to Damon, who grins like a lovesick teenager. "She's got some work to do before then."

"OK, OK. Bye, ladies." He jogs out and across the road, waving to people as he goes; as usual all we see is the way the denim of his jeans hugs his butt. Golly, I could stare at him crossing the road all day.

CeeCee raises her eyebrows so high she almost falls over backwards. "And you think he ain't crazy in love with you? You ain't got the good sense God gave a goose if that's what you think!"

I giggle. She's right. He's as happy as ever, and it's because we're getting married. All doubt gets cast aside, and I keep on with my cake pops.

"Close your eyes." Damon holds my upper arms as he leads me inside our cottage. "Keep going, I've got you."

"What is it?" I listen out for any sounds that might clue me in on what his surprise is but all I hear is the crackle of the fire.

"You're going to have to wait and see."

I take small steps, suddenly unable to remember where our furniture is placed now that my eyes are squeezed shut. He pushes me forward; he's so close his breath tickles my neck. The scent of roses hits me as I head closer to the sound of running water.

"Nearly there…and stop." He pushes a door open, and by the squeak it makes I know it's the bathroom. "Open your eyes."

I blink a few times as my eyes adjust to the light. "You ran me a bath? That's the big surprise?" I can't keep the laughter from my voice. Damon had been back over to the café to pick me up, and was gushing about all the things he was going to surprise me with.

He rolls his eyes. "If you'd care to look a bit closer you'll see it."

I scan the bathroom. My green terrycloth robe isn't on the hook—instead there are two new bathrobes hanging up. Flummoxed why he'd buy bathrobes, I say sweetly, "Thank you! I've always wanted a new robe! How did you know?"

With a chuckle he says, "Lil, you're the worst liar!" He pulls one of the robes down and hands it to me. On the right lapel in shiny gold embroidery it says, *'Mrs. Guthrie'*. "Oh! That's so sweet! And what about yours?" I take his down; sure enough *'Mr. Guthrie'*.

"I figured you spend half your life soaking in the tub… this way you won't forget me."

"I could never forget you." I lean in for a kiss.

"There's a bunch of bubble bath, and stuff there from Mary-Rose's shop. I thought you could relax, while I make us a fancy dinner…and then you'll get your other surprise."

"Another one?"

He grins wickedly. "This one is more for both of us."

I make a show of wiggling my eyebrows. "Can we skip dinner?"

"This is why I love you..."

I pull my boots off, and take down my jeans. "There's room for two, you know?"

His eyes are trained on my shirt as I unbutton it from the top down.

"Let me help you with that." He rips my shirt open, and we laugh as buttons scatter to the floor. "This is why I bought the dressing gowns..."

CHAPTER FOUR

Seven days

The next day I'm up early. Tiptoeing to the bathroom, I wash up, and rummage through the bag of make-up samples Missy gave me. Tossing aside the scarlet reds, and eye-popping oranges, I finally settle on a pink lipstick. It's still two shades brighter than what I'd pick, but I guess that's Missy's way of compromising. I apply foundation, which instantly makes my skin prickle. I figure the damage is done so lash on the mascara hoping I don't look like a clown. With two swipes my lipstick is on.

Sighing at my pink-lipped reflection, I amble to my wardrobe, careful not to wake Damon. Jeans, jeans, jeans, baggy tees, sweats. Golly, I had no idea my collection was so limited. The joys of being able to hide under an apron most days has had a severe effect on my apparel.

Nothing I have is even *remotely* stylish. I don't let this stop me from pulling out the bulk of my clothes in the hope I'll find some forgotten twin set or a fancy woolen wrap dress. I know things will be hectic at the café and I won't have time to come home and get changed before dinner with the soon-to-be in-laws tonight. As I step over the pile of clothes I've dropped to the floor it dawns on me how stupid I'm being. The way I dress probably won't make an iota of difference to Olivia. And why the hell do I care anyway?

With a grin, I pull out my favorite Christmas sweater, a Kermit-green knit that announces: *This girl believes in Santa!* With the token chubby Father Christmas embroidered to the fabric. So I won't win any prizes for my fashion sense, but if you can't wear an ugly Christmas sweater and not smile, then there's something wrong. I pull on my jeans, and head to the dresser to pick out a set of Christmas earrings.

The kitschiest, brightest outfit I own will do just fine today. Plus, it cheers up our customers, and I have a few local children that stop by daily and have a giggle over what I'm wearing. We make them welcome, and sit them near the fire with some Santa coloring-in pictures and a cup of warm cocoa.

The phone shrills from the depths of the lounge. I race out to find it, wondering who'd call so early. Damon still sleeps in the bed, his soft snores following me out of the room.

"Hello?" I answer.

"Child, what's with all the secrets? Just because I've been away does not mean you have a right to keep me out of the loop!"

And here we go. "Mamma, what're you talking about? We only just went through the wedding stuff a few days ago!"

She huffs. "And you neglected to mention Damon's folks are in town! You know your daddy and I need to meet them…"

Oh, golly. "Geez, Mamma, they arrived late the other night. It was news to me too. How on earth did you find out already?"

"None of your beeswax."

"So it was Rosaleen, I take it?" You have to give it to her: Rosaleen would make a fine detective.

Mamma sighs all dramatically down the line. "And so what if it was? At least *someone's* telling me what I need to know!"

"I'm probably the best one to ask, though, Mamma. *Not* Rosaleen."

"Lil, are you getting jittery? Is that what this is?"

Mamma's the second person to suggest I'm a bundle of nerves. I take a deep breath and silently count to ten. What is it about weddings that send everyone a little mad? "I'm not jittery, Mamma. I'm just busy. So how about you and Dad come and meet the Guthries at the café for supper?"

I picture my mother at the other end of the phone. Her dark blond hair falling in soft short curls around her face. She'll be wearing the usual sweat suits and sneakers, as though she can achieve so much more if she dresses as if she's going to the gym. She's been power-walking over to my house every few days, with her pencil behind her ear, ready to take notes for the wedding. Even a blizzard won't stop her from marching here. She's the softest person around though, truly wears her heart on her sleeve.

A tut drags me back to the phone. "You're expecting me to have supper with the Guthries…" she pauses "…and you tell me this now?"

It seems we all feel a mite uncomfortable around the distinguished Guthrie family. "Yeah, Mamma, why? You've got plenty of time between now and then."

Another drawn-out Mamma sigh wangles its way down the line. "Fine. But I do have quite a big wedding list to conquer, you know."

"Like what?"

She pauses, which I know means trouble.

"Out with it! What?"

"Now, honey…"

I groan. "Don't you honey me…what are you up to?"

"Don't think I can't tell by your tone that you're not open to this."

"This sounds ominous…"

"Just hear me out. Your cousin Jeremiah—"

"No!"

"That's not hearing me out!"

"Mamma, he is not coming to the wedding. Absolutely not!"

I can almost hear her mind tick while she thinks of a response that will convince me. My older cousin, Jeremiah, got himself so intoxicated before my first wedding that when I walked down the aisle he hummed the theme song for *Jaws* at the top of his voice. It didn't end there. I wanted to strangle his scrawny neck before the night was out.

"He's changed…he's more…together now." She uses a beseeching tone that she knows will guilt me into agreeing. "And, Lord, think of your Aunt May. She's been through the wringer with poor Jeremiah. It would be uncharitable not to invite them."

"Mamma, are you serious? How do we know he's not going to act the same?"

"Lil, please."

I think back to the one-man wedding wrecker. Jeremiah groped my bridesmaids, interrupted the speeches, knocked the two-tier wedding cake to the floor—not before splattering the groomsmen who sat next to it. His grand finale, though, was the worst. He lit up a bunch of fireworks he'd stolen from God knows where, which unfortunately went off before he had time to get away, resulting in his tight black curls setting alight. He looked like Lucifer himself.

"He's sorry. He wants you to know that. You know his hair grew back grey—surely he's paid enough!"

I'm truly bamboozled. Shaking my head at my mother's attempts to cajole me, I glance outside, to see snow falling heavily. Another cold and wintry day, the kind that favors snuggling in front of a fire with a hot cup of cocoa.

"Mamma. I just want it to be perfect. If he's there I'm going to worry about what he'll be up to…"

She exhales a huge breath. "Honey, weddings and funerals are family time. Let's just be grateful it's a wedding and not the alternative."

I shake my head at my mamma's reasoning. There's no way she's going to give in, I just know it. The guest list is swelling at the seams, and thinking practically we really can only fit a certain number at Guillaume's. But how can I say yes to Olivia, and not to Mamma?

"Lil, I admit his behavior could have been better—"

"Better!"

"Hear me out, Lil. But that was a long time ago…we're all different than we were back then. You'd be the first to say everyone deserves a second chance."

She's done it—her much-practiced mother guilt. "Fine, Mamma, but if he does one crazy thing, *just one*, you have to make him leave."

"Deal."

I sigh.

"And also, Jeremiah *is-bringing-his-family*." She scrambles the words so fast it takes me a moment to decode them.

"What? No! What family?"

"He's seeing a lovely lady with six kids…"

"Mamma!"

"OK, OK, I'll tell them to get a sitter. Now I'll see you tonight at the café. I don't know how I'm meant to get everything done in time. There are the ribbons for the chairs I need to pick up, they'll need ironing—"

"What ribbons? For which chairs?" Exasperation edges into my voice.

"For the reception—Guillaume said it was OK. Though I did have to say it was Cee's idea... Anyway, never you mind, Lil. I know you're busy at the café. I'm fine-tuning, that's all."

"OK..." I say warily.

"You've gone and thrown a spanner in the works by telling me about supper so late..." Her voice trails off as she says almost to herself, "I'll have to leave the wishing well until tomorrow..."

I don't bother asking what the bejesus a wishing well is for. I know she's worrying about the Guthries and what they'll make of her and Daddy so I say softly, "OK, Mamma, and they're just people like any other, so don't go feeling you have to act differently."

"I know that, sheesh, Lily-Ella. See you soon." And with that she hangs up the phone, no doubt about to burst into the bedroom and galvanize my slumbering father. I smile, suddenly feeling all warm and fuzzy that my parents are finally home. Like everything with my mamma, she'd planned a cruise, and a world trip to follow, with military precision. Just under a year they'd traveled the globe, and at one point I thought they may never return. I've always been close to my parents and I missed them more than I cared to mention when they were away.

Ambling back to the bedroom, I peek past the door and see Damon slowly rousing. "Hey, pretty lady," he says, and pats the bed next to him. Butterflies swarm in my belly. I don't know how a man can wake up and look so downright sexy. His wavy hair is mussed from sleep, he has pillow crinkles on one cheek, and somehow it all adds up to an invitation back to bed. Not that we had a whole lot of *sleep*...

Without a second thought, I pull back the covers and hug the warmth of his body. He weaves a hand behind me, and pulls me close. "We'll be late," I say.

He shrugs. "It'll be worth it."

I laugh, my mind focused on the man in front of me. "It sure will."

When I arrive at the Gingerbread Café CeeCee's standing behind the silver prep bench rolling out pastry as if her life depends on it. She's muttering to herself and shaking her head.

"Talking to your invisible friends again?" I joke as I unwind my woolen scarf, a favorite of mine that CeeCee knitted for me years ago. I hang my parka on the coat rack, and stand with my back to the fire, jiggling my legs when the heat sears.

"You've gone and caught me having an argument with this here pastry. I was a million miles away on account of it not complying with me." Dusting her hands on her apron, she walks to me and pecks me on the cheek. "You look…" Her lip wobbles, and she turns away. Next second she's slapping her knees and doubles over laughing.

I survey my outfit. I'm sure she's seen me wear this a million times over. "You got a problem with the fat man all of a sudden?" I point to the chubby Santa on my sweater.

She manages to stand upright and slowly turns to me. "Lil," she sputters, "you killin' me!"

Baffled, I look down at my outfit again thinking I've got my jeans inside out, or back to front.

"For someone who doesn't wear make-up you surely got it spread across your face real good!"

Shoot! I rush to the mirror in the office and check my reflection. Oh, God! It looks as if someone scribbled all over my face with lipstick. *This* is why I don't wear gloop. I scramble to find something to wash my face with, eventually unearthing a container of wet-wipes from the dusty recesses of the desk drawer. I swipe at the residue of make-up, including the black smears of mascara that are everywhere *except* my eyelashes, and curse myself for languishing in bed with Damon. We'd canoodled for a lot longer than we should have, knowing we were already late. There hadn't been time for coffee, or even our usual curbside goodbyes.

As I return to CeeCee she's still hawing and slapping the silver bench when laughter gets the better of her. "I don't want to *know* how that happened…"

I purse my lips, and try to think of a plausible excuse. "Well, you see…"

"Don't even try, Lil. I bet if I walked over to that *fine-looking* thing across the road his face would be covered in make-up too."

My eyes widen and after a high-pitched squeal I dash out of the café, my feet slipping on the icy pavement; I run on the spot, trying not to fall. Eventually, I catch myself, and walk a little more sedately over the road. Damon's standing in front of the coffee machine that's the size of a small car, discussing the merits of braising lamb shanks as opposed to baking them with a group of elderly women. They're not paying any attention to what he's saying; instead they're whispering behind their hands. Scrunching my eyes to a sliver, in case it helps minimize the damage, I look at Damon and see the reason for their distraction. The so-named Pink Passion lipstick is spread across Damon's face. He looks like one of those bobble-head clowns that you drop balls down the mouth of at an amusement park.

"Damon," I say urgently.

"Hey, Lil! This here's my fiancée, from the Gingerbread Café."

The ladies give me a knowing look. I wave limply and tug on Damon's arm. "I need a quick word."

Damon throws the ladies an apologetic glance, and leans down to whisper, "I'm in the middle of a cooking demonstration here."

"I'll be quick."

He wriggles his arm free. "Lil, can't it wait?"

"You have lipstick all over your face!" I yell a little too loudly. Everyone in the shop stops and turns to stare at Damon. "Sorry!" I say as I watch a blush creep up his cheeks, which, I must say, matches quite nicely with the Pink Passion.

"Would you excuse me, please, ladies?" he says to the women, who are outright tittering at his expense. "It seems I've...er..." He throws me a desperate glance.

"We er...had cupcakes for breakfast!" I holler. "With pink icing! Lots of pink icing!"

Damon breaks into a wide grin, and pulls me to him. "You, my lady, are going to ruin my reputation."

"That's my plan," I whisper back.

He kisses the top of my head, and I wave to the women before making my way back to the shop.

Shivering from the cold, I dash back inside the café, and stand by the fire.

"So, pumpkin, you had pressin' business over the road, I see?" CeeCee looks down her nose at me and continues to roll pastry dough.

Before I can respond the doorbell jingles and in walk Missy from The Sassy Salon and Sarah from The Bookshop on the Corner.

Missy click-clacks her way to me in her high-heeled boots, her big pregnant belly swathed in a bold zebra-print form-fitting coat. "We thought you must have been robbed or something!" Missy screeches. "What on earth were you running over the road like that for?"

Sarah, who's dressed in a more sedate grey pantsuit and black coat, gives CeeCee a hug and walks quickly to join us by the fire. "Lil, oh, my God, I snorted coffee up my nose when I saw you ice-skating your way over there. I called Missy straight away and told her to stick her head out the door and take a look at you!"

Missy smacks her hands together and laughs. "Your impression of running man rooted to the spot was darn right labor-inducing!"

It's my turn to blush. "Well...you see, we ate cupcakes..."

CeeCee trundles over with a tray of gingerbread coffees. "Oh, don't you listen to those lies she about to sprout!" she says knowingly.

Missy guffaws and eases herself on the sofa, a hand on her back, and one on her belly.

Sarah's eyes light up. "Do tell..."

I laugh, and know there's no way I can get away from spilling the beans. Sure as shooting it's going to end up on CeeCee's Spacebook. "Darn it, no one can keep any secrets in this town!" Everyone finds a spot to sit, and my heart lifts at us girls having some time together. Usually we gather at some point each day to shoot the breeze but of late, with all of us busier, we haven't had as much time. "Did you say labor-inducing?" I frown over at Missy.

"Not really," she says, "though my old bladder isn't what it used to be. It should be illegal to make a pregnant woman laugh like that, Lil." She takes a sip of her decaf coffee.

We giggle at Missy's joke. They're the type of girls that make your cheeks ache from smiling, and your belly hurt from laughter.

CeeCee closes her eyes and runs a hand over Missy's bulging belly. "Won't be long now, Missy."

Missy turns to CeeCee, her eyes wide. "I'm not ready!" she blurts out, high-pitched as though she thinks CeeCee means she's going into labor right now.

"He ain't ready right now, either. I seen it." CeeCee points to the spot between her eyebrows. We all tease CeeCee about her second sight but she's been scarily accurate in the past so a kind of silence descends as we think of Missy finally having the baby she's dreamed about her entire adult life. She's worried about being an older mom at forty-five, but none of us think that matters a damn. Forty-five seems as good an age as any to have a baby.

Missy says, "He can bake in there a little while longer." She goes all misty-eyed. We don't say a word, but I'm guessing we're each thinking the very same thing: that Missy's going to be a wonderful mother and sometimes the best things happen to those who deserve them most.

Missy wipes her eyes with the sleeve of her sweater and turns to me and says, "Don't think we've forgotten, Lil. What made you skip across the way like you're training for a bobsled team?"

"If only I had a Spandex one-piece." I muse. "Well, *someone*—" I put my hands on my hips and stare directly at Missy "—said I should try and wear make-up so I'd get used to it before the wedding. This *someone* also said it was colorstay! When it quite clearly wasn't!"

Missy leans her head against the sofa and giggles. "I gave you the wrong bag! Didn't you think it was odd the lipsticks were way too bright for you?"

I make my mouth a tight line.

The girls laugh into their hands. "And let me guess, your poor old fiancé had it spread right across his handsome face too?"

I cross my arms and nod, trying my best not to sputter with embarrassment.

The girls burst out laughing, as I color the perfect shade of Pink Passion myself.

CeeCee cocks her head and says, "I think we can imagine the rest o' that scenario. Pray tell, how'd the two o' you ride in the same truck to work and not notice each other's faces?"

I grimace. "We were *so* late...so we hurried to the truck and launched ourselves in cracking heads as we did. I drove with one eye closed, as pain kind of numbed one side of my face. Damon had one of those beanie things on with the side straps, and I just didn't see. The windscreen demister didn't work so Damon was frantically wiping at the screen... Golly, I need a new truck, *and* a new make-up expert..." I flash Missy a grin. "When I pulled into the street there were a bunch of ladies waiting on Damon's stoop, so I slowed and he jumped out."

"It could've been worse," Sarah says. "Could've happened when your future in-laws were here."

I gasp at the thought. "True. That would have been a nightmare! Speaking of which, they dropped in already."

Missy leans forward on her seat. "I thought they weren't due for a week yet?"

I throw my palms up. "They wanted to surprise us."

"Well, that's the sweetest thing I've heard," Missy says. "I bet they were excited to finally meet you." She fluffs her curls, and gives me a huge smile. Missy's one of those people that sees the good in everyone, and everything, so telling her I'm slightly uneasy about a few things Olivia said will only make her want to fix it.

"It was certainly interesting," I say.

Sarah cocks her head. "Interesting, Lil? That's like saying someone's shoes look comfortable when what you really mean is ugly. What happened?"

In deference to Damon, I don't feel right telling them what Olivia said. "Oh, you know, it was just so unexpected. And late, and I wasn't prepared. George, Damon's dad, fell asleep, and Olivia…I think she was probably jet-lagged herself. They're coming here for dinner tonight, they can meet my parents, and—"

"Lil," Sarah says gently, "you're wringing your hands so hard they're going to fall off."

I unclasp them and smile. "Weddings, huh? At Christmas. Do you think it's selfish having it at this time of year?"

"Why do you say that?" Sarah probes, a frown appearing between her smoky kohl-rimmed eyes. "You love Christmas. And it's your anniversary, after all."

"It's just I guess it didn't occur to me that our guests might have preferred to spend Christmas Eve with their families rather than attend our wedding. I mean, I know you girls wouldn't think that, but are other people thinking that?"

Sarah scoffs. "That's crazy, Lil. It's one more reason to celebrate." Sarah's an introvert among us more feisty personalities—she's the kind of girl you can tell your secrets to and know she's like a vault. A quirky, whimsical soul who I count as one of my closest friends after CeeCee.

I play with the handle of my mug. "I hope so."

"Put it out of your mind," Missy says. "There's no place we'd rather be than watching you two lovebirds get married. And I'm sure everyone agrees."

"Stop fussing, Lil," CeeCee says.

"Well, OK." Their coffee cups are empty. I stand and pick them up. "How about some hot chocolate?"

"I was wondering how long we'd have to wait," Sarah jokes. I've never seen a girl so addicted to chocolate as she is. And she's as skinny as a beanpole, the lucky thing. "I should've known you had a hankering." I smile and head to the stove.

I take a small pot down and pour in some milk. While that begins to boil, I break off chunks of dark chocolate and stir them in. It's like a big warm hug, the smell of the molten chocolate melting as it combines with the creamy milk. Once it's mixed through I pour it into four glass mugs and throw some marshmallows on top.

"Let me help." Sarah dashes over and takes two of the mugs, sipping hers as she goes. "Lil, gosh, that's good."

I laugh my thanks. We're quiet for a moment as we savor the rich taste, bitter and sweet at the same time from the quality of the dark chocolate, sweetened by the gooey marshmallows.

Missy rubs her hands together. "How's about we do that make-up trial soon? Now Olivia's here we can invite her too."

"Hmm," I say. "Let's just keep it us girls for now."

Missy raises an eyebrow. "OK. You just say when and we'll make a night of it, just us. I'm about to get a lot more time on my hands."

"With a baby comin'?" CeeCee says in mock consternation.

Missy hoots with laughter. "No, I mean, with the salon. My new girl, Becca, starts today, so I'm going to hand things over to her and go rest my swollen…everything."

"I can't believe it," I say. "It's going to be so weird not having you just a few steps away."

Missy's eyes shine with tears. "Oh, golly, here I go again." She plucks a tissue from the box. "You know, I can't wait until this urge to cry over every itty-bitty thing goes away."

"Hush now," CeeCee says. "Missy, you know where we are. It ain't like we're going anywhere. You still gonna visit us every day. I know I ain't going to be able to function without some cuddles from that little bundle o' joy you about to bring into the world."

Missy gives us a warm smile. "Thanks, Cee. I'm really looking forward to the whole motherhood thing. I'm scared, and excited and nervous. But mostly just plain grateful. There's times though when I worry about the salon. You know? That's been my baby for as long as I can remember."

"It's going to be in good hands," Sarah says and looks to me and CeeCee. "I met Becca yesterday. She's going to fit right in here. With one look at grumpy ol' Marjorie she had her figured out. They were firm friends by the time she left. She's going to treat that salon like it's her own."

Marjorie is Ashford's answer to the Grinch. She despises Christmas. Hates any form of celebration. Calls us all materialistic and brain-washed by consumerism. She sure is hard to fathom when you first meet her. "Geez, Missy, if she can handle Marjorie she can handle anyone!" I say. I go to the display fridge and take out some dark chocolate fruit mince truffles, and a handful of Missy's favorite, gingerbread and white chocolate.

Sarah gives me a thumbs up while Missy takes a deep breath and continues: "I know. I should be thanking my lucky stars I even managed to find a hairdresser that'd come live in Ashford. For a while there I thought I might have to close up for the duration. And Becca is sweet as sugar. I don't know why I feel as though I'm never gonna see anyone again. Anyway, listen to me! We're supposed to be organizing your wedding!"

"Missy," I say, "you're bound to feel that way. Your life is about to change for the better. And like Cee says, we might even see more of you now that you're a free woman. *Have baby will travel.*"

More composed, Missy nods. "You're right. I'll probably have my own sofa here at the café, with my own fluffy blanket. Cee can use that baby carrier thingy-majiggy and wander around with him tied to her chest, singing lullabies, while I catch up on my beauty sleep."

"That sounds mighty fine to me," CeeCee says. "Ain't nothing like rocking a baby to sleep, especially at Christmas. I'm gonna teach him a bunch of carols before he's even old enough to smile."

CeeCee is always babysitting for locals. She's affectionately known as a baby whisperer. Exhausted mothers often stop by the café and beg CeeCee to tell help get their infants to sleep. She laughs her southern haw, and takes the squawking bundle into her arms. We order the exhausted women to rest up, they'll amble to the recliner with a steaming cup of hot chocolate in hand. Drink it quickly and doze, safe in the knowledge Cee'll have their babies snoozing in no time.

I hope CeeCee will have the chance to hold a child of mine. And that she'll be around when they are old enough to bake alongside her. I don't think there's anything nicer than picturing that day. Almost as if I can see a little blond-haired girl standing on a step so she can reach the bench, listening patiently to Cee as she shows her how to mold fondant, or roll out pastry.

"I saw your mamma the other day," Sarah says, pulling me from my daydream. "That holiday definitely agreed with her. She's looking as happy as I've ever seen her."

She's been flitting around town since she came home, showing anyone who'll look her holiday photo album. "Did you see the pictures?"

"We *all* saw the pictures!" Missy says.

I shake my head, laughing, grateful she didn't invite everyone to the family slide-show night. Mamma learned the art of taking a 'selfie', which was adorable for the first few hundred shots. "You know she's gone and invited my cousin Jeremiah to the wedding?" The girls attended my first wedding, and know all about the disaster that is my cousin.

They dissolve into laughter again.

"You girls finished?" I arch my brow, and try to keep the smile from my voice.

Missy gushes, "Oh, he's just misunderstood! His hair grew back grey, after all…"

I gasp. "Mamma told you too?"

She shakes her head no. "Rosaleen. And…it seems, well, I don't know how to put it—"

"No! Please don't tell me Mamma invited Rosaleen?"

Missy pulls a face and says, "She's very excited. And so are her daughters…"

CeeCee clears her throat. "While we're at it… the three Mary-Jos were asking about bringin' their boyfriends." She shakes her head, as she's always ruffled by the outrageously flirty teenagers. "Seem too young for boyfriends if y'all ask me."

I curse under my breath. Mamma's gone and invited people left, right and center, without checking with me. With the extras that Olivia wants to invite, our intimate affair is going to be a circus. At this rate Guillaume is going to throw his tea towel down and cancel.

"Shoot. With that news, I better get to makin' more gingerbread wedding favors," CeeCee says, and lifts her bulk out of the chair. She turns back and says to Sarah, "Is that man-mountain o' yours gonna be here for the wedding?"

Sarah and I look at each other and laugh. Seems CeeCee is all set with giving our significant others a nickname, and sticking with it.

"He sure is," Sarah says. "Actually…he's not planning on going anywhere after that."

"What?" I ask. "He's moving here for good?"

She nods, her smile lighting up her doll-like features. "Yep. We figured it was about time. I mean, Ridge's practically living here anyway. But he's selling his apartment in New York, and moving in with me."

We screech our support and take turns hugging Sarah. She met Ridge a few months back after he came to do a story on a chocolate festival the town of Ashford hosted at Easter time. It didn't take long for love to blossom with the pair of them, and before we knew it Ridge was here almost every weekend after quitting his job at *The New York Herald* newspaper and doing freelance work instead.

Sarah says, "It's the weirdest feeling making room on my bookshelves for him. Is that odd? I mean, aren't I supposed to move half the clothes in the closet, or free up some room in the bathroom cabinet?"

"I think it's completely normal," I say. "I'm sure there are plenty of people who are quite fussy about who they share their shelves with."

After another fit of laughter, Sarah stands and shrugs her coat on.

CeeCee groans and says, "Let's make more o' those gingerbread wedding favors then, Lil."

"Be sure and send any mistakes my way. I'm craving gingerbread men so bad I'm worried I'm going to have a gingerbread baby," Missy says. Sarah clasps Missy's hands, pulling her bulk out of the sofa. "Let's go, gingerbread mom. I've got a customer, by the looks."

We hug our goodbyes and promise to catch up again later.

A few hours later I'm busy clearing tables when CeeCee wanders from the office, holding a piece of paper. "Lil, these orders have just come in on that gizmo." I suppress a smile at her reference to our antiquated fax machine.

"We better get a move on—the mayor's gone ahead and ordered a bunch o' cakes for his staff Christmas party." Her finger works its way down the list as she mumbles, "Black forest meringue, yule log, boozy fruitcake, chocolate-fudge cheesecake, and—" she chuckles "—lemonade pie. I knew he loved that pie. He done ordered it every week since I baked it for him a few months back."

CeeCee's famous for her southern pies. She makes them from scratch and when they sit cooling on the bench, their scent wafting down the street, you can almost count the seconds until we're inundated with customers. I've watched CeeCee make a million pies, followed her recipes to a T, mixed the ingredients with love in my mind, but they never taste as good. I don't know what her secret is, but they put the *comfort* into comfort food, all right.

"So." Cee puts the list on the bench. "Where should we start?"

I run through the order and say, "With the boozy fruitcakes. They'll take the longest to bake."

"You soaked the fruit already?"

"Yes, ma'am. I soaked a batch yesterday, good and proper with lashings of brandy, and some sugar syrup. I thought we'd make mini fruitcakes for the café, but we'll do that later now, and use this for the mayor's order instead."

"OK."

I wander to the stereo and press play. The café fills with the sound of Christmas carols. It's dark out despite it being the middle of the day. Outside people hurry from one shop to another searching for Christmas gifts, or buying groceries for their festivities. Snow rests on the dark wooden window panes almost like a framing for the cheery shoppers as they dash about on the cold day.

"I thought we could make some of those gingerbread in a jar gifts, too, Cee."

Last year we filled a bunch of mason jars with the dry ingredients for gingerbread men, and printed out the tiny recipes cards to go with it. We attached them with red and green festive ribbons, and a gingerbread man cookie cutter. They were fun and easy Christmas gifts, and all people had to do was add the wet ingredients and bake.

"Easily done, Lil," she chortles. "Ain't like we short of supplies for gingerbread." She bends down and unearths a box from under the bench and rifles through it. "We've got a bunch of cookie cutters here, and most o' them are Christmas themed. We sure can make those gingerbread jars again. Kids loved buying those last year for their folks."

I lean over and look into the box of still-wrapped cookie cutters. "Let's get this order done, and then we can make some, and put them in the window."

We pull out silver bowls, and I take the fruit mix from the fridge. The pungent smell of alcohol hits me as soon as I peel back the plastic wrap.

"Glory be, how much brandy did you put in there?" CeeCee hollers. She makes a huge show of covering her face with her hands.

"Enough." I smirk. "And a splash of rum for good measure." While CeeCee finds the remainder of ingredients the recipe calls for, I grease square loaf pans with butter, then turn on the mixer and beat sugar and butter, slowly adding the eggs, once again being drawn into the world inside the arms of the beater, hypnotized by the transformation and the way certain ingredients combine.

CeeCee whisks the flour and spices that she'll add to my bowl so we have one huge batch to add the alcohol-infused fruit to.

"The fruit is ripe with brandy, Cee." I lift a fat cherry aloft; it's plump from absorbing the alcohol. It seems festive—the red and green cherries and golden raisins shine out from the bowl. CeeCee nods and smiles at the small gem-like cherry in my fingers.

"Let's ice them white and mold some holly and ruby-red berries out of fondant." I throw the cherry back in the bowl.

"They'll look mighty Christmassy, Lil," she says, stirring while she gazes dreamily over my shoulder to the busy street outside.

We work in silence, humming along to *Silent Night* as the singer croons softly out of the speakers above us. There's something so healing about baking. I know CeeCee feels it too. Life just seems to make sense when you can plunge your hands into a bowl of brandied fruit, and chat away to your best friend about the most trivial things.

Once we've put the loaf pans in the oven, I scour the mayor's order to work out what's next.

The doorbell jingles, and in walks Damon's dad, George. He's dressed impeccably in a suit and wears a tie. "Good morning, ladies."

He's so much like Damon in the way he walks, and the tone of his voice. "You're a little early for dinner," I say, smiling.

He takes off his leather gloves and leans against the bench. "I'm blaming you. Since I came in here the other night I've had a hankering for gingerbread. I figured while Olivia was otherwise occupied I may as well satisfy my craving."

CeeCee hems and haws. "See? I told you that tree was a good idea! Draws folks like bees to honey…"

"It sure does," I agree. "Pull up a stool, George, and I'll make you up a plate." Dusting my hands on my apron, I meander off, searching the selections in the fridge for gingerbread flavors. I take some gingerbread macaroons, and a chunk of gingerbread fudge, and add them to the plate.

"Don't forget the gingerbread cake pops," CeeCee says, pointing. I take a cake pop, and a few dark chocolate and gingerbread truffles from the fridge. So we're a little addicted to gingerbread flavored treats? What kind of Gingerbread café would we be if we weren't! There's something so child-like and sweet about the flavor, and it only gets better once we fancy it up for adults in the form of a more gourmet morsel.

"So where is that wife o' yours?" CeeCee asks as she heads to the fridge and takes out foil-covered cream cheese for the chocolate-fudge cheesecake.

George's eyes light up as I put the plate in front of him. "Running errands. She said something about organizing the centerpieces for the tables. I guess you'd know more about that, Lil?"

She what? I only told her very quickly what we envisaged. I imagined we'd go into more detail tonight, and then if she wanted to help she'd at least know what we were looking for. "Oh? I mentioned it the other night, but we haven't actually discussed it properly yet."

George bites into a macaroon, and nods his appreciation. "You know Olivia." He shrugs, non-committal.

No, I don't know her at all.

He half laughs when I don't say a word and says as if by explanation, "Loves being involved." He shrugs, and gives me an apologetic look.

Maybe she's simply window shopping? Surely she wouldn't go ahead and buy something without checking with us first. "I hope she doesn't go to too much trouble," I say, with an edge of concern in my voice.

"She loves that kind of thing, Lil. Once you get to know her you'll see. She might seem…overbearing at times, but it's more that she wants to be useful, rather than outright in charge." He manages to blush, as though speaking this way of his wife is out of order. "But, it's your wedding, Lil. And if by chance Olivia does tug the reins a little too hard, I hope you feel comfortable having a private word with me."

It's easy to see where Damon gets his personality from. George is friendly and warm, and him offering to step in is a comfort. He obviously knows his wife well. "Thanks, George. Maybe tonight once we get into the finer details of the wedding, Olivia will feel more involved."

"I'd say so," he says amiably. "Until then, I might pay a visit to Damon. Thanks for these." He holds up a truffle. "I'll see you tonight, ladies."

A few hours later we've done the bulk of the mayor's order, and decide to finish it off later. We've tidied up and are ready to move on to the next thing on our list. The most exciting thing we've ever baked, too.

"Nothing for it, let's make that wedding cake o'yours."

I let out a squeal. We've spent the last two months searching for the perfect cake design. We settled on a three-tier cake, elegant and striking. We had folders full of design ideas, and it was so hard to narrow it down. After all, we're known for our cakes, and it has to be perfect.

"I'll start on the sponges, Lil, if you want to mix the different flavored ganaches."

I take the hand drawn design from the folder, and flip through the pieces of paper for the recipe we settled on. Reading through, I wonder if it'll be as delicious as we imagine. "Hazelnut ganache for the top layer, dark chocolate and orange for the second, and vanilla bean for the third. What do you think? That'll cater for all tastes?"

"Surely will. Ain't no one gonna see a cake as pretty as this, neither."

We set to work, excited to finally start the design we've been dreaming about for months. CeeCee's mouth is a tight line, and I can't stop my fluttery hands. She's concentrating hard, yet I can't seem to focus. I keep going back to the drawing, if we pull this cake off it's going to be the most elegant piece of artwork we've ever baked. And all for my wedding day. Just the thought is enough to send my heart racing. I picture Damon standing behind me as we cut the cake in front of our friends and family, and I'm giddy with love.

"It's spectacular!" The wedding cake sits safely in the display fridge, after we took out three lots of shelves to fit it inside.

"I ain't never seen a cake like it."

The first tier is round, full of snowflakes like a snow dome, which spill down the silver cake, settling at the base. It's like a silvery snowstorm come to life. With steady hands, we studded edible diamonds around each tier, and with a sprinkle of glitter it glimmers like an invitation to another world. Each layer has different flavored sponges, with mouth-poppingly luscious ganaches spread thickly through.

"I'm going to take the truffles out of that fridge, Lil. So we're not opening and closing the fridge all the time."

"It's not like it'll melt though, Cee." I laugh.

"I know, but the less we disturb it, the better. I don't want those snowflakes falling off. I ain't too keen on making those ever again. My eyesight ain't what it used to be, you know."

"OK, Cee. That was some finicky work, all right." Of course we chose to make snowflakes from palm size, right down to the size of a penny. As they became smaller we needed so many more to decorate the tier. After a while though your fingers freeze up on account of having to keep your hands stiff for so long.

"Saying that, though, I don't reckon I've ever liked creating something as much as I have this. And that's saying somethin'."

I amble behind CeeCee and rest my chin on her shoulder. "You think we should make wedding cakes now?"

"As long as I don't have to cut out itty-bitty snowflakes all day, I think I'd like that. Can you imagine what we'd come up with?"

I imagine the café stacked with cakes for weddings, birthdays, family celebrations. And it could be yet another financial back-up for us if the catering side of things falters. "I think we should give it a try." If I got to spend a day lovingly making someone else's dream wedding cake, it'd be a damn fine day to me.

At the end of a long day, I sit by the display window and watch the last of the late evening shoppers exit from the shops across the road so the owners can close up. It's dark out, and CeeCee's gone home, insisting dinner tonight is only for family.

With the café all toasty warm, and *Jingle Bells* playing merrily in the background, I get my second wind, and continue on with the mayor's order. We've only got the yule log and CeeCee's lemonade pie left to make and then we can deliver it early tomorrow.

Yule log is one of my favorite Christmas recipes. Making the cake resemble a log, with all the grooves and gouges, dusted white with snow, is a Christmas tradition in our family. My grandma used to make it every year when I was little. I loved watching her roll the sponge, and cover it with thick butter-cream icing, before running a fork down the length for her grooves. In that soft way of hers she'd share stories about her childhood, while I listened, rapt, occasionally dipping a finger into the chocolate icing.

When I make yule log, I'm transported back to her orderly kitchen, and it warms my heart as though we're still connected. If you share that kind of love, it can always be brought back to life when you bake. It's almost as if she's standing right behind me, smiling.

Glancing at the time, I realize everyone will arrive for dinner soon. Instead of making the base of the yule log, I take some gum paste from the fridge. I set to work, massaging it, to make it pliable to make acorns. They dry rock hard, and aren't the nicest to eat, but they finish off the woodsy look.

"Hey." Damon sidles up behind me and kisses the back of my neck, sending goose bumps down my body.

"Hey…" I say, turning to his soft smile.

"It's freezing in here." In my trip down memory lane, I hadn't noticed the fire is down to embers. I set the acorn leaves aside.

"Take a break. Put your feet up." He leads me to the sofa, and starts fussing with the fire to spark it up before joining me.

He surveys me. "Lil, you look a little…peaked. Are you OK?"

"Yes, I'm fine." I must look a fright. I push a tendril of hair back, as usual wearier once I've sat down for a moment.

"OK. It's just I don't want to be standing at the altar alone, while you're tucked up in bed sick or something."

I giggle at the thought of Damon all dressed up in his tux, checking his watch. "I'm no runaway bride. If I was sick I'd be there anyway. Happy to spread my germs with you. In sickness and in health, remember?"

He throws his head back and laughs. "I remember. Let's test the waters." He leans closer and cups my face, and kisses me slowly. A tingle of desire races through me, and I'm giddy with the fact I get to marry this man.

"Get a room!" We jump as if scalded to the sound of my dad's jocular voice and rise to greet him. He wraps me in a warm hug, and musses my hair. "Where's Mamma?" I ask.

Dad scratches the back of his neck. "She's running late on account of a wardrobe malfunction. I don't know what that means, but there you have it."

"A wardrobe malfunction?"

Dad shrugs and Damon takes it as a cue for drinks. "I'll uncork the wine. You guys catch up a while."

"Good man," Dad says and sits heavily. There's something utterly teddy-bearish about my father. He's got a pot belly from too many sweets, and wears red braces that make him look like some kind of professor. His bushy eyebrows stick straight up as if he's been zapped with lightning; they're longer than the hair on his almost-bald head.

I lower my voice and say, "She's dilly-dallying over what to wear, isn't she?"

He touches a finger to his nose implying it's a secret. "She said she'd just be a minute."

"I don't see what's wrong with what she usually wears." I have the grace to blush a little as I remember myself fretting about the exact same thing this morning.

Damon returns with a bottle of red wine, and glasses. "Now you're talking," Dad says, accepting a glass eagerly. I think his pot belly might also be a product of his penchant for red wine, which he claims is purely medicinal.

A second later Mamma arrives, her hair covered in snowflakes, which melt quickly as she rushes towards the fire. She unwraps her winter coat and throws it towards Dad. "Evening all!" she trills happily.

"Mamma!" My eyes go wide with surprise. "What are you wearing?"

Golly, I can see where I inherited my fashion sense from. Mamma is decked out in a silky pantsuit, with every color imaginable splashed across it making my eyes cross in confusion.

"It's gorgeous, isn't it?" she says. "I borrowed it from Rosaleen. She said shoulder pads are coming back in. *And* that the vibrant colors make me look a decade younger." She gives her newly styled hair a dramatic flick. Obviously she snuck in to see Missy at the salon this afternoon too.

"Where's Cee?" she asks.

"Gone on home. Says tonight is just about family."

Mamma's lips pucker. "But she is family."

I shrug. "She wouldn't hear a word of it."

CeeCee is more than an employee; she's my best friend and more like a mother figure, especially when my own was traveling the globe for nearly a year.

Mamma says, "Maybe she's beat, Lil. You've both been burning the candle from both ends."

"Yeah…I guess." I survey the café, making sure I haven't left any empty mugs or plates around. On the bench is the gum paste and the few acorn leaves I managed to mold so I wander over and pack them away. With one last look around I'm satisfied the café is as ordered as it's ever likely to be. I wonder what strangers make of it when they walk in. The sofas are so well loved they're worn. The dark chocolate walls have tiny chips where kids scuff up against them when they're hooting and hollering around the place. Christmas decorations hang down from silver hooks in the ceiling, and golden tinsel laces around every available surface. To me, it seems cozy and festive, and almost like a home away from home. Woolen throw rugs are bundled in a wicker basket by the recliners, and secondhand books are an arm stretch away. I want people to visit, and loll about as if they're at a friend's house. To stumble in on a cold day, take a deep breath, savoring the scent of what we're baking, and take their time while they're here.

Dad and Damon wander to the window display, wine glasses in hand, chatting away as if they're old friends. They've only known each other a few weeks, and already they get on so well, it makes my heart sing to watch them. Dad's one of those people that really listens when you talk. Looks you right in the eye and asks questions as if you've gone and solved the meaning of life or something.

Mamma pours herself a glass of wine and I take the opportunity to strike. "I hear we need a few more place settings at the wedding?" I purse my lips.

She fumbles with the stem of her wine glass. "Honey, it's only a few—"

"An entire bookclub, Mamma?"

"They're my friends…"

"And Rosaleen?"

She lifts a hand. "You ever think she's just lonely? I think she could use some friends, Lil."

"How're we all supposed to fit at *L'art de l'amour*? Mamma, I know you're excited but how can I make that work?"

"Well, I asked—"

A flurry of wind whips in as the front door opens and in walks Olivia with George in tow.

"Good evening." Olivia saunters over. She's wrapped a fine fur stole. She makes a huge show of kissing Damon on both cheeks before striding over to me.

Mamma starts to fidget with her shoulder pads. "Olivia, I'm Lil's mamma, Sue. It's nice to finally meet you." I hear the nervousness in Mamma's voice and I just want to hug her.

Olivia smiles that sugary smile of hers and says, "Wonderful to meet you, Sue. We've been looking forward to this for an age."

"Us too." Mamma smiles at Olivia.

Olivia takes off her stole, and begins taking her gloves off, finger by finger. "Lil, as we discussed I went ahead and found you the centerpieces. They're being delivered tomorrow."

I clear my throat. "About that, Olivia, we didn't actually—"

She grins at Mamma. "She's so busy, what with the café, and Christmas, it was the least I could do. I practically drove the entire length of Connecticut until I found them."

"That was really kind of you," Mamma says. In the background Damon makes a joke that has both dads sputtering into their hands.

I glance back to his mother. "But, Olivia—"

"They're gorgeous, stunning in fact. Big *fake* sweeping white *lilies*." She puts so much emphasis on the words fake and lilies that I almost reel. Is she calling me fake? "They sit in a crystal vase, quite tall, actually. I did worry about people being able to see over the top of them, but figured that isn't important in the scheme of things."

"They sound darling," Mamma says, and nudges my arm. "Don't they, Lily?"

Damon sits on the arm of the sofa, swishing his red wine before taking a mouthful. I try to catch his eye, but he's too caught up with a story my dad is telling. "Well," I say, "I'd hoped on getting poinsettias as part of the Christmas theme."

Olivia lets out a high-pitched laugh. "Oh, Lil. No! They're so old-fashioned."

Mamma nods. "I've been trying to tell her that." I stare at Mamma, trying to explain by the sheer look in my eyes that she's not helping.

Mamma touches Olivia's arm. "Let me get you a drink. Red wine OK?"

"Lovely." Olivia throws her gloves on the nearest table, and fusses with her jacket. "I hope you're not upset, Lil? I didn't do the wrong thing, did I?" For a brief second she looks contrite, and again I wonder if I'm making too much out of nothing.

"I'm sure they're lovely, Olivia. I guess we'll make them work. Although we had planned on a more festive—"

"Great." She cuts me off as she twirls her wedding ring on her finger, a dazzling diamond that probably cost more than my house.

Damon wanders over, smiling like a loon. He loops an arm around my waist. "Your dad says he's got the bachelor party all sorted. I intend to win big, and show the old men how it's done."

"Is that so?" I ask, arching a brow. Thankful he's finally beside me.

"Darling, I was just about to tell Lil all about Katie. All those tête-à-têtes you two have when you come to New Orleans…I thought maybe it's not too late to fly Katie here. She could definitely help with the menu."

Mamma returns with an over-full glass of red wine, and manages to slosh half out before handing it to Olivia.

Olivia grabs a napkin from the table and wipes the side of her glass. Poor Mamma looks mortified. I shake my head, trying to signal to her it's OK.

"Katie's a lovely girl, quite famous in her own right as a chef these days, works alongside a Michelin-starred someone-a-rather. Damon adores her! Always rushes straight over there when he arrives in New Orleans. Don't you, darling?"

I give Damon a closed-lip smile as my pulse speeds up. Damon has never once mentioned anyone other than

Charlie when he visits New Orleans. I take a step back from him; his hand falls from my waist. "You rush over where exactly?" I keep my voice neutral but I'm sure everyone can tell from the clench of my jaw it's the first I've heard of...Katie.

Damon has the grace to blush. "Katie's an old friend of mine from high school—"

"They were childhood sweethearts." Olivia puts a hand to her chest. "Such a sweet girl, lovely family too."

Damon says, "We were just *friends* in high school." He clutches my hand, and gives it a squeeze, but right now I have the most immense urge to ask Olivia what she's playing at here. And Damon, too. Lunches with his childhood sweetheart?

"So you catch up with Katie a lot, then?" I ask Damon, finding it almost impossible to keep the hurt from my voice.

He swallows hard. "Charlie and I go to her restaurant when I visit New Orleans. We talk shop, that's all. There's really nothing more to say."

We stand silently. Anger courses through me and in equal measure I feel like a fool. Olivia smiles benevolently, and I make my mind up about her. She's intent on creating a wedge between us for some inexplicable reason. My dad must sense the awkward vibe radiating from us. He scoops up a platter of oysters Damon prepared and waves it under my nose. Immediately I cup my mouth and run to the bathroom.

CHAPTER FIVE

Six days

Damon lifts the quilt up to my chin, and kisses my forehead. "I've left a pitcher of water here, and there's soup in the fridge when you're up to it."

I nod, truly miserable. Being sick this close to Christmas, especially with so much work needing to be done, and Cee having to take up the slack at the café is the worst possible timing. "Sure."

He sits on the edge of the bed; the slight movement makes me close my eyes against waves of nausea.

"You were angry last night," he says, stroking my hair back. "About Katie."

I bury myself further under the blankets. The night comes rushing back. "Yes, Katie. An old flame...one you catch up with when you go back to New Orleans. Which is fine, except you neglected to mention it to me."

He laughs, he actually *laughs*.

I scowl. "Which part of this is funny, Damon?"

"The Katie part. She's not an old flame, not even a teeny tiny flicker of a flame."

I let out a drawn-out sigh. "Right, well, your mother didn't seem to think that was the case."

He leans over me, his face close to mine, his wavy hair falling forward. I resist the urge to tuck it back for him.

"Lil, Katie was one of my best friends throughout school. We both loved cooking, still do, and now she's on her way to being one of the best chefs in America."

"She sounds like the whole package, Damon." I try to keep the jealousy at bay but it ekes out anyway.

He grins.

"Don't grin at me!"

He strokes my hair back. "You're beautiful when you're jealous, you know that?"

I scoff. "I don't know why you're not taking this seriously, Damon. Your mother blurting it out like that last night made me feel about this big." I hold my thumb and finger together. "I had no idea you spend your weekends in New Orleans gallivanting and doing who the hell knows what."

He throws his head back and laughs. "She's gay, Lil."

"So?" I pull the quilt over my head. *She's gay?* "But your mother said…" I muffle through the quilt.

He pulls it down and kisses the tip of my nose. "She's a great girl, and my mother has always assumed we'd be perfect for each other. Her family knows my family very well. But Katie hasn't told them she's gay, so when we were younger we let them think what they wanted. It was easier for her and everyone assumed we were a couple."

"I thought…"

"I know what you thought." He stands and grabs a sweater from the drawer, with one quick movement pulls it over his head. "I'd never hurt you, Lil. Ever."

My stomach is a queasy lump, and I blush. "I'm an idiot."

"No, you're not. In future I'll tell you when I plan on *gallivanting* around New Orleans. Or better yet, you come for a weekend with me."

He crouches by the bed. "I have to go. Will you be OK?"

I nod, closing my eyes against the roiling in my gut.

"The doctor should be here around lunchtime, but call if you need anything."

Exhaling slowly, I say, "Can you check CeeCee is OK? Mamma's going in to help her, but that could actually hinder her." My mamma is the clumsiest cook there is. She's liable to set the café on fire if you don't watch her.

"They'll be fine, but I'll pop over and check. Let me know what the doctor says." He kisses my forehead. "Sleep tight. I'll call at lunch to check on you."

I sink into the softness of the pillow. It's only a moment before I drift off into a restless dream-filled sleep.

An hour or two later I startle awake, suddenly sure I know what's wrong. I throw back the quilt, and race to the bathroom cupboard. In the very back are boxes of tests. I take one and rip the packaging open, hastily reading the instructions as I go, even though I've done so many before I've committed them to memory.

Two minutes. I'll know in two minutes. My somber mood is instantly replaced with hope. *Maybe I'm pregnant?*

One hundred and twenty seconds have never moved so slowly, as I wait with the stick sitting on the window ledge, as if it's not something life-changing, as it so clearly is.

I think of how I'll tell Damon. Sweet things, I've heard, like putting a bun in the oven, and asking him to open it. Will he understand? Or buying booties, and wrapping them up. Or…

Two minutes are up. With a deep breath I peer at the test. One line shrieks out in neon pink. Negative. Devastatingly, positively, negative.

I ditch the test in the bin, and head back to bed, not bothering to wipe at the tears as they fall.

A knock at the door wakes me. Glancing at the time, I see it's only eleven. Too early for the doctor. I amble out of bed, not bothering to check my reflection in the mirror.

I press my face up to the peephole. It's Sarah. I smile, in spite of myself. I have the best friends.

"Hey," she says as I motion for her to come in.

"Hey."

"CeeCee told us you were sick. She made you a basket of goodies, and I brought you some magazines."

I take the proffered bag, and say thanks.

"Get back into bed, Lil. You look positively green."

I give her a rueful smile. "I thought I was pregnant, but I'm not."

"Aw, Lil. I'm sorry." She follows me to my room and sits on the end of the bed. "Maybe, you know, once all the wedding stuff is organized, and after all your Christmas orders are sorted, your body will slow down, and it'll just happen." Her black bangs hang over her eyebrows, highlighting the genuine look in her eyes.

"It's stupid worrying over it, already, isn't it?"

"It's not stupid, Lil. You've wanted to be a mom your whole life. It will happen, but right now you've got so much on. It's just a matter of time."

I've been taking pregnancy tests almost weekly since Easter. But Sarah is probably right: once things settle down my body will just *know*, and it'll happen. The yearning for a child is almost indescribable sometimes, is all.

"You're right," I agree. "There's still so many little things that need to be organized and I feel awful leaving CeeCee at work. Is she OK?"

Sarah scrunches up her nose. "She's…" Her voice trails off.

"Mamma?" I know by Sarah's expression there's been some kind of drama at the café.

She nods. "I don't know how to tell you, Lil. So I'll just say it. She somehow tripped and knocked your display fridge over. The wedding cake…" Sarah pales. "I'm sorry, Lil. It's completely ruined."

I gasp, picturing the three tiers of perfection toppling over and smashing to the floor. "Please tell me you're joking," I whisper through my hands.

"I'm so sorry, Lil. Your mamma is beside herself with worry. But I'm sure we can fix it. We can all help…"

"But…how?" I'm beginning to feel as though my wedding is cursed.

She shrugs. "CeeCee said don't worry, you can make another one when you're back."

I'm too stunned to speak. That cake took us the better part of a whole day. Will we even have enough time to make another one? I want to weep with the worry I feel. "I can't believe it. How could she knock over a huge fridge?"

"She feels terrible, Lil."

I sigh, thinking of Mamma, I know she'll be upset, and I fight hard to let the anger subside. "I guess we can always make another one…"

Sarah presses on. "Good news. Missy said Bessie's finished our bridesmaid dresses and yours isn't far away."

I smile, Sarah's managed to change the subject to something more positive. At least that's one thing Mamma can't ruin. "I can't wait to see them." The girls have mink satin gowns, similar to my dress, but with a high back. They're cut on the bias and swirl out at the bottom like a creamy wave. When we hunted for material, and held up the color next to each of their faces, it suited them so perfectly they instantly agreed on that fabric. I'd expected the usual bridesmaid disagreements, especially as all of us can be vocal when we dig our heels in, but, so far, everyone seems happy with my choices. Bessie from the haberdashery shop designed them, and they're truly magnificent.

"When you're feeling better we'll all go and you can see what you think." Her forehead furrows.

"What?"

"There was one other thing, though, being relayed like Chinese whispers, we might have misunderstood, because it doesn't seem right…"

"What doesn't?"

Sarah takes a deep breath and says, "Well, Bessie told Missy that Damon's mother called in to see your dress."

"Really? I haven't even seen it!"

Sarah swallows hard. "She told Bessie to make it short, to cut it above knee length…"

I gasp. "What? Why would she do that?"

"So you didn't ask her? That is so odd! Don't worry. Bessie thought the whole idea was ridiculous so she said to Olivia that unless you come and tell her yourself, she's designing the dress the way you asked."

My mouth hangs open. Why would she do such a thing? I tell Sarah about the centerpieces, and about alluding to the fact Damon was visiting his so-called high-school sweetheart, and how they were perfect for each other.

"So when you add all those little things up, Lil, it does sound like she's plotting something."

"But why?" To have someone level-headed like Sarah agree makes me crumble inside. What's Olivia's motivation?

Sarah shrugs. "God knows. You'll have to ask her, Lil. Be upfront, and demand to know why she'd do that. Otherwise, what else has she got planned?"

My eyes go wide as I think of all the things she could undo without my knowing.

"This is like something out of a book," Sarah says, biting down on her lip.

"You'd know," I say, laughing. "It's so ridiculous it's almost funny." I sober when I imagine myself walking down the aisle in a short gown, and then being surprised by a venue change. "I'll have a talk with Bessie, and then see what Olivia has to say."

Later that evening I'm as sick as I was the night before. If the ground opened up and swallowed me I'd be OK with that. It's like being seasick, as I roll slowly over in bed lest I start retching again.

Damon arrives home as the snow falls hard outside. I've hardly moved all day, and I know the house will be arctic without the fire lit. He enters the bedroom, his complexion rosy from cold. "Lil," he says, and kneels beside the bed, surveying me. "Have you eaten?"

I shake my head no.

"How about I fix you some soup?"

"No, I'm OK." I'm still too queasy to think of food. I pat the bed. Damon shuffles around to the other side, takes his boots off and gently hops in beside me. He pushes tendrils of curls softly from my face.

"What did the doctor say?"

"He took some blood tests, just in case, but thinks it's just a twenty-four-hour thing. I should be OK tomorrow."

"I hope so," Damon says. "It was the strangest feeling, glancing across the road today and you weren't there."

"I missed you."

He groans, and pulls me in for a kiss. "I missed you more. Next time you're sick, I'll stay home. Everything else can wait."

I smile. "You'd close your shop, just like that?"

"I would."

I drop my gaze, collecting my thoughts so I can tell Damon without making it a blubber-fest. I feel silly crying over the fact I *thought* I was pregnant. "I took a pregnancy test."

His eyes go wide, and he pulls back and searches my face.

"Oh," he says, reading my expression.

"Not this time," I try to keep the disappointment from my voice.

He presses his lips together. I know he wants this as much as me. "It's OK. Maybe we just need to try harder." He gives me a silly smile, trying to lighten up the mood.

I laugh. "Well, OK."

We lay silently staring into each other's eyes. I commit every nuance of his face to memory. The tiny thin scar he has above one eyebrow, a relic from a childhood bike tumble. The starburst pattern in his deep brown eyes, like miniature fireworks. The love I feel threatens to swallow me up whole sometimes. Real love, it makes life come alive and when we're like this together, in the quiet, any doubts about Olivia float away. I'm determined to get to the bottom of her antics without Damon getting tangled up in it. But right now, I'm going to enjoy snuggling in Damon's arms while the snow falls heavily outside.

CHAPTER SIX

Five days

The next morning, still fragile, I head to the café.

"Well, lookie here," CeeCee says as I untangle my scarf and walk through the front door. "Oh, Lil, you pale as a ghost. This ain't good right before your wedding. How you feelin'?"

"I'm good, Cee. How are you? I felt so guilty leaving you here." The café looks the same as it always does; one day off and I half expect things to have changed. Well, aside from the gap where one of our display fridges used to be.

"Don't you worry 'bout me." She huffs, and I know she's worried about the wedding cake and what I'll say. "Lil, I'm so sorry…"

"Cee, don't be. There's nothing we can do about it now. I just hope we have enough time to make another one. And this time, we'll ban her from the café, just until it's safely delivered to the restaurant."

"Oh, Lil. It was terrible…when I saw the fridge come down, and your mamma fly through the air to catch it, golly…" We start laughing on account of Mamma's clumsiness. She has trouble boiling water at the best of times. Though without her we would have been in a pickle; there's no way CeeCee would have been able to cope alone.

Our talk is cut short as the doorbell jingles, and a flurry of customers arrive.

"Hey, Georgia," I say to a regular of ours. She comes in most mornings with her little boy Matthew. "The usual?" I ask.

"Yep," she says, smiling. "But Matthew wants two gingerbread men, says he's earned it on account of his school report."

I raise my eyebrows at Matthew. "Is that so?"

His big brown eyes look earnest as he says, "My teacher says I can read as good as the class above me. She sent Ma a letter and everything."

Matthew had all kinds of problems when he started school. He couldn't make sense of the words like other kids. Georgia struggled for the last two years trying to work out how to help him. She found an amazing tutor called Jo, who diagnosed his dyslexia. They've been working closely with him ever since.

I bend down to Matthew's height. "Do you really think two gingerbread men are enough? I mean, that kind of brilliance needs to be celebrated. How about I give you some gingerbread men to take home, and you can choose whatever you want out of the Christmas display?"

He claps his hand over his mouth and looks up at his mother. She nods yes. Turning back to me, he says in a hushed tone, "Out of the window display? *Anything?*"

I scruff his hair. "Anything. You earned it."

He shrieks and runs to the window.

Georgia and I exchange smiles as Matthew comes bouncing back with one of the chocolate Christmas boxes that are about the size of his head. "Whoops," I say. "I take no responsibility for the ensuing sugar high."

Georgia laughs. "I don't see any signage, Lil, that says I can't leave him here while I go shopping."

I tap my chin. "Er…it's around here somewhere."

Matthew sits in his favorite chair by the fire, and commences eating. Chocolate crunches and cracks and falls all over the floor in his haste.

"I'll bring your drinks over," I say. "And maybe a plate for Matthew." Kids and chocolate, there's no better combination. Customers look over at the small boy as he chews happily, not caring chunks of chocolate box fall to the floor with each bite.

Matthew's hands are smeared with chocolate as the fire crackles heartily behind him. My chest tightens as I think how lucky I am that these people are more than just customers, they're friends. Ashford is a small town, and I know all the ins and outs of Georgia and Matthews's life. It's been tough for Georgia, a single mom with a child who needs extra help, yet she's done it, she's worked tirelessly for her son. Whenever she needs a hand, her gardens mowed, or something in the house fixed, someone will step up; they won't expect payment, or even thanks. It's just the way things are done here. Folk look out for one another.

And their visits almost every day are a highlight for me. This place, with its mix of eclectic people, is so easy to live in. It makes me all warm and fuzzy like one of Sarah's heartwarming novels.

A young couple mill at the front of the café near our wicker baskets, which CeeCee has filled with shortbread shaped like Christmas trees. They flop against each other as they peruse, in that new love kind of way.

CeeCee and I set to work making gingerbread coffees, and hot chocolate for regulars who come in and hover by the fire. The café is a hive of activity this time of the day, friends catching up over plates of warm bagels, their chatter more animated as they cradle cups of steaming-hot coffee. They bunch closer when newcomers arrive, and stand back so they can warm themselves by the fire.

Missy struts in with a flick of her hair, and joins us at the bench. "Hey, sugar," she says, grabbing a gingerbread man from the basket and unwrapping the clear cellophane. "You had us worried there for a minute."

"It was nothing," I say, watching crumbs fall down Missy's front, which is somehow even bigger than it was just a couple of days ago. She rubs a hand protectively over her belly as she chews. I can't help but stare at it thinking back to yesterday and how sure I was that would be me soon.

"Earth to Lil," Missy says, waving her hand in front of my face.

I shake myself. "I'm a million miles away today!"

"You've got a lot on your plate. I've got some good news," she says between bites.

"Yeah?"

"Your dress is finished. I happened to walk past Bessie's shop, and thought I'd poke my head in. I had a teeny tiny little peep. It's truly gorgeous, Lil."

A ripple of excitement runs through me. "She's finished all that beading already?"

"She sure did, and it's as lovely as you are, Lil. I stood there, overcome again by one of those God-awful hormonal crying jags, and pictured you in it. Your long blond curls cascading down the open back of the dress, that bias cut sitting so well over your curves. You need to go try it on, Lil. Bessie said she can make any adjustments you need."

Bessie's the local dressmaker, and tailor extraordinaire. She runs a small haberdashery shop, too. Like most folk in Ashford, you need to offer as many services as you can to make ends meet. An unassuming woman who can take a piece of fabric and sew it into something magical. She'd sketched my gown, a while back, and I knew instantly from those black and white drawings it was perfect. Now it's ready!

It's like a satin sheath, with long sleeves, and a plunging backline, forties style, simple yet stunning because of the exposed back, which drapes into a cowl at the base of my spine. Bessie thought the front of the gown needed a little sparkle, so she hand-sewed some antique beads along the décolletage.

"It kind of makes it more real, doesn't it?" I ask. When I went for the first fitting a few weeks back I sat with it draped across my lap wondering what Damon would make of it as I walked down the aisle. Would he be expecting a more formal gown, or would he instinctively know I'd choose something classic, and unfussy?

Missy gives me her megawatt smile. "It's really real! Bessie said we can all scoot on down there whenever we're ready to try on our dresses. And we need to meet up, us girls, and discuss the bridal shower. That's if you still want to have one? I know getting sick has been a time suck…"

The thought of a late night out when I still have so much to do makes me sigh. Would the girls think I was no fun if I bowed out?

"Would I be a total party pooper if I said no to a nightclub?"

Missy struts around the bench, and gives me a hug. "No, definitely not, and to tell you the truth, with my ankles now canckles, and the need to pee a five-minute occurrence, I'm kind of relieved. How about we spend a night in watching soppy chick flicks and eating…" she surveys the cooling bench "…a few of those right there?" She points to a rack of butterscotch tortes.

"I been running over hell's high acre," CeeCee says, which is her roundabout way of saying she's been busy. "A night in sounds about right to me too."

Missy fills a paper bag up with cookies. "Golly, I'm going to be the size of a house when this baby comes out. And you know what? I don't give a damn." She rubs her belly. "OK, sugar, a night in… I'll scoot over and tell Sarah."

"You ain't scooting anywhere on that icy road," CeeCee says, her voice stern. "I'll go an' tell Sarah, and I may as well take this here pile of truffles for her. You know what she's like if she doesn't have a chocolate fix. It just ain't fair you girls so skinny."

Missy laughs, and showers me with crumbs. "I'm so skinny? I can't even get in the door sideways!"

CeeCee rolls her eyes. "That won't be for ever, Missy."

Missy winks. "I hope you're right. Lil, let me know when you're ready and we'll go see Bessie and try our dresses on."

"Sure," I say. "How about the day after tomorrow? I should be all caught up here by then."

"Done. Don't forget I want a piece of that pie when it's ready, Cee." She click-clacks her way out of the shop, somehow making pregnancy look glamorous.

CHAPTER SEVEN

Four days

It's well before dawn the next morning, and we're taking a break after making a huge batch of dough to make braided loaves for our lunch special. The yeasty smell of dough proving accompanies us as we sip our candy-cane coffee.

The doorbell jingles, and in walks Guillaume, gruff, and unsmiling. "Lily-Ella, what is the meaning of this?" He brandishes a piece of paper.

"What?" I ask. His face is dark with fury.

"You don't want your reception at *L'art de l'amour* any more? I have already ordered the supplies! Found extra staff! And you send me an email to tell me this!" His thick French accent rises with each word.

CeeCee frowns. "Let me see that." She rests her glasses on the bridge of her nose as she reads, mumbling as she goes, "Well, I'll be..."

Olivia. I don't have to read the email to be able to guess what it contains. I hurriedly reassure Guillaume. "Please don't worry. We're definitely having our reception with you. And in future, if anything changes, I'll speak with you in person. I have an inkling someone has their heart set on making trouble, but it won't happen again."

Guillaume's dark expression softens slightly as he gazes at CeeCee.

"Guillaume?" I say. "Everything can still go ahead as normal."

CeeCee flushes, and pretends to be interested in the fire all of a sudden.

"Guillaume," I say again, touching his arm.

"Oui?"

A grin splits my face; when he reverts to French I know he's dumb with love for CeeCee.

"I said, everything can still go as planned, right?"

He tucks his hands into his pockets. "OK. Yes. *Merci.*"

My anger at Olivia will have to wait as I fight the urge to question CeeCee and Guillaume about why they can't make eye contact.

"CeeCee," I can't help but tease, "are you OK? You've gone as quiet as a mouse."

She turns from the fire, her hands on her hips. "Yes, yes. I'm…deep in thought on account of the letter, is all."

"You're deep in thought?" Who says that? My heart lifts, thinking love can find a person when they least expect it. I may be jumping the gun, but the vibe radiating from these two is enough to make the most oblivious person notice.

"You gonna make something of it?" She stares down her nose at me.

I laugh and shake my head. "No, ma'am."

"I must go." Guillaume shuffles his feet, and stares resolutely at the floor. "Lil, I hope there is no more problems. I cannot cook unless I'm happy. And this email, it did not make me happy."

"I understand, Guillaume. It won't happen again. And we want you to be happy." I smirk at CeeCee, who looks away.

"Au revoir." He gazes longingly at CeeCee once more before spinning on his heel.

I wait two counts before saying, "What in the heck was that, Cee?"

"It's that soon-to-be mother-in-law—"

I wave her away. "Oh, I know, it's her. But I meant that…" I point to Guillaume as he strides past the front window, shrugging down into his jacket against the snowfall.

She clasps her hands and grunts to herself.

I place my hands on my hips. "CeeCee, spill already."

She takes a huge breath and says, "Fine! Glory be, you sure are nosey. You like a bloodhound or somethin'."

I fold my arms and raise an eyebrow.

She giggles like a young girl. "Well…we're just friends."

"I don't believe you."

She sighs, but it's half-hearted and she grins. "It just sort of happened, but it's not like you young things. He's a companion, someone to cook for on these cold winter nights. That's all it is 'fore you go thinkin' silly on me."

"Oh, Cee. That's so beautiful." I am stunned she hasn't told me, but I can see it's a sensitive issue for her.

She fusses with her apron. "I don't want folk knowing just yet, though it won't be long before Rosaleen finds out, I'm sure. Just till I know exactly how I feel. Sometimes, when I think of Curtis, guilt rips me up inside. I promised I'd love that man for ever."

I cluck my tongue. "You do still love him, Cee. But surely there's enough room in your heart for a friendship?"

She averts her gaze. "I know, just some days are harder than others. Especially this time of year, the memory of Curtis passing hits me hard. And at any rate, I s'pose hand-holding ain't a sin, after all…"

I smile, picturing CeeCee and Guillaume holding hands across the table as they share a home-cooked meal. Sweet.

"You should enjoy it for what it is, Cee. You'd be the first to tell me not to overthink it."

She shrugs. "I know, cherry blossom. I'm OK, I truly am. It's been real nice having someone to cook for again."

I pat her arm. "I'm happy for you."

"Why don't you scoot over the road and tell Damon about what Olivia did?" Like an expert, she changes the subject.

"I'll wait," I say, my mouth a tight line as I remember the last few days. "He'll be along soon, and I'll explain then."

"Well, OK. Let's bake."

"Good Lord, that syrup smells like heaven itself," CeeCee says, dipping a spoon into the mix of berry coulis I've just made. The doorbell jingles and in walks Damon with his mother.

"How're you feeling?" he asks, sidling up to me.

"I'm fine." I manage a tight smile as I think of Olivia running around behind our backs trying to make trouble.

Olivia smiles her huge smile, and says, "Whatever you're baking smells divine!"

CeeCee and I exchange glances, and she nods to me. I swallow the lump in my throat, unsure about confronting her, but knowing I have to.

"I'm glad you're both here," I say, clasping Damon's hand. "Guillaume paid me a visit early this morning…" I glance at Olivia expecting her to blanch, but she's still smiling as if nothing is amiss.

"What'd he say?" Damon asks.

"It was more of what he thought *we* said that was a concern."

"Do we have to guess? What is it, Lil?" Damon's forehead furrows.

I sigh, and find the piece of paper Guillaume left behind. "Read it yourself."

Damon takes the printed email, and reads quickly. "What? Who would do that? Is he mad?"

I hold back a guffaw. *Who would do that?* Does he have no idea? "He's OK now, we've sorted it out. But there's this—" I point to the email "—and a few other things. Olivia, do you care to explain?"

Her eyes go wide. "Care to explain what? What are you implying, Lil?" She puts a hand to her chest in mock surprise.

I sigh. "I think you know."

Damon scoffs. "Lil!" His eyes darken as he frowns over at me as if I'm crazy.

"What?"

He clucks his tongue. "I hope you're not suggesting you think my mother would send this, are you?" For a second I falter. His voice has a warning edge to it. I should have spoken up earlier.

I cross my arms. "Well, of course I am. She's the one who's been telling us we should change venues, and hire a different chef, one that was your supposed girlfriend..."

CeeCee wrings her hands on an apron. I know she's debating whether to speak up.

"God damn it, Lil. Why on earth would she do something like that? I can't believe you'd suggest it?" Damon's never spoken to me so sharply before; tears sting my eyes.

"Well, she did, Damon." My voice rises. "And she also visited Bessie and tried to get my dress shortened!"

Olivia inhales sharply. "I did no such thing!"

Damon clenches his jaw, as if he's furious. My heart races as I realize he doesn't believe me. "I don't know who's behind this but it certainly isn't my mother! I think you should apologize, Lil."

I fight the urge to stamp my foot in frustration. "Absolutely not!" I glare at Olivia. "Your mother has been making things hard since she arrived. She told me you hate small towns and that you were never planning on staying here. Is that right?"

Damon flinches momentarily.

"Oh, my God, Damon! You were never going to stay?"

He runs a hand over his face. "It wasn't like that, Lil. I was going to set up the shop, and just see."

"See what?"

He groans. "See if it made any money. If it did, I was going to hire someone to run it, and I'd go between here and New Orleans."

I want to cup my face and cry. "But you said when I first met you…"

He pulls me into a hug, but I push him away. "Lil."

"No, Damon. You told me you moved here so it'd be a safe place for Charlie to grow up. That you'd had enough of big cities. Now your mother is accusing me of taking you away from your child too. Am I? Do you want to move back to New Orleans?"

CeeCee's face is pure sadness. She's wringing the tea towel so hard that she's in danger of shredding it.

"Sometimes I think it'd be easier, but—"

I cut Damon off. "Then you should go, if you really don't want to be here."

"Lil, it's not like…"

Without another glance, I stalk off to the small office out back. Suddenly, it feels as though I don't know Damon at all. He lied to me when we first met, and this revelation shocks me to the core. It makes me wonder what else I don't know about him.

And I'm certain Olivia is happy she's finally made a wedge between us. I hear CeeCee mumble to Damon, and the jingle of the bell as they leave. Sadness overwhelms me that Damon wouldn't even hear me out when it came to explaining about his mother.

CeeCee finds me slumped in the chair, crying. "Lil, I think in the heat of the moment there was a lot said there that ain't quite right. You didn't stop to let Damon explain."

"Cee, he wasn't prepared to hear about how his mother is intent on wrecking our marriage before it's even started. I haven't seen him like that before…he wouldn't even take one second to consider what I said."

CeeCee tuts. "What would you do, Lil? If Damon sprung that on you about your mamma? Would you automatically assume he was right? Or would you think he was talking crazy?"

"It's not the same, Cee."

"Well, o' course it is! There's no way he's going to think his sweet-as-pie mother would stoop so low. Why would he? She's always laughing, and dishing out compliments, trying to help out. You're going to have to sort this out, with both of them."

I shake my head. "I'm the innocent one here, Cee."

"So?"

"What do you mean so? So why should I?"

"Because how else is Damon going to find out what you're saying is true?"

I huff. "Right now, I don't want to even look at him."

"Lil, there's four days until your wedding…just remember the fact you love that man, nothing else matters."

I swallow back any more conversation, knowing CeeCee'll just keep on telling me to fix it. I don't know if it's fixable. Damon was never going to stay here. And he thinks sometimes it'd be easier to move back to New Orleans. And there's Charlie. His gorgeous, bubbly daughter, who, by right, should have her daddy close by.

Not to mention his conniving mother, who he only sees as lovely. Suddenly the thought of getting married doesn't seem so merry.

I lock up the café. The icy wind blows my hair back as I dash to the truck. After spending the afternoon mulling it over, I know I have to talk to Damon, and sort everything out. My heart aches just thinking of him. I hate fighting, and I want to make it better. But there's no way I'm kowtowing when it comes to his mother.

Arriving home, I see the house is lit up. I sigh, relieved—for a moment I thought maybe he might have stayed elsewhere.

I walk inside. Damon's on the sofa in the front room.

"Hey," he says.

"Hey."

"Are we going to fix this?" He pats the cushion next to him.

I take my parka off and throw it on the end of the sofa. "I hope so."

"Lil, why would you think my mother would do something like that? You make her sound like some kind of monster."

I take my time replying, remembering CeeCee's stern warning about if our roles were reversed. "Since that first night in the café, she's been dishing out all these little comments that make me question everything. Bessie told me your mother walked in and started giving her instructions about my dress, Damon! You can go and ask her yourself! And she wanted to move the venue from day one, and then suddenly someone cancels Guillaume, from an email account in my name, that *isn't* actually my account? She wanted to make sure you were happy here. She said that to me. I feel like a fool, Damon. At first I doubted myself, sure I was reading too much into it, but now I am certain it's her. And then there's the doubt about you. Why did you say all those things to me when we first met if they weren't true?" As hard as it is to have this conversation, I feel better laying my cards on the table. I have to know Damon will support me now and forever. And I need to know where I stand.

"Lil, I had planned on moving here, but, like I said, I was going to go back and forth, if it was financially viable. But then I met you. We fell in love, and I had no intention of leaving after that. When I said I loved it here, and I wanted Charlie to have the experience of growing up somewhere safe, a town where people look out for one another, I meant it. I'd hoped that once she was old enough she might like to move here too. I don't want to move back to New Orleans, but sometimes, when we're fussing over sales figures, or worrying about the catering income, I yearn for a shop that makes a decent living because it's in a busy town. And that's all I meant by it."

I close my eyes, partly mollified by his answer, until I remember his mother, and her attempts to destroy the wedding. And maybe our relationship too. "Your mother managed to plant all these seeds of doubt. And you don't trust *me*. You believe your mother. I don't know how I'm supposed to get over that."

"I do trust you, Lil. But saying my mother is responsible for cancelling the venue…it's just not possible."

I resist the urge to scream in frustration. "Not just that, the other stuff too."

He sighs. "She's says she didn't do it, Lil. I know my mother—she's not like that."

"Well, who else would do it?"

"Let's just leave it for now."

Four days. And everything is up in the air. I'm angry at Damon. How can we just leave it? His mother for reasons unknown is set on ruining us and he doesn't even care. "I'm going to lie down. I'm not feeling great."

"Lil…"

I wake during the night and reach for Damon. He turns to face me, and in the dark room he says softly, "I'm sorry, Lil."

Half groggy, I say, "For which part?"

"For all of it. I've been awake all night worrying about it."

His skin is prickled with cold. I pull the quilt up, and thread my legs through his. "So what does that mean?"

"I guess…I need to really ask my mother if she had something to do with it all. It's not that I don't believe you—it's just that I can't see her doing any of that. I mean, what reason would she have?"

I run a hand along his arm to warm him. "I don't know. It doesn't make sense, but after the things she said I'm certain. I hope we can sort it out for all of our sakes."

"I'll talk with her tomorrow." He runs a finger across my hairline, and I close my eyes against the sensation. "I shouldn't have made you feel I wasn't on your side, Lil."

"It's OK. I probably would've done the same if you said that about my mamma."

CeeCee, as usual, was right.

CHAPTER EIGHT

Three days

"I'm glad you two lovebirds made up. I knew you would," CeeCee says.

I smile in response before saying, "I can't see how I'm ever supposed to work it out with Olivia, though. I can't see her admitting it, somehow."

"Wait and see, cherry blossom. You never can tell what's gonna happen; life sure can be complicated sometimes."

I blow my hair from my eyes. "It sure is."

An hour later, Damon walks into the café with his mother on his tail. *Here we go.*

I'm serving a customer who is taking his sweet time choosing. He can't decide between one of CeeCee's southern lane cakes, or a chocolate hazelnut meringue. CeeCee walks from the office out back to the sound of the bell jingling. Her mouth becomes a tight line when she sees Olivia.

"I'll serve, Lil," she says to me. "You go on and talk to Damon and his mother."

Olivia glares at me. I just shake my head, tired of the fight. "Let's go sit by the fire," I say.

Damon's face is taut with worry. He still pecks me on the cheek, which makes Olivia narrow her eyes. "I hoped we could sort this out, together."

I square my shoulders. "Great."

"OK, so…" he says slowly.

"OK, so, Olivia—" I decide I'm not going to pussyfoot around "—I know it was you who did all those things. *I know it.* Though why you did beats me. I think we can all move past it, though, if you admit what you did."

She surveys her fake nails before saying, "Really, Lil? It's ridiculous. I'm not that kind of person, and Damon knows that. What you're suggesting is pathetic. Something teenagers would do."

Damon sighs. "Well, there's no question someone did it. We have the email from Guillaume, and I talked to Bessie, and she said someone who looks remarkably like you came in and said Lil wanted her dress amended. I don't know what else to do here."

"To be perfectly honest, Damon, it's all too much for me." I turn to Olivia. "The centerpieces you found arrived. Did you want to explain those to Damon?"

She blushes. "What—you don't like them?"

I laugh at the absurdity of the situation. "Come on, Olivia! The *fake lilies* you bought are five feet tall, and are bright pink! I may as well put a flamingo on each table."

Damon looks from me to his mother. "What's this all about, Mother?" My stomach flips.

Olivia inhales sharply. "Well…I thought they were lovely."

I shake my head no. "They're comical, Olivia."

She doesn't even flinch when she says, "Damon, just because you're marrying a girl who said herself she wouldn't mind being wed in a field with a lame horse for a witness doesn't mean you need to take it out on me. Now, *Katie*, she would have made a nice wife."

I suck in a breath, bewildered by her resentment. Damon narrows his eyes. "What kind of thing is that to say? Jesus, Mother." His voice rises with every word.

"I'm sorry to say it, Damon, but I think you're making a bad decision. This whole—" she waves her hands around

"—place isn't you. You've made a rash choice. Your father and I are worried, that's all."

Damon rubs his face, and groans. "God! That's the dumbest thing I've ever heard. Dad definitely doesn't feel that way. I *know* he doesn't."

Olivia's face drops and she says quietly, "I'm looking out for you."

"By not accepting Lil? How's that looking out for me?" CeeCee serves customers, all the while darting glances my way. I nod almost imperceptibly, to tell her I'm OK.

Olivia's eyes shine bright with tears at Damon's outburst. Maybe she is just looking out for her son, but it sort of feels like being sucker punched when the reason she's behaving like a monster is because she feels as though Damon ran away and picked the first girl he saw, who in her mind isn't good enough.

"It's your life, Damon," she continues. "But I want you to know, I think your place is in New Orleans with your daughter."

"My place is here, with, Lil. And it will always be. I see more of Charlie now than I did when I was working all hours, so that doesn't wash with me."

I do feel for Olivia. There's obviously something lacking in her life to make her act such a way. And Damon finally believing me and standing up to her only makes me sad. Sad for her in a whole new way.

"I'll just butt out, then," Olivia says, her voice wobbling.

"Good idea," Damon snaps.

That afternoon we close up early. Mamma, Sarah and Missy sit at the kitchen bench finishing off their gingerbread milkshakes, slurping them back like kids.

CeeCee and I finish what we're doing, and get ready to close early. We bundle on our coats and scarves and walk up to Bessie's shop for the final dress fittings. I'm giddy with excitement, and hope my dress still fits after all the Christmas baking I've been sampling.

We're chatting away about the last few days and all that's happened when CeeCee stops dead in her tracks as her handbag vibrates. She pulls out her cell phone and plunges her hand into her bag for her reading glasses.

Her lips move as she silently reads the message to herself. "You go on ahead," she says as the light goes from her eyes.

My throat tightens. Something's wrong. "No, we'll wait," I say, my breath coming out with puffs of fog.

"It's Janey. I have to go…" Her voice cracks.

We instantly gather close and hug her. None of us speaks as we stand outside, the snow drifting around us, as we think of Walt and Janey, and what this might mean. Eventually Missy says, "Is she OK?"

CeeCee glances down to the message on her phone. "It doesn't say a lot. I better go. I'm sorry, Lil, sorry, girls." She turns on her heel and walks back in the direction of the café.

The four of us watch her retreat. She strides past the town Christmas tree, which sits in an apex on the side of the road near the Gingerbread Café. Its shrieking fairy lights don't catch her attention. Her head hangs low; she's lost in thought. I fight the urge to run after her, and squeeze her tight. I send up a prayer that it's good news about Janey that's called her away.

"Maybe Janey's better?" Mamma says almost in a whisper.

"Yes," Missy says. "Wouldn't that be something? She's better and she's home for Christmas." Her voice lilts.

"Imagine that," I say softly. "Let's hope that's what it is."

CeeCee's walked so fast she's only a speck in the distance. She must be going on home by the looks. Janey lives at the other end of town. I hope Janey is coming home for Christmas. And not because of any other reason.

We lace arms and walk with quick steps to Bessie's, eager to get out of the cold. I can't help picturing CeeCee's downcast face, and wish I could snap my fingers and make Janey better.

For a moment the sun peeks out and brightens the wintry day. With our boots on we trek through the slushy ice, passing shops along the main street. I wave at the local shop owners who stand on their stoops and ask about the wedding. I do my best to sound merry, even though my heart is heavy with worry for CeeCee. Each business façade is decorated with shiny tinsel, and flashing fairy lights. Wreaths of holly hang on doors. Mary-Rose's bath shop has a gorgeous Christmas tree in the window, made entirely from green bath bombs that she's stacked in a cone shape. "How don't they topple over?" Missy points to the bath bombs.

I shrug. "No idea, but I can smell them from here. Minty. We might need to detour in there on the way back."

"Sounds good," Sarah says. "I'll pick up some for Christmas presents."

We get to the small haberdashery shop, and push open the door to the sound of a sewing machine drumming into fabric. Bessie glances up from her work and cracks a smile. "Well, there you are, Lil. Girls." She pushes a tendril of silvery grey hair back into her clip. "Wait until you see your dresses now…" She takes her glasses off and blinks to focus.

Missy immediately goes to the oversized cane chair and tries to drop into it. "Give me a hand, Sarah. There's a chance I might get beached if I do this wrong."

Sarah laughs and guides Missy's bulk into the cavernous chair.

"Is CeeCee coming?" Bessie asks.

"No," I say, quickly. "She's got an errand to run."

Bessie nods. "Take a seat, girls. And I'll start the show, shall I?" We nod as Bessie trundles out back.

Missy pipes up, "Lil, enjoy this, OK? I know you're worried about Janey and CeeCee but it's not wrong to push it from your mind for a while. I know what you're like, but worry won't change a thing."

It's almost crazy how well my friends know me. "OK," is all I manage, knowing what she says is true. Guilt sneaks up on me at times, as if by enjoying this experience I'm doing CeeCee a disservice.

"Ready?" Bessie wanders back out.

"Oh, Bessie, I cannot wait to see them all!" Missy says, clapping.

I sit on a stool by the window. Bessie's shop is cluttered with swathes of fabric, and half-dressed mannequins. Sitting here makes me want to regress to childhood and play dress up. I can imagine pulling out lengths of shiny material and draping them over me or grabbing the feather boas and strutting around as if I'm a flapper from the twenties. It's like a Pandora's box of loveliness and Bessie holds the key. She can whip up an outfit in thirty minutes that would leave most designers envious. Missy gets most of her clothes made here—animal print and sequins are her weakness, though she'll give any loud, form-fitting fabric a go.

Sarah hunts through piles of sample fabrics, holding them up to the bright light to inspect up close. I wonder if she's contemplating her future wedding dress. Her relationship with Ridge is the stuff dreams are made of; he swept her off her feet, and treats her like a princess.

"Lil, I sewed those antique beads on, but you'll have to be careful you don't catch them on the satin when you're getting dressed otherwise we'll have pulls."

"Eek! So excited!" And suddenly I am. *The dress.* The kind of dress I've always wanted is seconds away from reality.

Bessie ambles over to a rack of clothes on hangers, individually wrapped in clear plastic bags, and picks the garment on the end. My breath catches. It's been a few weeks since I've seen my dress and I'm ruing the fact the candy canes we made have been so addictive.

Carefully, she takes the plastic away and drapes the dress over her arm to stop it touching the floor. "What do you think?" she says as she holds the coat hanger forward so we can see the beading.

Missy says, "Hoist me up, someone! I can't see!"

We laugh, and go to help her out of the chair.

Bessie points to the beads. "So I had to go slow, Lil, because I didn't want to pull the satin, but, as you can see, the beads are dazzling."

I gasp. It's the most gorgeous gown I've ever seen. The creamy satin shines in the dim shop. The antique beads glow as if they've got a secret, and I bet they have. I wonder where those beads came from—perhaps another wedding dress decades ago? The beading goes along the front of the straight neckline to give it some sparkle. They're burnished gold, with a tiny pearl inlay surrounded with diamonds that are so small they look like glitter. Added to the shimmer of the satin, it's almost as if the dress is lit up. "Wait until you see the back of it," Bessie says.

The gown is backless as the satin falls into a gathered cowl at the base of my spine. It's more daring than I'd usually do, but the effect is so dramatic, and timeless.

Mamma chokes back tears, "Oh, Lil, you're going to look like a movie star."

Sarah pats Mamma's back. "Lil, it's absolutely breath-taking. I haven't seen anything like it before."

Missy lets out a squeal. "Can you get on in there and try it, Lil? If I go into labor and miss seeing it on, there's gonna be trouble!"

I laugh, and nod. "Less of the labor talk, Missy. You need to wait at least three more days, you know."

She cackles. "Yeah, I know." She runs a hand over her belly. "I told the little man that a million times, so let's hope he's listening."

Bessie walks to the change room with the dress held aloft. "OK, Lil, it's time. Shout when you're undressed and I'll help you put it on so we're careful with the beading." She's a diminutive woman, with a soft smile, but her eyes, bright with excitement over the dress, remind me of us at the café when we've baked something amazing. The joy in crafting something from raw materials.

"Lucky I wore my best underwear."

Bessie grins, her eyes shining with laughter. "Trust me, girls, I've seen it all from so-called granny panties, to full-length body-suction underwear. I'm oblivious to anything bar the dress."

The girls laugh, and I shut the curtain and undress.

"Full-length body-suction underwear?" I hear Mamma say. "I don't know what that is but I need some."

Missy replies, "I've seen pull-me-in panties, but a full body suit, I don't know…the muffin top has to go somewhere. With a full length body suit on wouldn't it push it all the way up to my neck? I'd have neck fat!"

"The mind boggles," Sarah's voice carries through to the changing room.

I grin at Missy's muffin-top exaggeration. She's voluptuous, and flaunts her curves with pride. Her form-fitting ensembles make me shake my head in wonder.

There's not many people who could pull off that kind of style with such pizzazz. With her heavily made-up eyes, and big auburn curls, and her constant hair fluffing, she's like a screen siren from another era.

Pulling back the curtain, I motion to Bessie that I'm undressed. My skin breaks out in goose bumps despite the heating in the shop, half from nerves and half from cold. There's no mirror in the change room, so the girls will see the dress on before I do.

Bessie steps into the small space with me, and slides the curtain closed. She carefully unzips the side of the dress. "So, you'll need to step into it, Lil, and then I'll pull it up, and you gently ease your arms in the sleeves."

"OK."

Bessie holds the dress as I gently stand inside like she instructed. It's like a creamy wave at my feet.

"Here we go, Lil. Stand up straight, and I'll pull it up, and we can see how it fits."

I hold my arms out as Bessie glides the dress over my body, and zips it up. She fluffs it out at my feet. It feels deliciously smooth cascading down my body. I run my hands softly down the side. It's so different from when I had a fitting three weeks ago, when there were pins holding it roughly together.

"How does it feel?"

"Like perfection," I say almost inaudibly.

Bessie stands back to survey me, before straightening the neckline, and pinching the satin on one side to make it even. She stands back again and folds her arms. With a grin she whispers, "They're going to cry, Lil. When they see how beautiful you look."

I'm grinning like a fool as excitement courses through me. "Do I really look beautiful?" I think of myself compared with the other girls as more of a plain Jane. But on my wedding day, I want to be glamorous. I want to make the extra effort so Damon catches his breath when he sees me, a vision in satin, walking down the aisle to him.

Bessie gives me a kind smile. "Lil, beautiful doesn't even sum it up. Wait until you see it. You are a show-stopper."

I nod my thanks, not trusting myself to speak as my emotions roil around.

"What's going on in there?" Missy screeches. "Enough with the oohing and aahing—we want to see this masterpiece!"

I take a deep breath and smooth the fabric, wishing with all my heart that CeeCee were on the other side of the curtain with the girls. Bessie fusses with the train and says, "Ready?"

Nervous, I say, "Yes."

She inches out of the change room and says, "I give you the soon-to-be Mrs. Guthrie." Slowly she inches the curtain across. I step out of the change room.

The girls gasp, high and loud. Missy covers her mouth with her hand as her eyes go wide.

"Oh, golly, Lily-Ella that's absolutely…" Mamma chokes back a sob "…stunning! No one is going to be able to take their eyes off of you." Tears fall down her face, as she cries unabashedly.

"Thank you, Mamma. Don't cry! You'll start Missy off again!" I swallow back my own tears. I have a feeling Bessie's made some kind of magic happen for me.

"It's too late," Mamma sobs.

Sarah laughs; her eyes are glassy too. "Golly, this crying jag is contagious! Lil, I haven't seen a dress so dazzling before. The way the bias hugs your curves…"

"Wait." I hold a finger up. "Do you want to see the back?"

Missy screeches yes.

I turn slowly, careful not to step on the train.

"Sweet Jesus!" Missy yells. "Lil! You're killing me! *Give me the box of tissues!*" Sarah laughs and hands her the tissue box. "Lil, I've seen a lot of wedding dresses before, but nothing like this. It's out of this world, *stunning*! You're making me yell because I'm so freaking happy!"

Bessie laughs at Missy. "Happy yelling is a good thing. Lil, are you ready to see yourself?"

"Yes, I am!"

The girls gather behind me as Bessie wheels over a mirror that's covered with a sheet.

"OK, one, two, three." Bessie angles the mirror to my height, and pulls down the sheet.

My heart skips a beat as I take in the sight of myself in the mirror. The dress looks every inch as stunning as it feels. The beads along the front blink at me like friends. The satin shimmers as I touch it again, my hands drawn to the silky feel. "Bessie..." I can't form words. The girl in the mirror doesn't look like me. She's been replaced with a blond-haired girl draped in a creamy satin vision, her cheeks are flushed, and her blue eyes bright with happiness.

The girls giggle behind me. "Goddess, right?" Missy says.

"I'm completely besotted by it. Thank you, Bessie." I turn to her. "I knew it would be amazing, but this is just..."

"Ravishing?" Sarah adds. "Spectacular? Captivating? I can keep going."

I laugh. "Yes, all of those."

Bessie smoothes down her own dress. "I'm glad you like it, Lil."

"I love it. I don't want to take it off. It's not only the look of it, it's the way it feels." What I don't say is how different it is from my first wedding dress, which was all puffy sleeves, a voluminous frou-frou affair. This gown, being cut on the bias, accentuates my country-girl curves in a way that makes me feel beautiful. I can't wait to lock eyes with Damon as I enter the church, and walk to him, to my future.

Mamma dabs at her eyes. "Bessie, sometimes I think you should be in Paris, or Milan, or one of those fashion capitals, not stuck here in Ashford, but I'm mighty glad you are. You've made my daughter's wedding day even more perfect."

Bessie smiles. "I wouldn't last five minutes in a big town. But thank you, it was my pleasure. It's not often I get to make a bridal gown, so when I do it's extra fun for me."

Sarah says, "Let's take a few photos. Maybe CeeCee might like to see them?"

"Aww, that's lovely," Mamma says as Sarah pulls out her phone.

The girls smooth out the small train, and I beam, for once happy to be photographed.

"Right," I say once they've snapped away. "Let's see you girls in your bridesmaid dresses!"

CHAPTER NINE

Two days

The next morning, I wake an hour before my alarm. It's dark out and the wind is so fierce the shutters shake and *woo* as if there's an eerie presence outside. I know it's only my worry over CeeCee that's making me feel uneasy. I creep from under the covers so I don't wake Damon. I'd spent the better half of the night trying to call her but her phone went straight to voicemail.

In the pitch-black room, I fumble for some clothes as quietly as I can. It's too early for Damon to wake, and he has his bachelor party tonight and will probably be out much later than me. I'll be with the girls, having our movie marathon, and make-up trial ay Missy's house. I scrawl him a quick note to let him know I've gone in to work early.

Ten minutes later, I'm showered and dressed and race to my truck; the cold outside steals the air from my lungs. It seems every winter gets that little bit more frozen, and I'm careful not to slip on the fresh snowfall. The truck door makes an almighty creak as I pull it open and I wince, hoping I haven't woken Damon up. Though the truck doing its usual three-minute warm-up to start will wake up anyone in the vicinity who's not a deep sleeper.

"Come *on*." I push the accelerator and try to cajole the motor to roar into life. I turn the heat up, but it comes out in a frosty cloud until the motor warms.

Finally, it decides to start, and I reverse out, thinking I may as well have walked by the time it's taken to get the truck to comply. Driving at a snail's pace, I focus on the road, lest I suddenly slip and lose control.

I chug down the street, wiping the inside of the windscreen as I go. The main street is sleepy with no one about; as I drive closer the lights from the Gingerbread Café shine out. She's there. I knew she would be. When something's eating at CeeCee she bakes. We both do.

I park around back, and go inside. "Cee?" The furious clicking of computer keys travels from the office. It's the only space in the café that doesn't get the warmth from the fire. I shrug into my coat in the chilly room. "What're you doing?" I peek over her shoulder. "Is that your matron of honor speech?"

She stops and swivels on the chair to face me. "Yeah, Lil. Kinda difficult to express how I feel about y'all in just a few pages." Tears spill down her sweet brown face.

I crouch down to her level. "They don't look like happy tears, Cee."

She gives me a sad smile that almost breaks my heart in two. "They ain't, they surely ain't."

My stomach drops. "Go on, I'm listening."

She nods, and takes a deep breath. Her hands shake so she clasps them together. "I'm sorry I didn't get to see you in your dress yesterday."

I wave her away. "It doesn't matter. You'll see it on the day." I realize in our excitement we'd forgotten to text her the photos of us in our dresses yesterday.

A sob escapes her. "That's just it, Lil. I might not see you in it at all."

"What? Why?"

"It's Janey. He...they..."

I uselessly pat CeeCee's leg, wishing I knew what to do or to say.

"The doctors say there ain't…there…ain't nothin' more they can do for Janey." Her face falls; as she is wracked with sobs and fresh tears spill. I'm at a loss of how to help her. My mind gropes for words that won't form. I try so hard to keep it together for CeeCee's benefit.

"My best friend…my longest friend is coming home. Coming back to Ashford to say her goodbyes."

"Oh, Cee." My fight to stay reserved for her crumbles and my eyes fill with unshed tears.

She shakes her head, and again I notice how much smaller she seems. Her grief is somehow making her fold in on herself.

I grapple with the right words. "You need to be with Janey. Nothing else matters right now." I can't imagine getting married without CeeCee there. It wouldn't feel right, as if a piece of me were missing, but I know that Janey needs her. And that's what friendship is. Letting go, when you so desperately want to clutch on.

She looks up, and cracks a half-hearted smile. "You a good girl, Lil. Always have been."

"So…when's Janey coming home?"

CeeCee takes a long shuddery breath. "Tomorrow. They say…" her voice takes on a slight edge "…that she has a week, like she's planning some holiday or some such. I hate the way they guess like that…a week, almost like we should mark it on the calendar. How'd they even know such a thing? What about if we want *more* than a week? What if she ain't ready to go yet? They never think o' that, do they? What gives them the right to flounce around healthy as can be and put a number on someone's life? It ain't right."

"They don't know. How could they?"

"I know what the comin' days are gonna be like, Lil. I know from when Curtis passed on." She pauses, expels a shaky breath. "It brings it all back, and I know I need to find strength somewhere in here—" she taps her heart "—for Janey. I don't wanna tumble into that dark place again."

I move to hug her. She's dusty with flour, and smells like cinnamon. "Strength, Cee? You got it in spades. Strength is being there when it's hard. And helping out when your heart is breaking. And you've been there every step of the way for Janey. Not just now, but a whole lifetime. No question it's going to be a dark time. But we'll all be here for you, and Janey. And Walt. He's sure going to need a friend like you, Cee."

When CeeCee's husband Curtis died, she barricaded herself in her house. No one saw her for weeks after the funeral. It was as if she just stopped living. She didn't answer her phone, or her door. Stopped going to church. I'd only just opened up the café—it was so new all I sold back then were gingerbread men, and instant coffee. I wasn't making a dime. In fact I was losing money. But I knew CeeCee needed a reason to wake up every day. So I went and dragged her out of her house, and insisted she help me at the café. It wasn't long before she learned to smile again. And in the midst of it all, I made a friend I'll cherish for ever.

"Lil, I'm just…I'm *every* kind o' sad. How you gonna cope here all alone? What about the wedding? What if I can't make it?"

The thought of CeeCee missing my wedding makes my heart seize but it's nowhere near as important as being with Janey. "You never know, Cee—what if you can make it? What if Janey's doing better than expected? And if not, then I'll be more proud knowing you're with Janey."

"I know, you like a daughter to me, that's all. It'd be like missing my own kid's wedding. But we'll see, we surely will, cause, no matter what they say, I ain't giving up on my friend just yet. The good Lord performed miracles before, and there's still time to hope."

I nod sagely, knowing that deep down CeeCee knows what's coming but holds onto a tiny thread of *'what if?'*.

"What about the café, Lil? How you gonna manage?"

"Easy. I'm sure I'll have plenty of helpers." Once everyone finds out Janey's back and CeeCee's gone to care for her, folk around here will be lining up to give me a hand. It's the way things are done in Ashford. If you fall there'll be someone to lift you. "And if all else fails, I'll ask Mamma. She's already ruined the wedding cake—there's not much else she can do surely?"

"I'm gonna stow away our good pots and pans."

I smile. "Good idea. And maybe we'll hide the blender, and anything else she might be able to blow up."

We giggle at that. So Mamma's a little on the clumsy side—probably because she's always talking to someone and forgets what she's meant to be doing.

"Why don't you go on home, Cee? Take a break. You're going to need—"

She cuts me off abruptly. "I don't need to sit there and dwell on it alone, Lil. I want to be here with you."

I bite the inside of my lip to stop myself crying. "Well, OK."

She hoists herself up from the chair. "There ain't nothing for it except a bit of baking," she says, resolute.

We embrace in the small office, and I promise myself I'll do all I can to be there for CeeCee over the coming days. "So tell me all about that dress o' yours…" CeeCee says as we head out front to find some comfort in baking.

Later that evening, we're all gathered around Missy's kitchen bench, giggling like schoolgirls as she attempts to make up my face so I can choose what colors suit me best for the big day. Then we intend to sloth out for our chick-flick marathon.

By now Damon will be gambling up a storm with his friends at his casino-themed bachelor party. I smile, thinking of him trying to perfect his poker face. I'd know instantly if he had a bad hand. That little wrinkle near his mouth would deepen.

"Stop blinking, Lil!"

"I can't help it!" I squirm backwards. "It feels like you're gluing my eyelashes together."

"Listen to her! Being tortured by a mascara wand." Missy shakes her head, and cups my chin, trying to stop me from moving. It's difficult not to blink while she's batting at my eyelashes.

Sarah and CeeCee move to Missy's red leather sofas to chat about their latest bonk-buster reads. In light of what's coming for CeeCee I think tonight is just what she needs to revive her soul for the sadness approaching.

Mamma sits on a stool next to me and pushes her face close to mine. "What?" I say, trying not to wiggle as Missy continues torturing me.

"What, aren't I allowed to gawk at my own daughter?"

"It's the way you're doing it. It doesn't suit me, does it?"

Even though I asked Missy to go light with the make-up, it feels as if it's been trowelled on.

"It certainly does suit you," Mamma says. "If only you'd stop pulling those faces."

Missy stands back to survey me. "Hmm." She steps forward and dabs at my lower eyelashes with the brush, and says, "There. Done."

"Well, let's see."

Missy holds the round mirror to her belly, "Girls, you see it first—what do you think? More rouge?"

Sarah bounds up from the sofa first. "Wow, what a transformation. No, no more rouge."

CeeCee stands and snaps a photo. "That's going on Spacebook. Stop fussing." She slaps my hand away as I go to fumble with my eyelashes.

"Missy," Mamma says, "you're an artist. You made that blank canvas into something spectacular."

I roll my eyes. "Blank canvas, geez."

"Well, you know what I mean."

"Let me see!" I say, excited.

"Don't touch your curls!" Missy yelps. She spent the better part of an hour wrapping locks of my hair around rollers.

"No." Missy laughs and puts the mirror face down on the bench. "Let me finish your hair first."

I groan. "Just one little peep?"

She laughs and hands me the mirror. My eyes made-up look bigger somehow, and brighter. Missy used a special technique to contour my cheekbones, which takes away some of the fullness in my face. My lips are a natural pink with a little gloss to make them shine. "Geez, Missy, I don't look like this when I put make-up on myself."

"You're welcome," she says with a huge smile. "I am so jealous of your long eyelashes it kills me when you don't even appreciate them. Totally wasted on you."

I laugh. "Maybe not. Maybe I will start wearing gloop. I can't believe it…"

"Let's unwind the rollers and finish your hair. You're seriously going to be the best-looking bride I've ever seen."

"I'm dizzy with all these compliments."

"Get used to it," Missy says. "You're going to be showered with them soon."

I glance over at CeeCee, who's suddenly quiet, staring off into the distance. She's going to tell the girls about Janey tonight, but she was worried it'd cast a pall over the evening. I reassured her that they'd want to know, and being together whether we're laughing or crying is all that matters.

CHAPTER TEN

One day

The café seems lifeless without CeeCee's company. She came in early this morning to tidy up a few loose ends, but I sent her on her way with a basket of Christmas sweets, and a hamper I filled with ham and cheeses and fresh bread. I thought I'd drop fresh provisions at their front door each day so none of them have to leave Janey's side. I only wish there were something I could do to bring that light back into CeeCee's eyes. And make Janey miraculously better as well.

It was tough saying goodbye to CeeCee. Knowing what she's going to face. And sweet Janey home to say goodbye. This town won't be as bright without her. Gloom settles over me as I think of what their family is going through.

Mamma flutters around the café and tries to help but has the worst butterfingers I've ever seen. The day before the wedding and I've still got so much to do, including making another wedding cake, after the display-fridge disaster. My bridal party is coming in for the morning tea we'd planned to welcome Olivia. And now she's not even going to attend. While Damon and I are back on track, it seems as though everything else has fallen apart.

Taking a deep breath, I reach for a pencil, and decide to make a to-do list rather than let my mind spin with reminders.

Mamma ambles over, frowning. "What have I done this time?" she asks, holding what's supposed to be a red velvet cake with raspberry frosting, but instead looks like a science experiment gone wrong. For some reason she's smothered it with blue icing, which has run with the red, making a deep purple ooze.

"Did you follow the recipe? Why did you cover it in blue?"

"To make it pop. And of course I followed the recipe, Lily-Ella, but when Mary-Rose came in and I got to talking, well, I forget exactly what stage I was up to, so I took a guess. It'll be all right, won't it? What if I cover the icing with blueberries?"

It looks like a 'baking gone bad' after shot. "Have you tasted it?"

She tilts her head. "You know I haven't, Lil. Look at it. Does it look like there's a slice missing to you?"

It's hard to say whether there's a slice missing, as it doesn't resemble a cake as much as an erupting volcano. "Not even blueberries can disguise that, Mamma. Throw it in the bin and start over. And this time tick the ingredients as you go."

"You're too finicky," she says and eyes me as she places the cake on the bench. "I'm not throwing it out. That took me two hours to make."

While Mamma studies the recipe for the umpteenth time, I finish my fruit mince pies, by cutting a star shape out of pastry. They're our biggest seller right before Christmas and I know folk around here will be expecting some of the delicious little morsels, wedding or no.

Today is my last day in the café, and I want to make sure my regulars don't feel as if I've neglected them. Mamma says I'm being silly and should just shut the café and enjoy the last afternoon before the wedding, but I can't. This business means everything to me. It's not just about making money; it's about providing something for the town. They've come to rely on us, and I'd rather not leave them in the lurch right before Christmas. There are lots of folks who don't have family here, and we make sure they've got all they need over the Christmas break. Besides, going home after the morning tea wouldn't help. I'd sit there alone worrying over things I can't change, like the fact I've caused a rift between Damon and his mother. Even if it's no fault of mine, I still *feel* guilty.

I walk with the tray of fruit mince pies to bake in the oven when I trip over something, the tray shoots out of my hands and crashes to the floor, the pies a squishy mess, as fruit scatters every which way.

"Whoops," Mamma says. "I shouldn't have left those pots there. I was looking for one of those—" I stop her talking by holding up my hand.

She studies the floor. "I don't think they're fixable, somehow."

I close my eyes and count to ten, one step away from losing my mind.

"Lil?" she asks.

I'm clenching my jaw tight so I don't yell at her. "Don't. Don't say a word."

She shrugs. "It didn't take you long to whip that up. Come on…" She squeezes my arm. "Start another, everyone will be here soon."

"Please. Go to the other side of the bench. Take your mess, all of it, and don't move from that spot."

Mamma's spread mixing bowls from one end of the bench to the other. Eggshells litter the floor where she's knocked them off. She's pulled out every single pot from under the bench and left them sitting in disorderly piles on the floor. The sink is stacked with dishes that she hasn't put in the dishwasher next to her. For a completely orderly woman she is the extreme opposite in the kitchen.

"OK. OK. Sheesh, Lily-Ella, you make it sound as though I've set the place on fire!" Just as the words leave her mouth I do smell fire.

"Oh, my God!" I push past her and slam a tea towel down on the baking paper that has caught alight from being left too close the flame on the stove where she was boiling water.

The baking paper falls to the floor, still smoldering. I stamp on the lick of flame as the smoke detectors begin to wail overhead.

"Oh, dear." She leans over my shoulder. "That's quite loud. How do you make that stop?" she shouts in my ear.

I take a stool and climb up to stop the fire alarm. My ears buzz from the noise. I step down, and hold my head in my hands. If only CeeCee could see this, she'd be laughing her southern haw, and finding the funny side. When I peek through my fingers, I bite back on manic laughter. The kitchen resembles a kindergarten, almost as if a child came in and painted the place with food.

"So what's next?" she asks innocently.

I scoff. "Out!" I point to the door. I should've known Mamma would be no use. She's downright dangerous in a kitchen, and, as annoyed as I am, I really should've expected it.

"But...what?"

"Out," I say through clenched teeth.

She manages to slip on the gooey fruit on the floor and I catch her arm to right her. I raise my eyebrows.

She blushes, and runs a hand through her hair streaking blue icing through it as she goes. "It's not as easy as it looks, this baking caper, is it?" With a grimace she rips a section of paper towel and wipes uselessly at her hair.

"No." I know she means well, but it'll be easier if she's out of the way so she doesn't destroy anything else.

"OK, darling, well, I just hope it's cleaned up in time." She pecks me on the cheek and grabs her coat off the rack and walks into the snowy day. "I'll go see the girls, see if they need anything…" her voice is resigned.

The doorbell jingles as I'm bent over scooping up the mess with a dustpan. "Won't be a minute," I call without looking up.

"Did you have a food fight?"

I glance up sharply to Olivia's voice. As usual she's immaculately dressed, her hair perfect, and here I am on my knees with cake in my hair, the kitchen a screaming disaster.

She steps over pots and grabs an apron off the back door, sliding the tie over her head. "I'll stack the dishwasher first."

My mouth is opening and closing like a fish out of water.

It takes a minute for my brain to catch up with my mouth. "Umm, OK."

Without any fuss she piles the dirty dishes away, and wipes down the benches.

When that's done she clasps her hands together. "Right." She picks up the recipe from the bench, and checks off the ingredients before adding them to a bowl.

I tie my hair back and try to act as if I'm in control. Olivia appearing right when I need a hand without me asking her surprises me. There's been no word from her since the confrontation in the café. I hope this means we'll be able to work things out, but I'm hesitant too. I wonder if I can trust her after everything she's done? And maybe she's here to cause more trouble. I shake the negative thought away, until she proves otherwise I'll play nice.

"This won't take long," she says. "What shall I start afterwards?"

"It would be great if you could make some gingerbread men."

"Easy. I used to make those when I was first married." She's wearing one of our old aprons, which looks raggedy over her stylish grey pant suit. As usual she's coiffed to perfection, her hair clipped back into an elegant chignon, and her make-up naturally flawless. "We didn't have a lot back then, so made do with whatever we had." She shrugs, and gives me a small smile.

"But...?" The Guthries have always had money; it's gone back for generations.

"Yes, there's a shocking little skeleton for you. I was married before I met George." She looks into the space past my head as she recalls the memory. "He worked hard for us. Neither of us had much, and nor did our families. But that didn't matter a jot."

She was married before?

She hunts through cupboards for ingredients before returning to the prep bench. "He worked in a factory, long hours for little money. But I took great delight in packing him lunch with whatever I could fancy up, so he felt like we had lots. No matter the weather, I'd stand outside and wave him off as he walked the three miles to work each day before dawn."

I'm too bamboozled to respond, and it seems Olivia has no intention of letting the story finish there. "We were childhood sweethearts. We fell in love before we even knew what the word meant. Straight out of school, we married, and in my simple hand-sewn dress I felt like the luckiest girl alive." She lets out a hollow laugh. "But happiness can be taken away in the blink of an eye." She clicks her fingers.

"What happened?" I don't know why, but I have the feeling Olivia's story has a point, as if she's trying to make amends with me.

She measures flour into a cup before saying: "It was his twenty-second birthday, seems so young in retrospect, but back then we felt so grown up. I'd waved him off to work. Retreated inside and made an apple pie with fresh fruit stolen from the trees in a neighbor's yard. There it sat cooling, waiting for nightfall for him to come home. But he didn't. He didn't ever come home again."

I gasp. "Why?"

"There was an accident at the factory. He was rushed to the hospital. I sat in the dark at home, waiting, wanting to walk outside to find him, worrying I'd miss him if I left the house. There was a knock at the door. *And I just knew.* He was gone. I could feel it. The light was dimmer. Something was missing from the world. *He* was missing. For a long time I sat at that kitchen table, night after night, hoping he'd come back. That it was some horrible joke someone had played on me and he was really alive. How could he be taken from me? It seemed like the worst kind of cruelty." Her usual composure is gone, and her face crumples.

"Oh, Olivia." I place the bowl down, and move to hug her.

She wipes under her eyes. "It was a long time ago."

"But you were married? You loved him," I say, my voice soft.

With a sad smile she says, "I loved him more than anything, still do. He pops into my dreams every now and then, making sure I don't forget him. I guess, in a way it's why I also pictured Katie and Damon together. That somehow they'd find that magic too being childhood sweethearts. But—" she laughs "—I had no idea she was gay. Damon kept that pretty close to his chest."

"Why are you telling me this, Olivia?" I can't quite fathom how she's gone from treating me like an enemy to now a confidante.

"When I first met George, he sensed I was broken inside. I didn't tell him about my first husband immediately. I didn't want to tarnish the memory. He was so patient with me, so loving. I honestly didn't think I'd be able to fall in love again, didn't think I was capable, but George with his indefatigable patience and sweet soul was hard to resist. However his mother didn't like me. In fact she did everything she could to stop the marriage happening, said I was only after the Guthrie money. But I loved George with all my heart, and the fact he was wealthy didn't matter. Remember, I'd made do without much my whole life up until that point, and if he had to give all his money away to prove our love was real then that would've been fine by me. At first I didn't spend a dime of George's money, I was too scared to be labelled a gold-digger, but then we moved away from his parents, from Ashford altogether, and I became enraptured with the moneyed lifestyle. It wasn't long before that girl who baked whatever she could scratch together to make her husband smile married another man, and lost her way. And then treated you the very same way my mother-in-law did me."

My mind spins with questions. "Does Damon know about your first husband?"

Her eyes widen and she shakes her head. "No." Her eyes are glassy with tears and I know she's wondering whether she's done the right thing trusting me with her confidence.

I touch her arm gently, and say, "If you want to keep it between us, I'll never say anything, Olivia."

Her face relaxes, and she loses the pinched look from a moment before. "I'd appreciate that, Lil. I really would. Seems like it's stayed a secret for so long now, why not for ever?" She resumes adding ingredients into the bowl in front of her and I smile to myself. Yet again the magic of baking manages to distract her from her hurt.

"My lips are sealed. I'm glad you shared it with me." She's more composed so I move back to my side of the prep bench and continue with another batch of fruit mince pies.

Olivia takes a steadying breath. "I'm sorry it had to get to this. And I apologize again. I guess I didn't realize I'd grown too big for my boots until Rosaleen came and gave me a piece of her mind."

My eyebrows shoot up. "Rosaleen?"

Olivia leans against the bench. "Yes. We were friends a long time ago. She knew me when I first moved to Ashford, poorer than a church mouse."

"But she never said a word to me?"

"Oh, Rosaleen knows how to keep a secret…"

I go to speak, and then stop. If there's one thing I *wouldn't* associate with Rosaleen, it would be her ability to hold a confidence. "What did she say to you?" Surprise creeps into my voice, despite trying to keep it neutral.

Olivia throws her head back and laughs. "All manner of things, enough to make me realize what a fool I've been. She told me I'd done wrong by the twenty-two-year-old girl that came to Ashford with nothing. *Me.* And it made me think. I spent a whole day mulling over what she said. And I realized she was right. Where did that happy-go-lucky young girl go?" Olivia drops her gaze and spins her wedding ring around. She's silent for an age before glancing back up at me. "And what gives me the right to meddle in Damon's love life? And it was never about you really, Lil It was more I wanted him home, closer to us, closer to Charlie." She walks around the bench and takes my hand like a mother would do. "The way I've acted, it's embarrassing. Like some kind of crazed fool for thinking I know what's best, when I hadn't even had five minutes with you."

Her face is a picture of remorse, and for the life of me I can't dislike her. She's been so honest, and in some small way I understand her reasons, even if I don't agree with the way she's gone about it.

"I don't know what to say…" I hadn't expected Olivia would be so forthright in admitting her deception, and I especially didn't think there'd be a story like that behind it.

"I don't expect you would. You should, by rights, kick me out of your lovely café, because that's what I deserve. Some part of me just wanted Damon back in New Orleans closer to us when we're there. We don't see Charlie all that often any more because she flies here for school holidays…I guess I thought he was hiding out here after divorcing Dianne, and settling because he wanted to get away. I'm so sorry, Lil. I know how completely wrong I was. Damon gave me a piece of his mind. George isn't speaking to me because he knows I sent the email to Guillaume. I left it open on the computer. When I invited the Guthries that you hadn't, they said they wouldn't come, that if you wanted a simple wedding then what right did they have to barge in? It seems that I was wrong on all counts."

I smile at Olivia; for the first time it's genuine. "So where to from here?"

"Well, we have a morning tea to host, and a certain little girl is en route from the airport with Damon's cousin."

I can't help beaming. I love Charlie like she's my own child, and I'm beyond excited to see her. "She's landed?"

Olivia nods and returns my huge grin, sensing I think, how much Charlie *and* Damon mean to me. "Just before I came here. Damon's gone home to meet them there."

An aura of silent forgiveness passes between us. I can't help feeling overwhelmed with relief. "Well, OK. We better get these desserts done."

We set to work, my mind spinning with everything Olivia's confessed. I can't believe out of all the people to set things right it was Rosaleen. And it's not like her to keep a secret—that she knew Olivia half a lifetime ago. Wonders will never cease.

Olivia and I have just finished laying the trestle table with the finger food for the morning tea, when a squeal makes me jump. I swirl to see Charlie there, her blue eyes bright with excitement.

"Lil!" she yells out and throws herself at me. I pick her up and hug her tight. "Daddy wouldn't let me go in my bedroom! Says there's a surprise in there but I have to wait for you!" She speaks in exclamations as her words tumble out.

Her long blond hair tickles my face. "He made you wait?" I say, secretly glad he did. I've been desperate to see her face when she finds her flower-girl outfit waiting for her.

"Yep!" She wiggles in my arms as she sees Olivia over my shoulder. "Grandma!" I place Charlie down and she runs into Olivia's outstretched arms.

It's plain by Olivia's cry of joy how much she loves Charlie. She rains kisses over the little girl's face as Charlie squeals with laughter.

"Where's CeeCee?" Charlie says, scanning the café.

"She's helping a friend," Olivia says. "I'm sure she'll be along to see you just as soon as she can."

Charlie pouts. "But I was going to help her make a gingerbread house."

"Well," I say, "did you know your grandma is a pretty good helper too? How about we set you up now and you can decorate it while everyone's here for the morning tea?"

She gives me an impish grin. "OK."

Smiling, I go to the cabinet where we keep our gingerbread-house kits and take one out. I go to the kitchen and mix up a bowl of icing sugar, and take Charlie's apron from the door. It never fails to make me smile, her child-size chocolate-colored apron Damon bought her last Easter, covered with a smattering of smiley-faced gingerbread men.

I cover the coffee table with newspaper and set Charlie's supplies along it. She's chattering away to her grandma telling her all about the tree house my neighbors have, and the friends she wants to see in Ashford. For a seven-year-old she's well adjusted to the huge changes that have taken place in her life, but I'm always wary that anything could upset that fine balance.

Olivia's like a different person in Charlie's presence: her features are relaxed and happy; she doesn't hold herself so stiffly. Maybe things really will be OK for all of us going forward.

Charlie stands beside me, her hands covering her mouth as if she's trying to stop the glee from falling out. Olivia crouches down, and begins to arrange the walls of the gingerbread house so Charlie can ice them together.

The doorbell jingles and Olivia says, "You go, Lil. I'll keep Charlie amused."

Charlie claps her hands and throws a cushion on the floor to sit on.

I turn to the customer and see Walt. My heart leaps to my throat. A much older, faded-looking Walt. He's without his usual threadbare earmuff hat, and looks wrong without it, as if he's missing a part of himself.

"Hey, Walt." My voice carries the sadness from my heart.

"Lil, how you doing?" His voice is gruff.

"Good, good." I usher him into the warmth of the café, immediately wanting to ply him with food and drinks because that's all I know how to do in times of need.

"I came in to pass on my congratulations, and to thank you for the baskets of food you've sent over. Janey and the kids surely do appreciate it. And CeeCee says your pie is almost as good as hers.

That brings a faint smile to my lips. "How's Janey doing, Walt? Do you need anything?" My mind reels trying to think of what I could possibly do to help. But I know with CeeCee there, and Janey and Walt's grown-up kids, they'd have everything covered.

He runs a hand through his sparse hair, and takes a moment before saying, "We're lucky to have so many folk we call good friends, you included, Lil. Times like this I can't tell you how much it means..." His voice cracks. "CeeCee being there, it's like a balm for Janey. She sits there with her, praying for her, reading to her. It's taken some of Janey's fear away...of leaving us..."

"Walt—"

"No, it's OK. After all these months it still doesn't seem real. I keep thinking I'll wake up and find it was just a bad dream. But, anyway, Lil. We know how hard it must be without CeeCee here, and what with the wedding and all. I wanted to say thank you in person."

"There's no need for thanks. Nothing would keep CeeCee away, and nothing is as important as Janey right now."

He shakes his head; his eyes glisten with tears. "Janey so wanted to see you walk down the aisle, Lil."

I press my lips together to stem the tears that threaten to flow. Janey's been like an adopted aunty most of my life. Keeping up to date with everything through CeeCee. Those two are like little girls when they get together and start talking nineteen to the dozen. And Walt, a man who lives for his family, and his furniture shop. Who will he be without Janey?

"I would have loved that, Walt. But weddings, they're not so important as time with your family."

"Don't let this stop you from celebrating, Lil. Weddings are a joy, especially when it's a for-ever type of love… Cee's told us all about you and Damon. I hope it's everything you imagine it will be and more. It's rare: real love, so cherish it. I know I have…"

He shoves his hands into his pockets and nods, unable to continue talking. "I should go."

"Send all our love, Walt. And we're all here for you."

"Thanks, Lil. Be seeing you."

He heads outside, and doesn't give his shop a backward glance.

Olivia says softly, "Why don't you go freshen up? I can handle anyone who wanders in. Besides, your guests will be here soon." She gives me a comforting squeeze.

"Thanks, Olivia."

I check Charlie is OK, and then I wander to the small office and wash my face, musing about how much can change in one short year. My life has leaped to these dizzy heights where I've been full of every kind of happiness a girl can know. But my heart sinks as guilt barrels me over for feeling this way, when my friends are having the very worst year of their lives. I know CeeCee would berate me over thinking this way, but it seems wrong to be celebrating when I should be commiserating.

I throw my shoulders back, and walk out, pretending that everything is fine.

"Better?" Olivia says.

"Good enough. Let's set out the finger food."

We spend the next twenty minutes layering the table with cakes and slices, when Missy blows in. "Well, would you look at this?" she says, eyeing the laden table. "I'm sure going to have to sample one of everything. You OK?" She touches my arm and leans close.

"I'm fine. Walt stopped in."

Her mouth makes an O. "How is he?" She turns to the doorbell. "Oh, let's discuss that later when we're on our lonesome. Look, you're about to be inundated with friends." She points to a small group of women dressed up and rushing through the door out of the cold. Missy knows if I start talking about Janey and Walt I'll dissolve into tears.

Sarah wanders in with Mamma, who gives me a sheepish look. "Am I allowed back in here?" Mamma jokes.

"Just don't touch anything," I say mock angry. "Stay away from the fridges, the stove…" I stifle laughter when I see her nod, her face solemn.

"I won't touch a thing," she promises.

The girls see Olivia hovering in the background. Missy whispers, "What's all that about, then? Did she make good?"

"I'll tell you all later, but I have a feeling things will be OK from here on out." I won't break Olivia's trust by telling the girls, but I will have to think of something. Maybe I'll just say she apologized and leave it at that. "Olivia helped me out here today when I desperately needed it. There's a lot more to her than I first thought. And…she can bake!"

"Golly." Missy shakes her head. "That's great news, Lil. Just goes to show, there's good in everyone when you search long enough." It's Missy's way to always see the positive and it's one of the things I adore about her.

Sarah pipes up, "You've done a great job keeping it all together, Lil, with all you've had on. I hope you can relax after today, and enjoy some pre-wedding time off, even if it's only this one afternoon."

I sigh, thinking of my beautiful three-tier wedding cake that was relegated to the bin. "I'll have to make another wedding cake now, so I won't be able to close up until that's done."

Sarah and Missy exchange glances. "We can help you, Lil. Don't give it another thought, sugar." Missy pushes me in the back. "It's time for you to mingle. We've got a few things to organize, so you skedaddle, and we'll sort the drinks and food and whatnot."

I go to speak but Sarah cuts me off. "We won't let your mamma help!"

An hour later and I'm hot from standing so close to the fire. I move towards the front door to get some fresh air, when I see a striking girl hovering nervously by herself nursing a cup of coffee. Her long hair hangs in shiny curls down her back, and she has the most luminescent hazel eyes.

She must be Becca, Missy's new hairdresser. I introduce myself.

"I hope it's OK for me to be here?" she says shyly.

"Of course! The more the merrier. It's a good time to meet most of the local ladies, too." I guide her inside, away from the front door, which opens and closes frequently on account of people coming and going.

"Everyone seems so nice already," she says in a quiet voice.

"Most folk are." I think of Rosaleen keeping Olivia's secret when it truly mattered—just goes to show people are much more complex than you might think. "Where are you staying?"

She flicks her long hair over her shoulder. "With my cousin, Clay, just out of Ashford. I thought once things settle I'll look for somewhere closer to town."

"Clay?" I try to place the name.

"He's new here too," she says. "He just moved to our uncle's place, the Maple Syrup farm. He's looking to start it up again."

I remember the quiet guy with dark eyes that stopped in when Dad was here. "I know the farm well—we used to go there as kids…but what happened to your uncle?" Some people keep to themselves around here, and I think back to the old man who owned the farm, stooped with age and a life of hard work. He lived alone as far as I know. Years ago he used to sell bottles of maple syrup from a little shack set up at the front of his farm, the most glorious-tasting sweetness, but one day the hand-painted sign was gone, and we figured the work was too much for him at his age.

Becca shrugs. "No one really knows. He never kept in touch with the family. Next thing we hear he's left the farm to Clay in his will. We all kind of felt bad that we never really got to know him, but, you know, he was a loner. Seemed happiest on his farm by himself."

I tilt my head, remembering the old man and his quiet way. "Some people are like that, I guess."

She nods. "Now that he's gone he seems so mysterious, you know? Like, I wonder what made him tick."

"Is the farm still…?" I try to think of a word other than derelict.

She laughs, sensing my hesitation. "A little ramshackle?"

I grin. "Well, yeah."

"Clay's cleared the house and fixed it enough to be habitable. He's going to renovate it, and fix it up real nice, but for now the kitchen is functioning again, and the two front bedroom walls are boarded up enough that the snow doesn't creep through. It's an adventure living there."

My eyes go wide as I picture Becca with her silky curls and high heels living in a house with boarded-up windows.

She sees the look on my face and laughs. "It's not as bad as it sounds." She gives me a reassuring smile. "Clay's made it livable fairly quickly. I think that's why our uncle left the farm to him. He's the only one in our family that has any practical sense with things like that."

"Is he going to farm maple syrup again?" I immediately think of recipes with maple syrup. It'd be amazing to have a locally made product in stock in the café.

"That's the plan. He's got so many ideas, and, you know, I haven't seen him this happy in years. Clay's a little different from the rest of us. Actually, he's a lot like our uncle was, in that quiet, broody kind of way. There's a lot going on inside that mind of his, but what…who knows?"

The chatter behind me increases in volume by the minute. Our small morning tea has somehow morphed into most of the local shopkeepers squashed inside the Gingerbread Café. Women are clutching cups of steaming-hot coffee that Olivia is making as quick as she can with help from Sarah. Olivia must sense my need to help because she shakes her head and waves me away. I turn back to Becca. "We'll have to have you both over for dinner after the wedding. There's a few of us who catch up every few weeks."

"That'd be great! I've heard all about those dinner parties of yours from Missy." She blushes and plays with the handle of her coffee cup. "Are you all set for tomorrow?"

"I'm as ready as I can be." I realize if some things aren't perfect, then that's OK. All I need tomorrow is the man I love waiting for me. If the cake isn't spectacular, so be it. The table will be bare of centerpieces and that's fine too.

All I need is Damon. Thinking of marrying him tomorrow makes butterflies swarm in my belly in anticipation. Just when I feel slightly woozy at the thought of him, in he walks wearing that sleepy Damon smile that I love so much. "Excuse me, Becca, my groom has just made an appearance. If you're not doing anything tomorrow you're more than welcome to come to the wedding. I can squeeze you in on Missy's table."

She gasps. "Really? Are you sure?"

I know Becca is going to fit right in Ashford and I look forward to getting to know her after Christmas. Suddenly worrying about numbers and guest lists seems silly. "More than sure. We'd love to have you there."

"Thanks, Lil. I'll be there." I give her a quick hug, before walking over to Damon.

"Hey, pretty lady." He takes me in his arms; his aftershave tickles my senses. "I've been thinking of you all day."

We're back to our pre-wedding selves. Relaxed and happy together as if nothing else matters. "Likewise."

He stares into my eyes, and it's as if there's no one here but us.

"I know I'm not meant to be here, but I couldn't help myself," he says, his voice husky.

I pull him closer, so we're jean to jean. "Good. I was one second away from dashing over the road to find you."

He kisses me softly on the lips, and tingles race down my body. When we draw apart the deafening silence of the room hits me; I blush, knowing when I turn all eyes will be trained on us.

"Morning, ladies," Damon says, grinning like a fool. A cheer goes up as women yell out all manner of things.

Charlie runs to her dad and pulls him by the hand. "Come and see my gingerbread house, Daddy." We follow her to the coffee table and squat down to see her creation.

"What do you think?"

The walls of the house are thick with icing sugar that oozes slowly down. Brightly colored chocolate buttons are stuck all over the small structure, and slowly fall, pooling at the base of the house. "It's perfect," I say. "That icing sure looks like snow."

She beams. "And look inside." She points to the gingerbread people she's cut out from brown paper. "There's you, Lil, and you, Daddy, and that one there is me."

"Who's that?" Damon indicates a fourth cut-out.

"Oh," Charlie says, blushing. "That's a little baby. A baby boy." A ripple of joy floats through me. It seems Charlie might just adore a little brother or sister one day.

Damon musses her hair. "Looks like a perfect gingerbread family to me, Charlie Bear."

Behind us, the chatter has dwindled away again.

Missy claps her hands, and announces, "Thank you, ladies, and gentleman." She looks at Damon.

"I better go," he says, ducking his head.

"No, no!" Missy cries. "Stay. This concerns you too."

Damon throws me a questioning glance, and I shrug.

"Now," Missy continues, "as most of you know, CeeCee isn't here because her best friend, Janey, needs her more than anything right now."

The guests murmur, most dropping their gazes to the floor as we're reminded of the sadness.

"You may have heard on the grapevine that the lovebirds' wedding cake is no longer after a slight altercation with umm…Sue, and then a tiny little tumble…" She glances squarely at Mamma, who fidgets with her sweater.

Behind Missy there's a table with a sheet draped over a tall square box that I hadn't noticed them bring in.

Missy gives me her megawatt smile. "We're breaking tradition here today, because we wanted to show Lil something special from her best friend, CeeCee. And while she can't be here with us today, she's certainly thinking of you. So much love went into this, and once you clap your eyes on it you'll see what I mean. For CeeCee it's helped her, these last couple of days, to do something that brings her comfort. Sarah and I certainly assisted. And when I say assisted, I mean we got in her way and made her holler at us a number of times, but still..." She fluffs her auburn hair, her eyes twinkling.

Sarah steps forward and says, "So I'm sure Lil can guess what's under here. And I just want to say I have a whole new respect for you ladies now, after watching CeeCee make magic happen. Are you ready to see it, Lil and Damon?"

Damon squeezes my hand, and I nod.

"OK," Sarah says. "If everyone could close their eyes while we take down the sides of the box."

The room erupts with peals of excitement as we all cover our eyes. My heartbeat thrums in anticipation. Missy mumbles to herself, and Sarah giggles.

"On the count of three open your eyes."

"Wait," Mamma says. "On three or after three?"

I laugh. "Mamma!"

"On three," Sarah says. "One, two, three."

I take my hand from my face. And inhale so sharply I cough. "Oh. My. Goodness." Standing regally on the table is the most spectacular wedding cake I've ever seen.

The ladies squeal behind me.

The cake stands three tiers high. The bridal couple atop are made from fondant, the bride with a dress exactly like mine, her long blond curls cascading down. The groom is dressed in a tux and has a rakish Damon smile. They are so lovingly detailed, I'm in awe of CeeCee's handicraft.

The first tier is a dome similar to our original cake, decorated with miniature snowflakes that drift down the cake and settle at the base.

The second tier is embossed with white trees, whose branches join as if they're holding hands with a periwinkle-blue background.

The top of the third and final tier swirls 3D like waves. The base of the cake is a row of shop fronts that look like the ones in Ashford, with the café central in the picture. I pull Damon by the hand and inch closer to inspect it. Inside the 'café' there's a fireplace, roaring in red and orange. Minuscule gingerbread-men bunting adorns the walls, just as it does in real life.

Trees made from chocolate spill onto the cake plate making it seem like a forest come to life. And written in cursive writing along the very bottom is: *And they lived happily ever after.*

I stand back, looking from a different angle. Each time I see a new detail. "How did she…I mean…what?" I can't fathom how CeeCee could make something so intricate in a couple of days. I bet she hasn't slept in her race to finish it.

"She's amazing," Damon whispers.

"How would she even have time to do it?"

Damon holds me by the arms and gazes into my eyes. "She made time, Lil. Like she always does for her friends."

I nod, and swallow the lump in my throat. "I wish she was here."

Mamma wanders over to me, her face radiant. "That's the prettiest cake I've ever seen. So much love went into that, Lil."

"It sure did," I agree.

I'm missing CeeCee something fierce and only wish she were here. Everything seems hollow without her. Suddenly all the emotion of the last few days hits me like a brick and I rest my head on Damon's chest as a queasy feeling washes over me.

"Can you believe the wedding is tomorrow?" Damon says, turning his head on the pillow to face me.

"Time's moved fast, hasn't it?" The bedroom is dark bar a glow from the streetlights, which filters through the curtains.

"It sure has. Should we have organized a honeymoon? I'm thinking now we should have."

I shake my head. "Nope. With both our shops closed and Charlie here, what more do we need?" I'm truly looking forward to the week we'll all have together, snug inside our warm cottage, cooking purely for our own benefit, and languishing the day away playing puzzles or coloring in with Charlie.

Damon runs a finger back and forth along my hairline.

"You don't think we're jinxing ourselves by staying in the same house tonight, do you?"

His laughter rings out. "I don't believe in all that. Besides, where would I go? It's you and me for ever, tonight and every night."

"Well, OK." I laugh back at him. "I think I'm too keyed up to sleep…"

"I have just the tonic for that." He cups my face and sweeps his lips over mine. Closing my eyes, I kiss him back, knowing that waking up with him tomorrow and every day after is like living in paradise.

CHAPTER ELEVEN

The Wedding Day

"Shoo, shoo," Missy says, to a half-dressed, sheepish Damon. He holds a tee shirt to his exposed chest as he steps into his boots.

"I'm going, I'm going," he says groggily. "Aren't you girls a little early?"

She arches her brow as she hoists the biggest make-up bag I've ever seen onto the bench. "*No!* We aren't early! And you, huh? *Sleeping in on your wedding day?*"

Damon smirks at me and I blush. We weren't in any hurry to sleep last night, and, well…time just got away from us as one thing led to another. Now I'm in a pre-wedding daze from love, and lack of sleep.

He throws his shirt on and then embraces me. "See you soon, Mrs. Guthrie."

Mrs. Guthrie. It has a nice ring to it.

"That you will, Mr. Guthrie."

He whispers into my ear, sweet nothings that make me tingle with desire. Missy clears her throat.

"OK. OK." Damon smirks and holds his hands up in surrender. "I'm going to say goodbye to Charlie Bear, and I'll be out of your hair."

"Speaking of hair," Missy says, grinning, "I have one bride, two bridesmaids, one mother of the bride, and a cute as a button flower girl to do. So skedaddle."

Damon laughs as he goes down the hallway to find Charlie.

Missy rummages around her bag, pulling out lotions and potions and lining them up on the bench, when Sarah walks through the door.

"Happy wedding day!" she calls out in a sing-song voice before giving me a hug. "Where's your mamma?"

I shrug. "Probably going over her to-do lists, and ticking everything off for the twenty-seventh time."

Sarah delves into her satchel, and pulls out a bottle of champagne. "For the nerves."

"You read my mind." I take it from her and put it in the fridge. "I'll need that when Missy starts with the mascara torture."

"Now don't you even think of it, Lil," Missy says. "If you wriggle and jiggle like you did last time I know I'll poke you in the eye! There's no way in heck you're walking down that aisle with bloodshot eyes from a mascara-wand poke, not on my watch." She's all uppity with nerves.

"Still like a statue, Missy," I say, keeping my face solemn. Sarah laughs behind her hand, and Missy swats her with a bag of cotton balls.

"Morning, girls!" Mamma power walks her way inside. "Sorry I'm late, golly, your father had some sort of hair crisis, and then there was the small matter about the iron, and then the accident with your cousin's pants. I thought I'd never get here!"

"Mamma, I don't even want to know what you're referring to with the pants." She dashes forward, her hair in curlers, and her face ruddy from the cold.

"Did you walk here?" I ask, amazed. Snow falls heavily outside, and the sky is grey with cold.

"Of course! Just because it's your wedding day doesn't mean I can let myself go!"

I shake my head. Some things will never change. "No, of course not. Walking in a blizzard is good for the body, surely?"

She tuts at me as if I have no clue. "Missy, Sarah, what's the order of events here?" She takes out a pad, and starts slashing lines through her list. "Do I need to add anything here so I can check it off?" Mamma is one of those people that needs to be part of the process, every single step of the way, and she's usually organized, *except* in the kitchen where chaos reigns supreme.

Missy grins. "I just happened to make you a list, Sue. I know you're fond of them." She winks at me and I smile.

Mamma beams. "Well, OK. Let's see it." Missy hands Mamma a list written on the back of a dried-up make-up wipe.

"This isn't a list, Missy! It's a piece of rubbish!"

Missy guffaws. "It's all I had!"

Mamma frowns as she reads it. "'Number one. Pour Lil champagne. Number two. Make her drink it.' What? What kind of list is this?"

I laugh at Mamma taking it seriously. Missy is most certainly not a list person.

"Well, they are important steps…" Missy says, grinning.

Sarah wanders back from the bedroom with Charlie. Her little shoulders shake as she cries. "Honey," I say. "What's wrong?"

She swallows a sob as she takes a deep shuddery breath. "It's my lucky bracelet. I can't find it and I won't be able to play the…" She stops suddenly, and glances at Mamma.

Mamma crouches to Charlie's height and says, "How about we go turn that bedroom of yours upside down until we find it? I bet it's fallen off while you were sleeping."

Charlie gives her a half-smile. "OK, 'cause without it I won't be able—" she lowers her voice "—*to do you know what.*"

Mamma clasps Charlie's hand and leads her down the hallway saying, "We'll find it, honey bunch, don't you worry about a thing."

"Sugar, you want to get started?" Missy asks.

I sit on a stool at the kitchen bench. "As soon as Olivia arrives," I reply. "This time I have a little surprise for you girls."

Missy's face lights up. "Oh, do tell."

A knock at the door interrupts us.

"Must be Olivia," Missy says, "Anyone else would just waltz in."

And they would; most of us folk in Ashford don't lock our doors. There's no need to really. I walk over and open the door to Olivia.

"Good morning." She smiles warmly and gives me a peck on the cheek. "I bought you this." She hands me a small box. "Go on, open it."

Smiling my thanks, I flip open the lid. Inside sits an antique pair of earrings with a small blue stone.

"I figured, that's your old, borrowed, and blue all wrapped up into one. Though," she adds hurriedly, "if your mamma or anyone else has already given you something for luck then you don't need to wear them."

"Oh, wow! They're gorgeous, Olivia." I take one carefully from the box. "I'd be honored to borrow them for the day."

She steps over the threshold. "Not borrow, keep. You're the perfect girl for Damon and I want you to have them. You're family now. And maybe one day, you can hand them down to Charlie if she decides to get married. They were passed down by my mother, and, well…it's only right."

"That means a lot, Olivia." I put the antique earring safely back in the box, touched she's given me something so meaningful.

She unwraps her scarf and says, "Right, where is everyone?"

I lead her inside to the kitchen where Missy is humming *Jingle Bells* to herself while she's making up Sarah's face. The two girls wave to Olivia.

"Morning, Olivia," Missy hollers. "Come now, Lil. Watch how Sarah just sits here while I do her make-up. She doesn't fidget, or screw up her face. See?"

Sarah pokes her tongue out at me while Missy's back's turned.

"She just moved!" I screech.

Missy swings back to Sarah, whose face is neutral and clucks her tongue. "Now she's seeing things? Maybe we should give her a glass of that champagne…"

Olivia puts her handbag on the bench and says, "Allow me." She ambles to the fridge as though she's been here before.

"Glasses are the cabinet to your right." I point.

Mamma walks back with a cheerful-looking Charlie.

"Found it?"

"It was under my pillow, just like Sue said it would be." She blows her bangs from her eyes. "And now I can…" She claps her hands over her mouth, and I hide a smile. Whatever her secret is there's a good chance she's going to blurt it out before the wedding.

"Olivia," Mamma says. "Welcome to the madhouse."

Olivia rises to hug her. "Thanks for inviting me."

Mamma waves her away. "You're part of the family now. So, ladies…who's up for a little pre-wedding sing-a-long? I thought we could listen to some calming pan pipes and sing—"

I roll my eyes. "Mamma, no pan pipes. If I hear the instrumental version of *Hello* one more time…"

Sarah guffaws. "How about we listen to Christmas carols, instead? I think you've all forgotten that it's actually Christmas Eve."

Missy says, "That's right, it is, and, Charlie, that means you better put your stocking out, right?"

She squeals. "Right! Oh, wait...I didn't bring it!"

"Charlie," I say, "if you traipse down to the spare bedroom I think you'll find a little something in there with your name on it. You can go hang it by the..." she's already off and running before I can say "...Christmas tree."

"Done," Missy says, surveying Sarah's face up close. "Lord, Sarah, you've got the most beautiful eyes I've ever seen. What do you think, girls?" We wander over and lean up close to Sarah's face, murmuring our agreement. Sarah seems to have this idea that she's ordinary, when it couldn't be further from the truth. Her big doe eyes are accentuated by the artful way Missy's applied the eye shadow. She's beautiful in the most unique way with her rosebud mouth, and air of grace.

"Sarah, Ridge is going to go out of his mind when he sees you," Mamma says. "You're always gorgeous, but today, you're stunning."

"She's right," I agree. Her bobbed hair is swept into an up do, with her blunt bangs hanging just above her eye line, framing her dark eyes. "Gorgeous."

Sarah blushes and mumbles thanks. Missy hands her a mirror and she stares, jaw agape, at herself.

"I love that reaction." Missy giggles.

Once Sarah eases out of the chair I turn to the semi-circled women and say, "Before we go any further, I wanted to say a few things..."

Missy's mouth becomes a tight line. I hand her a tissue box.

"It's that obvious?" she says. "Thank the Lord for waterproof mascara."

I clear my throat as a wave of emotion sweeps over me too. How can a few simple sentiments be enough for the friendships we have? Knowing that I'll always have these girls around no matter what life throws my way, I press on and hope I can manage to say what my heart feels.

"You girls mean more to me than I can sum up in a few words. You've been there for me through the good and bad and everything in between. I know all I'd have to do is shout and you'd drop everything for me if I needed you. And I hope you know, I'd do the very same for you. This is a little bittersweet without CeeCee here…" I take a moment as my voice cracks "…but I know we'll be still sitting on Missy's porch when we're old and grey, God willing, and cackling into the balmy night air…"

Missy sobs, and manages, "We won't ever go grey, not if I can help it!"

I throw my head back and laugh. "OK, when we're old and part of the blue-rinse brigade, I know I'm going to look back on my life and count my blessings for having friends like you."

Sarah swipes the tissues from Missy. "Oh, God, is my mascara waterproof? Jesus, Lil, that is the sweetest thing I've ever heard."

Mamma rubs Sarah's back.

"Give me one of those." I indicate the tissues. Golly, at this rate we're going to resemble puffer fishes by the time we get to the ceremony.

I rifle through the brown paper bag on the bench and take out their gifts.

"Charlie Bear, you're first." I hand her the note and the small velour box. She mouths the words out loud.

"I'm a flower girl!"

"Yes!" I bend to hug her small frame. "Your daddy thought it would be a nice surprise for you today. If you think you'll be OK you'll be the first girl walking down the aisle."

Her eyes widen, and she shrieks. "Yes, I would love that!"

"And," I say, "you'll have a posy of flowers just like the bridesmaids."

"This is going to be the best day ever!" Her face is animated with all the joy a seven-year-old can handle.

Next I take out Olivia's gift. I hand it to her and give her a quick hug. "Olivia, we haven't known each other long, but I look forward to being your daughter-in-law. Damon is my *Mr. Right*. I knew it from the moment I met him." I laugh, remembering that moment, picturing myself hands on hips, screeching at him for stealing my customers. "OK, maybe not the very first few minutes, but not long after. So I wanted to thank you for raising a boy who grew into a loving, considerate man, who means everything to me."

She opens the box and takes out the locket inscribed: *Thank you for raising my Mr. Right.*

"Oh, Lil. It's truly beautiful." She runs a finger along the inscription, and smiles. "Thank you."

"Sarah, and Missy." I hand them their boxes and they open them carefully. They gasp when they see the pearl pendant. They read the cards silently, Missy still in floods of tears.

"Well, read it out," Mamma says. "I want to know what it says!"

Sarah pulls the bottom of her sweater down and composes herself before reading, "'Today I say *I do*, two tiny words that promise a lifetime of love and laughter, tears and joy. Thank you for walking this path with me. I'll say *I do* to the man I love, with you by my side; our friendship, I'll hold in my hand and in my heart now and always.'"

The room is silent as everyone smiles and collectively *aww*.

"And, Mamma." I hand her a jewelry box with her own special message.

"I'll open it later, Lil. I know I'm gonna blubber like a fool otherwise. You clearly got that gene from me…"

I grin. Weddings certainly turn into the sweetest kind of love-fests when you have friends and family like these.

There's a knock at the door, stunning us silent as the girls sit with half-empty flutes of champagne in hand. The excitement is palpable as we stand up.

"Fix her train…"

"Careful with your champagne, don't you spill it on her…"

"Let me check your make-up…"

"Where's my other shoe…?"

"It's really happening!"

We stop as our gazes meet, and double over laughing. The knock at the door becomes more insistent and that only sets us off again.

Sarah walks to the door, the first of us to regain her composure. "We'll be a few minutes, if that's OK?"

The driver muffles a reply.

She walks back and claps her hands together. "Right. Charlie, your shoe is by the front door. I'll fix the train. Missy, you check her hair and make-up. Olivia, if you can wrestle the champagne from Lil, and Sue, we might just be ready to go."

Olivia takes my flute and says, "You've hardly touched it."

My hands shake. "I'm too jittery for champagne. I'll need all my faculties so I don't tumble down the aisle."

Missy stands back from scrutinizing me. "Mmm hmm, that's true. She's not used to high heels. We've had to hold practice sessions so she can walk without looking like a newly born giraffe."

"Missy! You said I looked graceful!"

She colors. "Well, I didn't want to put you off…"

I guffaw. "I knew it!"

"What's all this racket?" my dad booms, peeping around from the front door. "Lil, take a look at you…" Tears spring to his eyes, which he hastily swipes away. "Give your old man a hug."

We embrace, and the comfort of his bulk calms my nerves a little. "Don't cry, Dad, sheesh, you'll make me start again, and it's like a chain reaction here."

Missy harrumphs. "There's not enough make-up in the world for this lot."

"Oh, yeah, Missy?" Sarah says, raising her eyebrows. "As far as I see it, you're the one leading the charge with the sob-fests today."

"Well, I got a good reason…" She smirks and rubs her belly.

"Sure you do."

Mamma bustles around, clasping her hands and muttering.

"Mamma, take a deep breath."

She stops, and puts her hands on her hips. "I know, I know. I'm just making sure we haven't forgotten anything. Where's my list? Where's the bouquets?"

"I'll get them," Sarah says.

"What about the rings?" Mamma asks.

"Damon's got them," I reply.

"Anything else?" Her voice is manic with worry.

"My veil, I just need Missy to clip it on."

"Sugar, I almost forgot," Missy says, clamping a bunch of bobby pins between her teeth as she takes the veil from its hanger.

Missy attaches the veil to a clip in my hair.

Charlie holds my hand and says, "You look like a princess come to life, Lil."

I squeeze her hand. "You do too, Charlie." And she does. In her silky gown, and faux fur stole, with her tiny tiara, and beautiful blond curls set loose around her shoulders, she's every inch the princess.

She beams up at me. "If my feet hurt can I change back to my boots?"

I laugh. "You sure can. It'll be our little secret. Besides no one will see your boots under your dress."

"You're gonna make the man sweat if you don't get going soon, Lil," Dad says, checking his watch.

"OK." I exhale quickly. "I'm as ready as I'm going to be."

The phone shrills in the background as the girls sort my train. "Now who would that be?" Missy asks.

"Leave it," I say. "Everyone knows it's wedding time now. It's probably a wrong number."

"OK," Missy says, fidgeting with my dress.

I step carefully in my heels so I don't catch the hem of my dress. Dad holds my arm when we get outside; the snow on the front porch makes me slip and slide.

"Oh, golly, she's doing her newly calved giraffe impersonation again," Missy screeches.

"If I had a free hand I'd swat you right now." I fall into the limousine as gracefully as I can in the circumstances.

The driver parks the limousine as close to the church door as possible. Snow drifts down pooling in clumps by the old brick building. It's like something out of a fairy tale, a little brick chapel, flanked by trees, an organ sounding from inside.

The reverend rushes outside and opens the car door. "Everyone ready?"

I nod. Smiling like a loon. *I can't believe it's my wedding day!* Inside, Damon will be standing there, his too-long curly hair brushed back into submission. Wearing a tux, his hands clasped in front of him, and that smile of his.

The reverend pulls his coat tighter. "Well, I'll get those doors swung open. Take care on the ice now, ladies. Lil, I'll see you at the other end." He gives me a warm smile. "Sue, Olivia—" he holds out his hands "—can I escort you inside?"

"Good luck, Lil." Olivia gives me a quick hug. "I can't wait to see you marry your Mr. Right."

Mamma says, "I love you, precious girl. And I'm proud of you."

They exit before I can thank them. I concentrate on taking deep breaths.

Dad holds my hands tight, no doubt aware of the sweat I seem to be producing despite the icy weather. Mamma and Olivia each hold the reverend's elbow as he walks them through the arched doorway.

"OK," I say.

"It's show time," Missy says, doing jazz hands.

Charlie laughs and mimics her.

Dad gets out first and holds a hand out to me, steadying me, before he helps the girls out. We're just out of eyesight of the open doors, so the girls fix my dress, and pull my veil forward, before pulling at their own dresses to make them sit right.

The organ sounds, and I take a deep breath, wishing once more CeeCee were here. I shake the selfish thought away and smile. I'm nervous, and excited and know CeeCee will want me to enjoy my day.

322 A Gingerbread Café Christmas

With a few more Lamaze-like breaths I say, "Let's go get me married."

Charlie walks in first, taking slow measured steps as Missy showed her how to do. The crowd let out an *awww* when they see her. Sarah flashes me a smile, then follows Charlie.

"Keep smiling, sugar." Missy moves inside.

"Ready?" Dad hooks his arm through mine.

I blink back tears as a heady feeling rushes through me. "Ready."

We walk into the warmth of the chapel as attendants close the heavy doors behind us.

I'm grateful that my hands are occupied so I can't fidget. All I can think is don't fall over, don't trip on the dress, don't cry—that is until I lock eyes with Damon, and everything except him flies out of my mind. He's wearing a black tux, and has his hands clasped in front just as I imagined. His smile goes all the way to his deep brown eyes. The girls stand together off to the side of the pulpit looking every inch glamorous under the colorful mottled light that streams in from the stained-glass windows.

We walk in slow, measured steps towards Damon's smiling face. People wave, and take photos as we pass, but I make eye contact with Damon and keep him in my sights, overwhelmed at the happiness that races through every fiber of me.

Dad turns to me. "Well, this is my stop," he says and kisses me on the cheek. "I love you, Lil."

"Love you too, Dad."

He sits next to Mamma in the front pew.

I turn to Damon's outstretched hand. "You're heart-stopping beautiful, Lil," he whispers, brushing his lips over my cheek.

"You're not too bad yourself, Mr. Guthrie." My voice shakes.

The reverend clears his throat and begins.

"We are gathered here today—"

He's interrupted by the chapel doors being swung open by two attendants. The guests murmur and a ripple of clapping starts from the back as they see whoever it is at the entrance to the church.

"Who…?" My voice trails away when I see them; my breath catches in my throat.

They make their way up the aisle; Mamma motions them to her seat and moves down the pew a way.

CeeCee and Janey.

CeeCee looks regal, dressed in a silk green jacket and long skirt as she pushes Janey's wheelchair. Janey has pillows either side to prop her up. She's so small, so pale, but her eyes are bright. I grab a handful of my dress and lift it as I run to them.

I hug CeeCee hard; my pulse races as I fight to control my emotions. *She's here!*

"Sorry we're late," CeeCee says.

"You're right on time."

I bend down to Janey and embrace her. Even though she's bundled in blankets it's obvious how thin she's become. Her complexion is sallow, and she wears Walt's threadbare earmuff, which makes me smile.

"I'm so glad you're here, Janey." I only wish I could make her better.

She lifts a hand to my face. "There's no way CeeCee was missing out on your wedding day, Lil, not on my account." The words fall laboriously; her voice is raspy. "Lil." She crooks a finger asking me to move closer. "Lil, I want you to make me a promise."

"Anything."

I lean close as she whispers in my ear. "Promise me you'll look after Cee?"

My chest tightens. "Always, you have my word. I'm so sorry, Janey…"

She puts a finger to my lips. "Don't be sorry, beautiful girl. It's the way things go sometimes. I've had a blessed life. My family, my friends, my church. God's calling for me, Lil. And I've made peace with that." One lone tear falls down her cheek, and I wipe it away gently. "I'm going to miss this place. And the people. But I know you'll all look after my Walt, and my very best friend. We'll meet again some day, that's what I believe, and I take comfort in that."

"I believe that, too, Janey." The church is silent; everyone is respectful of Janey making such a huge effort to be here.

With quaking hands she pulls the top blanket higher. "Being here, to see you marry, it's a gift I'll treasure. You go on now…I've kept you long enough. I want to see you smiling up there." She gestures towards Damon.

I half stand, and kiss Janey's cheek before I whisper, "Thank you for this." She nods, and gives me a radiant smile, and it strikes me that everyone will get a chance to say goodbye to her. As impossible a notion as it is, it's poignant and beautiful in its tragic way.

I glance at CeeCee. "You're as beautiful as I ever seen you, cherry blossom," she says. "Now run along, 'fore folk here think you've gone and changed your mind." I clasp her hand and kiss the top of it, holding on longer than necessary. CeeCee knows what's in my heart without me having to try and find the right words. "Go," she says softly; her eyes are red from crying.

With one last glance back at them, I take a deep breath, gather the soft satin of my dress and walk back to Damon, reaching out to clutch his hand, grateful he's there to prop me up as so many emotions roil through me.

"The good Lord has made today more special." The reverend bows his head and then looks at Janey. "We are gathered here today…"

Damon turns to me, and takes my hands again. He spends an age staring at me, as if he's committing this moment to memory. I take in his brown flecked eyes, the deep pools of emotion in them. His smile, which is just for me, now and for ever, and the way he holds himself, loose and relaxed, and not nervous at all.

My hands shake ever so slightly in his.

He clears his throat. "I happened to walk past the Gingerbread Café and see a blond-haired beauty laughing, crying, and singing, *all* at the same time."

A ripple of laughter comes from the guests.

"I was in love. That simply, that quickly. Even though we'd never met, I recognized you. I kept making excuses to see you, just to be near, my heart sped up each time, and not only because you threatened to drive me out of town."

I laugh.

"I couldn't sleep at night as my mind would flash with you, the girl from the Gingerbread Café, with the big blue eyes, that are kind of leaky at the best of times."

"Amen!" CeeCee calls out.

So I'm a blubberer?

"When we first kissed it was like a balm for my soul, and I knew my life was about to change for ever. Once-in-a-lifetime love. The kind that makes me want to watch you as you sleep. Hold you when you're crying. Cook alongside you for a fleeting glimpse of the passion you pour into what you do. The kind that makes me in awe of you when you do something selfless for others as though it's nothing. And it is nothing for you. You see people differently. You want to make things better. You're like this great big constellation, a glittery, starry, all-consuming galaxy…and you brighten every day by being with me. I promise to cherish our love, from now until for ever."

"Can I kiss him now?" I ask the reverend.

The crowd titters.

"Not yet."

I squeeze Damon's fingers. So touched by his vows.

CeeCee jumps up. "I've got mistletoe!" She walks over and holds the green leaves over Damon's head. "What?" She gives the reverend an innocent smile. "It's tradition."

He shrugs, laughing. "We haven't got to the '*I do*' part yet…"

I lean forward and kiss Damon quickly and in the brief second our lips touch a vision flashes in my mind of us old and grey, and holding hands like young lovers.

"Sorry, Reverend. But I didn't want to break tradition…"

He tuts. "Well…we're breaking tradition again, it seems. Before your vows, Lil, there's someone else who wants to show you how they feel."

Charlie wanders to the piano that sits a step higher on the pulpit. She gives me a little wave, and then sits on the stool, smoothing her skirt down.

Damon looks as proud as Punch staring at his little girl, who doesn't seem nervous in the slightest. In her cherub voice she says, "I wanted to play a song for Lil, because I know it's her favorite. And I've been practicing since Easter. I love you, Lil. And you too, Dad," she adds quickly.

She puts her hands to the ivory keys, and begins the most hauntingly beautiful rendition of *Amazing Grace*. Her sweet little voice lilts and warbles as she pours every bit of love she has into the song. There's not a dry eye in the house as we watch her tinkle away, as if she were born to sing.

Ever vocal CeeCee says, "Mother o' Mary, that girl is pure gold."

I rest my head on Damon's shoulder as we make our way along the slick wet roads to *L'art de l'amour*.

"How does it feel, Mrs. Guthrie?"

"Nothing short of perfect."

Charlie's head lolls on the seat opposite, the excitement of the day too much for her already. I lean over, and try to lay her down without waking her.

Damon takes off his coat, and drapes it over her small frame. "She's even prettier when she's asleep."

"She's angelic."

Damon sits back, and pulls me close. "What did CeeCee say when she left?"

After the ceremony CeeCee took me aside to talk, cry and laugh after one of her launch hugs. By then Janey was exhausted, and needed to get back home. I worried for them being in and out of the cold like that, but CeeCee had Janey so rugged up, she said she was OK.

"Oh, lots of things," I reply. "I can't believe she made it. And Janey. I'll never forget it." I think of them both with peace in my heart.

"It made the day complete," Damon says.

"She did say one thing about Missy."

"What?"

"She said Missy's having a little girl, not a boy, like they've been told."

He tries to hide a smile as he shakes his head. "How does she always know?"

I shrug. "No idea. But if she says it's so, then I know it will be." After all, CeeCee said she'd seen it with Damon and me. And she couldn't have been more right.

We're standing near the entrance of the kitchen behind folding doors at Guillaume's restaurant. "Nervous?" I ask Damon, clutching his arm. Pots and pans slam down in the kitchen, chefs talk in raised voices as they prepare the three courses of our wedding menu.

"Nope, I can't wait to twirl you around that floor." He runs a finger up and down my exposed back, making me shiver. "Are you nervous?"

I grimace. "A little. I don't want to fall over."

He kisses the top of my head. "You won't."

We peek through the double doors as Missy taps a spoon on a champagne glass. "I'd like to introduce you to Mr. and Mrs. Guthrie…"

With one last kiss we walk out as our family and friends hold up glasses to toast us. We head straight to the middle of the dance floor. Damon puts a hand to my back, and pulls me tight.

Missy continues, "And they'll be sharing their first dance, and we ask you to join them when you're ready."

I take in the restaurant as we wait for the music to start. Tables circle the small dance floor. They're covered in white tablecloths and are adorned with poinsettias, which someone, I'm guessing Olivia, was able to find. Mamma's ribbons are tied artfully around the wooden chairs. The seating area is plunged into darkness as above us hundreds of little fairy lights glitter like diamonds. I can make out the smiley faces of our family and friends who gaze back at us as the song *A Thousand Years* begins.

"Ready?" Damon asks, cupping my face, his lips a whisper away from mine.

I reach for his hand, and rest my other on his shoulder. "Ready."

He moves a hand to my back, and raises an eyebrow. "Did I tell you how much I love your dress?" We dance slowly, shuffling, and swaying, our bodies pressed tight as we listen to the song. It's almost as though it were written for us. I mouth the words to Damon as we gaze into each other's eyes, love sick in the nicest possible way. "Did you ever think you'd feel like this?" I ask.

Damon puts his lips to my ear. "As soon as I saw you."

With a smile, I wave the bridesmaids and their partners to the floor. I search for my dad's face, and find him off to the side and motion him and Mamma over.

They sidle up and begin dancing next to us. It's not long before the bridesmaids and their partners join us, Missy standing two steps away from Tommy on account of her belly.

Sarah and so-called man mountain Ridge wander over, and join in.

I think of CeeCee. Missing her boisterous laugh, and her warmth. Would she have stolen Guillaume out of the kitchen for a quick dance? I rest my head on Damon's chest, smiling at the thought.

"We're proud to call Damon a part of our family, and with that his parents become part of us too. Please raise your glasses and toast to the bride and groom, Mr. and Mrs. Guthrie." My dad lifts his glass and takes a sip. I raise mine to him and take a sip and grimace. "Does your champagne taste weird?" I ask Damon.

He rubs the fabric of my dress under the table. "No, it tastes as fine as it looks. Do you want something else?"

I cup his hand. "No, it's OK."

With the speeches finished I signal to the waiter to play the music.

"I never knew you collected stamps!" Damon says. "*Stamp camp?* What is that?"

I groan. Dad's speech was not so much sentimental as embarrassing. "There wasn't much to do in Ashford when I was a kid, so I went to stamp camp to be with my people." I pretend to be outraged. "Some lifelong friendships were made at stamp camp, I'll have you know."

He chokes back laughter. "And *your people* were avid stamp collectors?"

"Well," I scoff back, "what about your creepy skeletons? You were a *goth* in high school?" I wrinkle my nose, picturing Damon with jet-black hair and nose piercings.

"For about two minutes before I realized chicks do not dig guys wearing eyeliner."

Laughter barrels out of me. "This chick digs you. Even if you do sound like a throwback from the eighties."

He nuzzles my neck; my skin breaks out in goose bumps.

"Enough, you two, your honeymoon hasn't started yet!" Missy struts over looking glamorous in her gown.

"He started it," I joke.

Missy sits heavily next to me, trying to catch her breath. "I'm beat," she says.

I lean my head on her shoulder, debating whether to tell her about CeeCee's premonition.

"Golly, would you look at those two?" She points to Ridge and Sarah, who slow-dance under the fairy lights, almost as though they're under a spotlight. Ridge looks every inch the Harlequin hero Sarah pegged him for: tall, dark, handsome. And Sarah, with the sheath of satin trailing down her body highlighting her lithe frame, looks perfect in his arms. They kiss as if they're the only ones in the room.

"They'll be next," Missy says. "By then I hope my canckles are long gone."

I pat Missy's arm. "You'll have a little baby soon. It's like it's all coming together for us."

"It surely is, Mrs. Guthrie. What a year it's been…"

We watch Ridge and Sarah dance slowly around the floor, and my heart swells. Sarah thought she'd never find love, but she has, and, like me, it was worth the wait. I think of CeeCee's special friendship with Guillaume, and how important that will be to her in the coming weeks. Missy'll have a gorgeous baby to cuddle any day now.

And we all have each other and men in our lives who love without fear, whole-heartedly and passionately.

My mamma and father sit off to the side with Rosaleen. I have a new respect for her now, and realize even though you think of a person a certain way, there's always so much more to them than that. Like Olivia. Once her secret was out, she became the person I envisaged as my mother-in-law. She and George are staying for a few weeks now, and she said she's decided to tell Damon about her first marriage, so she can move on and not worry about someone mentioning it to him. That's why she didn't want to be here at first—too many people knew her other life—and after a long chat, I asked her what was so bad about it. It's not the kind of secret that hurts people.

And Missy's right, it's been an amazing year. Buoyed by friendships that will span a lifetime. Love that will make us rise each day with a smile.

That's all we need. *Love and friendship.*

The door to the restaurant opens, sending a shock wave of icy air through.

"Is that Dr. Skerlew?" Missy asks, narrowing her eyes at the shadowy corner of the restaurant.

"Yes," I say, turning sharply to Missy. "Did you call him? Are you OK?"

Missy laughs. "I'm fine, sugar. I didn't call him."

He walks with quick steps to our table. "I've been trying to call you," he says, his face pinched.

My mind spins. "What is it?"

"Can I chat to you privately?"

Missy hoists herself out of the chair. "I'm just going to find that hunk of a man of mine," she says, and winks.

The doctor's face is ashen, and I suddenly remember the blood tests.

Damon stands. "What is it, doc?"

The doctor's expression softens as he picks up my still-full champagne glass. "Can't drink, Lil?"

Puzzled, I say, "It tastes funny."

"That's because you're pregnant." He grins. "Congratulations."

Damon's eyes go wide as I let out a shriek.

The doctor continues: "The blood tests came back a bit later because of Christmas…you'll still need a sonogram. But, lay off the champagne." He smiles fondly. "I tried to call you at home, figured you'd want to know." I recall the phone call we missed as we rushed out the door to the church.

Our friends and family gather around. Damon raises his eyebrows at me and I nod yes. There's no way we'll be able to keep this to ourselves.

He runs a hand through his hair, and shakes his head as if he can't believe it. "Lil and I have a little announcement to share with you."

Charlie bounds over, holding the hand of another little girl. "What is it, Daddy?"

He lifts Charlie to his hip. "We're delighted to share with you that we are expecting a baby! It's early days yet, but well…you'd figure it out anyway."

A cheer rises from the group and there's more hugging and kissing. It's been such a huge day for all of us, I don't think my cheeks will ever be the same.

Charlie isn't as boisterous as I would've imagined. She's quiet and playing with the pearl on her necklace. "What do you think about a little brother or sister, Charlie?" Damon asks.

She drops the pearl. "Oh, I can't wait. CeeCee told me all about it at the church today…he's going to be the cutest little thing."

We look at each other over the top of her head. So CeeCee already 'knows'.

EPILOGUE

Christmas Day

"My own baking set?" Charlie squeals as she tears open the box. Cheery Christmas wrapping paper litters the floor in a circle around her crouched figure. "Santa remembered everything on my list!"

Damon sits beside her and balls the scrunched-up paper together. "You must have been a good girl all year."

"Oh, I was," she says with a serious expression.

I'm still buzzing from the wedding and the baby news, even though it's barely dawn and we haven't slept much. I know we'll all fall in a screaming heap this afternoon. We'll nap after breakfast before we wake to prepare a late Christmas lunch for our families.

"I'll start breakfast," I say, forcing myself from the comfort of the sofa.

Damon stands quickly. "You take it easy, Lil." His gaze drops to my still-flat belly. "Put your feet up. I'll cook."

"All protective already?" I smirk.

He laughs. "It's not too soon, is it?"

"Come here." I pull him to the sofa. He takes me in his arms, and lifts my sweater, exposing my belly. Charlie dashes over to look. "Is he kicking?" she asks.

"Not yet, Charlie Bear." Her little face is lit up as if she can't wait. I'm thankful she took the news well and isn't threatened by a sibling. She leans right up close to my belly button. "Hello?" she says. We hold back laughter as she waits for a response.

"Good morning, sugar!" Missy and Tommy let themselves in. "I didn't think we'd get here with the amount of snow falling," she says. "What's going on there?"

"Charlie's introducing herself to the baby." I pull my sweater back down and stand up, holding Charlie's hand. "Merry Christmas." I kiss Missy and Tommy.

"I don't know about you, Lil, but I am completely shattered today. Sarah and Ridge slept in but they'll be along soon." We thought having Christmas breakfast together would be better so Missy can rest up for the day.

Damon saunters over, his jeans clinging to him, and his shirt open a few buttons. In my groggy state I have explicit thoughts that make me blush. He grins at me like he can read my mind. We all wander into the kitchen. "Sit down, ladies. Tommy will help me sort breakfast."

Tommy takes his beanie off, and goes to the kettle. "I can possibly make instant coffee," he says, "or toast. I'm not as fancy as you guys." He winks at us.

"I'll have a glass of water." Missy holds a hand to the table to steady herself as a low groan escapes her.

I push my chair back and rush around the table. "Missy, is it the baby?"

She scrunches her face tight.

I grab a chair and try and ease Missy into it. Before I know it, I'm standing in a puddle.

"Oh, my God! Her water's broken. Help!"

I'm almost frantic when Missy laughs. "Lil, relax, I just need a minute. Well, I'll be darned. I think it's really gonna happen. My boy is on his way…" I grab some tea towels and line the floor, worried she'll slip when she stands. There's no time to explain it might be her little girl who's on the way.

Tommy crouches down, and searches Missy's face.

"It's show time," she trills and flashes her jazz hands.

"Oh, my God. Tommy, make sure they don't give her any drugs. She obviously doesn't need them, crazy as she is." I shake my head at her cool.

Missy throws her head back and laughs, then grabs a fistful of Tommy's shirt. "If I ask for the gas you make sure they give it to me. That's your job, mister."

Tommy widens his eyes. "Drugs it is."

"Lil, can you call the doctor and tell him we're on our way? I want to leave now. The snow's falling hard and I don't want to get stuck." Tommy helps Missy out of the chair.

"Of course!" My heart hammers in my chest as I search frantically for the phone.

"Relax, Lil, you look like you're going to pass out!"

I stop and exhale as if I'm the one about to give birth. "OK, OK. Give me a hug and get going."

Later that day phone shrills, startling me from sleep. We'd all been exhausted after the wedding, and the excitement of the last couple of days and had eagerly fallen into bed for a daytime nap. I grope the bedside table for the cordless phone as the time flashes neon green. It's a touch from noon.

"Hello?" I say.

I strain to hear; there's faint chatter in the background.

"Cee?"

"Cherry blossom, were you asleep?" She's so quiet I can barely hear her.

"No, no. Is everything OK?"

Damon turns over next to me and rubs his eyes, turning on the bedside lamp. I mouth the word, "Cee." And he sits up, pulling the quilt against us.

"She's gone, Lil. Not even an hour ago. My best friend… gone to God." Her voice breaks, and I close my eyes against the heartbreak of it. She chokes back tears.

"Cee, I'm so sorry."

After a minute she says, "Me too, Lil. But seeing her so frail and in pain…she was ready, she said she was ready to go. And then she drifted off, just as quick as that. In its own way it was beautiful, Lil. With a soft sigh, she was gone. And now she's outta pain."

"I can't believe it. At the wedding…"

"I know, she gave living that one last push, and enjoyed every second of it, Lil. But you know, I don't think Janey's gonna be all that far away…"

"What do you mean?"

"We had to ring the doctor, and he just happened to be delivering Missy's baby. She delivered a little baby girl right around the same time as Janey passed on. The *same time*, Lil."

I gasp as tears well. "At the same time?"

"The very same. The doctor told us." She sobs; the distance between us seems like a gulf and I want to go to her. "That child gonna be something special, all right."

My heart thuds as I think about the two happening simultaneously. It's got to be a sign.

"So Missy doesn't know any o' this yet, she's sleepin', according to the doctor, but you know somethin' else…"

"What?"

"You know what Missy called the baby?"

I close my eyes as goose bumps break out over my body. "Tell me…"

CeeCee chuckles as if she can't quite believe it. "Angel."

Wide awake after CeeCee's call, I turn to Damon and explain what she said. He's sits there quietly, his head resting against the bedhead.

"That has to be one of the most amazing things I've ever heard," his voice is wistful.

I nod. "It's so special, and I know it'll be something for CeeCee to hold onto in the coming months."

We sit there silently, lost in thought. My mind whirls with Missy having a little girl, and of Janey being out of pain.

Before the maudlin sets in, I say, "We better get dressed. Our family will be here soon."

Damon pulls me in for a tight squeeze. "Yes they will, Mrs. Guthrie. And we have lots of cooking to do before we go to the carols by candlelight tonight."

I squeeze him back, hugging the warmth from his body. In a last minute rush, my dad helped one of Walt's friends at the community center rally around and organize a last minute town gathering to celebrate Christmas. It was done quickly in the hopes Janey would be there. But now, we'll sing in her honor instead.

If there's one thing Ashford does well it's come together as a community when we need to.

We get dressed and head to the kitchen to start preparing our Christmas dinner. My hand itches to call CeeCee back but I know her, and I know she'll need some time alone.

Olivia throws her napkin on the table and stands to clear the dinner plates. I go to help but she shoos me away. "Relax, Lil. Take a break. That has to be the most delicious turkey I've ever tasted, you two certainly make a fine pair." She shoots us a sweet smile. "Let me wash up."

My dad flicks his braces. "One day off the diet, and look." He points to his belly.

Mamma raises an eyebrow. "One day? Don't think I don't know you sneak into the Gingerbread Café and charm Lil into serving you things you aren't meant to eat."

I go to protest, but she gives me one of her knowing mom looks and I close my mouth. Moms' *always* know. She says, "I'm going to help Olivia with these dishes, so why don't you see how Charlie Bear is faring, and then we'll head down to the carols?"

Damon's dad George snores loudly in his chair, his napkin still tucked into his shirt.

We laugh and Damon says, "I've never known him to sleep like that in company. Must be the country air."

Olivia turns, her gloved hands covered in suds. "Well, we'll find out, won't we? We plan on spending a lot more time here in future." We exchange a glance, as happiness courses through me.

"I think," I say. "That sounds mighty nice."

With one last offer of help, they wave me away, so I go look for Charlie, who has retreated to her room to play with her Christmas presents.

I lean against the door jamb and watch her pretend play with her dolls, holding up conversations in different accents for each character.

She stops when she sees me and laughs. "I'm still learning how to talk southern," she says, after throwing in one of CeeCee's one liners into her role playing.

"You sound exactly like Cee."

"Really?"

"Really. And hopefully you can show her soon. I know she wants to see you as soon as she's able."

Charlie puts the dolls carefully back into the dollhouse.

"I know, Lil," she stares up at me. "I know her heart's sore. She told me all about it. But I can wait."

It never fails to amaze me the way CeeCee connects with people from age seven to seventy. She's just got that way about her.

I cross my arms against the chill of this side of the cottage. "Are you ready for the Christmas carols? We've got some teeny tiny candles that are LED, so there's no danger my mom can set anything on fire. And we can huddle together in the town hall, and sing 'till our heart's content."

Again she gives me a look that seems so much older than hers years. "Let's sing for CeeCee."

"She'd like that," I say.

"And for the baby." She glances at my tummy.

I smile. "Perfect."

She jumps up and I grab her in a hug, inhaling her innocence and marveling at her sweet heart. "Let's go, and sing for everyone we love."

We head to the kitchen where everyone is busy throwing on jackets and winding scarves around their necks.

"Ready?" Damon asks, and scruffs Charlie's hair.

We nod, as Charlie pulls her mittens on.

Damon loops a hand lazily around my waist and I clasp Charlie's mittened hand. Damon opens the door to the blustering snow. We decided to walk slowly to the town hall since we won't all fit in the one car and while it's artic out, at least we'll all be together. And that's all I want right now. To be with those I love. To be thankful for what I've had, and what I've got. To celebrate the joy of life, including the new one inside of me, and to be there for my friends when they most need me. Again I think of CeeCee and wish fervently I could go to her now.

Damon senses my mood, and grips my waist tighter, searching my face as I look to him. "You OK?"

I nod. Our parents walk behind us chatting away about all the places they've traveled to, and how much more they want to see. We turn the corner into the town hall and see Sarah and Ridge clutching steaming cups of coffee. Their breath blows out like fog. Sarah waves us over, her face shining with happiness.

"Lil!" She embraces me. "We've been waiting. Come on inside. CeeCee is here. And Guillaume." She winks.

"They're here?"

"Everyone is here," she says. "What kind of Christmas would it be if we weren't?"

Damon rubs my back through the thick parka I wear and whispers. "Go to her, Lil. I'll escort everyone else in in a few minutes."

I nod and kiss him on the cheek. He senses what I need, always.

Sarah takes my hand and leads me into the warmth of the hall. Charlie races in after us, so I stop, and throw an arm around her shoulder as she catches up. We continue through the crowd of locals who sing and wave candles in the air in front.

She sees me before I find her in the throng of people. "There you be, sugar plum. And what's this I hear you've gone and got yourself a little bun in the oven?"

I launch myself at her in proper CeeCee style, and as she hugs me back I notice Guillaume sitting next her, his face lit up by love.

"Well," I say, looking into her deep brown eyes. "I think *you* knew about it before I did."

She lets out her southern haw and picks up Charlie in a huge bear hug. "Well o' course, didn't we Charlie Bear?"

Charlie giggles. "That was such a hard secret to keep."

Damon and the gang meld their way over to us. CeeCee makes room so we can all sit on a rug she's laid out.

Everyone spends a minute saying Merry Christmas and Sarah hands out candles to our folks, and we sit quietly together. I lay my head on CeeCee's shoulder so grateful to be close to her. She pats my hand, we don't need to talk, we each know how we're feeling.

Charlie stands and tries to sit between us to cuddle CeeCee. I inch out of her way and scoot over and wrap my arms around my husband. He kisses the top of my head, and lays a gentle hand on belly.

While carolers croon out from the little stage in front, I close my eyes and absorb the meaning of the words. It's been a big year for all of us, my friends, my family, and me. And I can't help but feel life has come full circle. I smile, for once, certain I'm not going to blubber. There's too much to be thankful for.

What if a tragedy struck and you only had yourself to blame?

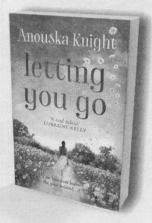

Alex Foster lives a quiet life, avoiding the home she hasn't visited in eight years. Then her sister Jaime calls. Their mother is sick and Alex must return. Suddenly she's plunged back into the past she's been trying to escape.

Returning to her home town, memories of the tragic accident that has haunted her and her family are impossible to ignore. As Alex struggles to cope, can she ever escape the ghosts of the past?

'A fresh new voice in romantic fiction'
—*Marie Claire*

Everyone has one.
That list.
The things you were *supposed* to do before you turn thirty.

Jobless, broke and getting a divorce, Rachel isn't exactly living up to her own expectations. And moving into grumpy single dad Patrick's box room is just the soggy icing on top of her dreaded thirtieth birthday cake.

Eternal list-maker Rachel has a plan—an all-new set of challenges to help her get over her divorce and out into the world again—from tango dancing to sushi making to stand-up comedy.

But, as Patrick helps her cross off each task, Rachel faces something even harder: learning to live—and love—without a checklist.